D0953010

WIDOWS-IN-LAW

WIDOWS-IN-LAW

MICHELE W. MILLER

BLACK
STONE
PUBLISHING

Printed in the United States of America

First edition: 2019
ISBN 978-1-5385-5691-7
Fiction / Thrillers / Suspense

1 3 5 7 9 10 8 6 4 2

CIP data for this book is available
from the Library of Congress

Blackstone Publishing
31 Mistletoe Rd.
Ashland, OR 97520

www.BlackstonePublishing.com

For Kai, Shane, Jerome, and Ellen

Friday, November 8

Explosions burst from the big man's gun, the noise muffled and distant even though he was close enough that Jessica could see the flashes. Return fire ricocheted, heading toward her and Lauren where they'd flattened themselves against the wood floor. Splinters stung the backs of Jessica's hands from a bullet that blew through the planks nearby. She cried out, hyperventilating, her ears still ringing from the blow to her head. She forced herself not to throw up, the floor spinning like Dorothy's bed leaving Kansas. It felt as if she'd been trapped for a million seconds, each one ticking by like a whirling, off-kilter metronome.

Jessica felt Lauren grab her arm and yank her toward a nearby window, a way out. She followed. More blasts filled the room, one after the next. The women hit the floor again. The big man charged toward the door, shooting, shouting. He stopped suddenly, propelled backward. He took one stutter-step back, his gun firing wildly as he fell to the floor.

The room went mute, buzzing now. Dizziness and shock overtook Jessica, the room seeming to darken. She sensed running nearby, Lauren's hand grasping her again, pulling her to get up *now*. Jessica followed, moving toward the window, a bright rectangle in the dimness around them. But Lauren suddenly froze and held her back. The attacker stood in the doorway, gun trained on them.

CHAPTER 1

Brian usually called Lauren's office at night so he could avoid actually talking to her. Unless he wanted something. But mostly it was Lauren who wanted, needed, left messages, anxiety blooming in her chest like an innards-eating alien whenever Emily acted up or bills were overdue. Lauren hated being the nagging first wife and, more than anything, she hated that she needed Brian. It went against the grain of how she saw herself. That was what she was thinking as she walked from Manhattan Family Court to her office, dodging an obstacle course of meandering tourists heading to their double-decker buses at City Hall.

In her office, the desk phone's red light flashed at her as if winking in confirmation of Lauren's thoughts. When it came to Brian, texting and emailing didn't work any better than calling. He was old school like that, a landline kind of guy, at least when it came to Lauren. New hookups probably received witty, solicitous texts at just the right moment … unless Brian wanted to avoid incriminating evidence landing in Jessica's hands. Lauren didn't know whether Brian cheated on Jessica, and she didn't exactly wish it on her. But the idea that Jessica was somehow better than her, had tamed the savage beast that had once been Lauren's husband, picked the scab on Lauren's low self-esteem that only Brian still managed to scrape.

So, Lauren had gotten the glib thing down, calling Jessica her "wife-in-law," while always maintaining an innocent I'm-not-mad smile on her face. Wife-in-law was a term Lauren learned in family court. The first case she'd prosecuted. The City had charged a prostitute with neglect for leaving her children alone. The prostitute claimed she'd left the kids in the care of her stablemate, her "wife-in-law." But after the mother had gone off to work, the pimp ended up assigning the wife-in-law to other duties and put a six-year-old boy in charge of three younger kids, including an infant. The boy's babysitting gig fell apart quickly after a rousing game of match-toss set the apartment on fire. Luckily, no one was seriously hurt. All the kids ended up in foster care.

Lauren's days in her jet-speed, often heartbreaking job at Family Court made her ex-wife drama seem bland as tofu—but it was *her* drama. So she tended to refer to Jessica as her wife-in-law, mostly to avoid giving her the dignity of a name and—secretly—because she was sure it would annoy Jessica and Brian if Emily ever repeated it. Lauren tried to be grown-up about Brian's remarriage, and she didn't love him anymore, but she had an ocean of pettiness hiding under her adult self, just like she had low self-esteem floating under the confidence the world saw on the surface.

Her first time in the office all day, Lauren perched an armload of files on a free corner of her City-issued gunmetal desk. Bathroom-sized and mildew-scented, the narrow office resembled a foxhole. The desk belonging to Lauren's office mate took up most of the wall near the door. Lauren's was next to a dirt-streaked window at the far end of the room. It wasn't a space worthy of hanging a framed law-school diploma. All she'd put up on the wall was a calendar that Emily had made on Snapfish.com, with photos of the two of them on vacation. Lauren sat and logged into her voice mail.

The female voice spoke. "You have seven calls. Call number one from an external number, received yesterday at nine p.m."

Brian. The beginning of their extended round of phone tag that usually ended with Lauren giving up and enlisting Brian's secretary for help. Some people still had secretaries in Brian's world, even though they called them admins or executive assistants now.

"Lauren, I'm in Miami for a couple of days," Brian said. "I'll take care of the check when I get back."

Out of town again. She would have to dig into savings to pay the maintenance and mortgage on the apartment. Still, she was lucky to get anything to supplement her low-paying job working for the City of New York. So much for the experiment in fatherhood, though. For the past five weeks, their sixteen-year-old, Emily, had been living in Westchester County with Brian and Jessica, not with Lauren. Always the shrewd lawyer, Brian had structured the divorce settlement so he'd pay Lauren alimony rather than child support and get a tax deduction for the payments. Lauren didn't receive an extravagant amount of money because Brian's career had only taken off after their divorce, but his monthly checks paid the mortgage on the Washington Heights apartment they'd bought together twelve years ago. At the time of their divorce, neither of them had imagined Emily would live with him instead of Lauren and he'd still be stuck paying child support disguised as alimony.

But after a year of fighting with Emily about her going to school and getting home at a decent hour, and Lauren's gut-wrenching anxiety when she didn't, Emily had sauntered in at dawn one day, reeking of marijuana and tobacco, "too sleepy" to go to school. For a moment, Lauren had hoped that Emily smelled that way because she'd been *around* people smoking, but one look at her slit eyes, red as campfire embers, had slam-dunked Lauren's notion. It killed her to let go of Emily's daily presence in her life, but she'd called Brian and asked him to take her. He could control Emily in a way Lauren couldn't, no matter what she tried.

Lauren reassured herself that Brian's greater ability to put Emily in check wasn't about Lauren's maternal shortcomings. Emily was desperate for Brian's approval. She was just one more female in Brian's life who was obsessed with an unavailable man. Underneath that truth, though, Lauren couldn't help thinking that Brian's superior ability to control Emily was a statement about herself as a mother. Deep down, she finally believed Brian's criticism that she was too lax and didn't know how to parent a teenage girl.

It's not like she hadn't tried. She'd breastfed, taught Emily baby sign language before she could speak, watched useless Baby Einstein videos with her. She'd done all the PTA-mom things, including getting her into the best public schools, a melee in Manhattan where they lived, and volunteering at school auctions. But really, how would Lauren know how to parent a teenager? Lauren had basically missed her own teenage years completely, her parents so coked up they'd barely noticed when she'd *become* a teenager. Lauren's teenage years made Emily's look like a *Brady Bunch* holiday special.

Still, Lauren was scared, terrified that Emily was on a path that would lead to the same dark place that she'd been in at Emily's age—only now, drugs were stronger and deadlier. Kids died if they didn't get turned around in time. Lauren had wide-awake nightmares of heroin, Fentanyl-laced pills, and synthetic marijuana, any of which could easily kill Emily or scar her for life. And Emily's life had been painful in ways Lauren would have given a body part to prevent, making Emily more vulnerable to addiction.

When Lauren asked Brian to take Emily, she'd expected excuses: "I'm out of town too much" or "I've got a big trial coming up," that sort of thing. But he'd surprised her. "I'll find out about school registration up here." He'd paused, likely looking at the calendar on his phone, because next he said, "We'll move her this weekend, get her started in school Monday morning."

"Don't you want to talk to Jessica first?" It was clear he didn't, and despite the outward civility between Lauren and her wife-in-law, Lauren got a charge out of it. She could imagine how Jessica would feel about the full-time invasion of her kingdom. Her duties would now include cooking, shopping, and the sundry childcare duties that Brian would be way too busy to do. Lauren wondered if it would fit in with Jessica's *intention*—cue the creepy music—for her little life. Lauren thought back to Jessica speaking politely to her through the window of Brian's Lexus during a post-visitation drop-off, recommending that Lauren check out the *Law of Attraction*. Lauren was sure Jessica was still bending over backward trying to figure out how she'd attracted Emily, the teenage she-wolf.

"Emily's my daughter," Brian had said. "There's nothing to talk to Jessica about."

After that, Emily's daily calls often included complaints about the arguments between "Jessica Rabbit" and Brian. The tension had mounted in the idyllic Silverman household with the addition of the unruly teen.

Lauren could count on Emily telling her all about that and anything else that might feed Lauren's doubts about sending her to live with her stepmother in the upscale Westchester town made famous by Bill and Hillary Clinton. Today, Emily had called before school, telling Lauren how the town was going crazy because they didn't want low-income housing built near the Metro-North train station. Emily had said, "Are you sure you want me to live in this town? Daddy's not even around, and *she's* bugging out again."

"Yes," Lauren tried not to snap. "Get ready for school, or Jessica's going to have to drive you again."

Emily had been firing blanks. Jessica might be a self-absorbed one-percenter who could overdose Emily on nail polish fumes and teach her a hundred ways to charge a credit card to its limit, but anything was better than the weed-smoking delinquents Emily hung out with in the city.

Lauren scribbled notes as she listened to a couple of messages about her court cases, mostly scheduling issues.

"Call number seven, received today at three thirty p.m."

"Lauren …" A voice came on the line, the woman's words strangled. Lauren knew the voice, but it was different, strange. The choked whisper turned into a cough, then words. "Lauren, this is Peggy." Brian's secretary. *Huh?* "Please call me … Brian's been injured. Please call." Then silence.

Lauren jumped to her feet, gasping, all the air gone from her lungs. "Oh, my God. No," she said aloud, frantically punching in the number to Brian's office, dreading Peggy's news.

CHAPTER 2

"The burns are bad." Lauren laid her head back against the cool vinyl headrest of a mini-Prius.

Her anxious fingers twisted her hair into long curls over one shoulder. She felt as if an invisible hand were squeezing her heart, pumping blood at triple the normal rate. Above all else, she was so damned worried about Emily. After Lauren gave birth to Emily, she stopped eating for two but took on the pain of two. She still ached when Emily ached. Codependence is what the self-help books called it, although Lauren didn't put much stake in self-help books.

Lauren turned her head sideways to look at Constance in the driver's seat. "Brian was probably smoking in bed. I don't know how many times he ignored me about that. And here I am, pissed about the same old shit, and I don't even sleep with him anymore. On top of that, now I feel guilty for being pissed at him." Lauren shuddered, feeling queasy. "I hope he lost consciousness."

Dry heat hissed as it filled the car. A green-and-white sign hung over the right fork of the highway: NEW YORK AIRPORTS. Constance steered to the right, over the RFK Bridge, then down onto the Grand Central Parkway. Lauren and Constance had become close, sharing an office for four years since they'd started working at the Administration for Children's Services, their first jobs after law school. Dreadlocks to the small of her back, Constance spoke with a crispness born of private school education. "You don't have to worry about the Winston hearing. I've got your file and I know the case."

"This is too weird, traveling with Jessica."

"You're going for Emily. It has nothing to do with Brian or his wife."

"Right."

Two endless cement walls cradled the road as the car traveled below ground level through Astoria, Queens. They emerged and passed the remnants of the 1964 World's Fair at Flushing Meadows Park. Lauren stared at a huge metal globe in the flat park.

"How do you get along with her?" Constance asked.

"Jessica? Okay. Nothing overt ... although, between me and you, she's a total princess. She's one of those wackos who think they only need to have an intention to magically manifest the results they want. For her, I think it's just a fancy way to package self-obsession. Narcissistic personality disorder disguised as a spiritual quest."

"That's a big diagnosis." Constance chuckled. "Narcissistic personality disorder. You've been reading the DSM for bedtime relaxation?"

"You've seen those parents in Family Court, the ones who name all ten of their kids after themselves, like George Foreman, but their only claim to fame is a long rap sheet. And they still manage to feel superior. Luckily, I don't have to spend much time with Jessica.

"Really, I can't complain. She's good to my kid, as good as she knows how to be ... takes her shopping, that sort of thing. I've gotta be grateful for the effort. Brian has sole responsibility for screwing me over, and her being with Brian is its own reward. Jessica will get whatever comes with the territory." Lauren shook her head, remembering the reality. "If he comes through okay."

"Well, the trip to Miami is only two hours and change. It shouldn't be too bad."

"She's a better woman for him than I was. She wants more of the things he wants—the country club, the material stuff. Did I ever tell you how they met?"

"No."

"She was an operating-room nurse in Los Angeles until she witnessed an anesthesiologist leave the room just before the patient, a little kid, aspirated and died. I remember when Brian got the case. Back then, it was a big one for him, and he was really scared he'd lose it. No one who was in the operating room would talk about what happened. They were one big happy family—doctors and nurses sticking together. Then Jessica came forward and broke the case wide open. Brian was so excited when he called home from California to tell me about it."

"Wow."

"So Jessica was on the outs at the hospital after that, but she was on the ins with my husband, literally."

"Jeez."

"Our marriage was just a shell of itself by then anyway, and it wasn't his first affair. It was kind of a relief when he left. But before he did, he made sure I knew that it was Jessica's outstanding moral fiber that made their love inevitable."

"You would have come forward—and quicker."

Lauren pushed aside the old pain of believing Brian at first, about how Jessica was somehow this amazing person that Lauren wasn't. During her lowest moments of depression, Brian had provided endless ammunition for her old self-hatred. "You can't help but question her valiant motives. She was husband shopping. He probably had on his wedding ring, but I can imagine him looking at her with a sick-puppy expression, that my-wife-is-for-shit look. She probably thought she'd *attracted* Brian to her because, together, they were going to get justice for that child's family, all wrapped up in a nice bow to make Jessica feel good about herself. To a person like Jessica, Brian's wedding ring was probably an engraved invitation. But to hear him tell it, she was Mother Teresa … a saint with big tits, I guess." Lauren looked down at her own small chest. "I hate to be catty, but when I see a woman as thin as her with a chest that big, the thought of surgical implantation just flashes across my mind."

"Catty?" Constance said. "I would have asked to see the scars."

The traffic slowed on Union Turnpike, becoming stop-and-go. Lauren took a deep breath, bracing herself for whatever lay ahead. "I can't believe this is happening. The recovery from burns is supposed to be so long and hard. Even if Brian survives the surgery, his life will never be the same, and neither will Emily's … just when she was getting used to the new school and starting to have a real relationship with him."

Constance took a double-lane exit, and they entered the sprawling JFK airport. They said goodbye with a long hug, and Lauren walked alone through the automatic doors of the departure terminal. In the distance, Jessica and Emily waited beside the check-in kiosks. Emily appeared tiny, thin and unprotected. Lauren thought wistfully of the chubby girl Emily had been, all innocence and hopefulness, until her transformation at puberty. Emily had Brian's coloring, her long curly hair a light-brown version of Lauren's. Jeans clung to her hip bones, and she wore a short leather jacket Jessica had given her.

Emily turned and saw Lauren approaching. Tear-smudged eyeliner bruised the undersides of her almond-shaped gray eyes. She ran, crying. "Mommy."

Lauren took Emily in her arms and stroked her hair, murmuring, "It's all right, baby. Everything's gonna be okay."

Jessica's pale-blue eyes were puffy, her face drawn. She was six inches taller than Lauren with legs up to her now-bloodshot eyeballs. Jessica had a dancer's posture and six-pack abs you could sense even through her bulky black sweater. Lauren was five years older than Jessica, a working mom who fit workouts in during lunch hours if she wasn't on trial. No one had ever accused Lauren of being ugly, and she was in good shape, but some women were trophy-wife material and some weren't. Jessica was. She looked frail now, though. Stooped and skinny, in as much need of a mother as Emily. Lauren had to do her part to disarm the minefield that separated them, she knew that. For Emily's sake. Lauren's eyes met Jessica's, and Lauren reached for her, awkwardly, a part of her brain shouting at her outstretched arms: *no, no, don't hug her, not that.*

Jessica broke into sobs. "Oh, God, Lauren. What are we going to do?"

Lauren brought Jessica into a three-way hug. She flinched inside when she felt Jessica's hair against her face and the fragile bones of her shoulder under her hand, but she hugged her anyway.

***

It was approaching midnight in an ICU waiting room in Miami General Hospital when the green-clothed surgeon turned and left. The wailing started. Brian was dead.

Not my baby, too. Lauren flashed back to her own pain at fifteen, losing her father. Now, Emily.

Jessica and Emily hung onto each other, sobbing. Brian's law partner and his wife huddled with their arms around the two. Lauren wanted to embrace her daughter but stepped back, placing her palm against a cool windowsill to balance herself, confused by the onslaught of feelings: loss, shock, and a tinge of anger, too, that a group of people were entwined around her daughter, weaving a barrier between mother and child at the worst moment of Emily's life. But Emily had to share her loss with those who loved Brian. Emily knew Lauren didn't love him.

Of course, Lauren had once loved Brian intensely, almost from her first day of college when they met. Lauren remembered the icy face of the NYU registration clerk. "I'm telling you, Miss, your financial aid check hasn't arrived. You can't register."

Unlike the other students who filled the cavernous room, Lauren didn't have a single adult in her life who loved her and could step in when systems failed. The drug program had basically put eighteen-year-old Lauren on the bus to college and slapped its rump. Tears welled up.

She felt a hand on her arm and looked back into deep gray eyes. "Ask that guy over there," Brian said. "He's a supervisor." He talked over Lauren's head to the clerk. "Hey, buddy, she doesn't have to wait in line again after she straightens it out, right?"

The line behind them snaked the length of the registration hall.

"No, she can come right to me."

"Thank you." She smiled at Brian, amazed once again how the counselors at the program had been right: life would take care of her if she didn't pick up a drink or a drug. People would even help when she just showed up for life and didn't run from it.

Brian was older than her, starting law school that day. He took a half-chewed licorice root from the corner of his mouth and smiled. "Thank me at coffee after, I'll wait for you."

"It might take all day. Look at this crowd."

"All right, on second thought, when you get done here—you know where they play chess in Washington Square Park, at MacDougal and West Fourth?"

She nodded.

"Meet me there. I'll be out losing my shirt to the chess sharks."

An hour later when she showed up, Brian waved a twenty-dollar bill. "Come on, I'll buy lunch."

Lauren was impressed: a college guy who could hustle the hustlers in Washington Square. She wasn't looking for a he-man—or at least her better half wasn't—but she couldn't see dating a guy who needed *her* protection if some crazy New York shit went down.

"Mom."

Emily had left Jessica's embrace. Lauren took her daughter into her arms. Jessica's perfume then her arms surrounded them. "Lauren, oh, God," Jessica cried, the heat of her breath touching Lauren's ear.

Lauren realized with a jolt: Jessica was trying to comfort *her*.

"Jess," Brian's law partner spoke, gently. Steve was Brian's best friend. Wearing an Italian suit—having come straight from his Manhattan office to the Miami hospital—Steve was tall, his dark hair and facial structure politician neat. He put an arm around Jessica's shoulder. Steve's wife, Nicole, reached for Emily. Nicole was a lawyer, too, and Steve's perfect female counterpart, wearing a designer suit and a thousand-dollar highlight job on her short, flawlessly styled hair. With Nicole's arm around her shoulder now, Emily listened, her eyes fixed on her father's best friend.

"It's time to go, Jessica," Steve said, patiently. "I have my plane. I'll fly you all to Westchester Airport and take care of everything here. I'll talk to the hospital about flying Brian back and get them the address of the funeral home."

Over Jessica's head, Steve's eyes flicked to Lauren's for an instant.

Lauren didn't know if she'd imagined it, but she saw a hard, challenging glint in his eye. As if he were sizing up an opponent. She didn't mind that Steve was taking control of the arrangements. Jessica was in no shape to do it, and the last thing Lauren wanted was to take charge of burying her ex-husband. Still, why had Steve looked at her like that? Although atrophied from disuse, Lauren's street-honed antenna set her nerves on end.

CHAPTER 3

Monday, October 21

Steve sent an SUV to pick up Emily and Lauren for the funeral. Emily's chest clenched as the car turned down a narrow block lined with double-parked cars. Apartment buildings bookended the funeral home. They cast a tall shadow over the one-story brick house with its white shutters meant to make the house-of-the-dead look like a home. They weren't fooling Emily. She backhanded away tears. She didn't want to go in there, a place of only one truth: her father was dead. The thought vibrated through her: her father was dead. She said it to herself again, trying to make the idea less shocking, waves of sadness flowing over her. He was dead. Daddy was dead. In her mind, she was wailing, doubled over on the pavement, even when she was shaking people's hands and accepting hugs from those who waited outside in the cold. She felt her mother's arm around her, anchoring her.

Jessica and her stooped-over parents stood on the short path that led to the funeral home's entrance. Jessica looked nice, as usual, thin as a model in a long black coat. She'd left her fur coat at home, but there were enough fur coats in the crowd to populate a small forest. Lauren never wore fur. She wouldn't, even if she had the money. It was one of the few things Emily and her mother agreed on.

Emily tried to make eye contact with Jessica to say hello. But Jessica's eyes were unfocused, half-open. She'd been dipping into the medicine cab-inet, or a doctor had prescribed something new to help her. No help for the kid though. If Emily had done that Amy Winehouse shit, swaying on her feet, eyelids weighing a million pounds, they would have sent her to a rehab boarding school, poof, no questions asked. The kid had to feel all her feelings, no matter how hard. At least it was a consolation that her mother had to feel hers too. She didn't drink or do drugs. She said she'd used up her quota when she was a teenager. She'd told Emily a little about it—running away, living on the street, sleeping in a drop-in center. Emily didn't think her mother told her everything because the stories she told weren't that bad. And she got through it in the end, became a mom plus a lawyer.

Except her mother did become a crazy woman, screaming and turning all shades of red in the face when she smelled weed or alcohol on Emily. A couple of times, Emily told her: "I'm not half as bad as you were at my age and, look, your life turned out okay." Her mother really went out of her mind when Emily said that, which was like the only power Emily had when she was about to get a "consequence." Her mother said her own recovery was a miracle, and lightning might not strike twice. Plus, drugs were stronger nowadays and a lot of kids died before they got help. Jeez. Like Emily hadn't read about all the kids dying? Her mother was always overreacting. Emily had never even tried heroin or pills, none of her close friends had, not that her mother would believe her.

Crisp, gold leaves gusted down from a big tree onto the lawn in front of the funeral home. Car doors slammed. It was almost time to go inside. More people crowded the sidewalk, coming from their cars, surrounding and hugging Jessica.

Jessica's father seemed even shorter than the last time Emily's father forced her to spend part of her Disney vacation visiting Jessica's parents in Florida. Jessica's father hovered, shrunken to below his daughter's height now. Jessica's mother held Jessica's arm, the top of her head reaching her daughter's chin. Steve Cohen appeared, towering over all of them. He and Nicole each kissed Jessica, the two women air-kissing. Nicole's eyes scanned the crowd, her mouth set in a funeral-sad smile, not really listening to whatever Steve was saying to Jessica. Emily always admired that about Nicole, how she was so smart that people only required half her attention. Emily edged closer to the small group, wondering where Jessica's friends were, the college friends she must have had or the ones Emily imagined she hung out with after spin class or Pilates. Emily looked around, seeing no evidence of anyone.

Steve didn't have a coat on, and Emily watched to see if he'd let it show that he was cold. Daddy said Steve's suits cost ten thousand dollars each, and Daddy had started buying suits like that too. Her father was "on his way up," people kept saying. He and Steve had whole towns for clients. They sued toxic-waste dumpers and companies that poisoned workers with asbestos or lead. Emily's dad had been one of the good guys. He'd said that now that he was a *partner* with Steve instead of an employee, he'd be rich enough to retire in just a few years, at the rate he was going. But that was all over. She used to imagine becoming really rich, but she didn't care about any of that stuff anymore. She felt as if she were standing under a huge, endless sky with nothing to ground her now that her dad wasn't in the world. She wiped tears from her eyes and turned back to see her mother greeting an old man with a wide hat.

"Emily, this is Chief Judge Clark," Lauren said. "Your dad clerked for him, and he married us."

"My condolences, Emily. Your father was a good man and a brilliant lawyer."

Emily could tell the judge meant it. Hearing good things about her father poked a pinhole through her darkness for a second. "Thank you."

Lauren gave Emily one of those around-the-shoulder hugs that mothers gave when they were proud of you for just acting like a human being, remembering to say thank you and stuff like that. After the judge moved on, a van double-parked and a bunch of kids from Emily's old school tumbled out. She straightened her black-and-white dress that she wore under a leather jacket. None of her friends had ever seen her in a dress. She ran over to them, beyond the edge of the crowd of adults, and her friends each hugged her. Someone handed her a vape that looked like a pink magic marker. She inhaled, feeling the soothing nicotine hit her bloodstream. One of the girls held her hair back when the wind blew it in her face, making her feel like she wasn't alone in a crowd, the way she'd felt before.

Emily's friends were all different races, diversifying the place. It was a little embarrassing that her father had only white friends and family. Emily wasn't used to that in Manhattan, where even one person's family often contained all shades of people. She scanned the crowd again. She did see her mom's friend, Constance, and her dad's secretary, Peggy, who were black; and there were a couple of guys waiting to go in, one Latino, one black. She wondered who they were. They looked like cops, stiff in wool coats over suits and shirts buttoned tight around their thick necks. Probably investigators who worked with Daddy on cases. They seemed too uneasy to be lawyer friends, unless they were just uncomfortable being in this sea of pink faces in the age of Trump and the alt-right.

From the circle of her friends, Emily saw her mother approach a couple of her cousins. Emily's grandmother didn't show; not a surprise. Emily's mother hadn't seen her in years, and Emily had only met her a few times. Lauren didn't want Emily to have anything to do with her grandmother, who usually asked for money whenever she saw Lauren. Emily's mother made less money than the rest of the lawyers here, less than their legal secretaries, too. She said she couldn't afford to support drug addicts. She probably hadn't called Emily's grandmother to tell her about Dad.

The crowd rippled and moved toward the funeral home entrance. Thick mauve carpet muffled their footsteps inside the large chapel, and the hum of two hundred hushed voices formed a blur of words. The closed coffin was at the front of the center aisle. Emily stiffened, taking a step back. She felt the arms of her two best girlfriends around her. "I'm okay."

Like a wedding, friends and family of the wife and ex-wife divided themselves up. Jessica and her family took the front row to the left of the aisle, in front of a podium. Lauren, her cousins, and her friend Constance sat in the second pew on the right side of the aisle. Lauren turned back to Emily. Emily was torn about where she was supposed to sit. Leaving her friends, she went to her mother. "I'll sit with Jessica, Mom."

Lauren squeezed her hand, permission to leave, a worried look on her face. Jessica slid over and made a space for Emily in the front pew with

Jessica's immediate family. Jessica put her arm around Emily's shoulder. Emily exhaled with relief that she was part of the important family at her own father's funeral, not just a bystander. Emily saw her mother watching, making sure she was in good hands with Jessica, as if Emily were a toddler who couldn't take care of herself. For a change, Emily didn't mind.

A rabbi who seemed to know Brian—which was amazing because her father never stepped foot in a synagogue except for weddings and bar mitzvahs—talked about him. Friends took turns at the podium. They mostly talked about work, until Steve Cohen loomed over them at the podium. Steve had a set of index cards but talked without looking down. His eyes scanned the front pews, making eye contact with Emily for a split second then settling on Jessica.

He smiled sadly at her and recounted the Jessica-Brian love story and how they first met during a big case. Emily winced. Steve knew her mom and dad were still married then. Now, in front of hundreds of people, he was telling how Brian thought Jessica was a heroine and irresistible as if Brian marrying Jessica zeroed out his cheating on his wife. Emily looked over at her mom. She was staring ahead, expressionless. Emily's father traded her mother in for a newer model, that was the whole effing story.

Steve looked out at the audience. "He was my best friend. We sailed together, we flew together. When we first met, he taught me everything I know about toxic tort litigation. He was brilliant and generous with his knowledge. We sat up late into the night at the office, talking about the issues. He loved the law, and I know he particularly loved practicing before the Honorable Betsy Clayton of the Southern District Federal Court."

An older woman a few rows back nodded and smiled at Steve. Her father and Steve must still have had a case before her. Emily groaned inside. Even she knew it was tacky to brownnose during a eulogy.

Before Emily faced forward again, she caught sight of the two hulky investigators, smirking. The Latino one put his head down, hiding it. They didn't seem to be good friends of Emily's father, and they obviously didn't think much of Steve. Emily again wondered who they were, but she faced front and listened to the end of Steve's eulogy.

***

Rick Stuart blew his nose as Carl Cintron drove away from the funeral home. "The widow was pretty," Rick said, wiping with a napkin.

"Pretty stoned."

Rick half laughed, half snorted in agreement. The auburn skin of Rick's nose was ruddy and irritated where he'd rubbed it raw over the last couple of days. Rick never listened to Carl about vitamin C and echinacea. Loosening his tie with one hand, Carl guided the car around a curve that led from the Cross County Parkway to Sawmill Parkway. "Judges, fancy-ass lawyers, politicians. The place was packed with them."

"Jordan Connors didn't show up. Not much of a friend."

"Unless trouble kept him away. I keep thinking someone got to Silverman first, pulled him right out from under us."

"The fire marshal's preliminaries are in," Rick said, loosening his tie, too. "There was no irregular burn pattern."

"I guess. But you heard the audio of Jordan Connors. He's scared. Connors is in way over his head, and so was Brian Silverman. Now Silverman's dead."

"Jordan's definitely been playing with fire," Rick agreed. "He should be scared."

Carl and Rick rode silently for a while, Carl mulling over the funeral service. "Did you hear Steve Cohen's story about how Silverman met his wife? Silverman was married to someone else then."

"Yup."

"Guys like him make life hard for the rest of us."

The eulogy had brought Carl's thoughts back to Kansas City, returning home at dawn after a grueling night of surveillance at a trap house. His wife leaned against a wall, her eyes red from crying. "You know I heard something funny, Carl. From the other wives. I heard the guys all back each other up when they're out whoring. That there's no way of knowing whether your husband is really working a stakeout on radio silence all night, and half the time he's not."

"Misery likes company. You've found some miserable friends." He passed her, angrily, wanting only to sleep. "You know that's not my thing."

Carl's wife hadn't reacted well to living far from her friends and family in New York, and Carl could have reacted better to her. Now long-divorced, Carl drove across a small bridge from the Bronx to Manhattan. Blazing fall colors on the New Jersey cliffs painted the Hudson blood orange.

"I felt slimy just listening to Steve Cohen," Rick said, "'Brian was my best friend, he taught me everything.'" He roofed his eyes with his hand. "'Oh, and where is that federal judge whose ass I can kiss?'"

"Do you think Steve Cohen could have been involved in Jordan Connors' operation?" Carl asked. "Maybe he had something to do with Brian's death."

"We've got nothing on Brian's death and even less on Steve Cohen. Tackiness isn't a criminal offense, last I checked."

"That's a damn shame," Carl said. "It would bring a certain satisfaction to lead that guy away in handcuffs."

CHAPTER 4

At dusk, the dining room lay shrouded in shadow. Light from the adjacent kitchen illuminated a vast array of food on the dining room table, which the caterers had moved to one wall to make room for the guests. Through a haze of Klonopin, Jessica watched the faces of friends and family who had come back to the house after the funeral to share the beginning of shivah. They stood, hands clasped in a large circle, while the Jewish Prayer for the Dead droned.

Jessica felt her mother's cold, wrinkled hand wrapped around her own. Jessica's father stood on her other side, eighty-two years old and withered from the days when he'd so intimidated Jessica. She'd been their miracle baby, born when her mother was already in her early forties and her father was fifty. He'd always been larger than life to Jessica, but now that she needed his protection, he had no strength left to give. That didn't stop her from imagining his criticism: *The lox isn't cut thinly enough, the bagels aren't hand thrown. And why are you so damn skinny? Am I going to have to stop my life in West Palm to rescue you?* As if he were a ventriloquist speaking through her, the berating thoughts inside Jessica's own head always seemed to have his voice. Even when he was thousands of miles away.

The prayer over, Jessica's parents released her, and the buzz of conversation resumed. The guests converged on the food. She swayed on her feet, light-headed. She felt Nicole's palm on her arm. "You have to eat something, Jessica."

"She hasn't had anything to eat or drink all day," Jessica's mother chipped in as if Jessica weren't there. Jessica's father harrumphed in agreement or maybe oblivion, chomping his dentures on an everything bagel, cream cheese coating the corner of his lips.

"I'm okay," Jessica said, not sure whether anyone heard her or whether she'd only imagined herself saying the words.

Time floated by. She sat in the family room, a homey space of intentionally mismatched country furniture, a fireplace, and a flat-screen on the wall over it. Nicole had brought her a glass of juice. It waited untouched on the antique end table next to Jessica. She couldn't bear to drink it. She pulled her feet up beside her on the thick couch, its soft greens, browns, and ample cushions the closest thing to a cocoon she could find.

Guests came and went. After a while, the hum of voices softened as the crowd thinned, and goodbye hugs interrupted her dark fugue every few moments. Jessica managed her best schooled smile each time, her lips pulled upward. But all the while, she was with Brian, reliving their life together, needing him, missing him, conjuring him. She was at dinner with him, where the waiters greeted him, knowing his name. She was with him as he helped the landscaper with his immigration papers, patiently explaining concepts that he'd needed to research himself because immigration wasn't even his area of law. Then there was the time when one of Emily's friends had lost everything in an apartment fire and Brian donated a thousand dollars to the family's Kickstarter campaign. Jessica would never have thought of doing something like that. A hundred dollars, maybe. But Brian was truly her better half, a mensch, smarter than her, funnier, connecting with people in a way that had never come naturally to her. She had loved being by his side, enjoying the sunshine he brought.

But her memories of Brian looped around, always ending with their last time together. Five days ago, jogging, orange and yellow leaves splashing down around them from the tall trees that lined the road near their house. She'd inhaled deeply, appreciating the thick must of autumn, grateful for the life she'd manifested and dreading winter only for its indoor treadmills and StairMasters. She'd mused, a silent joke: it would soon be time to "manifest" a trip to the Caribbean. She didn't really take the Law of Attraction stuff that seriously. Yet she didn't dismiss it either. She found the ideas comforting.

But the thought of vacation led her mind back to the Emily situation, about how they'd have to take their trips during school holidays now, surrounded by crowds who flooded airports and resorts during those weeks. She was having a tough time feeling good about all the things that came with having a child full time, inconveniences that were only gradually becoming apparent. She tried to repress her anger; the wicked stepmother was a no-win role. But the lack of a child of her own made all the changes feel like an irritating blouse tag at the back of her neck, invisibly scraping at her simmering resentment. It was unjust. Still, as she'd heard on a recent podcast, you either rowed with the rapids or crashed into the rocks. That had struck a chord with her. She had a bad habit of fighting anything in her life that wasn't perfect. If she was powerless over 99 percent of her life like the podcast said, she was wasting too much energy fighting back, and to no purpose.

Sun flashed between breaks in the trees, casting a golden glow over the country-club golf course. The semirural road was silent except for the sound of Jessica's and Brian's feet and the two sets of paws that pounded behind them. Hazel and Nuke, Jessica's muscular Labrador retrievers, one chocolate and one black, kept a steady pace.

For the first fifteen minutes of the run, Brian had talked about a lead-poisoning case. An entire housing project had been built on a site contaminated by a nearby lead factory. Two generations of kids who grew up there had developed learning disabilities and other medical problems. Brian had come a long way from the malpractice cases like the one that had originally brought them together. He'd said that if he won the case, he could retire early on his fee and help those poor people too. Not that Jessica believed him when he said he'd buy a beach bar on a Caribbean island and chill out for the rest of his life.

Brian had been working closely with the congressman who had referred the case to him and Steve. Jessica knew he got a kick out of having the respect of powerful people and wasn't about to give all that up. Brian had come from a lower-middle-class family, his father a journeyman printer back when newspapers were printed with machine-applied ink rollers. Brian's mother had been a homemaker, a great cook of traditional Jewish dishes like stuffed cabbage and kugel, but not known for much else. She'd died two years after Brian's father, neither of them making it to seventy. Brian had grown up in a cramped Queens apartment and attended deficient New York City public schools. To Brian's family, a "good job" meant one with union benefits. No, Jessica smiled to herself, she didn't believe Brian would retire when he had just begun to realize his dreams. Having a comfortable home in the suburbs and gaining the respect of people he read about in the newspaper meant a lot to him.

At the sound of a car approaching, Brian pulled ahead of Jessica to run single file until it passed. She watched, appreciating him. She'd never stopped appreciating him—six feet tall with a lean body from his morning runs and power meetings at the Sports Club. He wasn't handsome in a hunky sort of way, which had made her underestimate him at first. His generally unruly hair had started to recede and his face hadn't been chiseled in perfect proportion like some of the frat boys at her college, but he had a sexual charisma combined with a stunning intelligence that went beyond his looks.

Until Brian, Jessica had dated for years without getting into a relationship. She'd had the "patience of a saint," her friends used to say, although patience really had nothing to do with it. Brian had been brilliant with a promising future, a good sense of humor, and what turned out to be incredible skill in bed. She'd been lucky to put off sex long enough for him to fall in love with her before they made love. Otherwise his skill in bed might have shifted the power so much that she could have strayed into obsession before he'd become equally obsessed with her, the surest way to lose a potential mate, especially a man like Brian. Instead, she'd hit the jackpot, marrying a man who still made her shiver when he brushed his fingertips against her arm. They'd lived together for over five years and been happily married for the last two of them.

Once the car passed, Brian fell back into place beside her, and she'd dared to mention (she couldn't help herself) the issue that had been on her mind constantly as of late: having a baby.

Brian spoke easily, his breath measured, the pace they ran together easier for him than her. "Listen, Jess, I've got my hands full with Emily right now. This isn't the time."

Jessica's words came out between thick breaths, her immediate anger and the run clipping them short. "You're out of town half the time … it should be me worrying about whether my hands are full."

Brian's words hardened into commands. "Don't start, please."

She'd wanted to pitch a fit. He acted as if she didn't care for Emily, even love her. She'd taken care of Emily two weekends a month for years already. But one day, Brian had just come home and announced that his incorrigible teenage daughter would be living with them full time.

Overnight, Jessica had acquired a sixteen-year-old who made messes, texted eighteen hours a day, argued constantly, and had to be driven from place to place, even to school at 8:00 a.m. because she always missed the school bus. Then every weekend, she went back to Manhattan, back to the delinquents Lauren let her hang out with. When she returned to Westchester each Sunday, kicking and screaming, it took Jessica three days to get her reacclimated to school and a normal life away from Lauren's marginal Manhattan neighborhood. And just when Emily began acting like a human being again, she went home for the weekend and the cycle started all over.

Jessica forced words out, both intimidated by Brian's temper and breathless from the pace that kept getting quicker, "Lauren practically parachuted Emily down on us … and now … we can't have our own children?"

Brian shot her a seething eyeful.

She added, "Inheriting a teenager is not the same as having one of our own. I'm thirty-two. If we wait too long—"

"Goddammit, Jessica," Brian raised his voice, "I don't need this shit right now. I've gotta be at the airport in an hour, so give it a fucking break, okay?"

She'd been ready to say one more thing, but before she could speak, Brian put an extra kick into his pace and left her staring at his back as he stretched out the distance between them and disappeared around a bend.

Shame flooded her, as if she were a girl rejected after a one-night hookup. She felt the deepest echo of old pain, muscle memory that didn't produce pictures of events, only the deep stab of long-buried feelings.

The shame subsided as she jogged home, but then an even worse thought surfaced: he was making her into Lauren. She'd heard him use that same tone of voice with Lauren on the telephone before they'd separated. She'd made sure to overhear their calls on a few occasions, walking quietly near a closed bathroom door, or passing through to the kitchen in her California apartment when he was speaking in the living room. She'd felt reassured by what she'd heard, that it was only a matter of time for his marriage with Lauren to end. She'd heard the disdain in his voice, the anger of someone trapped in a cage.

She started to weep as she ran, trying to talk herself through it: *you're not going to lose him, stupid woman.*

Twenty-five minutes later when she arrived home, he was already packed and headed to the car, his hair still wet. He nudged past her, anger in his eyes. He never even said goodbye. It was the first time he'd gone on a business trip angry, without them making up first. That would have been painful enough to put her in bed for the rest of the morning, if she'd allowed herself. But she'd never expected those angry words to be the *last* words she'd ever hear, that his disdainful tone would resonate in her head for the rest of her life. There would be no flowers or gifts to dull the memory of it. No long talks to reach a better understanding. No intense lovemaking to bury it. Brian was dead.

***

Steve Cohen stood over Jessica. "Jess?"

She emerged from her memories as if stepping into a Taser-field of pain. She reached her hand up to his. "Steve."

"Does Brian have a password on the PC downstairs?"

"Oh, um, sure. Five-six-one-A-G-F-dollar sign."

Steve patted her hand and made his way past groups of mourners toward Brian's basement office. She looked around from her seat on the couch, seeking out her mother, the bearer of pills, the pill expert after fifty years with Jessica's father. Instead, Mr. Manley, a large bespectacled man of close to sixty, approached.

The guidance counselor from the local high school had a deep, comforting voice. "Mrs. Silverman, I'm so sorry."

Looking up, she put out her hand to shake his. "Thank you for coming."

"What will happen to Emily now? She's doing much better in school …" Mr. Manley appeared to get lost in his own thoughts and his voice drifted. "Such a shame to uproot her now."

"Yes." Jessica paused and closed her eyes, the lids too heavy to hold open. What would happen to Emily? Despite what she'd said during her last argument with Brian, things had begun to get better with Emily over the six weeks she'd been living with them. Feeling guilty for putting the whole burden on Jessica, Brian had virtual-commuted more when he wasn't away on a case. Emily had taken to doing her homework downstairs in Brian's home office while he worked on the PC. It brought a warm, companionable feeling to the house even though Jessica had felt a little left out sometimes. Brian had showered Jessica with affection for chauffeuring Emily around their suburban community and engaging her in shopping trips and mani-pedis, things Lauren would never do with her.

The whole situation wouldn't have been bad at all if she'd been the only mother raising Emily. The real problem with being a stepmother was that she wasn't the one Emily loved. It was mostly a thankless role. Emily could never be Jessica's and that made giving so much to Emily feel more like unrequited love than parenthood. Brian had told her that being the biological parent of a teenager wasn't much better. He pointed out how many times Emily had shouted *I hate you!* when Brian set rules she didn't like. Jessica knew he had a point.

Jessica opened her eyes, remembering Mr. Manley's question about Emily's future, one to which she had no answer. But he was gone. She'd closed her eyes for longer than she'd realized, resulting in an untethered fast-forward. In Mr. Manley's place, Hazel and Nuke sat and stared up at her. She unfolded her legs. "I need to feed them."

"I can do that, honey," Jessica's mother said from beside her on the couch.

When had she sat there? Jessica thought about asking for another Klonopin, but decided to do a trial run on clarity. "No, I'll do it."

The dogs leading the way, she passed through the sprinkling of people who chatted in tight clusters. The bright whiteness of the kitchen brought her closer to a sober surface. She squatted to retrieve a bulk-size bag of dog food from under a counter, scooped generous portions into the dog bowls, and brought the water bowl to the sink for refilling.

A window above the sink overlooked the front lawn and circular driveway where several people mingled. It was dark. She could mainly only see large movements of the body, but she recognized Emily, standing alone, hugging herself as her van-load of friends pulled away. A lit-up end of a cigarette rose and fell, carried by the shadow of Emily's arm. Jessica couldn't believe she was doing that. The thought struck Jessica hard: Emily's life hung in the balance of what happened next. She could go back to her working mother who couldn't control her, to a city school where she cut classes more than she went, to the dangerous boys in Lauren's iffy neighborhood, to drinking and probably smoking weed and who knew what else … or Jessica could do something about it, the way Brian would have wanted her to.

She knew Lauren wouldn't take Brian's parental wants seriously, even in death. Lauren always seemed to have a smirk on her face whenever she saw Brian and Jessica, as if their entire life was a joke to her. Lauren was all bluster and self-righteousness, but Jessica was sure she was really riddled with guilt that she'd totally failed with Emily, while Brian and Jessica had begun to succeed. Just thinking about it made Jessica feel a steadying sense of purpose. She began to rehearse in her mind what she'd say to Lauren, nervous of being shot down but determined. She could at least offer to keep Emily and see what happened. So be it if Lauren responded with her typical sarcastic, condescending attitude. Jessica was doing this for Brian.

CHAPTER 5

Steve's wife, Nicole, stood at the center of a small group of state senators and a US congressman who all listened, enraptured, to her retelling of a hedge fund deal that only Nicole could make interesting. Lauren thought Nicole could have held their attention with her tits and ass alone, but the politicians were just as hot for the money she wielded as a donation-bundler. When Brian first met Steve and Nicole, he'd told Lauren all about Nicole's dinner parties where she collected huge checks—Lauren thought with an inner smile, "yuge" checks—to political action committees.

Nicole was a good storyteller with her razor-wire smile and impossibly white teeth—the whole package. But Lauren quickly had enough. She looked around for Emily.

In the kitchen, Lauren spoke to Jessica's back, "Have you seen Emily?"

Jessica turned. "She's outside. Her friends just left."

"Mr. Manley asked what we're going to do." Lauren pulled a chair from the antique oak table, reluctant, but needing to talk with Jessica. "I don't know how she's going to survive this, and I don't know what to do about school."

Jessica sat. "We could keep her in school here."

Lauren looked in Jessica's pale, devastated eyes. Lauren felt sad for her. But the idea of leaving Emily to live alone with Jessica was beyond a nightmare. Lauren sighed, forcing herself to face the situation. "I'm afraid of what will happen to her if I bring her back home, how she'll react now that Brian's … gone."

"Brian would have wanted her to stay at least through the school year. He was so happy with the improvement since she's been here."

Was that a dig? Lauren tried to restrain the anger that tightened her face. Jessica acted as if Brian—and Jessica for that matter—had no part in causing Emily's problems in the first place. She was like one of those crazy nurses who took credit for resuscitating a patient after she gave him poison.

Jessica took in Lauren's anger, her eyes widening, becoming wet.

Oh, jeez. Lauren tried to soften the expression on her face. She hadn't meant to hurt Jessica at a time like this. And if Lauren were honest with herself, she did care what Brian would have wanted. He was the father of her child, and he'd loved Emily. Although, without Brian, what was the reason for Emily living here, away from home?

Lauren took a deep breath, thinking aloud. "Emily has bad judgment and she's impulsive. In her traumatized state, God knows what will happen if I pull her out of school here and she comes home wanting to run wild with her friends again. Maybe I could move up here myself, but I'd have to find a new job—mine has a New York City residence requirement. And I'd need to sell the apartment." Lauren wondered whether Brian had left money for her to take care of Emily, enough to risk leaving her job without having another lined up. "How could I move that quickly?"

"Please, Lauren, I'm happy to keep her."

Lauren placed her face in her palms. Was Jessica capable of caring for Emily over the long haul? She was gung ho now, but Brian's memory and desires would fade, and Jessica would soon become as self-absorbed as always. Yet could she rise to the challenge? And was there any choice? Lauren looked at Jessica, who waited expectantly, seeming to give Lauren a pass for acting as if Emily's staying with her was as bad as waking up from a nightmare on Elm Street.

"Okay, we'll take it a day at a time," Lauren said, "but if she could finish out the school year …"

Jessica brightened. "It's settled then."

Lauren smiled, bleakly. "She's going to explode when she hears." Emily was old enough to think she should have a choice in the matter. Not.

Jessica sat back in her chair, appearing to dread telling Emily, too.

A male voice cleared at the doorway. Both women looked up. Steve. The sleaze barometer hit the ceiling. Lauren barely restrained her eyes from rolling into her head. She was still burning from his eulogy.

"I'm glad you're both here," he said, condescension already dripping from his voice. He sat down at the table across from Lauren, catty-corner from Jessica.

"I've been downstairs going through Brian's files and PC. I haven't found a will." He spoke to Jessica, "Do you know where he might have kept a hard copy, a safe-deposit box maybe?"

"No. He didn't keep a safe deposit," Jessica said. "I don't think a will was a top priority yet. He was always too busy."

Lauren knew what that meant. Brian had died intestate. It was basic estate law. Since there was no will, the first fifty thousand dollars of the estate would go to Jessica. Jessica and Emily would split the rest down the middle.

Steve sat for a moment as if contemplating the significance of Jessica's statement. "Well, he has a moderate IRA plus sixty thousand in the checking account. You have automatic deposit for the mortgage payments," he said to Jessica. "Ninety-eight hundred a month. So you don't have to worry about that. Your next real estate tax payment will be due in December. You can deal with that later too."

Lauren took in what Steve was saying. Brian had also been paying another thirty-five hundred a month to her, which covered her maintenance and mortgage. She barely netted that much a month at her job, so his payments were vital. She knew Brian and Jessica didn't have much equity in the house. They'd bought it after the market had bounced back in Westchester, so the house wasn't something that could be cashed in.

"Fifteen hundred a month for the cars," Steve said to Jessica. "You're locked into leases on both of them."

"Three years," Jessica said.

"Two thousand dollars a month for the plane, hangar rental, and insurance—a three-year lease, too. No escape clause."

Lauren ticked it all off in her head and saw Jessica frown as if she were trying to do the same, addled by whatever medication she was taking. The amount of money Brian had in the bank wouldn't keep Jessica in panty-hose let alone pay Brian's debts and keep two households afloat for any length of time, at least not two households in Manhattan and Westchester County. The real estate taxes for a house like this in Chappaqua could easily be forty thousand dollars a year. Brian spent money like a drug dealer. "Fast money goes fast" was an expression people used to say in the streets. Jessica would need to downsize (until she found someone else's husband to marry) but even downsized, it was only Brian's share in the law firm that would provide for Emily and Jessica. Lauren, too.

Aside from Lauren's alimony, the divorce decree entitled her to 10 percent of Brian's profits from his business. Now that there would be no alimony, that 10 percent of the value of Brian's cases with Steve would be what would pay her mortgage. Lauren found herself literally sighing with relief as the thought occurred: Brian had several big cases that would settle over the next year or two. He'd told her about them. When he was traveling and had nothing better to do, he sometimes called to shoot the shit with her. He'd said his share of the contingency fees would be worth millions. Lauren took another look at Steve. Why was he acting as if the cash in Brian's accounts was the extent of Brian's estate?

She didn't ask. She didn't want to put Steve on the spot on the day of Brian's burial. This wasn't the time to get into the weeds of the estate business. Steve had probably been talking about Jessica's petty cash needs until they could officially settle the estate. He was Brian's best friend, and it was only habit that made him speak like a cautious lawyer. She could call him at his office later in the week to talk about it.

After a few rote words of comfort, Steve left them.

Jessica put her hand on Lauren's arm. "Don't worry about money, Lauren. Brian and Steve have a couple of huge cases coming down the pike. We'll all be okay. Brian was talking about retiring early when the fees came in, not that I really believed he'd stop working."

The kitchen door slammed open and the two Labradors rushed to their feet from under the table. A smell of cigarettes entered with Emily like Pig-Pen's dirt cloud. Lauren felt a deep anxiety about it, as if she'd inhaled electric voltage with the tobacco stink. Emily's darkly circled gray eyes were Brian's for a moment. She appraised Jessica and Lauren with the same piercing intensity and hard-set, stubborn jaw as her father. She hugged herself and spoke pliantly in a tone that would only last for as long as she got the answers she wanted.

She looked from Jessica to Lauren. "What's going to happen to me now?"

CHAPTER 6
BRIAN

Eighteen Months Ago

Cars honked in rush-hour traffic. Pedestrians moved faster on Park Avenue's wide sidewalks than the vehicles. Behind potted plants, couples and groups of friends savored happy-hour tapas, drinks, and warm spring weather in a cathedral's courtyard café. Brian walked uptown, returning from Grand Central Station where an adolescent techie had fixed his glitchy phone. He'd left his office for the errand between one of many drafts of motion papers he'd been writing, wanting to relax his eyes before pouring over the words one more time to make sure they were perfect. Pointedly ignoring his vibrating pocket, he swore off looking at his phone while he walked. He wanted just a moment to enjoy the warm breeze and blossoming cherry trees on the Park Avenue median. Their pink only lasted a couple of weeks before morphing to green. He tried to really take them in, not to get lost in his head thinking about all the tasks he needed to do.

Brian stopped at a light, his phone vibrating again. He finally looked at it. A Facebook message on his home screen: Jordan Connors. Jordan was one of Brian's hundreds of Facebook friends whose posts didn't show up on his news feed. Neither of them had liked or shared each other's posts in years, and they hadn't seen each other since college. If Brian had wanted to find Jordan, he could, but he hadn't the vaguest idea what the guy was up to.

For Brian, social media was about business. Selfies and self-published books of his acquaintances didn't interest him. But in case someone was in a plane crash or mass disaster, or knew anyone looking for a lawyer, Brian was a click away. From time to time, he got a case that way. He never failed to send Facebook birthday messages. For him, they were the modern version of the birthday postcards dentists snail-mailed as a checkup reminder.

He looked at the message from Jordan: *Can you give me a call? 917-555-2424.* That was it, terse, no explanation. Brian would have expected some explanation from someone he hadn't heard from in years. But Jordan was no regular guy, never had been.

Brian and Jordan had gone to Queens College undergrad together, meeting because they'd lived in the same garden apartment complex on the outskirts of the commuter campus. Jordan was one of the smartest guys Brian knew, maybe smarter than Brian himself, and there weren't many people Brian thought that about. Jordan could be a sarcastic asshole at times too, but he had been funny as shit, an encyclopedia of politics, history, video games, sports, you name it. Maybe Jordan had been too smart for his own good, dropping out of college just four months shy of graduation, the degree superfluous to Jordan even when he was so close to getting it.

Brian remembered wishing he had Jordan's courage. Brian went off to the safety of law school, while Jordan moved to Las Vegas like an Old West settler pursuing a gold rush.

Waiting on the corner of Fifty-Second Street for another traffic light to change, Brian clicked onto Jordan's telephone number.

Jordan picked up after a ring. "Hello."

"Jordan, hey, it's Brian."

"Brian, thanks for calling."

"It's good to hear from you. How are things?"

"I'm good. With people now and can't talk, but, listen, my mother needs a lawyer."

"Everything okay?"

"She had some shitty plastic surgery. I figured if there's any shyster I can trust to get her a couple of bucks, it's you."

Brian laughed, reminded of Jordan's sharp-edged, born-and-bred New York attitude. It had always made Brian feel at home in a way he didn't feel around his friends who'd transplanted themselves to New York after the Ivies. "Thanks for the vote of confidence. I'm sorry to hear about that. What kind of injuries does she have?" Nerve damage was most likely, Brian thought, which could be permanently debilitating and an excellent payday if it weren't for the age of the plaintiff here. She would be too old to feel the pain long enough to push the verdict into the millions.

"Why don't you stop by my place?" Jordan said. "I'm on Fifty-Seventh, only a few blocks from your office. I'll be done with my meeting in fifteen if you're free."

Brian didn't have a reason to say no. Jessica didn't expect him home. He worked sixty hours in a good week, so there were many unsupervised breaks, and his motion papers only needed one more read-through before he headed home for the day. He couldn't help but be curious about Jordan. He'd been one of Brian's degenerate college friends, enamored of cocaine and wild women, two of Brian's favorite things about college. It was a side of Brian that few people knew about. He'd kept the different parts of his life sharply separated. And he'd sworn off all that when he started law school.

But one thing he knew from that experience was that good genes had been the only thing separating Brian from becoming an addict. He had an addictive personality. He'd easily left the hard drugs alone after graduation, but leaving the women alone had been more challenging. The problem with Brian and women was that he never knew when an obsession with a woman might hit him. He could be going about his business, focused on nothing but work, friends, family when, out of nowhere, he'd meet a woman's eyes or accidentally brush against her—even someone he already knew—and something about the connection would send him hurtling down the path to her bed.

He'd managed to stay away from cheating on Jessica since they'd married. He loved her and was sick of hurting people. He felt as if the harm he'd caused Lauren and Emily had scarred him too. But underneath it all, he doubted he'd possess the inner strength to resist that spark when it happened again. The way the craving for a woman could sucker punch him, he fully understood what it meant to be a drug addict.

Jordan had been a kindred spirit, enjoying a good party, although he probably lacked the baggage of a conscience that Brian had. But for all Brian knew, Jordan could have a paunchy wife and five kids by now. Brian walked to Fifty-Seventh Street, wondering if Jordan would live in one of the street's few remaining rent-stabilized apartment buildings, or was he a denizen of the Fifty-Seventh Street known as Billionaire's Row? The two realities were woven into the same street. Brian wanted the best for Jordan but he halfway hoped Jordan had ended up struggling, just to reassure Brian that he'd made the right call by going to law school and playing life safe.

When Brian reached Jordan's glass-walled building, its hundred stories casting a needle-thin shadow over Central Park, the answer became clear: Billionaire's Row. A Cy Young Award–winning pitcher nodded to Brian and put on sunglasses as he passed, leaving the elevator as Brian entered.

Ninety-two floors above, Jordan opened his apartment door, wearing jeans, sneakers, and a backward baseball cap, the uniform of an internet start-up guy. The two men hugged, slapping backs. Brian took in the wall of windows at the far end of a sleek living room. The apartment was socked in, surrounded by white cotton and moisture as if they were in an airplane flying through cumulus clouds.

Jordan followed Brian's gaze. "On a clear day, you can see all of Central Park plus Queens and Jersey. The view is never the same twice. The clouds and sky are always changing. Want a beer?"

"Thanks."

"I see you traded in your jeans for Armani suits," Jordan said, carrying cold Brooklyn Lagers from behind a bar.

"It's the uniform." Brian noticed the clouds taking on a pink cast as an unseen sunset unfurled behind them. "Nice place."

"It's a corporate apartment. I've got one here, one in the Hollywood Hills, another in South Beach."

Brian opened his beer. "Last I heard, you were in Las Vegas playing poker."

"Fifteen years ago I got eighty-sixed from the casinos for counting cards at blackjack. The casinos do everything they can to make it hard for a professional gambler to make a living. But getting eighty-sixed was the best thing that ever happened to me."

"How so?"

"I ended up in Samara, Costa Rica, a little beach town on the Pacific coast, running an internet gambling site. I was at the right place at the right time." Jordan grinned, "And here I be."

"Isn't internet gambling still illegal?"

"I'm cool. I'm set up in a country where it's legal. I can't process money transactions in the US, so our US bettors funnel their transactions through proper IP addresses. There's plenty of money to be made within the legal constraints. As bullshit and protectionist as those constraints are."

"How do you get business?"

"I advertise, mostly on sports news sites, and a lot of my business comes from agents who get a piece of the profits for each person they refer. I've also got a niche business that's a big moneymaker. There's a group of billionaires, Chinese, who love to gamble, mostly invitation-only poker games. I host and process the action. My business is perfectly legal if done right, and it captures a different market than the legal sports-betting casinos. But there are those who would begrudge me my goal of being rich without slaving to Wall Street."

"The Chinese government probably isn't very fond of you," Brian guessed. "Isn't gambling illegal in China?"

"I never step foot in China." Jordan took a joint from an onyx box and lit it. "I'm not looking to do life in a reeducation camp for letting their baby billionaires gamble."

Brian accepted the joint and took a drag. "Do they even bother to reeducate foreigners?"

"Ha, a very good question. I'm staying the fuck out of China, and all is good."

"Wow. I envy you," Brian spoke smoke. "I'm up to my ass in pleadings, interrogatories, motions, chained to my desk most days. Pretty much seven days a week. Don't get me wrong—I'm not whining."

Jordan laughed smoke. "You're whining."

Brian grinned, feeling woozy. The weed was strong, and he hadn't smoked in a long time. "I love a good day in court, especially with the amount of money up for grabs. But the work to get to court, getting prepared, it's grueling … I truly hate being a lawyer. My wife thinks I'm joking, but if I ever get a big enough payday, I will happily set up a bar and restaurant on an island in the Caribbean. I've been stuck on that idea since Jessica and I went to the Chat 'N' Chill in the Exumas."

"Oh yeah, I know the place, on Stocking Island. Owned by a guy with an MA in finance from University of Chicago. An impressive dude. Killer smart. A damn beautiful island to have a restaurant on. I rented a private island near there a couple of years ago." Jordan accepted the joint and inhaled. "It was a glorious week with a supermodel on the rebound. Thirty-eight thousand a night. Can you believe it?"

"For the woman?"

"Ha ha. Dude. Come on. For the island. Although some haters might say it adds up to the same thing … which is like saying Donald Trump pays for it, or Demi Moore." Jordan patted his own nearly concave chest, grinning. "It's the whole person they're attracted to."

"You have a point."

"Anyway, we would travel to that restaurant by seaplane. The plane and pilot came with the island." Jordan smiled, nostalgically. "I loved the Exumas."

Brian took a long swig of his beer. He imagined getting off the treadmill that was his life, which felt even more like a treadmill now that he was getting a whiff of Jordan's life. But he knew Jessica would never go along with the kind of simple life he craved. He didn't need a private island. He just wanted off the treadmill.

And, of course, it wasn't only Jessica that tied him down. Emily was in New York. She was growing up fast, a freshman in high school. There would be college tuition in four years. He would be tethered to his job and New York for a long time to come. He knew he should be grateful for his life, which was good by any objective standard, but he found it hard to stay in that attitude. He always felt as if something wasn't quite right.

"Gambling, my friend, is the pot at the end of the rainbow," Jordan continued. "But I read your website bio. You've got a lot more karma in the bank than I do. You're helping people. That's worth a lot. I try to give away money to good causes, but that's not the same as actually rolling up your sleeves and helping people."

Brian shrugged. Winning for his clients made him euphoric, but he worked years for each victory, and the thrill didn't last long. Plus, until joining up with Steve Cohen, he'd been on a salary. He was only now working on cases that would give him a piece of the verdicts, which he hoped would make the thrill a lot more thrilling. "That ballplayer I saw in the lobby? Was he a friend of yours?"

Jordan stretched his legs, crossing them at the ankles, no socks on. "I will say this to you as my attorney. Attorney-client privilege. Yes. A lot of these sports guys are big rollers, but money changes hands the old-fashioned way with them—cash—not credit cards or wire transfers, which are easy to trace. My athletes aren't fixing games. They just love to gamble and need to keep the appearance of impropriety at bay. Once playing ball in front of forty thousand fans stops doing it for them, and beautiful women become a blur in their beds, the athletes need other activities to spike their adrenaline. They're adrenaline junkies. Life is boring without risk. But, unlike them, I'm ever mindful that the house always wins, and I've chosen to gamble on the house. I just make sure not to trip any land mines belonging to the FBI, IRS, or local district attorneys." Jordan reached for his open laptop. "Let me show you my site."

A couple of clicks past a menu of gaming icons and an online poker game appeared, Jordan's passion. Cards were moving fast on an animated green table. Brian tried to adjust his eyes to figure out what was going on.

"We can see all the hands now because I have admin rights," Jordan said. "It's unbelievable how much money some of these Chinese guys play in the nosebleed games. They're not the real pros who make a living at it. Few pros, myself included, would risk a million dollars on a hand. Pros count on natural variation. You win some, you lose some. If you know the game better than the next guy and play it strictly by the numbers, not by emotion, you come out ahead and make a decent living. You've got to be a billionaire not to care about losing a million on a hand because of dumb bad luck." They watched a few hands and Jordan pushed the laptop aside. "I'm starving. You?"

Brian laughed, his own voice sounding distant. "Starving."

"You still like sushi?" Jordan said, scrolling through his contacts. "We can talk about my mother while we wait."

"Okay," Brian said, way too high to return to the office to proof motion papers.

He was glad to hang out longer too. He wanted to hear more about Jordan's life. Like Sean Penn chasing El Chapo, Brian always found himself trying to fill a void, searching for something he couldn't get from his safe life. He wanted to get closer to Jordan's life, get a taste of the thrill of it. Jordan could see it in him. They could both see it.

CHAPTER 7

Monday, October 28

After a week, Lauren's daily shivah calls to Jessica's house ended. On her first day back in Family Court, Lauren was relieved to return to her normal routine, although she missed Emily. Her instinct to protect Emily during a crisis created a painful maternal yearning that felt like a vacuum imploding her chest. Letting Emily go—allowing her to stay with Jessica—was among the hardest things Lauren had ever done, and that said a lot.

Lauren approached a Haitian woman and showed her the signature page of a document. "Ma'am, did you sign this document, placing your child in foster care?" A Creole interpreter echoed her words.

The woman appeared sad but sure. "Yes, I did," she said in accented English.

Lauren smiled, sympathetically. "Just a few questions then." Lauren returned to stand beside dozens of overstuffed court files piled on the table. She glanced down at sticky notes on an open file. "Ma'am, why did you place your child into foster care?"

The woman sighed and teared up, switching to Creole. The male interpreter's voice followed hers: "My daughter is fifteen years old ... She will not obey my husband or me. She will not go to school, and she has already been pregnant once."

"Do you want your daughter to remain in placement?"

The woman paused to listen to the interpreter. "Yes."

The case was like most of the voluntary placements: an incorrigible teen and frightened, fed up parents with no escape hatch, as Brian had been for Emily. A group home or residential treatment was the parent's last resort. In Lauren's own case, when she was sixteen, city lawyers had to do the same thing with her own mother, although for different reasons. Lauren had signed herself into rehab, but the program needed parental consent. Lauren's mother had to be tracked down by caseworkers. Lauren imagined them refusing to stop interrupting her mother's endless crack party until she consented to Lauren's treatment.

"Your honor," Lauren said, "I ask that the court grant the Commissioner's petition and find that the natural mother knowingly and voluntarily placed her child in care."

Judge Quiñones was a grandfatherly man with a deep cappuccino complexion and white, close-cropped hair. He spoke kindly to the mother. "Petition granted. Thank you for coming, ma'am." He turned to the uniformed bridge officer, who managed the flow of courtroom traffic. "Fifteen minutes, please."

"All rise," the bridge officer said, as the judge stood.

The moment the judge's robes disappeared through the chambers door, Lauren pulled her cell from her purse and rushed out, checking for messages while she race-walked through the noisy waiting area full of families. She dodged around a sprinting toddler, an older boy running after him, before she stepped inside a tiny windowless office with a desk, three vinyl chairs, and a coat locker reserved for the city attorneys while at court. She called Brian's house landline, now Jessica's, she mentally corrected herself. She'd left a message for Jessica that morning on her cell but had received no return message. Now, voice mail picked up after the third ring.

Brian's voice: "We're sorry, no one can come to the phone at the moment ..."

Lauren shuddered. The beep sounded. "Is anyone home?"

A pause, click, and Jessica's weary voice came on the line. "I just noticed your message, on my cell. Hi."

Lauren pushed aside the knee-jerk dislike she felt whenever she first heard Jessica's voice, even after spending a full week around her. "How are you?"

"Okay. My parents left this morning. The fire marshal called. They found a cigarette butt." Jessica's voice cracked. "That's what caused the fire. The marshal said that cigarette butts are the most likely thing to survive … the flames and heat." Jessica exhaled and began to weep. She blew her nose then sniffled. "The filters are designed not to burn so it's easy for them to tell when a cigarette caused a fire."

"I guess we figured that's what happened," Lauren said, tearing up, imagining how Emily would feel when she heard what had happened to her father. "Does Emily know?"

"Yes. She seemed relieved to have an explanation."

"Okay … that's good. How was school?"

Jessica lowered her voice. "Mr. Manley called and said she was absent. She's home now. She came back on the bus at the regular time."

"Damn."

Jessica whispered, "I didn't say much. It was her first day, and I don't know how hard to come down on her. She's really depressed. Mr. Manley thought maybe she should start therapy here—he gave me a couple of names."

"If she'll go along with it … I'll talk to her. Emily's on Brian's health insurance. I'll call Steve on my next break and find out about her coverage."

"She's in the basement, in Brian's office. I'll get her."

Lauren looked at her watch, mindful of the time. She had only five minutes before she had to be back in the courtroom.

The phone clicked, an extension picking up. "Mom?"

"Hi, honey."

"Mom. I'm worried about Jessica. She's not eating and won't talk to anyone who calls. You see how she's screening her calls?"

Lauren cringed. Was she the only thing keeping Jessica above water? How long could she give Jessica to pull herself together before bringing Emily home? It was Jessica's first day alone with Emily, and at least Jessica had taken Mr. Manley's call, but Lauren still worried. Lauren had basically been raised by wolves and knew how bad it was when the adults in your life checked out.

Of course, Lauren's situation had been much more extreme than

Emily's. When Lauren was twelve, her parents added crack to their burgeoning drug addictions and completely retired from the real world, locking themselves in their bedroom, smoking obsessively, draining their bank accounts, and selling things out of the apartment if times got rough. Lauren had lived with them in a rent-controlled walk-up in the East Village. They'd managed to pay the rent, but Lauren had to tell herself when to get up in the morning, what to eat, and when to go to school. Her only respite from her constant loneliness and plotting about how to keep her family situation secret occurred during the periods when her father tried twelve-step meetings.

"You're the only thing between me and the bad stuff, pumpkin," he'd say during those phases, taking Lauren with him everywhere like a bulletproof vest.

But those times never lasted long. Lauren would come home from school after days or weeks of being his bodyguard and find him locked in the bedroom getting high with her mother again, the sweet smell of cocaine smoke inundating the house. Lauren would beat herself up when it happened, thinking she should have stayed home from school with him. Her feelings of frustration and self-hatred were so bad on those days she'd felt as if the inner pressure would bust her wide open.

Unlike Lauren's father, her mother never tried to stop smoking coke and never seemed to feel any remorse about what they were both doing to Lauren. But perhaps her mother's total withdrawal from parenthood was better, less heartbreaking than the hope Lauren's father generated in her, which he shattered over and over, sending her spinning every time.

The beginning of the end came when Lauren's father won a lawsuit, every addict's dream. He'd been in a car crash six years before that had left him with broken bones and jump-started his addiction. Her father always told her he was going to get clean before the money from the lawsuit came, so they could live happily ever after. Of course, he couldn't get clean, and when the money came, it wasn't enough to make two crackhead dope fiends and their daughter live happily ever after. Plus the money attracted an entourage of stinking, conniving addicts who circled around them like restless border collies.

So while he still had some money, Lauren's father started copping weight, supposedly selling it, so they could have enough money left over to live happily ever after. A literal pipe dream. He told Lauren about it when he was high, talking at superspeed, licking his lips, pacing their living room. Her father and mother were their own best customers.

Lauren's nightmare was totally different than Emily's, but the rupture of Emily's family life felt all too familiar. Lauren had to remind herself to separate out her past drama from what was going on in the present or she could misread things entirely. She couldn't tolerate Emily staying in Westchester for any length of time if Jessica wouldn't behave like a parent. Lauren was having a hard time tolerating Emily being there at all, but she reminded herself that Emily was not reliving her own adolescence.

"I think you're the only one Jessica talks to," Emily was saying now. "The rest of the time she just stays in bed."

"Emmie, listen, don't worry about Jessica," Lauren said with more confidence than she felt. "She'll snap back, she's a strong woman."

"You think?"

"Have you ever met anyone who could stay on a StairMaster as long as her?"

"No," Emily laughed, a good sound to hear. "But no one would want to."

"Believe me, that takes a strong will. She'll be back to her old self in no time. So just try to take care of yourself."

"Mom … I've been thinking. Will I be able to go to college?"

"What do you mean?"

"Will we have the money?"

"We both depended on your dad, but you don't have to worry about money. Your father has some big cases pending, and then there's the overall value of his partnership with Steve."

"When Steve finishes the cases, we're still supposed to get Daddy's share?"

"Right, or Steve may want to give us a settlement instead of waiting for each case to finish. So what you need to worry about is getting your butt to high school, or there won't be any college."

"Jessica told you?"

"Mr. Manley said you cut today."

"I couldn't go in." Emily's voice lowered, becoming watery, maybe sincere or maybe just to manipulate her way out of trouble. "I couldn't stand the idea of people saying things to me about Daddy."

"The teachers are just concerned and the kids are trying to be nice."

"I know."

"Where did you go?"

"Nowhere," Emily responded, her voice becoming surly.

"Emily." Lauren's exasperation bent the syllables. She listened to the momentary silence. "I know you tried it before, but I think you should try seeing a therapist again."

"But, Mom—" Emily started to protest.

"It doesn't have to be forever. But they can help you get through this."

Emily sighed. "Okay."

"Great. We'll find someone good. Jessica has some names already. So, please, baby, try not to make things any worse for yourself. Go to school tomorrow."

After promising to call again later, Lauren double-timed it back to the courtroom and took her seat at the prosecution bench just as the judge entered. She tried to force her daughter out of her mind for the moment. At least Emily had agreed to accept help. Now Lauren only had to swallow her pride and call Steve.

She'd never known Steve well. By the time Brian had met Steve, her marriage to Brian had been near its end. She never met up for happy hours with Brian and his friends, pretending to be his Stepford Wife like she'd done before Brian's cheating had become an open secret. But Brian would still come home from his playdates with Steve and tell her all about the expensive champagne they'd drunk, the yachts his friends owned, and the women who couldn't smile with their whole faces because of premature Botox. Having powerful acquaintances made Brian feel important, but it was like a tree falling in the woods. It didn't count unless other people knew, particularly the wife who had little respect for him.

"They think having money is a sign of superiority," Lauren remembered telling him once.

"It's not a sign of inferiority either, Lauren," he'd say with disdain. "And I'm helping people. I don't have to take a vow of poverty to help people."

Now, as much as Lauren disliked Steve, she reflected that it was comforting that Brian's business partner had also been a friend who she and Emily could depend on. The irony wasn't lost on Lauren, the benefit she still received from Brian's lifestyle that she held in such low regard. She was wary of Steve though, and his help. She'd learned long ago that there was a cost for everything, and not just the price tag you saw before buying.

CHAPTER 8

Carl Cintron looked out of his boss' corner office. Below, on the Reade Street side of the Federal Building, Federal Police used a mirror attached to a long metal selfie stick to scan the underside of a delivery truck. An explosives dog, a black lab, sniffed the truck's tires. Carl turned from the window.

Tall, red-haired, and freckled, the ASAC—Assistant Special Agent in Charge—signaled Carl and Rick to seats in front of his large desk. "The Brian Silverman connection, we're not going to pursue it anymore."

"You've gotta be kidding," Carl said.

Rick shot Carl a hard "shut up" look.

The ASAC steepled his hands. "Brian Silverman is dead. We need to focus on Arena."

Carl leaned half out of his chair. "There was a cash transaction, twelve million dollars through Silverman's attorney escrow account two days before his *mysterious* death. We've been tracking Jordan Connors for months. We all know Connors has been dealing with the Chinese billionaire Xi Wen, to name just one. Silverman had to be helping Connors run the gambling money. I haven't been able to find anything in court data systems to indicate why Silverman would be receiving and paying out that kind of money."

"Listen, Carl, Xi Wen is, as far as we know, a legitimate Chinese businessman who's committed no US crimes. He places big bets, likes nosebleed poker games with stratospherically high stakes. His gambling would not please the Chinese, who don't want their billionaires sending large sums of money out of their country. But the FBI is not in the business of assisting Chinese law enforcement.

"We're on an austerity budget. We've got to triage the most promising cases and follow the best leads. Realistically, we'd hoped to catch and turn Silverman. One greedy lawyer running internet gambling payouts is a good media bust. But now that Silverman's dead with no indication of foul play, he won't be an example for other lawyers playing fast and loose with their escrow accounts." The ASAC spoke in the tone of Carl's fifth-grade teacher. "So, I want you to shift your focus from the dead lawyer to the living criminals."

Carl blanked his face, knowing he had to quickly adjust to the idea that months of his work was skittering away. Nobody liked a complainer.

The ASAC paused, assessing Carl, and continued. "Jordan Connors is routing bets through a server in New Jersey, ergo, breaking US law by operating here."

"Nice," Rick said ironically.

The New Jersey server really was a great find, Carl knew, and it was very bad news for Jordan Connors, whose foreign headquarters were little more than a villa where he vacationed. The internet betting sites needed servers closer to the US bettors or the online action was too slow. Local servers tempted internet bookies like second base tempted runners with a lead off first.

"So we've got him where we want him, but our top priority is still Arena," the ASAC said. "The evidence is piling up that the Arena syndicate has infiltrated Connors' operation. Jorge Arena is fixing sports bets and extorting internet gaming sites all over the world. We've recently turned another guy who's in with the Arenas. I'm hopeful he'll get us to the goal. He was selling drugs on the side that his people didn't know about. So they have no idea we busted him. He's above suspicion. We'll bring down the whole crew, including Jordan Connors. We'll even have a crack at the twelve million, wherever it is, if it has anything to do with Jordan's operation."

"Fair enough," Carl said, making sure the ASAC knew he had Carl's full buy-in to the investigation's shift.

"Good, because I have an assignment for you. I want you to work at the Home Game sports bar in Hell's Kitchen. Our informant manages it. His name is Juan Lachman. They call him CB, short for college boy. He's American-born Dominican. His family comes from the same town where Arena has his roots.

"There's an illegal casino upstairs at the sports bar. Jorge Arena is a silent partner. They run blackjack, roulette, poker. They cater to the investment-banker crowd, young men who are always looking for ways to give away their excess money to unworthy causes. We've already got a warrant to set up a stingray to listen in on the phones. But folks are sensitive nowadays about the way stingrays catch innocent signals going through their cell tower, so we can't overuse it, especially given the *upstanding* citizens who frequent the place. We've got to get closer."

***

Knowing he'd have a late night, Carl stopped at the gym, which was midway between work and his apartment in a middle-income complex on the far-west side of Tribeca. The gym was nearly empty. The lunch-hour crowd from the nearby government offices was gone. The after-work correction officers from the Tombs, cops from One Police Plaza, and prosecutors from the DA's office hadn't arrived yet. Only a sprinkling of locals who lived in Tribeca's multimillion-dollar condos and set their own hours were working out.

An iPhone strapped around his thick biceps, Carl mounted an empty treadmill with a view of a baseball game playing on an overhead screen. Embedded in the side of his thigh, a long white scar ended in a knob-shaped indentation. That and a two-inch scar over his eyebrow were the only remaining evidence of the accident that had ended Carl's own hopes of a baseball career. It happened just after his eighteenth birthday. The first responders cut him out of the car where his best friend and both of their dates lay dead. He'd been lucky, miraculously alive in a crumpled tomb, but he hadn't felt lucky. He was the designated driver. He'd only had one drink, well under the legal limit, and the accident wasn't officially his fault. But the question roiled in him for years afterward: Would his reflexes have been better if he hadn't drunk at all? Half measures had availed him nothing that night. He never lost sight of that lesson if he could help it.

His feet pounding the moving mat, his thoughts fast-forwarded to Brian Silverman's twelve-million-dollar transaction. Before Silverman's death, Carl had gotten subpoenas on Silverman's telephone toll records. Toll-record subpoenas only gained you access to the list of calls made and the caller's locations. That information would at least continue to trickle in about Silverman's last days without Carl violating the ASAC's orders. The sports bar was a good opportunity for Carl, he knew that. But he wasn't ready to let go of the Silverman issue just yet. He was sure there'd been a screwup or rip-off, and that was why Brian Silverman was dead. Silverman and his twelve million dollars were a loose end Carl meant to tie up.

CHAPTER 9

Jessica lay in bed in a fetal position, holding Brian's pillow tightly. She'd always loved their home, a remodeled old Dutch Colonial with a large front lawn, separated from the road by a line of tall trees and cradled in back by a patch of woods. It was a low-lying, rambling place with two bedrooms and ample living space on the first floor. Only the slope-ceilinged master bedroom suite occupied the second floor in what had once been the attic. With every window shuttered tight, the once-romantic wood-paneled room had become dark and coffin-like. Floating within that airless cocoon, she found herself wondering whether she would lose her home too. She felt a fresh stab of pain: she wanted to ask Brian what he thought. She wanted to ask Brian or tell him something a hundred times a day only to realize that she couldn't.

She could still make out Brian's scent on the pillowcase, but it was fainter. It would be gone soon. The thought threw her to the edge of abyss. She could barely breathe.

A knock sounded at the door. She opened her eyes and looked back. Emily stood in the doorway, silhouetted by the light from the staircase. Jessica spoke blurrily, her mouth too relaxed to form clear words. "Don't you have to go to school?"

"It's after school, Jessica. Remember? You already told my mother on me." Emily approached, haltingly, carrying a small bowl. "I brought you some fruit salad. The lady next door brought it."

"No. I can't." Tears leaked from Jessica's eyes. She wanted to be strong for Emily, but she hugged the pillow and turned her back on the teenager. For the umpteenth time that day, a horrible picture played in Jessica's head: Brian burning, screaming, dying. She tried to muffle her cry in the pillow, hating herself for being so fucking weak.

"Why don't you get up, Jessica?"

Jessica shuddered and shook her head, using all her will just to do that. She could feel Emily staring at her back and turning away. She could imagine Emily's own eyes burning. Emily had lost her father, and Jessica was useless to her.

When Jessica opened her eyes again, Emily was gone. The meds were wearing off, weighing her down less. She coached herself, scolded herself: *Get up, Jessica. You're breaking your promise. You promised you'd take care of Emily. If you don't get up now, you may never get up.*

Her thoughts floated to the last time she'd given in to the darkness, letting herself burrow in it, starving in the dark like a wounded animal. It had been so hard to dig out from that and return to life. During her teenage years, her father had been a popular figure in their suburban town, friends with everyone, holding court in the local diner each weekend. He had even served a term as mayor after he retired from his corporate job. But at home, he'd flown into rages, terrorizing their household for little apparent reason. Fearing criticism and desperate for his praise, Jessica did well in school and tried her best to be the perfect daughter. Meanwhile, her mother was keeping the plastic surgery industry afloat, and she expected physical perfection of Jessica too. So at twelve, Jessica had the mandatory nose job, and when her ballerina's body rebelled and sprouted large breasts that screwed up her mother's ideas about Jessica's premarital dancing career, Jessica had needed to fight with all her teenage fury to avoid reduction surgery. Her breasts had been too mixed up with her newfound womanhood to chop up so easily. Luckily, the dancing had been her mother's obsession, not her father's.

In the end, Jessica had made her parents proud. She overachieved in high school, stayed away from keg parties where girls humiliated themselves on a weekly basis, and headed off to college. She'd worked hard to get into an Ivy League school and had been more than ready to get out of her parents' house. She'd made big plans for herself, including medical school. She had a roommate she liked, and everything seemed to be lining up perfectly.

But it took only one fraternity party two weeks after Jessica arrived on campus to turn the whole thing around on her. She never knew what happened that night. Memories came back to her afterward in hazy flashes. She never knew whether she'd been roofied or had a weird reaction to alcohol. She remembered how heavy her arms had been, how she'd battered her fists against the chests of the three men who had sex with her, her strikes as light and ill-coordinated as thrown tissue paper. She pieced together that they dropped her back at her dorm afterward, as if they were dropping off a date.

She filed a complaint with the school two days later, but it only made things worse. That was long before women started carrying mattresses around campus and tweeting #metoo. Jessica remembered how her roommate told her she'd seen her go to the room with the men as if she'd wanted it. "Why didn't you scream if you didn't?" her roommate accused. "You can't ruin their lives because you were too drunk to think straight."

Jessica couldn't believe life had taken a hair-turn on her again. The old despair had returned. It was the same hopeless sinkhole that had changed the course of her entire life after the rape. Jessica's memories paused long enough for her to feel a surge of self-hatred for thinking about her own life, her own losses, so self-involved at a time when Emily was much more important. Emily was just a child. She'd lost her father. Jessica was sick of herself for being all she thought about. She couldn't do this anymore.

She groaned and, with all the energy she could muster, swung her feet out of bed. The bottle of Klonopin her mother had left was sitting on the night table, staring at her. Pills were always her mother's solution. Sometimes Jessica wondered whether her mother had so much plastic surgery just so she could have an excuse to do more pills. A consolation prize for aging. Jessica angrily grabbed the bottle and got to her feet.

In the bathroom, she flushed and watched the pills circle the toilet, horrified at the thought of facing her ruined life. Alone. But she had no choice. If she chose the darkness for another minute, she knew she would lose herself in it for good this time.

CHAPTER 10

Four blocks from Family Court, the phone was ringing when Lauren opened her office. She answered with her coat still on. "Hi, this is Lauren."

"Lauren, this is Peggy Hall."

"Oh, hi. Thanks for coming to the service last week. It was good to see you."

Since Lauren and Brian's separation, the two never saw each other, but they'd spoken many times. Peggy had always been formal but friendly and Lauren could count on her to remind Brian to send his support payment if she called.

"Steve asked me to return your call. Emily's insurance will be in force for another year."

"That's great."

"I'll email you all the information. You can change the contact information online."

"And about the support check … to tide us over." There was a silence, a long silence, as Lauren waited for Peggy to pick up the ball and relieve her discomfort about asking for money the way Peggy normally did.

"They only instructed me to tell you about the insurance …"

It wasn't the words Peggy spoke but something else—her pause—that punched Lauren like Marvel's Jessica Jones. Instantly, Lauren's head spun with calculations for her mortgage and maintenance payments and the last payment to Emily's orthodontist and—Lauren caught her breath. "Peggy, is there a problem?"

"No."

"If there's a problem, could you ask Steve to call me?"

"I'll ask, yes."

"Thanks."

"Sorry." Peggy said goodbye and hung up.

Lauren leaned back in her chair. Why was Peggy saying "sorry"? The thought came to her loud and clear: *Brian was murdered and Steve is going to screw us.* He wasn't going to make good on the money he owed. Lauren's lungs tightened. For days since she'd first heard about the fire, she'd had a bad feeling that it hadn't been an accident.

Stop, she ordered herself.

She had no reason to think that. So Peggy had seemed uncomfortable. Many people were uncomfortable with death and its aftermath. So Steve hadn't bothered to call back personally after his solicitousness at the hospital and funeral. Well, he was back in his world now, caught up in court and the old self-centered swing of things. Brian's needy family wasn't his priority.

Lauren felt a shot of shame, as if she were an embarrassing relative asking for money. It was an old tape, humiliation she used to feel when visiting her father's family on rare holiday dinners. Lauren was the poor relation, the one with stained, too-small clothes and inebriated parents. Asking for her own money now made her feel low as a coffin termite, but she knew it shouldn't. Her emotional baggage affected her perception.

No one who dealt with her as a parent or lawyer, or even a friend, could see the world of memories that roiled under her calm surface. She was like a duck gliding along the water but paddling furiously beneath it. She thought back to her first year of high school, doing homework in the living room. She tended to sit there when she studied because it gave her a vantage point on her parents' bedroom door, so she'd be ready to deal with any drama that might crop up. Her parents smoked back there, day and night, with an ever-changing crew of slimy characters they called friends. Lauren's home felt as safe as an East Village subway station at three in the morning. And on the occasions when Lauren's dad went away to detox, her mother had men in. Lauren never told her father but the first time she realized what her mother was doing was the last time Lauren had said more than three words in a row to her. Lauren's father wasn't much but at least he was loyal.

On the day he died, Lauren's mother found him in the bathroom and began yowling. Hearing her, a slew of people ran out of the bedroom, crack smoke billowing after them. They took one look inside the bathroom and jetted from the apartment. The front door slammed behind them, leaving mother and daughter alone.

Lauren's mother was screeching, her whole body shaking, "What do we do?"

Lauren's dad lay sprawled out, already stiffening in the bathtub, a needle still jutting from his arm. Lauren didn't have time to cry or scream like her mother, even though she felt as if every cell in her body had been pulverized. The police would be there soon. They'd take Lauren's mother to jail and take Lauren to foster care, maybe to juvenile detention, arrested for the crap they found in the house. Lauren grabbed a black plastic garbage bag from the kitchen and rushed around her parents' bedroom, picking up crack pipes and vials, needing to clean the house before the cops came.

After Lauren dumped all the pipes and torches into the garbage bag, she opened an unlocked safe inside the closet. She took out her father's illegal gun and freezer bags full of cocaine and threw them into the garbage bag too. She raced from the apartment with all the illegal goods, her mother still jittering in place in the bedroom. Lauren never came back. There was nothing left for her there. That day she concluded that her nightmare would never end, and she'd set about figuring out how to survive within it.

Years later, in the wake of Brian's many betrayals, Lauren finally glimpsed how, despite her adult life appearing normal on the outside, her past still controlled her. She began seeing a therapist. It had done wonders, giving her the courage to finish college, go to law school, and become emotionally self-sufficient without depending overly on men as she'd done with Brian. Lauren's therapist had warned her, though, that the extreme circumstances of her childhood might lead her to catastrophize and feel irrational shame or fear over situations that reminded her of her past. He'd said: *If it's hysterical, it's historical.* That had been an aha moment for Lauren, explaining so much about her reactions to life. With his help, Lauren had broken the mind-habit of feeling as if she were about to careen off a cliff at the least provocation. And she wanted to keep it that way.

Lauren felt suddenly claustrophobic in her cramped office. She pictured Steve sitting in his luxurious corner office, secretaries treating him like King Trump. He was still flying away for weekends in his private plane, still hosting his soirées. Steve was making her grovel for money that was rightfully hers and Emily's. And she didn't know what the hell to do about it.

She looked at the time on her phone. She could see her therapist's kind face telling her it was time for a little "self-care," and that was exactly what she was going to do. She grabbed her gym bag and walked west, past expensive lofts, restaurants, and construction cranes that satisfied the never-ending thirst for Tribeca condos for the ultrarich. She breathed in cool air. Peggy's call had put her on edge, but in the final analysis, she was just having a hard time believing that Brian could smoke a cigarette in bed the way he always did and that it killed him. Neither Steve nor anyone else had spoken about what case Brian had been working on, not even during the hours of waiting-room purgatory while the surgeons tried to save Brian's life. She could surmise what that meant: a woman was involved.

Still, the question that bugged her was, if there had been a woman in the room and the fire occurred while Brian was sleeping, where was the woman at the time? She hadn't died in the fire. That couldn't have been kept secret. Of course, if Brian had been with a prostitute, she might not have slept over. But why would Brian go all the way to Miami for a prostitute? Lauren contemplated that. Maybe the Miami woman was married. She would have left early. There was plenty of room for paranoia to breed in that soil. A jealous husband set the fire?

Lauren pulled open the glass door to the gym and walked down a ramp past the check-in desk and an open area of StairMasters, treadmills, and bikes. After a stop in the locker room, she entered the mirrored free-weight room, wearing loose shorts and a racer-back T-shirt. She was old school about her workouts. She liked to do a simple free-weight routine with dumbbells and bench presses.

She saw a dark-haired man sitting on the end of a bench. His upper arm leaned against the inside of his thigh as he did slow bicep concentration curls. When his arm lowered, it created a diamond-shaped triceps indentation. When he curled, the vein stood out against his well-developed biceps. He wore a T-shirt and running shorts. Nice legs.

He watched his working bicep, focused on the exercise. Very attractive. She smiled, her mind looking for distractions anywhere today. It had been longer than she wanted to admit—even to herself—since she'd been with a guy. She hadn't taken to the internet-dating scene, which usually ended up with her and the man boring each other to death in a Starbucks, since she didn't drink alcohol. And then there were the guys who were shocked about that, who said stupid, deprecating things about her not drinking because it made them uncomfortable. Truthfully, it would be easier to meet a guy for the first time over drinks, but she'd had her lifetime ration of mind-altering substances before she'd reached drinking age. She'd never even had a legal drink, which was no doubt a good thing.

She placed twenty-five-pound weight plates onto each end of a bar, which hung between poles attached to a bench. She nodded hello to a gray-haired trainer who walked out of the room. That left the dark-haired man and a woman doing calf raises with a dumbbell in each hand in the far corner. Lauren lay down and bench-pressed ninety-five pounds of plate and bar, eight reps, no problem.

Resting a minute between sets, she sat up and looked around. With the idle curiosity of a single woman, she casually sought out the dark-haired guy. He was facing the mirror but staring into the distance as if in deep thought or memory. He looked pained by something; a slight grimace crossed his face, making him appear vulnerable as if his dark eyes belonged to a young boy, not a man in his late thirties. Then his eyes met Lauren's in the mirror. He blinked and his head reared back as if struck. Lauren flinched in surprise at his sudden reaction.

He looked away momentarily. When he looked back at her, any expression of surprise was gone.

Lauren tried not to stare. The moment had been eerily intense—as if she were a mind reader who'd intercepted his deepest secret. She half wanted to apologize, to reassure him that his secret was safe, but he looked down, picked up a weight, and returned his attention to his exercise.

She got up and placed an additional ten-pound plate on each end of the bar. The guy looked vaguely familiar. Maybe she knew him, maybe that was why he reacted to her. Did she know him from her past life, his looks so transformed in twenty years that she didn't recognize him? She tried to dismiss the thought, not liking the idea of running into anyone from those days. New York City was a big place and she didn't go to places where she was likely to see the old people, if they were even still alive. She'd put time if not distance between herself and her old life, using Brian's last name before the divorce and keeping a nonexistent social media presence.

The mystery was starting to irk her as she lay down on the bench. The guy's failure to smile or say hello when their eyes met felt like a dis by some arrogant asshole who thought she was somehow interested in him. Nice-looking guys could be such jerks.

She lay down, breathing in deep. A 115-pound bench press was a lot for a 125-pound woman to lift. She'd done it before, but she usually used a spotter. It was because she was pissed, that was why she was lifting so heavy. And it wasn't because of the hot dark-haired guy. No, she'd been on edge all day. It was Brian, always Brian—dead or alive—who could get her pissed off like that. If he'd been alive, she would have killed him for smoking in bed, leaving Emily with yet another lifelong scar, all because he was likely screwing around with some woman rather than staying home and learning how to be a father.

Lauren pushed and lifted the weighted bar off the metal lip that secured it above the bench. With arms locked, she balanced the bar over her, the weight pressing down against her palms. She allowed her elbows to bend and lowered the bar to tap her chest and up to straight arms. One rep, no problem. She lowered the weight again, her arms shaking as she controlled the speed of its descent until it reached her chest.

She exhaled sharply and pushed. The bar rose one inch, two. Then nowhere. Her triceps clenched, quivered. Nothing. She couldn't budge it.

"Uhh," she let out the weight lifter's version of a karate *kiai*, a sound from deep in her belly to mobilize all her energy to push the weight up. But the bar didn't budge. She used all her remaining energy to keep the bar from crashing into her with sternum-crushing force. The 105 pounds landed softly against her chest. She was stuck, at a stalemate with the weight, still pushing upward just to lighten the weight against her.

Hoping everyone hadn't left the room, she called out, breathlessly, "A little help here."

She sensed quick movement. A lightening of the weight against her chest. The bar lifted. One assisted shove upward and she hooked it onto the metal lips. She looked into dark eyes, a scar above his eyebrow.

He smiled down at her. "Are you all right?"

She caught her breath. "Yeah, thanks."

"Hey, counselor." A voice called from the room's entrance. Gary, the bridge officer from Judge Quiñones' courtroom, entered the room.

She looked over. "Hey, Gary, I didn't know you belonged to this gym?"

"I usually come in the morning, took off early instead."

"Me, too. I usually come at night." She looked back at the dark-haired man, who was turning to leave. "Hey, thanks again."

"No problem." He walked to his bench and picked up a white towel, smiling back at her before he headed for the door. "Nice lift, but use a spotter next time."

She got up and took a weight plate off each side of the bar. He had smiled at least, but there was something annoyingly patronizing about the way he said that. She turned to the court officer, who looked so different with his long skinny legs out of uniform. "Gary, can you spot me a set?"

CHAPTER 11

Brian's Red Bulls were still lined up in the fridge like gravestones. Emily took one and headed down the steps to her father's basement office. As usual when Jessica was away, the dogs followed her. She felt furry pressure against the back of her legs, the dogs pushing past her on the stairs. She loved that. She opened the sliding glass door that led up a couple of cement steps to the side of the yard. Sunlight and a cold breeze poured in. As always, the dogs ran out for a piss-patrol of the property. They'd run around in the woods behind the house before they came back.

Emily pulled a flattened pack of Newports from her pants waistband and fell backward into a slouch on the hard sofa bed that Jessica had brought from her old apartment in California. Emily leaned forward and bent between her legs, probing under the sofa until she felt her father's glass ashtray. She'd spent enough time in this room with her father to know how to smoke in the house without Jessica finding out, although this was the first time it was Emily and not her father with a cigarette down here.

She took a deep inhale. She didn't have a habit, not yet, although she'd been smoking flavored e-cigarettes for a while with her friends. When her father died, she'd switched over to the real thing. She just couldn't give a shit about a cigarette habit anymore. The hot smoke filling her lungs was the only thing that cauterized the open wound her father had left behind, for a couple of minutes at least.

She stared out the door, watching Nuke lift his leg to mark a tree and run off. She'd hated it here in Westchester when she first came. She had no friends, and her father was hardly around. But one day, he brought home a PlayStation 4 and asked her to show him how to play. After that, if they were both home, he'd ruffle her hair and say, "Come down and play *Call of Duty*," which was like heaven for a kid like her. She wasn't too old to blow a whole weekend playing *Minecraft* or *Call of Duty*, although only her father, not her mother, let her buy the violent games.

Her father got hooked on the games, too. She'd laughed a couple of times when she came downstairs to find him already playing. He would look at her, startled by the noise (she never came down a staircase quietly). "You caught me," he'd say, and his face really did look like she'd caught him. He'd cover it up, joking, "Come down to my man-daughter cave."

He started working from home a lot after Emily moved in full time. So, even when they weren't playing, Emily would come downstairs and do homework while he worked. She had a little secret about that, though, which she would take to her grave. Her parents thought she was doing much better in school in Westchester, and she was. She had started having more fun once she got to know some of the kids, but half the reason she'd been doing better was because of Adderall. She never saw so many kids on Adderall before she moved to the suburbs. It seemed like everyone was doing it to keep up their grades and still have energy left for all the volunteer work and extracurricular activities they needed for their college applications.

It only took a couple of weeks going to her new high school before a gangly kid came up to her and said, "Well, we checked you out and you're not a narc."

Emily just smirked and said, "Really? Have the cops started hiring sixteen-year-olds?" Duh. The kids in her town could be really stupid about stuff all kids in the city knew, and they were super obsessed with going to the best colleges. That was true in Manhattan, too, but the kids in the city weren't so obviously desperate. As for Emily, she was always, like, whatever. Maybe she'd go to one of those colleges. (Everyone said she was smart.) But worst case, she'd stay in New York and go to City University and save her parents a shitload of money.

Still, she couldn't help but get happy when her parents nearly started dancing with joy when she brought home her first A on an exam once she moved here. After that, Emily studied and did homework for hours in this room with her father, breathing his nicotine and buzzing off the Adderall, though not so buzzed that he could tell. They got in a pretty good habit of hanging out together in the man-daughter cave.

Those were the best times she had with him since he moved out of the apartment with her mother. It seemed the rest of the time, all Emily ever did was fight with him, Jessica, and Lauren by phone. Emily's mother had ruined her life, chasing away her father, then Emily, too. And Jessica had been there both times, waiting with open arms, pretending to want Emily.

Emily turned on the PlayStation, deciding to log in to her father's profile and play as if she were him, just to feel closer to him, even if it was ridiculous. She clicked into MESSAGES. His messages with her, Distressed Damsel, were still there, things they'd said to each other when playing together online while she was in Manhattan on the weekends. He'd also been messaging with somebody named MacroRaptor. *Unlocking 5 mm, 2 pm eta. CU @ Next Level.* She frowned. There was no five-millimeter gun in *Call of Duty.* They didn't even measure guns in *Call of Duty.* She scrolled up. Another text in October with MacroRaptor, two weeks ago: *Unlocking 12 mm, 4:30 Roadtown. Leveling up.*

Emily dropped the controller as if it were hot. Her chest squeezed tight, feeling as if she was about to lose something else important and didn't even know what it was. For the first time in her entire life, there was something that she might not want to know.

Still, she swiveled the desk chair toward her dad's PC and turned it on. Road Town was the capital of Tortola. Daddy had honeymooned with Jessica on that island. Emily had seen the videos: turquoise water, pastel houses, him and Jessica sailing. Why had he mentioned Road Town to MacroRaptor, and who was that?

The landline rang. The trill of the extension on the desk nearly knocked her off her chair. Her mother had called the landline the other day out of desperation when Jessica wouldn't return her calls, but other than Emily's mother and Jessica's parents, robocalls and fund-raisers were the only calls that came on the landline. Emily picked up the phone, thinking maybe her mom was trying to reach Jessica again. "Hello."

"Is this Jessica Silverman?"

"No. Who's calling?"

"I'm a friend of Brian's … are you his daughter?"

"Yes." Emily doubted he was her father's friend. She smelled a salesman or maybe someone trying to buy the house. Steve had warned Jessica and Emily about people who read the obituaries and figured they could get one over on the widow. Steve said people might even tell them they were from her father's bank and ask for account information. "What's your name?"

"Jordan Connors."

Emily lit another cigarette. "Where did you know him from?"

"Look, I'm in a hurry. College."

"Really?" He was hyper, his words staccato. Emily had good intuition about people, could tell right away when they were assholes. He wasn't just impatient, he was arrogant, as if whatever had made him so stressed out was everyone else's fault but his. And Emily was the convenient one to dump it on because she was unlucky enough to have picked up his call. Her father never talked about any friends from college. This guy was bogus. "Donations can be sent to Mothers Against Drunk Drivers."

"Look, I've been calling for days. Your father and I had business together, and I need to talk to your mother."

Emily grabbed a sticky pad from the desk and began to doodle. "She's not my mother. And she's not real into returning calls right now. She's a little upset. You can call my father's office number anyway. His partner is there."

"Look, tell your stepmother to call me." His voice had picked up a threatening edge. It gave Emily a jolt. He exhaled hard, pissed. "It's important."

Now she was sure he didn't really know her father. Her father's friends would never treat her like that. She wanted off the phone, now.

"You have a paper?" he asked, calming his voice down. She could hear the effort it took him.

She pulled out a pen and a hot-pink sticky. "Yeah."

She wrote down the number he rattled off and repeated it back to him. The she hung up without saying goodbye as the sound of tires on gravel grabbed her attention, startling her. The dogs ran out the sliding door. Emily quickly opened the glass doors wider to get a fresh burst of air and hid the ashtray under the desk.

"Emily? Are you home?" Jessica's voice carried from the front hall.

"Down here."

Jessica appeared on the staircase, wearing jeans and sneakers, her eyes deeply circled and red from crying in the car. At least she'd gotten up and dressed, but her cheeks were more hollow every day. "It's cold in here." She shivered. "I went by school to see if you wanted a ride."

"I took the bus."

"I saw Mr. Manley …"

Emily let out a long breath, feeling tears coming, holding them back. "I know, I know."

"He said you didn't go to school again."

"So?" Hot tears filled Emily's eyes, and her throat tightened. She jumped up. "I can't go to school. My father's dead," she screamed. "My father's dead. Why don't you all leave me alone?"

Emily ran, pushing past Jessica. She might have accidentally knocked Jessica down if her stepmother hadn't sidestepped out of the way. Emily felt a flash of regret, swiftly buried by rage. "At least I'm not starving myself to death," she cried, her feet pounding on the stairs.

Emily pulled open the front door and ran across the lawn and into the road, ran until the cold air made her lungs ache. She stopped a couple of houses down the road and looked around. She had nowhere to go, and it was cold. She crossed the road and walked to a boulder next to the empty golf course. She sat and cried.

A few minutes later, a gust of wind sent a rack of shivers through her. She wiped her eyes and stood, putting her hands in her front pants pockets. She felt a piece of paper against her fingertips. She took it out and looked at it. It was that asshole's number, the salesman.

She crossed the road again and started back to the house. When she reached the driveway, she lifted the lid of a garbage can. Jessica would never call the guy back. Emily would save her the trouble of even thinking about it. She threw the hot-pink sticky in the can and went inside.

***

It was dark outside and the house was silent. After their argument, Emily had returned and shut herself in her room. Once again, despite a good start, Jessica had accomplished nothing today. She'd gotten rid of the pills before they could become a problem, but she couldn't break free of the depression that had straitjacketed her, making even the most minor tasks Herculean. She rose from where she sat and swayed on her feet, dizzy, her vision going black from low blood sugar. She closed her eyes and held onto the kitchen chair for a moment, waiting for the blackness to pass. Emily was right about her not eating.

It had been over a decade since anyone had considered Jessica anorexic, but she'd never entirely shaken it. After her one and only hospitalization, she'd always exercised a lot, feeling safer burning extra calories. She'd gone through minor bouts of undereating on occasion: when her mother had cancer eight years ago; during the months after she'd fallen in love with Brian, while she waited for him to leave Lauren; and sometimes, during their own marriage, in the aftermath of arguments. But what was happening now was as bad as she'd been since her miserable college years. The part of her that wanted to die kept her stomach locked up like a bank vault.

Anorexia was what did her in after the frat-party incident. She never told her parents about the rape, sure that her father would react like her roommate, judging and blaming her. Without support from anyone, Jessica tried to take control of her life and body. She began a never-ending diet and exercise regime that took on a life of its own. Only when she returned home at spring break, resembling a walking corpse, did her mother—a member of the "never too thin or too rich" club—stop complimenting Jessica's weight loss and hospitalize her. Jessica remembered the expression on her father's face: disappointment, disgust. She remembered his tirade because he'd already paid the tuition for spring.

The harsh memory opened Jessica's eyes now. Her dizziness had subsided, and the ground was steady under her feet. She forced herself to the refrigerator, sick of how hard life was. If she wasn't worried about taking too many Klonopin, it was anorexia; if it wasn't that it was anxiety—her heart palpitating in her chest for no apparent reason; or it was depression—sadness even when things were going well. She felt as if she'd been poking her finger in a dike her entire adult life. All the new age hokum she'd tried hadn't made a bit of difference in the end. She'd already erased the Law of Attraction app from her phone.

She surveyed the contents of the refrigerator full of leftovers from dishes people had brought. She passed over the containers of foods prepared with hidden fat, hidden gluten, hidden antibiotics that fattened the chickens and people who ate them. All the bogeymen of her anorexic self. She sighed, telling herself she could stick to something simpler. She'd restock basic items—milk, bread, yogurt. Over the last couple of days, she'd become able to focus on what Emily needed in a way she couldn't do for herself. Even the estate business that had motivated her this morning would have failed to get her out of bed if she had only been looking out for her own interests.

She pulled an organic yogurt shake from the refrigerator. If she couldn't bear to chew, she could at least replenish her blood sugar. The yogurt quelled the emptiness of her belly, and anger washed over her. Once all the bills were paid, she and Emily had only a couple of months of liquid assets in the bank accounts. That was what she'd been too hungry to think about. Brian had expected to bring in millions when the cases he'd brought to Steve's firm came to fruition. So this morning, she'd decided to start on whatever one did with estates so she could settle up with the firm. Her first step had been to call Steve to get his recommendation of an estate attorney. Instead, Steve's secretary transferred her to Peggy, who said she was supposed to handle any of the questions Jessica might have. So she left a message that Steve should call her with an attorney referral. Simple enough. But nothing. No return call.

At five, she called Peggy again, but Peggy didn't know anything and thought that Steve might have been in court all day. Well, it was seven o'clock now, and still no call back. It made no sense. Even if Steve were busy, attorneys loved to refer business to each other. Jessica knew that from Brian. Referrals led to referral fees or at least reciprocal referrals. It meant money, and if there was anything that Steve cared about, it was money.

She threw out the yogurt container, remembering that she hadn't checked the landline messages when she returned from the store. In the darkened front vestibule, the telephone sat on a spindly antique table. The red light was blinking. She pressed the play button, hoping Steve had called on the landline instead of her cell. She erased her mother's message halfway through her lengthy chitchat with the machine. After the next beep, Jessica heard the annoyed voice of a man she didn't know. He didn't state his business, and his voice smelled of salesman, a stressed-out salesman. Maybe he needed to make a quota or he would lose his job. There was nothing she could do to put a dent in that, least of all buy phony timeshares or sell her house. Exasperated, she pressed the erase button again. And that was it. No call from Steve or his office.

She looked up to see Emily coming from the hallway that led to her bedroom. Emily's face was slack, half-awake. A pillow indentation line ran from the outer corner of her eye to her mouth. "Did you hear from Steve?" she asked.

"Steve? Why?"

"I heard you talking to Peggy before. Is there something wrong?"

"No," Jessica answered quickly. "I was trying to reach Steve to get an attorney referral for the estate. It's no big deal, he was probably in court all day."

"That never stopped him from calling Daddy back. They used to talk a couple of times a day when Dad worked at home, and on weekends."

"Maybe he's having a hard time, too. He *was* your father's best friend."

"Yeah," Emily agreed, but her eyes bore into Jessica as if watching the demeanor of a witness. Once again, Emily reminded Jessica painfully of Brian. "Have you talked to Nicole?"

"I haven't heard from her. She's out of town on a deal."

"I'm sure they have cell service there. Some friend." Emily shrugged. "Anyway, you can call my mother. She'll get us a lawyer."

Jessica turned away and Emily followed through the bright kitchen doorway. "I don't think your mother would know anyone," Jessica said, annoyed at the idea. "I mean, she works with abused kids, not this sort of thing."

"She *is* a lawyer, Jessica."

The sudden bitterness in Emily's voice snapped Jessica's head back around. She'd put down Emily's mother. *Shit.* Things turned so swiftly between Emily and her. "You're right … I'll speak to her later."

"Whatever." Emily's face took on the blank, noncommittal look she cultivated. She picked up a bunch of bananas that lay on the counter and ripped one off. "I'm going downstairs."

"What are you doing down there? Anything interesting?"

"Homework," Emily said quickly, and turned away.

Jessica watched Emily head toward Brian's office. It was hard to believe she was doing homework, but on the occasions when Jessica checked on her, nothing was amiss besides the slight smell of cigarettes—just like when Brian smoked there. That was bad, really bad, but she didn't know what to do about it and hadn't mentioned it to Lauren yet, fearful of her reaction.

Jessica picked up her phone from the table. Emily was right about one thing. Jessica could call Lauren to see if she knew any estate attorneys. She couldn't deny it any longer: she was getting bad vibes about Steve not returning her calls.

CHAPTER 12

Across from City Hall Park, a solo estate practitioner sat behind a scuffed desk in a modest office in the Woolworth Building. Its window over Broadway let in little light due to scaffolding and nets that covered the less expensive bottom floors during facade repairs on the old landmark. Not knowing enough about estate work to handle things herself, Lauren had asked around for an attorney for Emily and her. This lawyer was relatively cheap by New York standards and had a good reputation even if his office reminded her of *The Maltese Falcon*. Lauren fingered the seam of a stiff leather chair as she talked. "I received a call last night from Jessica, Brian's wife. Luckily, she doesn't seem to want an estate fight—with me or Emily, at least."

The lawyer's U-shaped bald spot left a lonely tuft of hair at his crown, and his sympathetic smile puffed his thick cheeks. "That must be a relief."

Lauren smiled back, halfheartedly. "The possibility of a fight had occurred to me."

"Money has a way of skewing more natural family relationships than yours."

"She's really committed to Emily right now. The problem seems to be Steve Cohen. He's not returning our calls. Since Jessica and I have a conflict of interest—technically at least—I gave her the name of a separate attorney, one of my law school professors. He has a Park Avenue overhead and charges lots of money. She'll feel more comfortable if she pays through the nose."

He laughed. "You're giving me ideas."

"It took a lot for her to call me. She doesn't think I'm a real lawyer like Brian and his sleazeball friends. I'm a City lawyer, Family Court to boot, and God forbid I had to raise a kid so I couldn't take one of those top-of-the-food-chain, hundred-hour-a-week jobs. Not that I'd want that."

He nodded, sympathetically. "I've run into some prejudice myself."

"You can see how much Brian's friends are doing for us."

"We'll see." He looked down at his legal pad then back at Lauren. "The first thing I need to do is call Steve Cohen and see what we can do to free up Brian's money. But you know this is a litigation firm you're dealing with. If they want to fight you, they don't have to pay anyone to represent them. They can keep you in court for years with little downside. For Emily, the litigation costs could easily run into hundreds of thousands of dollars. Even if she wins, the legal fees will still cut heftily into her recovery. As for you, since you only get ten percent of Brian's profit, litigation would probably wipe you out, win or lose."

Lauren leaned forward. "There has to be a way to avoid that."

***

Carl sat at his desk. An empty coffee cup rested amidst strewn pens and half-read reports, pages flipped over, one on top of the next in a lopsided pile. Carl listened to Jorge Arena's voice coming from his PC's speaker. "Have you heard from the wife?"

Jordan's voice responded, jittery bravado, "We're talking. No worries."

"Don't fuck with me. When will I hear from you?"

"Jorge, where is the faith? Give me some credit. Tomorrow."

"Come see me tomorrow. We'll talk, either way."

Jordan's voice cracked, "Wait." The phone clicked. Jordan spoke alone now. Carl imagined him looking at the phone for answers it couldn't give: "*Fuck. Fucking shit.*"

Carl closed the audio file with a click and turned to Rick. "Jordan's in trouble. Brian Silverman has to be the key."

"Silverman is dead."

Carl looked away, irritated. He'd spent a couple of nights at the sports bar, working security and greeting customers, grueling hours that dragged as slowly as an airport security line at Christmas. It was a long-term assignment, he knew, so he wasn't expecting instant pay dirt. Once the Arena crew got to know him, he could present himself as a betting agent, a guy with clients. Anyone who brought business to a gambling website received commission. So Carl had to get into Arena's confidence and cut a deal to bring clients to Jordan. If he could get specific actions by Arena to set him up with Jordan Connors here in the States, that could be the linchpin to put Arena away. But so far, Carl had gotten nothing but flirtation from the well-endowed cocktail waitresses.

"I'm telling you, Rick, Arena had to be talking about Silverman's widow. Where did the twelve million dollars go that Silverman withdrew from his account? Now the wife may be in danger, dying for our help, or maybe she was in on it, too. If we get her, she'll talk."

"Your imagination is way ahead of the proof. We already have evidence on a dozen people involved with fixing games and individual plays. Why go for the spokes of the wheel—a tangential guy like Silverman, a dead guy no less, when we're so close to an excellent RICO bust on the entire criminal conspiracy? Maybe we'll even snag big-name athletes."

Rick sounded like the US Attorneys, who always compared RICO conspiracies to chains, wheels, and pyramids, diagramming the relationships of each defendant on a whiteboard before trial, snaring every minor participant in a dragnet. Carl felt no joy at catching ball players.

"If the bet-fixing led to Brian Silverman's murder, it would make it a much bigger bust," Carl countered. "With the kind of evidence we're gathering about Jorge Arena's gambling activities, he'll spend less time in jail than we spent investigating them."

"You're a pessimist, Carl." Rick rolled away, spanning the couple of feet to his desk. Spotless. As if he never read a report or used a pen or drank a cup of coffee. Rick logged into his computer. "We just put you in Home Game. Arena and his crew are so greedy, in a few weeks, they'll jump to take on a new agent, especially with CB backing you. Plus, everybody likes you, even killers, I can't exactly say why. ..." A spreadsheet appeared on the screen in front of Rick. "Look at these reports of weird betting patterns on blackjack games. And remember the strange poker plays on Jordan Connors' site? Somebody has to be taking a cyberpeek at the other players' cards."

"If that kind of bet went sour, Silverman might have been caught in the middle while delivering money."

Rick turned in his chair and took a long look at Carl. "Do me a favor—we're making good progress, so save me the nightmares about you doing illegal searches or wiretaps on the Silverman angle. Not on his wife, definitely not on his law firm."

"What?" Carl grinned. "I believe in the Constitution."

"I'm gonna hold you to that."

Carl had no plans for illegal taps or anything of the sort. But he also had no plans to tell Rick about running into the ex-wife at the gym—not yet anyway.

When he'd last seen Lauren Davis, she'd told the guy she was talking to that she usually went to the gym after work. Carl intended to be there. As pretty as she was, it would be no sweat for Carl to put in a little unofficial overtime on the Silverman angle. Carl tossed his empty coffee cup into the garbage and got up. "I'm taking Mookie for a run."

Rick swiveled to face him. "You need to give that old dog a break."

"Man, he's in better shape than you."

Rick looked down at himself, not an ounce of flab. "I hope so, because you're a sorry motherfucker about that dog. Personally, I don't understand that kind of attachment to an animal."

"You should try it. It would do you good."

"It makes me wheeze just thinking about it."

***

The scent of microwave popcorn filled Lauren's office as the afternoon sun faded. She read the day's email and munched. Her cell phone rang, and she wiped her fingers on a napkin before picking up.

"I heard from Steve Cohen," her new attorney said. "I hate to be the bearer of bad news, but I think you have a problem."

"What?"

"Cohen said Brian was an employee, not a partner. He claims the firm doesn't owe anything on his cases either. According to Cohen, the only thing Brian got beyond his salary was at year's end—a major appliance like a microwave or a washer-dryer—*if* the firm did well that year."

"A major appliance?" Lauren's voice raised with blindsided anger. "Brian paid for two homes. He leased a plane and lived like a goddamn multimillionaire. Even our divorce decree says I get ten percent of profits, so there have to be profits."

"Have you checked with your divorce lawyer to see if Brian's agreement with Cohen is in his file?"

Lauren felt a twinge of embarrassment. "Our divorce was uncontested, before I went to law school. Brian drafted the divorce papers. I didn't ask to see the agreement he had with Steve."

There was silence on the line for a beat before Lauren's attorney spoke. "Brian might have wanted to keep his deal with Steve Cohen unwritten, under the table, to save paying you the ten percent on the big cases. If Brian didn't want a paper trail, that could work to Steve's advantage now. Ex-husbands hiding assets is very common."

"That bastard … I mean Steve, not Brian. I don't think Brian would do that. He felt too guilty to be petty after we divorced, and he liked showing off how much money he made. That alone made it worth paying me."

"Okay, then. When Brian's widow retains her lawyer, have him call me. Maybe she'll find a partnership or profit-sharing agreement, although I doubt it exists if Steve is claiming it doesn't. In any event, Jessica's attorney and I can put our heads together on how we're going to deal with this. At least we can join forces to cut costs if it comes down to it."

"Okay." Lauren exhaled, trying to calm herself. "In the meantime,

I'll try to get Jessica to search Brian's files at home to see if she can find something written about fee-sharing."

"Most courts know that the attorney who brings in the business gets a piece of the firm's fee, even if there's no partnership."

"That alone would be millions."

"Cohen has a lot to fight about if he's greedy," the lawyer said.

"Then he has a lot to fight about."

Lauren hung up and dialed Jessica. She recounted what her attorney had said about Steve denying he owed them money.

"Could Steve have actually taken the partnership agreement?" Jessica asked, gathering strength as they talked. "He was down in the basement the day of the funeral, remember? He was the one who told us there was no will. I can't believe I gave him the password to the computer. What an idiot I am. Up until this minute, even with his not answering our calls, I still thought Steve was my friend."

"It's hard to believe he would take the agreement. I mean, who does stuff like that? Especially an attorney who could be disbarred if he were caught."

"There are some case files in the basement. A lot of the cases were cocounseled by out-of-state attorneys. Maybe I can find out who they are. We could contact them and they could confirm if it was Brian, not Steve they referred cases to. Maybe Brian told them what kind of financial arrangement he had with Steve on their cases."

"Right," Lauren said, surprised at Jessica's energy. "Their statements may not be admissible in court but it can't hurt. Just look again to see if you find a fee-sharing agreement."

Lauren hung up, feeling better than when she called. She looked out through the black speckles of soot on glass that served as her office window and thought about it: Jessica was nowhere near as wilting and delicate as she'd once seemed. Maybe she had an inner strength Lauren hadn't seen before.

CHAPTER 13

At dusk, a roller skater wearing a multicolored Afro wig glided on Hudson Street toward the Village. It was Halloween. Lauren had forgotten about the holiday without Emily around. She walked toward the health club's long, green awning. Near the curb, tied to a narrow metal pole that supported the awning, was the most pitiful rottweiler she'd ever seen. As she approached, he stared at her from beneath white eyebrows. His tail bumped against the pavement as if he just knew she was a dog lover. She would have thought him a puppy if the signs of his age—all bones and speckled fur—hadn't been so evident. She put her hand out to let him sniff and leaned down to pet him as he rose onto all fours.

"Mookie."

Lauren stepped back, startled. "What?"

A man appeared out of nowhere, the same guy who'd helped her with the weights earlier in the week. Lauren shook off her fright at his sudden approach on a dark street, even right outside the gym.

He smiled. "His name is Mookie. Mine is Carl."

She dismissed a distinct impression that he'd planted the dog. There were easier ways to talk to women. "The Mets?"

"Right, Mookie Wilson. You know baseball?"

Lauren scratched Mookie behind the ears as she spoke, noticing how the dog lay on a small blanket. "No. Gotta go, puppy." She headed toward the glass door to the gym.

The man reached around, pushing the door open for her, and followed her inside. The thought crossed Lauren's mind but left just as quickly: Where had he come from if his dog was already tied up, but he wasn't *leaving* the gym?

When Lauren finished her cardio and started loading weight plates at the bench press, Carl was there. "You need a spotter. You're gonna kill yourself."

She acquiesced and next thing she knew he was working in sets with her, benching during her between-set rests. He didn't say much while they worked out, which was good because she hated idiotic lines, and it was already obvious that he was pursuing her. They worked out hard, and she ended up initiating their sparse conversation, asking where he lived and worked.

"I manage a sports bar in Hell's Kitchen," he told her, taking his plates off the weight bar after his set.

"Interesting."

He seemed embarrassed. "I fell into it."

"Your mother wanted you to be a doctor?"

He smiled, "Yeah, something like that."

They continued their workout, moving on to shoulder presses. She watched him lift. He was definitely easy on the eyes and had a great body, which was more attractive because he appeared so unaware of it.

"Can I ask you something else?" she asked, one thing irking her.

"Shoot."

"No offense, it's none of my business, but do you always leave your dog outside by himself for so long?"

"Mookie's okay. Too old to steal, and it's not so cold out tonight. Anyway, he gets to meet lots of girls out there and he's got his blankie."

"His *blankie*?" Oh, God, that was the cutest thing she'd ever heard a guy say. "I guess he didn't seem too unhappy."

"To tell you the truth, I promised Mookie I'd take him to the Halloween Parade. Want to take the walk with us?"

Lauren smiled. "It was Mookie's idea, I guess."

"We go every year."

She started her next set before answering, ten reps until her shoulder muscles burned. She thought over his invitation. Maybe it was faulty reasoning, but she doubted anyone who carried his dog's *blankie* around with him was an ax murderer—and she trusted the dog at least. She could make sure they stayed on busy streets as they walked the dozen blocks to Houston Street. A parade would be public enough. Since Brian, she'd been gun-shy of men, had to convince herself to take any risk at all. But in this case, what did she have to lose?

***

They headed north through Tribeca and past the restaurants and galleries of Soho. The sidewalks became more crowded as they neared the Village. Many of those who walked uptown wore lavish costumes, especially the drag queens who always had a strong presence at the Village Halloween Parade. By Houston Street the noise level had picked up with the sound of percussion instruments and the shouts of those who watched and participated in the parade. A forty-foot dinosaur floated by, followed by a hundred elementary school children in costumes. Lauren remembered Emily in her first princess costume and the year when she decided to be a Power Ranger amidst all her princess friends. For some reason, that had made Lauren so proud. After the kids passed, a muscular man marched by, wearing nothing but a thong and seven-foot butterfly wings.

Carl laughed. "He's gotta be cold."

Next, the political Bread and Puppet Theater sauntered past—huge papier-mâché figures that were the spitting image of the president and mayor.

Carl and Lauren watched, talked, and laughed. She finally felt a reprieve from her worries of the last couple weeks. Eventually, the wind picked up and temperature began to drop as the parade neared its end. She shivered. Carl stood close to her, as if he were tempted to put his arm around her to keep her warm but wasn't sure he should. She smelled the leather of his jacket and his fresh, just-showered scent. She imagined his arm strong and comfortable around her shoulder and wished he'd just risk it. She liked him, more than she wanted to.

He put a palm on her back. "It's cold, let's get coffee."

As they walked, she cajoled herself, silently: *You are a mature woman, Lauren, act like it.* She took in a deep breath of the bracing air and glanced at Carl. Something about him was getting to her. Maybe it was all the stress she was under, but she was sick of being mature.

They ended up sitting close together at the outdoor café tables of an espresso house on Bleecker Street so Mookie could hang out with them. Carl took Mookie's baby blanket from his backpack and spread it under the table. "It's funny how, once you get a dog, you start looking for outdoor café tables to eat in, and Fido-friendly hotels for vacations. My kid loves Mookie. I think he misses the dog more than me."

"How old is your son?"

"Ten."

"Do you see him often?"

"Every other weekend. I'd rather have joint custody, but my schedule is too unstable to keep him weekdays. It's not all that easy weekends either."

They ordered sandwiches and drank coffee to stay warm.

"I feel guilty about that … and about taking Mookie. But I didn't have much choice. My ex didn't want him. She had too much on her plate." Carl fed pieces of meat to Mookie under the table and absentmindedly petted the dog with his free hand. "Which was lucky for me, or I would have died of loneliness without my son."

"Are you on good terms with your ex?"

"Not bad. It was hard being married to a guy who works nights." He grinned. "Now she only gets pissed when I do background checks on the guys she dates."

"Background checks?"

Carl appeared startled for a moment, as if he'd let something slip. "You know, online," he said quickly. "Google, LinkedIn, Ancestry.com. If a guy is going to be around my kid, I have to do my due diligence." He laughed, taking in Lauren's wary expression. "Come on, I'm only kidding about Ancestry.com. But I think it's perfectly natural to google."

Lauren took a long look at him, wondering if he'd been stalking his ex, even though, truthfully, she'd googled Jessica. She said, "You lose a lot of control when you're not living with your kids. That's right up there in my top ten problems right now."

"You have kids?"

Grateful for someone to talk to, Lauren told Carl about everything that had been driving her wild since Brian's death: Emily, the betrayal by Steve, her paranoia about how Brian died. Carl nodded and asked occasional questions. He seemed to understand her so readily, almost as if he knew what she was going to say before she said it.

"So, how are you and the new wife getting along?"

"It's a pretty strange relationship. I talked to her this morning. She's dropping Emily off Saturday for the weekend, even though Emily could easily come by Metro North. Jessica said she wants to go shopping in the city and asked me to come. I don't know whether she made the offer out of politeness or some weird bond she feels. And it seems like it's not just Emily who she thinks binds us together. It's Brian. As if I'm the only one who can understand what she lost. Frankly, I didn't want him dead but losing him was one of the best things that ever happened to me." She mused, "I needed to move on."

"Are you going shopping with her?"

"Jessica? No. I told her I wanted to spend time with Emily, even though Emily won't last five minutes before she runs out to find her friends. Truthfully, Jessica has been doing way better with Emily and the estate problem than I would have expected, but I'm still not interested in this merry co-widow shit. Putting aside the fact that Jessica lassoed my husband, we still have nothing in common." Lauren held her palm up before Carl could interject. "I know, we're both Jewish, in our thirties, both work out a lot, and both slept with Brian." Lauren grinned and leaned forward. "Honestly, Carl, there's probably a thousand woman who could say that."

Carl was laughing. "You're both raising Emily."

Lauren paused, half wanting to tell him more about the difference between her horrible childhood and Jessica's upper-middle-class childhood of suburban synagogues, private schools, and charity picnics, but Lauren held back. She didn't tell people the whole soap opera of her childhood until she'd known them a while, if ever. "She's a Republican, for God's sake."

Carl's eyes met hers, and they broke into laughter.

Lauren said, "Okay. That's not a good reason and I think she's an Independent now. No offense if you're a Republican." Lauren took a piece of meat from her sandwich and started to reach under the table to feed Mookie.

"He'll be hooked on you too if you do that," Carl said.

Lauren caught the message and smiled slyly. "I'll take my chances." Mookie licked the piece of meat from Lauren's hand and sat heavily against her leg. She petted him and looked back at Carl. "There could be worse things."

Carl's phone rang in his pocket. He pulled it out and looked at the screen. "Give me one minute," he excused himself to take a call inside the espresso bar. When he returned, he insisted on paying the check, and they walked down Bleecker Street toward the subway. "I really like you," he said.

"I like you, too." She smiled up at him, happier than she'd felt in a long time.

He stopped, "Let's exchange contacts. I don't want to depend on running into you in the gym."

Carl took his phone from his pocket. "I'll call you. You can save my number."

Lauren watched him punch her number into an iPhone—which she was surprised to see had a blue cover. She'd have sworn it was black when he took that call. She waited while his phone connected to hers and added him to her contacts.

After she tucked the phone back in her purse, Carl's hand slipped into hers, the heat between them making her want to lean in and kiss him. "Okay, now tell me," Lauren said, swatting that thought away. "How did you get into the sports bar business?"

"I had a college scholarship for baseball but I had an injury before I could go."

"That's terrible."

"I ended up at City College, did some bartending." He turned and leaned down to Mookie. He felt Mookie's nose, looking concerned. "His eyes are watery."

The dog began wagging his tail the moment Carl spoke to him.

"He looks okay," she said, frowning. Carl seemed uncomfortable talking about himself. It was sort of charming, Lauren thought. Humble, hopefully not neurotic.

"Yeah, I don't know whether he's a hypochondriac or just likes attention."

Lauren laughed. "You're both nuts."

They left Bleecker Street and walked up broad Sixth Avenue. Small storefronts and jazz clubs gave way to fast food and big-box stores. They neared the subway entrance.

Standing next to the fenced-in Third Street basketball courts, a game going under floodlights, Carl took Lauren's arm. "I'll ride with you. It's too late to ride the subways alone, especially on Halloween."

She looked up into his dark eyes and smiled, knowing better than to tempt her hormones. "It's safer than riding home with you, Carl."

"You're something else." He kissed her lightly on the lips, holding her for a moment. "Would you call me when you get home to let me know you're all right?"

"I promise."

He released her and she descended the subway stairs, smiling like an adolescent girl with a crush.

CHAPTER 14

Friday, November 1

Jessica sat on the edge of her bed, the room dusky as the sun set outside. She dialed Brian's office. "I'd like to come by and clean out Brian's things," she told Peggy.

Peggy responded, solicitously, "I can send them to you."

"No, Peggy. I need to do it."

Peggy paused. Jessica sensed her wariness—Peggy had always been wary of her. She'd never let an ill word slip, but Jessica had always thought Peggy was on Lauren's side. It was as if Jessica had inherited not just a stepdaughter but a stepsecretary. Jessica pushed the ancient feelings away—they were obsolete now, ludicrous.

She reverted to the familiar half whisper of the pitiful girl in mourning, her first time faking it. "I need to do it, Peggy, *really*."

Peggy paused again, probably wondering whether she should ask Steve or just do something nice and, frankly, normal for Brian's widow. Peggy had worked for Brian for over a decade, and Jessica was counting on a little trust and loyalty here, in Brian's memory at least.

"I have to pick up my grandson. Can you come Monday, earlier?"

"You don't have to stay. I have Brian's key."

An even longer pause. "Okay."

Forty minutes later, Jessica used Brian's passkey to open the glass doors to the law firm on East Fortieth Street in Manhattan. She walked casually past an empty reception desk and waiting area. Even on a Friday night, there would be at least a couple of young associates around, but she was the widow of a partner and had a right to be there. It was only Steve she wanted to avoid. Jessica opened the door to Brian's office and stepped inside.

She stood still, her eyes adjusting. Dimly lit by city lights through two walls of windows, everything appeared untouched since Brian's death. Jessica walked to the large desk, ran her fingers over the polished surface, and came around to the other side. A picture of Emily and Brian at a soccer match, and one of Brian and Jessica on their honeymoon in Tortola occupied the desk's back corner.

Their honeymoon had been a dream come true for Jessica. She'd gotten in way over her head with Brian when they'd started dating. She'd been a serial dater before Brian, always keeping the upper hand. It had taken her years to become self-assured again after her college nightmare and, deep down, she'd never wanted to give that power away to anyone. She certainly never intended to fall in love with a married man. She'd chosen Brian because he was as unavailable as a man could get. He was married and lived clear across the country. You couldn't get more unavailable than that.

But, stunningly, she ended up becoming so damned obsessed with him—she'd never experienced anything like it. She'd known he loved her. But the months leading up to his separation from Lauren had been a constant struggle. She maintained her female friendships, yoga practice, and work at the hospital. Yet, underneath all her effort to maintain normalcy, her mind was a NASCAR racetrack of torturous thoughts: What would happen next with Brian? What if he was the kind of guy who strung a woman along for years without leaving his wife? What if he wasn't *ready* to leave Lauren and Emily? What could she do to convince him to fix the situation?

She hid from Brian how freaked out she'd become over the entire, unexpected mess. Desperation was the surest path to losing a man. And while she was totally absorbed in how afraid she was of falling off an emotional cliff, she knew she was unworthy of his love. She was a woman who was unable to think of his wife and child as anything other than an obstacle to getting her own way. It wasn't pretty, and if Jessica gave herself even a moment to think about it, she had a hard time painting it as anything other than an ugly scenario she'd created by her own pathetic self-centeredness.

Despite that, she'd still had to make the situation turn out in her favor. Every cell in her body had told her it was a fight for survival. Although she hadn't actually imploded now that Brian had died, had she?

"Excuse me," a startled Russian voice and the sudden brightness of the hall lights made Jessica take a frightened step back from the desk. A dark-haired woman, buxom in a pink uniform, entered. "Oh, I didn't know anyone was here. You are his wife, no?"

"Yes."

"I recognize from the picture. I am so sorry. A very nice man."

Jessica caught her breath as the cleaning woman entered.

"Thank you. I was just coming to get some of his things."

"Such a shame. I come in now and make sure to dust and vacuum even though no one works in here. You don't want lights?"

"I just got here."

The woman pushed a switch, flooding the room with light. "And your daughter, she is all right?"

"Oh, yes, thanks."

The woman brushed a long dust mop over the desk. "Such a shame." She clucked her teeth and shook her head. "Such a shame. Take care of your beautiful little girl," the woman said as she turned to leave.

Alone again, Jessica looked around. Sleek ivory-colored file cabinets lined an unwindowed wall near Brian's desk. Jessica knelt and pulled open the lowest drawer. Bloated accordion files filled it. She used both hands to lift out the first one.

Magic Marker lettering identified a name she recognized from a Florida toxic-spill case Brian had talked about. Was that the case that brought Brian to Miami? No. Brian had told her it was close to settling. It would have come up in conversation if that was why he was going. Funny, though, how she'd never heard what case brought him to Miami. She'd never even received a condolence call from the attorneys who had been with him the day he died.

She took her iPad from her shoulder bag and placed it beside her on the carpet. She thumbed through the tops of the manila folders inside the case's larger accordion file. She pulled out a file labeled COMPLAINT and flipped through it, scanning for the dollar figure Brian had been suing for. At the end, she saw it: one hundred million dollars, a big one even if the demand was inflated. She jotted down the case name and amount.

Now she needed the name and number of the Florida attorney who'd farmed out the case. The way Brian had explained it, the person who was injured hired a local attorney, who referred out the big cases he couldn't handle. The local attorney needed attorneys like Brian and Steve, who had specialized expertise and capital to cover the years of expenses before judgment. Both things were necessary. That was why Steve had recruited Brian. Steve had an ongoing firm with support staff and seed money to pay for expenses like travel, expert witnesses, investigators, photocopying—easily half a million dollars—in a big case. Meanwhile, Brian had a reputation as a litigator he'd gained working for other firms. He had relationships with local attorneys around the country who were happy to refer to him for a cut of the fee. Even if their statements were inadmissible in court, Jessica could spread the word about Steve to all the attorneys who planned to refer directly to Steve now that Brian was dead. Let Steve sue her for slander if he wanted. She had virtually nothing to lose. Thanks to him.

She smiled, some consolation in the thought as she put the file back. She remembered a conversation last year during a dinner out with Steve and Nicole, something the two couples had done frequently. Brian had been talking about a lawyer he and Steve worked with. "He's a thief, that's the bottom line," Brian had said.

Nicole had looked around at the neighboring tables to see if anyone had heard. Her eyes glinted mischievously—they'd all had plenty of wine with dinner. "Watch your ass, Brian. He'll sue you for slander if it gets back to him."

Brian had leaned over and grabbed Nicole's hand. "Truth is an absolute defense to slander, you know that."

Steve laughed. "Right, let the old guy sue us. I'll have the time of my life proving he's a thief in open court. He'll end up disbarred before we're done with him."

It was ironic that Jessica felt just like Steve now—except she didn't have her own litigation firm to help her prove Steve was a thief.

She pulled out a second, slim file marked INTAKE. She spotted the name and phone number of the referring attorney typed on the top sheet of paper. She laid it on the floor and copied the information into her iPad. The rest of her job would be easier now. Brian was as fastidious as he was smart. There would be a slim folder at the back of each case's accordion file that would have the local cocounsel information. She worked quickly, listening for footsteps over the distant street sounds.

She closed the bottom drawer and moved up to the next one. She pulled out the accordion file for a case Brian had talked about a lot lately: the Etta Houses, an Indiana housing project contaminated with lead. She knew who'd referred that one. Steve and Nicole had been doing campaign fund-raising, hosting fund-raisers and bundling donations. The congressman's referral of that case was the first big one the firm landed as a result. Jessica wrote down the congressman's contact information but doubted she'd ever call him. She could guess where his loyalties would lie.

The next accordion file had an address in the Bronx written on it. No case name. She opened it, curious. It wasn't full like the other accordion files, wasn't divided into several manila folders either. Inside, she found a single document she recognized from the purchase of her home. In bold caps, it said CONTRACT OF SALE.

She frowned. Brian didn't do real estate. He hadn't even done the closing on her parents' house. When they came to him wanting to sell the home Jessica had grown up in so they could downsize to a golf-course condo, Brian gave them the name of a lawyer he knew. He said he didn't know enough about real estate and didn't have time, in the middle of a busy trial schedule, to learn. Of course, just from the closing on their own house in Westchester, Brian had probably soaked up enough to do it himself, but he'd never expressed an interest. He had a lucrative practice, and the two fields didn't mix.

A dark pain pricked at her. What else didn't she know?

The contract said it was for a "multifamily residential building." She took down the names of the seller and buyer. The buyer was Bronx

Development, LLC. The seller was a company called Inwood Partners, LLC. Jessica had never heard of them. She'd read in the Sunday *Times* real estate section that wealthy people used limited liability corporations, LLCs, to hide who bought luxury property. The selling price was five million dollars. She shook her head, trying to adjust her eyes to the print in front of her. This closing was no favor to a friend buying a house. A person doing a five-million-dollar deal could afford a real estate specialist.

She flipped to the back page of the file. Brian had signed as the representative of the seller. Someone named Jordan Connors had signed for the buyer, the word "president" printed next to his name. Jordan Connors, it sounded familiar. She'd heard that name before, recently. She couldn't remember when, but she was sure she hadn't heard it from Brian.

She looked inside the file for phone numbers. Nothing. No number for the buyer or seller. Her nerves stood on edge. Every other file had contact information for the clients and opposing counsel. She put it back in the drawer and flipped to the next accordion file, a thick one with a case name printed across it. She pushed past it to the next one and the next, then slammed the file drawer shut. She looked at the time on her phone. She wanted to get out of there. The longer she stayed, the harder to explain her presence. And the longer she stayed, the more frightened she became that she was in the middle of something she didn't understand, in a place she didn't belong.

She pulled open the next drawer. Four files in, she found a file with an address. The Bronx again. The corporate buyer was another LLC. A twelve-million-dollar sale price. What the hell? Again, Jordan Connors signed for the buyer. Jessica scribbled the address and corporate names.

Suddenly, it hit her. Jordan Connors had called. His message had been on the answering machine. She'd erased it, thinking he was a salesman. What could he have wanted?

Then the sale's closing date shot out at her: October 15. Two days before the fire … the day Brian left for Miami. She looked at Brian's handwriting and the now-familiar signature of Jordan Connors. A deep sense of foreboding filled her again. Somehow, instinctively, she knew Jordan Connors hadn't been calling to offer condolences—and that he would be calling again.

***

Emily hadn't stepped foot out of the man-daughter cave since Jessica left. She'd gone through every piece of paper in the file cabinet and skimmed through her father's accordion files, lined up against a wall on the carpeted floor. So much paper. Old school. Her father had said that lawyers still needed paper. Jessica had been down here earlier, looking through the stuff before she left. She thought Emily hadn't noticed. Something was going on and, like usual, the kid was the last to know.

Emily sat down at the PC, planning to put an end to that particular status quo. Her father's user account on the computer asked for a password. She typed it in—the license plate number of his car. He'd told it to her because he was the PC's administrator and she couldn't download any *Minecraft* updates on it unless she had his password.

She double-clicked on her father's Outlook. She would never have done that when he was alive. Unlike most adults, she respected people's privacy, and that was probably why her father trusted her. But he was dead, and she was too old to think everything was all right just because the grown-ups in her life said so. It wasn't like anyone woke her up the morning her father died and said, hey by the way, your dad will be gone forever today, so don't go around thinking it's a regular school day or anything. No, Emily had trusted things would be normal—half-assed, boring, depressing, but normal, just like every other day. Now she wanted to know what was going on, why her mother and Jessica were so tense, and not just about Emily's father dying. Something more was going on. Since no one trusted her enough to tell her anything, she had to take it upon herself to find out. She didn't want any more surprises.

Emily scrolled down through her father's emails. Spam, fantasy football, ESPN news alerts. She doubted he used this email account much, probably used his work network more. There wasn't much here overall. Emily came to an email from PayPal: fraud alert. Idly curious, she clicked in, knowing the PayPal password for the same reason she knew the computer's administrator password. He used to bitch about how she'd buy a video game and then, right away, she wanted an in-game purchase, a map or whatever. He would tell Emily to pay with PayPal. He didn't want their Visa number on any of those sketchy sites.

Emily typed in her address in Manhattan: 440w181, to enter the PayPal site. Her dad had said that was his ATM code too, ever since he and her mother bought the apartment in Washington Heights, the first place he'd ever bought. Thinking about it, Emily was sure Jessica didn't know Daddy's PayPal password, or she would have figured out it was Lauren's address and made him change it. The one downside of being a home-wrecker was that you always had to worry about another woman doing the same to you, even the baby mama you stole your husband from in the first place. Jessica had to have known Emily's father was basically fair game.

Once Emily was logged into PayPal, she clicked into the message about the fraud alert. It said there was a charge at a bar in Road Town, Tortola, BVI. Road Town again. The hairs on the back of Emily's neck tingled. Plus, there were a bunch of other charges. She started scrolling, shocked. Besides Emily's online purchases, she'd thought her father only used the family Visa and his firm's American Express card.

His charges stopped on October 17 when he paid for a hotel in Miami.

Emily moved down to the next item in reverse chronological order. October 16: the Virgin Islands Yacht Club in St. Thomas. She sat back hard in her seat. Her father had gone sailing in St. Thomas? What could make him take a one-day sailing trip right in the middle of a case? Emily distinctly remembered, back when her father and Jessica were planning their honey-moon, he said St. Thomas was too touristy. They'd gone to Tortola instead. He'd explained that it was forty minutes from St. Thomas by boat and that even though the two islands were close, one was American and one was British.

He must have sailed to Tortola and the bar charge in Tortola was real, not fraud at all. But Emily couldn't imagine him going for one day, and she also couldn't imagine Jessica letting him leave her behind on a trip like that. He always left Emily behind but not Jessica. The glaring answer lit up Emily's brain: Jessica didn't know. It was another woman.

"Ugh," she said aloud, totally frustrated. None of it made sense. He used a separate, private credit card. He went on a trip he didn't tell Jessica about. He was talking in code about it on the PlayStation. What "other woman" would put up with talking in code on a video game? Emily remembered the look on her dad's face like she'd caught him when she came downstairs while he was on the PlayStation. Was it even possible? That he was texting with a girl? Emily laughed aloud. No way. Her father could not possibly have dated a gamer. He was over forty, for God's sake.

Her mind spun with all the confusing stuff. She was only vaguely disappointed in her father when it came to cheating. He'd never been exactly the best role model anyway. But she couldn't come up with an explanation that fit all the pieces together. Her father was dead. Her mother was totally through with Steve. She'd even hired a lawyer. Jessica was being secretive. And why *was* Steve dissing them? The simplest explanation was that Jessica and Lauren had pissed Steve off somehow. Emily could easily imagine that—they sure pissed Emily off on a regular basis. So maybe, if that was the problem, Steve would talk to Emily. Maybe she could get to the bottom of things even if Jessica and her mother couldn't. That would be a surprising twist for the adults in her life.

Emily pulled up her father's Outlook contacts and looked up Steve's number. She dialed and listened to it ring twice.

The sound of Nicole's hello took her aback. Emily stuttered, "Nicole?"

"Yes."

"It's Emily. Isn't this Steve's line?"

"It's the landline. Hi, Emily."

"I thought you were out of town."

"I flew in for the weekend. How are you?"

"You haven't called."

"Oh … I've been involved in an important deal. So much pressure. I've meant to."

Hurt slipped into Emily's words against her will, "Why hasn't Steve called? He's been in town. My mother's trying to reach him."

Nicole's voice took on the tone of an adult talking to a little kid, "Oh, sweetie, I'm sure it's just that Steve's busy. I'll remind him."

"My mother's mortgage is going to be late."

"Emily." Nicole sounded irritated now, like it was slipping out of her, too, "Let the grown-ups take care of their business. These things are complicated. Your mother is a lawyer, she knows."

"What difference does it make that she's a lawyer if Steve won't call her back?" Emily wiped away tears. Nicole and Steve used to be so nice to her.

"You worry too much, and you always want to grow up before your time. I'll remind Steve … okay? And we'll talk soon. Gotta run."

Emily heard a kiss noise before the phone disconnected. She pulled her cigarettes out and angrily paced the basement, the dogs scurrying out of her way. Plan A—trying to call Steve herself—hadn't worked, not at all. But she wasn't done yet, not by a long shot. She might only be sixteen, but that didn't mean she was mentally handicapped. She was so effing sick of everyone treating her like she was. She was going to figure out what was going on if it was the last thing she did.

She sat down at the PC and thought for a minute. She opened the desk's center drawer and began pulling out papers. There was nothing particularly interesting—pens, paper clips, sticky pads—until she felt something deep inside the drawer. A thumb drive. It was probably nothing, just a backup for her dad's work, but she plugged it into the PC and double-clicked to open the file. Hieroglyphics instantly populated the screen. *Oh.* She took back what she'd just thought about her being beyond surprise. He had an encrypted file. She could see him having encrypted messages if he were cheating on Jessica, which he clearly was doing. But a whole file? She couldn't help but marvel at how many questions she had after only a half hour of trying to find answers in her father's basement.

She knew exactly what she had to do next. She picked up her cell phone and scrolled through her contacts to find Hector, a kid she knew from her old school in the city. He lived on the Upper West Side in the Douglas Projects, not far from their school. She remembered a story he'd told her. He was so proud of himself that his cousin was from Anonymous. Or at least his cousin *used* to be in Anonymous before he ratted his friends out. Everyone but him went to prison for a really long time.

Emily had to find out more about her father and she could think of only one way. She texted: "Hey H. Ur cousin, Tabu. Can U intro? Em."

She would be the one keeping secrets now.

CHAPTER 15
BRIAN

Six Months Ago

On a hot spring day, Brian walked alongside the congressman up a cement path, weeds growing through erupted veins of time and weather. The congressman—white-hair, blue eyes, and exact smile—had talked nonstop for the ride from O'Hare to an area where Chicago ghettos leaked into Indiana.

"Over seven hundred children live here," he said. "Every single one of them has elevated lead levels."

"The contamination started in the eighties," Brian said, knowing all the stats. He always did his homework. "That means a couple of generations. Thousands of people damaged."

The three-story garden apartments were like those where Brian and Jordan had lived during college, except the lawns here were dirt and sparse crabgrass, the trees scrawny skeletons, not a canopy of oaks and maples in a sea of green like Brian's old home. There was a bleakness here, a place that had been destroying lives since its inception thirty years ago. Brian couldn't help but think of Emily. How would he have handled the news that his daughter had been slowly lead poisoned into a life of compromised IQ, poor concentration, and personality disorder? He couldn't even imagine living with that truth.

Two hundred people, all African American, had packed into a

community room, sitting in metal folding chairs and standing in the back. There were no cheery posters on the off-white walls. They all just wanted out.

A woman stood, her two children sharing a folding chair beside her. "I let them play out in the dirt in front of our building for years. No one told us. Now we hear the dirt is poisoned with lead from the old plant they never bothered to properly clean up. We just want to be moved like the mayor promised—and they're not even offering enough money to live anywhere decent. The kids are going crazy, locked up in the house like prisoners. They don't understand." Her mouth wrenched into an angry grimace. "Neither do I."

The congressman spoke, looking glumly at the woman, "As to the move, the checks will begin to be distributed next month. We've got counselors coming out here to try to help folks figure out where to go. Let's have Brian Silverman fill us in on the lawsuit."

Brian stood and looked around. "Thank you for meeting with me today. We've filed the complaint in this case. The first step will be to get certified as a class so you won't each have to litigate the case separately, which would be prohibitively expensive. Unless the refinery settles with us, it will take years to get you what's owed. They will put as many hurdles as they can in our path. But we have a strong case and we'll need your cooperation. Many of you have met the team from my firm. They are continuing to gather documents. If we don't already have them, we need medical records for your children and yourselves. We'll need school records."

Heads were bobbing in the audience. They seemed empowered by what Brian was saying, which gave Brian an infusion of energy too. People were taking notes. "Money won't reverse the damage. These are hard facts. But money will ensure that your children receive the best interventions and be taken care of to the extent needed." Brian's eyes followed a toddler squirming in his mother's arms. He felt a disconcerting wetness in his eyes, remembering Emily again. "But I will fight for you. I will make sure you can take care of your children and yourselves."

An elderly woman raised her hand. "What about the offer they're talking about?"

Brian turned toward the side of the room where she sat. "I know the amount of money they're offering sounds tempting, but their formula doesn't pay enough for the damages to the children and teenagers. It is simply not enough for the lifetime challenges many of them will have to face. So we need to continue our trial prep. The most convincing argument for a favorable settlement is that we're ready and able to take the case to trial."

Brian shook hands or hugged nearly every person in that room before leaving. He knew money was a poor surrogate for getting people their health back. Every dollar they won was in exchange for a dollar's worth of health and peace of mind. They weren't winning the lotto.

Yet his clients tended to be grateful for anything he could do, which was a humbling experience, gratifying but ultimately inadequate because he couldn't make the sick healthy. Plus the pump Brian got out of dealing with his clients often had a boomerang effect, leaving him with a feeling of dread that he'd fail them. For a week after a meeting like this, he'd wake up in the middle of the night from dark dreams about things he had to do on the case—a deposition, a response to interrogatories, a motion; his mind fixated on each task that needed him, the thought returning repeatedly that he was an impostor, not nearly the superhero-attorney they imagined he was.

He rarely shared with anyone how these cases twisted his insides. He never dropped the facade that things came easily to him. He didn't even let on with Jessica, knowing his vulnerability would scare her. And he certainly didn't talk about it with Steve, who looked at people as numbers with dollar signs in front of them, not as real people whose lives could be raised up or dashed by the quality of his work product. Walking toward the congressman's car, Brian's unease deepened. He looked out at the housing project as they drove away, feeling as if all of life was balanced on the edge of a cliff.

He took out his phone and scrolled though messages and emails, which tended to soothe him like cyber-Xanax. He'd received messages from Jessica, Emily, and Lauren. The familiarity of the three women was a protective nest when his emotions threatened to get the better of him. Even Lauren with her nagging and jabs. Once he and Lauren had overcome the worst of their hurt, things had been okay between them. The part he'd regretted most about the divorce was letting go of the idea of family—Lauren, Emily, and him as a unit. Not that he was unhappy with Jessica.

His phone vibrated in his palm. Jordan. Brian didn't return the call. Instead, he forced himself to listen to the congressman's political small talk for the ride back to the airport. Brian shook the congressman's hand when he left the car, promising to see him at the next dinner party Steve and Nicole were hosting for him. "All righty, then," the congressman said, slapping Brian's back as if greeting voters outside Wrigley Field.

Brian tugged his compact carry-on into the terminal. He dialed Jordan as he waited on the abbreviated security line for private travelers flying their own planes. "Hey, J, what's up?"

"Can you come talk to me, attorney-client?"

***

After landing at Westchester Airport, Brian went straight to the Home Game sports bar on Manhattan's West Side. It was on a warehouse block midway down the street from the Intrepid, the aircraft carrier that served as a military museum. Car washes anchored each end of the block, and yellow taxis lined up outside them for the cabbie special rate. A forklift driver steered into a warehouse's garage next door to the building where Brian's Uber left him.

A broad-shouldered man unclipped a velvet rope to allow Brian to enter the sports bar at the bottom of a brown-brick building. A black awning but no sign out front made anyone who entered feel like an insider. Brian might have wondered about the place if he were passing by—or he might have overlooked it completely.

Brian took in the sleek, red-backlit bar that ran the length of the right side of the large open room. Cocktail waitresses in skimpy black outfits outnumbered customers at the moment. This place was no raucous beer joint like most sports bars. At the center of the room, a few men drank at high tables on bar stools, wearing suits or corporate casual. Mixed martial arts and a Mets game played on flat-screens.

Seeing Brian, Jordan broke away from talking to a small blond man near the bar.

"What are you having?" Jordan walked with Brian to the bar, ordered, and handed Brian a gin and tonic. "Come upstairs."

Brian followed Jordan to the back of the bar, down a hallway lit by floorboard lights, and up a carpeted staircase. A bouncer opened a door for them, and they entered a black-carpeted area more crowded than the bar downstairs. There were blackjack and roulette tables. Brian could make out poker games in progress at the far end of the room. The women working here wore shorts that were barely more than thongs. Low-cut belly blouses pushed up large breasts. They were extraordinarily beautiful. Jordan brought Brian to a VIP area in the back, a cocktail waitress smiling at Jordan in recognition as they passed. Behind velvet ropes, circular leather couches surrounded low coffee tables arranged into seating groups.

"Check out the tables over there," Jordan pointed with his forehead after they'd sat.

"Yeah?" Brian took in the sight of men at a poker table just outside the VIP area. Women massaged their shoulders. Brian watched the men play.

"See the two young dudes."

Brian knew who he was talking about. Two well-heeled men in their twenties, wearing shirtsleeves, their shirt buttons open. Women whispered in their ears as they rubbed.

"Most of the guys who come here are bankers, hedge-funders, a few trust-fund kids. They play high stakes. Not millions but thousands on a hand. Are you wondering how they concentrate?" Jordan asked.

Brian laughed and shook his head. "Exactly."

"They've drunk too much and probably snorted too much. You see the other guy who's getting a massage, a little older? Now, watch him. He's not a banker, and he's barely touched his drink. He's playing teams with two other guys at the table. They're telling each other their cards. He's saying something at the table like, 'I love the boobs on that one.' That means he's got two queens."

"No shit."

"Word to the wise: never do what they're doing, Brian."

Jordan and Brian watched the table for a few minutes, nursing their drinks, not seeing the cards but able to tell when the hands went sour for the young bankers.

Jordan put down his drink. "I have a business proposition for you. I want you to help me."

Brian felt a shot of adrenaline but made sure not to show it.

"It's safe and very profitable," Jordan explained.

"I'm all ears."

"I told you about my Chinese players. They're so desperate for action, they'd bet on a fly crawling up a wall if they had a taker. But the only thing they hate worse than losing is getting caught by the Chinese authorities. So, the house—that's me—gets its cut off the top and delivers the winnings in ways that avoid traceable records. They win some and lose some but, while they're at it, they get to funnel money out of China just in case things go sour for them there, which can happen without warning."

"Interesting."

"I want you to help me move the money. You could easily help me on this, and the cut is very generous."

"Interesting," Brian said again, watching a woman walk away from the poker table toward the front of the room, the lights shining on miles of smooth exposed skin. Brian had no moral compunction about Jordan's business, no more than he cared about people who smoked marijuana, used prostitutes, or the greedy schmucks getting ripped off at poker nearby. He'd heard all the stuff about how internet gambling preyed on the weak, how it brought an addict's fix to his fingertips. But in Brian's estimation, the Feds were only protecting the profits of the old-money casinos when they illegalized internet gambling. He had no ethical problem with internet gambling, especially when it came to billionaires. He certainly had no ethical qualms with their hiding Chinese money.

He imagined not working day and night, never enough hours in the day to make him feel comfortable that he was doing enough for his clients. He pondered how much easier the simple life would be if he had the kind of money Jordan had. Money would solve his Emily problem too. He allowed himself a momentary fantasy of flying Emily to visit him in the Bahamas every weekend. The proverbial cake and eating it too. Still, what Brian didn't want was to get caught up in anything that would threaten his law license or lead him to a simple life in prison.

Brian leaned over and stubbed out a cigarette. "If we were caught doing this, we'd get five years, easy. They could throw in a RICO conspiracy along with the tax evasion. On top of that, I get disbarred and Jessica and I die in poverty."

"Don't be a drama queen," Jordan said. "It's foolproof and not even illegal. We're a foreign corporation conducting perfectly legal overseas business. Technically speaking, there's no US profits to report, so no tax evasion."

"Technically speaking, right."

"The US government has no problem with us helping the Chinese get their money out of China. Think about it. We're doing our patriotic duty, and we'd be appreciated for it."

Brian couldn't help but notice Jordan's use of the word "we." He liked the sound of that and pictured freedom. He smiled. "You should have had one of those girls massaging *my* shoulders while you proposed that."

Jordan laughed. "Does that mean you'll do it?"

CHAPTER 16

Saturday, November 2

At six thirty, the sun burst through Lauren's fifth-floor window. A prewar radiator hissed, deceptively warm on a frigid day. She shuffled to the bathroom. It was a weekend, but she always woke up at dawn, no matter what time she'd gone to bed. Emily accused her of being rigid and controlling even while asleep, and there was an element of truth to that.

She washed her face, still feeling mortified as if she'd hooked up with someone against her better judgment. She'd tried to put it out of her mind yesterday, but it hadn't worked. She'd liked Carl so much that she'd ignored her instincts when she'd thought him evasive. He'd clammed up every time the conversation turned to him. And even when she first saw him with Mookie, she'd gotten a fleeting sense that he was somehow manipulating her. Now she could see that he'd planned every move of Thursday night like a chess game, ten moves ahead of her.

And the coup de grâce: he had two phones. When they were at the café, he'd excused himself to take a call on a *black* phone. When he put her contact info into his phone, he'd used a different phone, one with a *navy blue* cover. She wasn't sure at first, but it jelled in her mind in the hours after she left him: he was married, not divorced, and had a burner phone. He couldn't give her the same phone number his wife knew about, and he couldn't talk with his wife on his real phone in front of Lauren. He hadn't made a serious pass, but he was obviously one of those guys who played it cool until the woman gave it up.

She felt like an adolescent trapped in an adult body, hollowed out by her vulnerability, once again. Her remorse and shame about her neediness with Carl felt all too familiar, even after so long. In the quiet of her brightening living room, she remembered walking to a makeshift drop-in center on Saint Mark's Place in the East Village, alone, unprotected, an invisible speck in a fast city. She remembered thinking that her father was probably in the morgue by then, waiting for one of his cousins or aunts to put up the cash to bury him. A crowd of recovering addicts milled around outside the ramshackle building, smoking cigarettes, talking and laughing. Her father had brought her there when he attended Narcotics Anonymous meetings. There were big rooms downstairs where recovering addicts played cards, hung out, and had meetings. Anyone could walk into the sooty-dark place where all the windows were covered to protect the anonymity of the recovering addicts. There was no security or staff. Homeless adults roamed the rooms, lounging across metal chairs, sleeping, or talking to themselves in the back row of meetings until it was time to claim their beds at the Bowery Mission.

When Lauren was there with her father, she'd seen homeless kids too. So that first night after he died, she trailed behind when she spotted a group stomping upstairs like Peter Pan's gang after a day of boosting at Macy's and Tommy Hilfiger. She still carried her father's cocaine hidden in her knapsack, although she'd thrown his gun in a dumpster behind a sushi takeout place, wanting no part of it. On the third floor, two dozen chattering teenagers, girls and boys, tugged mattresses onto the empty dance floor of a sober nightclub that only opened for dancing on weekends. The building's owner stored mattresses for them and let them sleep in the disco when the dance floor wasn't in use.

Lauren pulled her mattress toward a wall of the disco, thinking she would feel safer there until she saw a moving shadow, a cockroach, at the baseboard where the dance floor met a peeling plaster wall. She switched directions and dropped her mattress in the center of the dance floor.

A tall, handsome boy with a crooked-toothed Denzel Washington smile pulled his mattress near hers. "You're new." He signaled to the other kids in the room. "Stick close to us. The addicts downstairs are cool, but there's older guys down there who aren't really in recovery. They'll try to pimp you."

He became her boyfriend, starting that night. At least he held her when she cried for her father, which was the closest thing she had to a funeral. He helped her keep her orphan's terror at bay. And she joined their group. They were fed and used the showers in an apartment next to the disco. They slept in relative safety in exchange for chores like dumping the garbage, mopping and cleaning the bathrooms downstairs, which resembled a nightmare Port-A-San at the end of a county fair.

The group helped her sell off her father's cocaine, all the kids buying new clothes at the Gap on the corner of Second Avenue, plus weed at Tompkins Square Park. The twelve-step meetings ran twenty-four hours a day at St. Mark's, white noise for the teenagers. Lauren and her friends passed through or napped in meetings, never actually participating, but they kept their weed and booze hidden from sight out of respect for the recovering addicts who would buy them coffee or cigarettes sometimes if they asked.

One night, Denzel didn't come back. They all figured he'd been busted, but there was no way to find out. Another of the guys became her boyfriend. Then another. And then there were the nights when she just needed company in the dark, it didn't matter who.

She felt that same yearning now, to be held and protected in the face of her upturned life. She hated that in herself, just as she'd hated it twenty years ago. Was that what drew her so rashly to Carl? Lauren dried her face, feeling shame welling up, much of it so old and firmly repressed that it flowed out like a gusher of underground oil. She'd worked so hard to craft a new life and leave her teenage self behind. She was such an idiot for opening herself up to some asshole, she of all people, who thought she was so damn streetwise. As if marrying Brian hadn't been enough of a lapse.

So yesterday, she'd forced herself to do the logical thing. She ghosted Carl, deleting and blocking his number before she could give herself time to back out. She didn't want the temptation of having his number or receiving his calls. She didn't want the chance to confront him, which would be a denial-trap if he tried to give her any half-assed explanation.

In answer to her thoughts, an ascending-beat ringtone sounded nearby. Only disaster rang so early. She banged her toe running for the phone. "Shit." She grabbed her toe. "Hello?"

"Lauren, it's me, Jessica."

"What's wrong?"

"Nothing, Emily's asleep. I scared you?"

"Yeah." Lauren sat, rubbing the pain out of her toe.

"Listen, I went to Brian's office last night."

"Get out."

"I found some things I didn't expect. Did you ever hear Brian mention doing real estate work?"

"What? No."

"I found sales contracts for buildings. Sold for millions of dollars. He was the lawyer."

"He didn't know anything about real estate. He said he had no interest in learning."

"Right. That's why I'm so freaked out. I googled the addresses and found pictures. One was a rundown house, maybe even abandoned. It sold for five million dollars. Another sold for twelve. Apartment buildings that size in that part of the Bronx aren't selling for half that much. And it gets worse. The files didn't have the phone numbers of the companies involved. I couldn't even find websites for them. There was a guy who signed for the buyers, the president of the company. He was a Facebook friend of Brian's, but he has a private page, so I couldn't get any information there. The thing is, Lauren, the building that was sold for twelve million … it must have been the last thing Brian worked on before Miami."

Lauren didn't know what to say. She was baffled, as if the world had turned on its axis and all the light in the room was suddenly shining for the wrong time of day. When you'd been married to someone for over ten years there were things you came to expect and things you didn't. She knew Brian would cheat on a woman and maybe cheat on his taxes, but his having an entire hidden professional life he didn't boast about was, frankly, too far out to fathom.

"What do you think?" Jessica asked.

"I don't know. Things have been weird but—"

"I have the addresses of the places. Would you come with me, just to see? I mean, Google Earth photos can be years old, and it's hard to figure out what's up unless we see the neighborhood."

"We sure can't ask Steve," Lauren mused. "Okay. At the least, it could be interesting."

***

Jessica and Emily arrived just after noon. Lauren kissed and hugged Emily, then made gluten-free turkey sandwiches that she knew Jessica would eat. Emily had told Lauren all about Jessica's myriad food restrictions. They sat in Lauren's square, eat-in kitchen with a window overlooking the mom-and-pop stores of West 181st Street—a bodega, a Russian delicacy shop, a glass-walled threading salon with Pakistani women bent over reclining ladies in barber chairs. Big-box stores had tried to pry their way into the gentrifying neighborhood, but raucous community meetings had kept them out.

Jessica and Lauren stalled, eating lunch and drinking tea, in the hope that Emily would get bored and go out as she usually did. That would spare them the need to explain their afternoon activities. But Emily milled around, lazily ate her sandwich, munched pickles, picked up the *New York Times*, put it down. She started texting on her phone, an activity that could keep her entertained for hours.

After a bit, she looked up at Lauren. "So, you went out with a guy?"

"Uh-huh."

Jessica smiled. "Oh, that's nice."

Lauren grimaced, not at all happy to be placated by Jessica about her love life.

Emily looked up from her phone again. "Did you slam dunk him yet?"

"It was nothing."

"It's always nothing—by the time you figure out all the bad things about them."

Lauren picked up her sandwich, wanting to kill Emily for talking about it in front of Jessica. Lauren took her last bite and rinsed her plate off before sitting back down. Emily had begun eating again but seemed to be chewing in slow motion, concentrating on her phone.

Jessica looked at Lauren, imploringly, clearly anxious to get going.

Lauren reached out and stroked Emily's hair from her face. "What are your plans for the day?"

Emily shrugged. "Dunno. Hang out. What are you doing?"

"The Bergen outlet mall, shopping," Jessica said quickly.

"Get out?" Emily looked at Lauren. "You're going shopping? You never go shopping—like for fun? What, you two are celebrating Steve screwing us out of our money?"

Lauren let out a clipped laugh of surprise. Jessica reddened, embarrassed that she'd failed to keep Emily oblivious to everything. She'd mistaken Emily's air of indifference for inattentiveness. Lauren could have warned her about that.

"Come on, I'm not stupid. Something is going on with Steve, something to do with Daddy, and now you two are going to the discount stores together. You think because I'm a kid I'm totally stupid. Well, whatever's up, I'm coming with you." Emily smirked. "I need school clothes."

"You hate that mall," Lauren said. "Remember? It's always crowded and they sell last year's clothes."

Jessica pitched in, "I'll take you to New Roc next week."

Emily sat back and crossed her arms. "Nah. That's okay."

Jessica looked desperate. "What about the friends you wanted to see?"

Emily smiled. "Don't you guys *always* tell me they'll still be here when I get back?"

"Okay, okay," Lauren gave up. "We're going to look at property that your father did real estate deals on."

"Get out." Emily laughed. "Daddy didn't do real estate. Even I know that."

"Exactly. That's why we want a look-see."

Emily's mouth opened, half-shock, half-excitement. "Oh."

The three of them retrieved Jessica's car from a one-hour spot downstairs. Emily spotted a group of her friends coming out of the corner

Starbucks with Frappuccinos. She ran to the girls; they began hugging, whispering, and laughing together. Lauren thought Emily might change her mind about coming but she didn't. A moment later, she trotted to catch up and dove into the back seat with her normal excess of energy. "Okay, so where are we going exactly?"

***

Jessica entered the address of the first building into the dashboard GPS. They rode across town, then north, the neighborhood changing as they drove. Flashy Dominican restaurants took up entire blocks. The sidewalks filled with racks of inexpensive clothing and crowds of brown-skinned people from countries Jessica had only encountered from the safety of all-inclusive resorts. Spanish-language signs provided overhead subtitles for beauty parlors and clothing stores, their display windows populated by full-figured mannequins in tight dresses.

The GPS led the car over a trestle bridge. Elevated train tracks ran overhead, blocking out the afternoon sun. Jessica didn't trust her GPS to find the quickest route. She often talked to the device as if it were an erratic relative, but not today. She watched the unfamiliar neighborhood, feeling a dread that kept her mouth stitched.

"We're getting close," Lauren said, looking over at the GPS.

Gas stations, auto body shops, and car-glass stores lined both sides of the street now. They approached a grimy store with tires leaning on a cinder-block wall. At the curb, a tiny man was jacking up a car with a hand pump. A sign advertised handwritten prices for new and used tires. The man looked at their slow-moving car and smiled, probably hoping they were shopping for tires.

"Arriving at 2506 Jerome Avenue," the GPS said.

"Jesus," Lauren said. "We're looking for a five-million-dollar building."

Jessica groaned as they slowly passed the dilapidated tire store.

Beside it, Jessica took in the sight of a small building, its windows boarded up. "It's the one I saw on Google Earth."

"It wouldn't fit more than four small apartments if there's one in the basement," Lauren thought aloud. "It could never be worth five million dollars."

"I don't get this," Jessica said, her eyes burning and knuckles aching from her two-handed grip on the steering wheel.

Emily snorted. "Daddy's building."

"Not your father's buildings," Jessica barked. "He was the lawyer."

Lauren's gaze snapped to her. "*Jessica.*"

Emily blinked hard, crossed her arms, and looked out the window. "Whatever."

"Look, Jessica," Lauren said, "You can turn the car around and Emily and I can go about our business."

"I'm sorry." Jessica turned back to Emily, her face hot with embarrassment. "I'm really sorry. You didn't do anything wrong. I'm just freaking out a little here."

"Okay." Lauren took a deep breath. "We're all stressed."

"I doubt anyone lives there," Emily said.

Several Latino and African men emerged from a car wash, drying all sides of a shining car that pulled out of a driveway a few yards up the block.

Jessica watched them but was thinking about the building. "It's worse than the picture."

"It's better than Dad having a whole secret family or—" Emily interrupted herself, shutting herself up, apparently thinking of Jessica's feelings. The first time ever, Jessica thought.

"I don't know anything about him anymore. What connection could Brian have had with any of this?" Jessica said, mortified that Lauren was witnessing what an idiot she'd been when it came to Brian. Jessica hadn't been the big winner after all—she'd been the biggest idiot. Brian did have a secret life. Jessica felt so diminished by it all. But she was still glad Lauren was here. She couldn't have done this alone, and she was beyond grateful that Lauren wasn't gloating. If she'd been in Lauren's place with a woman who had stolen the man she loved, Jessica didn't think she could be as nice.

"And why such a high price?" Lauren said. "My first thought was that it was some sort of speculation, but if there were going to be a rise in property values in the area—because of a shopping complex or zoning changes or something—you wouldn't buy at already inflated prices or there would be no profit."

"If it had anything to do with Daddy, it had to be about money," Emily said.

Jessica looked at Emily, the whole thing so unreal she felt as if she could spin out of control.

"Emily's right," Lauren said. "We need to figure out how money could be made on the sales of the buildings, and we'll have the answer. Let's just go to the next building."

Jessica wiped away a tear. "Okay." She programmed the GPS. "It's pretty close."

They left the auto parts street and made their way through a mismatched patchwork of five-story apartment buildings and clapboard homes. The Bronx streets wove in haphazard curves up and down, sometimes connected by staircases that ran between buildings, one block stacked over the next. Jessica drove up a narrow street on a hill of prewar apartment buildings. The block bent in a hairpin turn with two-family homes at the top of the hill and apartment buildings at the bottom. Halfway down, a ramshackle five-story building wrapped in scaffolding stood in the center of an abandoned lot. Two brick wings embraced a rubble-strewn courtyard. The GPS announced their arrival.

"Oh, God," Jessica breathed, stopping the car at the curb in front of it.

"Twelve million dollars," Lauren said.

On impulse, Jessica exited the car. A matted-down path through the courtyard, resembling the dirt jogger tracks that ran beside Westchester roads, led to the entrance. Above her, some of the windows gaped empty and black, but others seemed to have life behind their glass.

Lauren approached her. "What are you doing?"

Jessica started to march angrily toward the building. "I'm going to ask who the owner is. People live here."

Lauren grabbed her arm, "It's not safe. It looks abandoned."

Jessica wrenched her arm back, "I don't care, Lauren. If people can squat here, I can knock on some doors and find out who owns the building."

"Really? You've got to be kidding." But Lauren walked alongside her.

"I'm coming, too," Emily said, jumping out of the car.

"No!" Lauren and Jessica said simultaneously.

Lauren spoke firmly, "Wait for us in the car and lock the doors."

"Mom," Emily whined.

"I'm not kidding."

A hardness in Lauren's eyes convinced Emily, who about-faced to her seat in the car. The locks clicked.

At the building's steel front door, head height, was a square opening meant to hold a pane of glass. It was too dark to see more than shadows beyond. When they walked inside, it became obvious what had happened. A fire had charred the first floor. A burnt smell clung to the air, mixed with a stink of mildew and urine.

Jessica and Lauren walked through the lobby. Their shoes crunched glass particles as they watched their step in the near darkness. They saw signs of life at a far corner: a flickering candle, discarded meal wrappers, an empty bed of flattened cardboard boxes.

A ragged woman with tattoos hanging off flaccid arms rounded the corner from a hallway behind the campsite. She fanned a hand toward her chest, "Oh, fuck, you scared the shit outta me." She pulled at her pants and zipped them up; apparently, they had been too tight to lounge in comfort. A muffin top of fat hung over her waistband and her breasts sloped low on her chest under her shirt.

"Sorry," Lauren said.

The woman gave Lauren a once over and glanced at Jessica, "If you're looking to buy, this ain't the place."

"No. We're looking for the landlord," Lauren said, taking over as spokesperson even though it had been Jessica's idea to ask people.

The woman cackled. "Oh, lord, do you think the landlord would be found here?"

Lauren pressed, "Do you know who he is or who manages the building?"

That really tickled the woman. She bent over laughing with a hand on the wall. "Does it look like this dump is being managed by anyone? Where the fuck you bitches come from? Wait a second, don't I know you?" She pointed a finger at Lauren and peered at her, "Don't you work at Family Court?" She stepped toward them.

Jessica worried that maybe Lauren had taken the woman's children. What would happen then?

"Could be." Lauren seemed unfazed, reflecting back the woman's toughness.

"You got a couple of bucks?"

Lauren paused and took a twenty from the front pocket of her jeans. "It's yours if you tell me about the landlord."

The woman grinned, grunted, and reached down to shove the bill into her sock. "I don't know for sure, but there were some guys here this morning that maybe own the place. Hard men, you could tell. They looked around then went to an apartment down there." She pointed to an apartment without a door at the opposite end of the lobby, nearly invisible in the dark. "They didn't see me, and I checked it out afterward just in case they accidentally left something there. But I'm not lucky like that, never am. Anyway, it seemed more like they were looking *for* something, not leaving anything. They were talking up a storm."

"What did they say?" Lauren asked.

The woman shrugged. "I don't speak Spanish."

"You don't know who they were?" Jessica asked.

The woman sized up Jessica as if just noticing her. "Nah. But they were not happy."

"Let's just check it out," Lauren said. Jessica followed. They walked through a fire-widened doorway, the floors made of wood plank, the place unfurnished. All the windows were boarded up except one that let in light at the far right side.

A sudden noise wheeled Jessica and Lauren around, and they both jumped back. A bottle skittered across the floor. A figure stepped into the doorway. "Mom?"

"Emily? What are you doing here?" Jessica held her belly. "Oh, my God, you scared me."

"Emily, what the hell?" Lauren said, angrily.

Emily whispered close to her mother, "I got nervous out there by myself. A car passed, slow. They looked at me … sort of weird, like maybe they knew me. Chinese guys. I didn't know them."

"They were probably just wondering what you were doing here," Lauren said, coming to her.

The woman stepped into the room, following behind Emily. "Ain't this some shit. You know if I had *my* baby in this godforsaken place, *you* would be taking her away from me right now. *Again*."

Lauren put her hand on Emily's back, "Let's go." She spoke to Jessica, "There's nothing more to see here.

CHAPTER 17

Monday, November 4

It was a cold, gray afternoon and Carl had a case of the Monday blues, wishing Sunday with his son hadn't ended so quickly. Yesterday had been one of those days when the simple moments with his son had filled Carl up, like the early days when his son had graced him with a first gummy smile. They hadn't done anything special together. They'd just stretched out in Carl's bedroom on a dreary day, Carl's arm around his son's shoulder, their heads propped up on pillows watching TV, talking and joking about whatever came to mind.

Now, a half block from the West Side Highway, where the Intrepid lorded over the highway's intersection with West Forty-Sixth Street, Carl arrived at the Home Game sports bar. He pulled open the bar's outer door and passed through a vestibule into a dimly lit twilight. The place was empty except for a Central American day worker who was pulling upside-down chairs from tabletops and placing them on the floor in preparation for the first customers of the day. The day worker turned on flat-screen TVs with a remote control as he proceeded around the room. A replay of Game Six of the World Series emerged on one screen above the bar. Another opened to a soccer game. Beach volleyball players in bikinis were on a third TV over a lounge-seating area near the back of the room. Several more screens were still dark.

A man in his twenties approached Carl from a shadowy hallway past the lounge area. Wearing a silk T-shirt under a dark suit jacket, the man's eyes were a piercing blue and his hair was the streaked-blond of a California surfer. He extended his hand to shake. He could have been a model except the top of his head barely reached Carl's collarbone. "*Qué tal*, Carl?"

Carl shook his hand. "I'm good, CB. What's up?"

CB peered around. "I'm glad you left your partner home. You two look like Miami Vice."

"Aren't you too young to remember that show?"

"I spent my summers in DR when I was a kid. The television pickings were slim. Come in the back."

A group of women clattered in the door, and one of them approached. She wore black spandex leggings and a white leather jacket that stretched tight across her chest. She had stark cheekbones, jet-black Farrah Fawcett hair, and the physique of a fitness model except for her oversized breasts. "CB, I need to go home early tonight," she said in Spanish. "The babysitter has to leave by eleven."

"*Coño*," CB answered in Spanish, "you need to fire that babysitter."

Although CB had no trace of Latino features, he spoke Spanish with the accent and slang of a native Dominican. CB's great-grandfather, a suspected Nazi, had taken refuge in the DR after World War II. He left behind a slew of Aryan offspring in the same town where Jorge Arena grew up. Before CB was born, his grandfather and Jorge Arena's father worked as secret police together during Trujillo's brutal dictatorship. The families stayed close after that, although CB's grandfather immigrated to the US, and Arena's father spent time in a Dominican prison. It was all in the Bureau's files. Carl thought Arena's father must have taught his son some tricks. People tended to end up dead around Jorge Arena, and they suffered before they died.

"Daisy, have you met Carl?" CB said to the raven-haired Farrah Fawcett. "He's the new assistant manager."

She put out her hand and smiled coyly, "*Mucho gusto,* Carlos."

Carl smiled at her appreciatively, although he wasn't personally attracted to her. When he wasn't working, he was a homebody. He liked it that way, although he mentally acknowledged that, if these girls had a choice, many of them would prefer to be homebodies too.

CB spoke to Daisy. "I may have a few extra hours for you if you want to make up the time."

"*Gracias, papi.*" She leaned down and kissed CB on the cheek.

Carl followed CB to his office in the back, a room with a glass desk, mirrors, and cameras. It had been designed to count money with transparency.

"I called Jorge Arena's cousin, Pedro," CB said. "He's Jorge's body man, his executive assistant you could say. He just came back from Miami with Lucho Arena. Lucho is another cousin and the muscle, a smart guy but meaner than a python. Even meaner than Jorge. Something was going on in Miami."

Carl knew about Lucho Arena, had heard his voice on the taps from time to time. Carl sat in a leather armchair. "What do you mean, something was going on in Miami?"

"I think the trip to Miami had something to do with the missing money."

Carl modulated his voice, hiding his level of interest. "So, there's money missing?"

"Yup. Last trace of it was in Miami." CB sat at his desk and pulled out a pack of cigarettes.

Carl gave him a hard look. "Really?"

"Okay, all right." CB dropped the pack on the glass surface. "Pedro tells me they're expanding their search, looking in New York too. No rock unturned, you know? From what I'm hearing, the money was private action between a gambler Jorge was agenting and a Chinese dude. The bet was processed through Jordan Connors' website. Arena's gambler lost a big pot." CB rubbed his face and unconsciously reached for the cigarette pack before dropping it again. "I guess Arena's not used to being the one who owes the money, although I'm halfway surprised he's so hyped about still owing it. The Chinese guy must have a lot of juice." CB shrugged. "Notable fact: I haven't seen Jordan in a while. He stops by here a lot. He likes live-action poker upstairs, if we make sure none of the con-teams are at the table when he plays. We let him take a turn beating up our regular customers, fair and square. He buys some coke while he's here, maybe takes home one of the girls after work. But I haven't seen or heard a word about him in a couple of weeks. He didn't mention he was planning a trip. Are you sure he's still among the living?"

***

Red rays bathed the sides of the Tribeca loft buildings that Carl and Rick walked past. "I spoke to the cops in Florida today," Carl said.

Rick raised his eyebrows and looked at Carl. "About what?"

"Brian Silverman."

"Damn. You can't take no for an answer."

Carl pulled open the door to the gym. Warm air hit. Carl spoke quietly, "The cop said they sent the cigarette butt to the ATF for analysis. It was a Newport." Carl continued to talk despite Rick's annoyed exhalation. "Silverman smoked Marlboros."

Rick pushed open the door to the men's locker room. "What does that mean? He had an urge for a menthol. It's known to happen. He bummed a cigarette and died smoking in bed. There was no evidence of accelerant anywhere near the fire."

"The cell records came back on Silverman. He made calls from Tortola the night before the fire. Tell me, my man, what was he doing in Tortola the day after he withdrew twelve million dollars? And who would go all that way for only one day?"

Rick stripped off his button-down shirt and replaced it with a T-shirt. "The Virgin Islands?"

"The British Virgin Islands—an off-shore banking spot. Silverman had to be Jordan's runner. I'm telling you, something went wrong, that's why Arena's people are all over Miami and New York looking for missing money … and why Jordan's gone MIA."

"Yeah, well, how do you kill a guy with a cigarette? You haven't even begun to answer that."

Dressed in sweat shorts and an old T-shirt his mother had sent him from Puerto Rico, Carl slipped on his leather weightlifting gloves. "Let me ask you this: He was in surgery for hours before he died. With all the Valium and Propofol the doctors pumped into him, how do we know he wasn't slipped a roofie before he burned?"

When they reached the weight room, Rick pointed to the lat pull-down machine—they'd work their backs tonight. With Carl standing behind him, Rick sat and grabbed the metal bar, which was attached to a pulley and weight plates. He pulled it down to his shoulders behind his head and did several unassisted reps.

"One more." Carl pressed down on the bar with two fingers to help as Rick's breathing turned into a groan.

The bar touched Rick's shoulders, and he let it rise upward. Breathless, he spoke to Carl as they switched places. "You know that theory about the fire being intentional is far-fetched."

Carl swung his foot over the low seat and gripped the bar. He pulled it down and began his set. He watched Rick through a strip of mirror in front of him that separated two windows with a view of the Nautilus and stretching room. He spoke between breaths. "Let me ask you this, Rick: What are the odds of accidentally dying in your sleep if Arena's involved?"

Rick placed his palm on the top of the bar for an assisted rep. Carl pulled with the last of his strength, but suddenly Rick's help was gone. The weights pulled Carl to his feet with a violent jerk. "Are you trying to kill me?"

Rick bent over and spoke quietly near Carl's ear, "Shit. That's Lauren Davis."

Carl saw her through the glass window. She was doing hanging leg raises from an overhead bar, raising her muscular legs to a ninety-degree angle before she lowered them. Her hair was tied up in a thick ponytail, and she wore a black sleeveless T-shirt and stretch shorts. She looked great. "She has a membership here."

"You knew that?"

"Can't say I didn't." Carl smiled wryly, covering up his disappointment. "She hasn't called me though, and I can't seem to get through to her. I don't know what happened."

Rick let out a clipped laugh. "You're kidding?"

"Just tell her you work with me at the sports bar if she asks."

"If the boss hears about this, you're fucked." Rick raised his eyebrows. "You're not fucked, are you?"

Carl frowned, always uncomfortable with locker-room talk. "No."

"If the other guys hear about you doing business in our gym, you'll really be in the doghouse. We'll have to work out strapped if word gets back to her pal Arena that we're all here."

Carl patted Rick on the shoulder. "Don't worry about it. Arena's not her pal."

"Have you read her file? She's no Mother Teresa," Rick hissed as Carl walked away.

Carl headed toward the door, watching Lauren hang then jump down from the overhead bar. Despite what her file said, she'd been a kid when she'd last been on FBI radar. A victim, for all intents and purposes. Almost a dead victim. He'd spent enough time with her to know she didn't have a drop of criminal blood in her veins. He had reliable instincts about such things. She was a mom and a lawyer, and a good athlete. That was it.

Carl didn't think she'd seen him, her head bobbed to iPhone music as she reached to the floor and picked up a water bottle. Carl's sneaker toe caught on the carpeted doorsill between rooms just as she looked up and noticed him. He couldn't help but look down at the feet that had tripped him. They'd always embarrassed him, size thirteen Saint Bernard–puppy feet by the time he was twelve. He quickly corrected himself, smiling sheepishly. "Hi."

"Hi," she said without taking out her earbuds. Her first glance at him had turned glacial.

As if he'd been found out, he felt a shot of guilt for deceiving her. Things had gotten a lot heavier the other night than he'd expected. He tapped his ear and mouthed, "How are you?"

She pulled one ear bud from an ear. "Fine."

"Your daughter? Emily, right?"

She smiled, politely—a polite smile if he'd ever seen one. "She's fine, thanks." She pushed the earplug back into her ear.

Ouch. He reached to touch her arm. She hesitated then unplugged her ear again.

"Did I do something wrong, Lauren? I tried to call you a couple of times."

"I have an appointment in an hour, and I want to get in a quick workout. I don't have time to talk."

The woman was like Jekyll and Hyde. She hadn't seemed like the bitchy type. He'd heard about things like this, how people who were dating would simply disappear the other person from their lives, ghost them, not even providing an explanation. In this case, they'd only had one date, but it hadn't felt like it. He had to be honest with himself: she'd really hurt his feelings. "Call me, okay? You have my number."

She flashed a false, irritated smile that said he shouldn't hold his breath. She put the earbud back in her ear and walked away.

Carl returned to Rick in the weight room. Rick had obviously kept an eye on things. "She seemed real enthusiastic to see you. She dissed you, didn't she?"

Carl sat at the lat pull-down machine to do his next set. "I wouldn't call it that."

"What *would* you call it?"

Carl thought it over as he pulled the weighted bar behind his head. He looked at Rick in the mirror. "Okay, she dissed me."

Rick laughed, "Man, I read that a mile away. You've got a way with women, I'm telling you. You're a regular Bond," Rick's accent turned British, "James Bond."

CHAPTER 18

Hector was waiting for Emily at the 103rd Street subway station, across the street from Central Park. She'd taken Metro North from Westchester to Grand Central and from there, the subway. She'd told Jessica she was staying at the computer lab at school for a couple of hours and that she was thinking about catching a school basketball game. Jessica had seemed happy. Emily hoped she wouldn't get caught. Being mean to Jessica had started becoming unpleasant. Jessica was trying hard to be good to Emily, probably too hard, although Emily would never be the one to tell her that. Emily liked the benefits.

She also hadn't told Jessica the things she'd found out, that her dad was probably cheating on Jessica in Tortola. Emily didn't tell her mother either. She wouldn't want to be in Jessica's stilettos if everyone knew but her. So, with much effort—Emily almost blurted it all out a couple of times on Saturday—she'd kept her father's cheating and the encrypted file to herself, thinking it would be better to find out what was on the file before telling. And after their real estate tour in the Bronx yesterday, it looked like Emily had more important things to think about than who her father was hooking up with. She wanted to know what was going on with the building they'd seen and what was going on that would make Steve cheat them out of her father's money. Emily thought the encrypted files might be the key to all of it. Maybe she should have told her mother about it once she realized there was more going on than her father cheating. But if her mother knew, she would never let Emily do what she was doing now.

"You've gotta be chill with Tabu when you meet him," Hector said. "I'm not supposed to tell anyone he's back on the internet. He's on parole."

"No problem."

Hector must have been the geekiest kid in the projects. He always looked like he was wearing a school uniform even when he wasn't, and he played Dungeons & Dragons, which was as geeky as you could get. He didn't hang out with Emily's main group of friends, but she still thought he was a cool kid. They'd been in school together since the sixth grade, until she moved to Westchester.

It was already dark out and Emily tensed up as they neared the Douglas Projects. She usually walked around, not through, the projects, even though they were right in the middle of the Upper West Side within sight of a Whole Foods. She scanned her surroundings as she walked beside Hector. Surprisingly, the Douglas Projects were pretty with huge, old oaks lining the walkways between brown buildings.

"He used to do business with people online and never met them," Hector continued. "That was the way it was back when Anonymous was new. But now he's not supposed to be on the internet at all, so he said he has to meet you before he'd risk it."

"There was a documentary about it on YouTube," Emily said. "He ratted out all his friends, and they did like ten years."

"Yeah, it's kind of embarrassing. He had to do it, though, so he could help my mother with us kids. She raised him since he was a kid, before we were even born. My mother lost her job during the recession, and he was the only one making money. If he hadn't cooperated, he would have done twenty years." Hector led Emily down a path past a playground, toward a building entrance. "He stays inside most of the time since he came home from prison. I mean, it was in the papers that he turned state's. Luckily, he only ratted out a bunch of white boys who nobody in the projects cares too much about."

Emily smelled rice, beans, and cilantro-laced tomato sauce the moment they entered Hector's apartment. Three dark-haired preteens watched a flat-screen TV in a sparsely furnished living room with spotless, glossy-white walls.

"Those are my sisters. *Mami*, I'm home," Hector called, and brought Emily toward the alley-kitchen with space for a table at the end. "This is my friend, Emily, from school."

"Hello," Hector's mother said to her.

"Hi."

"Come on," Hector tugged on Emily's arm, relieving her of the awkwardness of his mother clearly checking her out. Emily figured Hector didn't have many girls visiting him.

Hector knocked on a door halfway down a long, dim hallway. A heavyset man in his late twenties looked out and walked back into his room. Hector led Emily in and closed the door behind her. The room was lit by a single desk lamp. A laptop sat open on the desk.

"I can't keep a lot of equipment around, in case my parole officer makes a home visit," Tabu said, almost apologetically. He looked Emily over, grimacing. "Loli. That's all I need."

"What did you expect, Tabu? I'm Loli."

"Boys can't be Loli."

"What's Loli?" Emily asked, annoyed at them talking as if she weren't there.

"Underage girl," Hector said.

Tabu shook his head. "Like I don't have enough problems."

"Well, I'm definitely not gonna *do* anything to make that relevant."

Tabu chuckled, seeming to like that answer. "She's a smart one, coz." He sat and swiveled toward Emily. "Okay, so what's going on?"

Emily pulled out the thumb drive she'd found in her father's desk. "It has an encrypted file, and I need to know what's on it."

He looked at it as if it were coated in Russian skin-eating poison. "Whose is it?"

"My father's."

"I've gotta be careful what I do. If I get caught hacking, they'll send me away for ten years."

Emily pulled out two hundred dollars. "My father died. He was just a lawyer, but something cray-cray is going on with his partner. I want to know why my father had an encrypted file."

"Your dad wasn't a terrorist or anything?" Tabu took the money. "I can't afford to get involved with some stupid Loli shit."

"You must have googled me, seen about him."

He took the thumb drive and wheeled away toward his desk. "Yeah, shit. I saw the obit. I cannot tell a lie. Lemme look at it."

He inserted it and Emily watched the unintelligible characters populate the screen.

"It's simple. A backup file for Whatsapp. I can create a clone account."

"Yes!" Emily exclaimed, so proud of herself for finding Tabu.

"Do you have his phone?"

"No. We never got the phone back. It must have burnt up."

"Oh, dude, I'm sorry. I need that."

"It's okay." Emily felt close to tears, crestfallen. She was always just a few inches from tears since her dad died. It didn't take much for her to start slobbering and embarrassing herself.

He must have seen it on her face because he gave her a sympathetic smile. "Look, you need to get hold of a device where he had the app."

Emily clenched her jaw, struggling not to cry.

"Listen, I know how you feel. Both my parents died when I was a kid. So I'm going to help you. If you don't have the phone, your only chance is his PC. Since he had a thumb drive backup, I gotta assume he had the app on it."

"So we can do something?" Emily asked, swiping away the tears that had managed to seep out.

He handed her the thumb drive. "I don't know what you think is on here, but take this phone and call me on my burner phone when you're home." He handed Emily a cheap black flip phone. "My burner number is the only one in the contacts. I can't risk you calling my regular phone or getting caught out there on yours. Once you're on your dad's PC, I'll walk you through what you need to do. Okay? On your honor, you have to destroy the phone after we're done with it."

"Okay, I will. Thank you!"

Tabu patted Emily's shoulder before she left his room. "I'm sorry for your loss." He turned to Hector. "You got good taste, little coz. Make sure she gets back to her train safe."

CHAPTER 19

The Broadway local arrived just as Lauren reached the platform of the Brooklyn Bridge station half a dozen blocks from the gym. She sat in a bright-orange seat and her mind wandered back to its current puzzle. For two days, she had reenvisioned, step-by-step, Saturday's trip to the Bronx. She had tried to think like Brian, to figure out what the hell he'd been up to with that building. She thought of illegal tax shelters, money laundering, speculation. Even though Brian had always stayed on the right side of the law when they were married, careful about attorney ethics and guarding his reputation, the one thing Lauren felt sure about was that Brian would never be an unwitting accomplice to anything. So she could only conclude that safety had become boring for him, and he'd been down with whatever shady stuff had gone on.

It didn't take much for her to make the next couple of logical leaps. First, shady deals were done by shady people who were often dangerous and could have killed Brian for some reason. Second, Steve was Brian's partner, perhaps the closest person to him and certainly a shady person. So, third, Steve could be involved in whatever led to Brian's death. Maybe that was too big a jump—but he did seem to be the X factor, the biggest change in Brian's recent life other than Jessica, who Lauren couldn't imagine as a thought-leader for Brian. And besides, Jessica was as mystified as Lauren.

Supposing it were true about Steve being involved, Lauren thought, would that make him dangerous? Lauren couldn't picture him pulling a trigger or lighting a match, but she'd known enough bad people to sense he had it in him to pull the strings that pulled the trigger. The main question was why. She didn't even have an educated guess on that.

Of course, if Brian had been murdered, maybe Jessica and Lauren should stop trying to figure out what was going on before they ended up in danger themselves. But they had to pursue Brian's share of the legitimate partnership money, even if they stayed away from the real estate mystery. Emily's future was at stake. And that brought Lauren to her conclusion: they had to know the whole story. Otherwise, if Steve were involved, they would be fighting him blindfolded.

Then, as if in direct response to Lauren's decision, just before she left the office for the gym, she'd received the most surprising call. "Lauren?" The voice had spoken quietly. Lauren had to strain to hear.

"Yes."

"This is Peggy."

"Oh," Lauren frowned. "I didn't recognize your voice."

"Listen, I need to talk to you. I shouldn't … but you need to know. Would you meet me after work?"

Although mystified, Lauren jumped at the chance to find out anything that might shed light on things. Still, she felt a distinct sense of unreality meeting Peggy under these unbusinesslike circumstances. Aside from the funeral, she hadn't seen Peggy for years and never outside of Brian's office. Peggy had always been formal, nearly ceremonious, in the way she treated Brian and everyone else. Brian had trusted and depended on her completely. It was familiarity that bred indifference and contempt in Brian, and Peggy never got familiar.

So now, going to meet Peggy was like a confirmation that, since Brian's death, nothing remained the same. Relationships were shifting like subterranean plates of earth during an earthquake. Steve, from Brian's friend to enemy; Jessica, from home wrecker to comother; and Peggy.

And Carl. The thought entered Lauren's head before she could stop it. She hated being bitchy to him, but when she saw him stumbling over his feet as he approached her, she felt such a strong impulse to catch the poor guy that she had to snap herself out of it. She'd blocked his number, so why was she still even thinking about him? Well, she was. And that was exactly why she'd ghosted him. She didn't trust herself. She'd come to feel even more strongly that Carl's wouldn't-hurt-a-fly aura just didn't fit with his evasiveness. He had a flip side, a strength, maybe a stubbornness. Combined with his evasiveness, it made her suspect that his shy, nice-guy facade was even more than a bullshit act to get laid, maybe more than his being married. He had to be "in the Life," as they used to call it back in the day—a hustler, a drug dealer, or a gangster. Lauren couldn't get past that idea, even though he had the cute, vulnerable thing down. Even killers loved their dogs. She could attest to that.

It stunned Lauren that so much low-life shit seemed to be going down around her, sucking her in. She would have sworn her gangster-dar would set off all kinds of alarm bells before she'd get involved with a guy like that. For over twenty years, she'd managed to stay away from people who exuded even a whiff of danger, especially men who seemed too good to be true, like European settlers with smallpox blankets.

The train pulled into the Astor Place station, and she found herself smiling at the memory of how Carl fed Mookie under the table. She thought about how Carl's face lit up when he talked about his son, and how she felt during their brief goodnight kiss. Lauren's chaotic childhood, life on the street, and Brian had left her deeply untrusting, a logical survival instinct after all that. But was she letting her imagination get away from her? She hadn't been in a relationship in years. She used to tell herself that Emily wasn't ready for her to begin anything serious, but deep down Lauren had always known that was a crock. It was Lauren keeping herself alone, thinking it was safer posing as Mother Teresa than risking a normal life. It was also Lauren who thought that any club that would have her had a hidden angle. And she was doing it again.

She'd had her perfect opportunity tonight to at least ask Carl about the two phones, to give him a chance to explain. She needed to get honest with herself. He probably wasn't a gangster, and maybe he wasn't even married. Maybe she was just afraid he *could* explain.

***

Starbucks at Astor Place was constructed industrial style to blend in with the touristy East Village loft area. The place reminded Lauren of a cement waiting room at Rikers Island. She spotted Peggy at a table. Peggy smiled when she looked up and saw Lauren approaching. It was a tense smile that furrowed the skin around Peggy's lips. Sitting ramrod straight, she wore a dark suit and a light green blouse, her coat draped on her shoulders. Her hair was cut into short brunette curls, swept back from her face.

She stood and shook Lauren's hand, something Peggy never did when Lauren used to visit Brian's office. The handshake said that today they weren't meeting as secretary and wife but were instead there to discuss serious business. Lauren lay her coat over the back of her chair and left to get a latte.

Once she returned, Peggy leaned forward, anxiety in her wide, brown eyes. "I worked for Brian for thirteen years, came with him when he switched from Satlin and Satlin to Cohen's firm. I've been at Cohen for five years, so it is my job … but aside from things like sharing a copy machine and microwave with the other secretaries, in my mind, Brian and I were separate from the rest. We were a team, and wherever he went, I would have gone."

"Brian appreciated your loyalty."

Peggy sat stiffly, all business. "Given my age, the latter half of fifty now, I'm going to stay on at Cohen. So, you can never repeat what I'm telling you. This is my last task for Brian … for Emily's sake. He would have expected that much, and I expect that much of myself."

Lauren inhaled a lungful of coffee-scented air, unnerved and mystified. "Thank you."

"I came to you instead of Jessica because of the sensitivity of this matter. I don't look at you as a petty person, so I trust you won't use the information to hurt anyone innocent …" Peggy searched Lauren's eyes.

"I'm not looking to hurt anyone."

She nodded then continued. "I overlooked Brian's weaknesses because they were none of my business. But you and I both know he did better in his business than his personal life."

Lauren smirked. "You could say that."

"I know you're surprised at what Steve is doing—not calling back, not wanting to give up any of the firm's money. But there were things going on between Steve and Brian that no one knew about. Over the last few months, I heard things, couldn't help it, and it got to a point where Brian didn't care so much, because he knew I would never comment on his personal life …"

Lauren nodded and waited.

"I believe what's happening now has to do with Nicole."

"Nicole?"

"Yes, Steve's wife."

"Oh, shit." Seeing Peggy's let's-not-lose-decorum frown, Lauren blurted out an apology. "Sorry, you took me by surprise."

Peggy waved it away. "I got a whiff of things early this year. Nicole and Brian were having an affair. They weren't terribly discreet about it. Brian tended to get carried away when he became infatuated. He became careless at such times. Well, I don't know how it happened; maybe Nicole told Steve in a moment of viciousness. I suspect Nicole is not someone known for kindness. But I overheard Brian and Steve arguing some months ago."

"Wow. That would explain it—but why wait until Brian dies to cheat his family? Why did they keep working together?"

"Well, I'm no fool, I figured it out for myself along with the bits and pieces of the argument I heard. Steve inherited the firm from his father, but he didn't have his father's talent in court. It was Brian who was the brilliant one—attorneys all over the country looked to Brian as the best lawyer to try toxic tort cases. They always came to him, not Steve. Even Steve's political friends who referred cases knew Brian would handle the actual work. Without Brian, Steve was just an ambulance chaser. Brian was his cash cow."

That made perfect sense. "Right."

"So basically, Steve sold his wife. He had to think about the planes he owned, the fancy cars, the expensive home in East Hampton." Peggy sat up even straighter, as if passing judgment. "He was a cuckold."

Lauren thought out loud, "Now that Brian's dead, Steve has nothing to lose by cheating him, and Brian's not around to fight back."

"Brian never stopped seeing Nicole. Steve didn't have the spine to sacrifice his business for his self-respect. Now he doesn't have to. I wanted you to know so you could be prepared to fight. You don't have to fool yourself that there was some vestige of friendship between Steve and Brian that will make him see the light and do right by your child. Their friendship was long over."

"Peggy, do you think Steve could have killed Brian?"

Peggy pulled her coat tighter at the neck. "Would a man who didn't have the courage to risk his business risk going to jail for the rest of his life?"

"He could have paid someone to do it."

Peggy got up. "I only know what I know. In Brian's memory, I needed to share it with someone who could look out for his family's interests." Peggy slipped her coat sleeves on and picked up her pocketbook from the table. "I wish you all the best."

Lauren rose with her, didn't want her to leave yet. "A couple more questions, please, Peggy."

Peggy paused and let out her breath. "Okay."

They sat back down, and Lauren sipped her latte to buy time to think. She needed to ask the right questions.

"Did you ever hear of someone named Jordan Connors?"

"No, can't say I have."

"Did you know anything about Brian doing real estate transactions?"

Peggy frowned. "No."

"Did you see any files that were labeled with addresses instead of case names?"

Peggy's eyes looked toward the farthest corner of the room, obviously focusing on Brian's file cabinets rather than her present location. "I did see a couple of files like that, within the last several months. I supposed they were asbestos cases. I never gave them much thought. I didn't look inside because Brian never needed anything from them … I guess it is strange that they just sat there, never needing any work."

"Please don't mention them to anyone. I don't know what they're about yet."

Peggy halfway smiled. "We never met, remember?"

Lauren watched Peggy leave. Lauren sat for a moment and stared, unseeing, at the pedestrians on the dark street on the other side of the coffee shop windows. Beyond Lauren's initial surprise, Nicole being such a lowlife didn't shock her, not with Nicole's *Devil Wears Prada* demeanor, as if everyone were a lesser species on the planet to serve her. What surprised Lauren more was that Peggy knew who Brian screwed yet knew nothing about the real estate deals. There was still no indication that the fire was anything other than an accident, but Brian's life appeared more hazardous by the minute.

So now, what was Lauren supposed to do with the information about Nicole and Brian? It was good to know, but for the time being, she would keep it to herself—for Jessica's sake. Betrayal by a ghost you couldn't even confront, Lauren wouldn't wish that pain on anyone. She smiled inwardly, amazed that she would go to any trouble to protect Jessica from having her feelings hurt. Would wonders never cease?

CHAPTER 20
BRIAN

One Month Ago

A cloud passed by Jordan's Manhattan apartment windows as he spoke. It darkened the room and cast a shadow across Jordan's face. Brian brushed away a thought that it was a sign of bad things to come. Walking from the window toward the couch, Jordan wiped sweat from under the brow of his backward baseball cap. For the first time, Brian noticed that Jordan was balding under the cap.

Catching Brian's glance, Jordan quipped, jittery. "Baldness is imperialistic ... like Russia during the Cold War."

"Your hair is falling like Eastern Europe?"

"It's weird how fast ... stress, I think." Jordan sat, turning deadly serious, his face grizzled. "I'm being blackmailed."

"Get out."

Jordan exhaled and lay his head back, taking in the ceiling. "If I don't work with them, they'll shut me down."

"Who?"

"The bookie from Home Game, Jorge Arena. His crew."

Brian sucked hard on a cigarette, the end glowing hot. "How would they do that?"

"DDOS attacks in the middle of the Super Bowl, World Series, or any playoff game. It's the easiest thing to do. Just flood my website with requests to place bets, a million automated requests. Bottom line, my friend, it has become clear to me that we all live every minute of every day by the suffrage of strangers, every time we walk down a street safely, every time we cross a street and no one attacks us like in *The Purge*. Same thing online. If evil dudes decide you're their target, that's it. They already shut me down once. A shot across the bow. They wanted to show me how easily they could put me out of business."

Brian thought it through, imagining how freaked out Jordan must have been when that happened. On the surface, he seemed laid back, but he was really a control freak. Jordan had to be jumping out of his skin right now: Everything he'd created was at the mercy of a DDOS botnet. "How do you work with them?"

"Take their side bets. Don't bitch when I see their guys collude at the virtual poker table."

"What are you going to do?"

Jordan stared off. When he met Brian's gaze again, Brian could see how the energy had drained out of Jordan's face, his eyes wide and frightened. "They're going to destroy all the good will I've built up. They'll suck my business dry. They don't give a shit about word getting around to my clients that my site can't be trusted. Arena will reduce my business to ashes, cash out, and run like the hedge funds do in corporate takeovers."

Brian poured himself a drink. He stopped at the window to look at the Central Park Zoo, Sheep Meadow, and the reservoir, small dollhouse pieces amidst the green, orange, and red of trees just short of prime. He turned back to Jordan. "Shut down shop for a while. You have enough money to stop completely. Why would you bother?"

Even as he asked that, Brian knew that it was easier to tell Jordan to stop than take his own advice. He'd made some bad decisions lately and, like Jordan, he felt incapable of putting the brakes on. Jordan's weakness was money and maybe power. For Brian, the effect women had on him was as insidious as drug addiction. The alcoholics were right about "one is too many and a thousand never enough." Once Brian had cheated on Jessica, the floodgates had opened.

He'd been at a club in Miami with Jordan, and the women had been amazing, their nearly bare breasts and the space between their thighs beckoning to him like an oasis in the desert. That party had released the proverbial beast in him and, like usual, eventually led to far more entanglement than he'd planned. Not right away, but soon after. He couldn't feel any sleazier. He didn't love Nicole. She wasn't exactly lovable. But his obsession with her had been all-consuming. He remembered something else Lauren had told him about addiction: if you were hit by a train, it was the first car that killed you, not the caboose. He totally got that now. It was the first woman who had led him to Nicole, which had risked everything. His marriage, his business, his friendship with Steve … and their partnership. He and Steve weren't seeing eye to eye on anything anymore.

Brian knew Jessica was getting double-screwed too, not having a baby. But he hadn't even done that to Lauren, knocking her up and betraying her at the same time. The first affair hadn't happened until after Emily was born, and he hadn't planned it. But he knew he was a piece of shit when he told Jessica that Emily wasn't ready for a sibling so soon after the divorce or that his career was taking off and he didn't want the added stress. When they argued, he pointed out her issues with anorexia or the way she'd screamed at him in an argument, as if she weren't stable enough to have a baby, even though he knew she'd make a great mother. It was the father, him, that was the problem. He'd read an article that said abusive men distracted their wives from the abuse by blaming them for unrelated things. Once he'd read that, he couldn't unknow it. So he knew what a lowlife he was. But he couldn't stop. He could give up the gambling business and the money that came with it, but he couldn't judge Jordan.

"Arena and his guys are the scum of the earth—crazy, sadistic," Jordan said. "I don't know what they'll do if I refuse them. They could do more than shut me down. One of the girls at the Home Game told me some stories about Arena." Jordan picked up a cigarette, his hand shaking as he lit it. "Arena won't let me get out now, and I can't shut down and leave town until I have the books straight. There was a bet, a very large bet. Xi Wen won. At least Arena didn't win that one, or I'd probably have a lot of explaining to do. The money needs to be delivered. Twelve million this time."

"That's some bet." Brian studied Jordan, worrying about him. Jordan wasn't the type to get hysterical, but whatever the woman at Home Game had told him, he'd bought it. Brian was surprised Jordan took a coked-up conversation with a call girl so seriously.

"We get Xi Wen his payoff, and then I'll close down shop. I'll get out of town. Lay low somewhere for a few years. But I need to get Xi Wen his money first. The loser already transferred the funds. I can't do the money transport without you. I could never trust anyone else. I'll make it worth your while, the six hundred thousand house fee, all yours this time. Not bad for a one-shot deal. Then I'm done. We'll both be done. I've got a few million saved. Some property. That's enough. I'm done."

Brian thought it over. He could do this for Jordan. Then walk away. Walk away from this, walk away from all the insanity he'd created, walk away from Steve's firm, and Nicole, too. He'd have seed money to start his own firm with it. Freedom money.

CHAPTER 21

Sunlight streamed through the kitchen window, and Jessica smiled, appreciating its warmth through the glass. All her security and dreams were gone and, God, she was confused. But still, it felt good to feel pleasure again, even for a moment. Maybe it was a sign that the merciless darkness of mourning was starting to lighten. Maybe it was just a hint that it would eventually pass.

It seemed Emily was getting better too. She'd gone to school—yesterday and today—with barely a shove from Jessica to supplement her alarm clock. Lately, Emily spent all her time after school working on the computer downstairs, and Mr. Manley had told Jessica that Emily used the school's computer lab during lunch hour. He said Jessica and Lauren should encourage her. A hobby, a passion for something, anything, could make all the difference to a troubled adolescent, and she wasn't just playing video games. He said she was interested in coding and cybersecurity.

Jessica went to the sink, rinsed out her coffee cup, and watched the dogs run around on the front lawn. She took a leather jacket from the hall closet and put it on over her running tights and long-sleeved T-shirt.

She opened the front door and shouted out, "Hazel, Nuke!"

She patted them as they strode past her into the house. She reached behind the door and pressed the activate code on the house alarm system. The air was crisp and still, the only sound the gravel under her feet as she walked to her car. She got in the car and drove onto the winding road lined with tall, graceful trees, their branches half bare. It took her aback. The last time she'd noticed, they'd been fully ablaze, raining down around her while she ran this same road with Brian.

After a short drive, she pulled into a parking lot behind the small strip mall that housed her Pilates studio. A long stand-alone building surrounded by woods, it was her first time there since Brian. She found a spot next to a row of cars. A car pulled in behind her.

The sky had begun to cloud over. She found herself wishing for snow, even though she would be on her own to deal with that contingency this winter. She brushed away a shot of fear and grabbed her gym bag. She didn't need to deify Brian. It wasn't as if he shoveled snow. She could call for a plow as easily as he did.

She opened the door and set her feet on the ground when something slammed her from behind. Her shoulder and hip crashed against the door. The air flew from her lungs. An instant vision flashed: carjack, robbery, rape. Letting out a breathless, terrified half scream, she tried to unpin her body from the door, tried to twist and run. Something shoved painfully into her ribs. The man's body pressed against her back. *Oh, God.*

He hissed into her ear, "We're getting in your car. Don't scream."

She nodded. His body pressure let up, but the sticking in her ribs pinned her against the door while he bent to pick up her keys from the asphalt. Jessica looked back at him for the first time, every muscle in her body seized with fear. He unfolded from his crouch with the keys in his free hand and pushed her toward the driver's seat. He'd made no attempt to disguise his face. Not even a stocking cap covered his sparse hair. That meant he'd kill her when he was done.

"Move."

Jessica looked to her ribs as she bent into the car. It *was* a gun, a very big gun.

Praying, crying now, she couldn't help herself, she scrambled into the car, over the stick shift, and into the passenger seat. He picked up her gym bag from the ground, threw it over the seat into the back and sat in the driver's seat.

She unclenched her jaw, and her voice shook. "What do you want?"

He turned the key in the ignition and looked behind him. "You know," he said as he backed the car out of the spot. "You have to know."

"No."

"Bullshit."

She thought of her phone in her gym bag, in the back seat. Miles away.

"I have important business to discuss, and you are so fucking hard to track down," he said with disgust, turning the car onto the road. "I could find my dead relatives on Ancestry.com faster than I found you. I would also add that I tried to make an appointment to see you, to do things in a civilized manner, but you didn't return my calls. I had to hire a private detective to get your address. Jesus-fucking-Christ, Jessica. Are you Queen Elizabeth?"

His words struck like a physical blow. "How ... how do you know my name?"

He pulled into the stream of traffic. "I was a friend of Brian's."

"*No.*"

He glanced at her. "No? What do you mean no? What's that even supposed to mean? No."

Jessica forced her brain to function. If this maniac hadn't been kidnapping her at gunpoint, would she have considered it possible that he and Brian were friends? He wasn't exactly material for the Westchester Country Club—scrawny, reeking of body odor, liquor stinking through his pores. But his leather jacket was expensive, very expensive. She looked closer. His face was bruised. He'd been in a car accident or beaten up. Maybe he didn't always look like this. She wasn't planning to join the Insane Carjacker Debating Society anyway. She forced words out: "You knew Brian?"

"Look, I'm out of time. You've been avoiding me. You've got to give the money back. They're going to kill me, and they'll kill you."

"The money?" Jessica stared at him. If he stopped at a light, could she unlock and open her door, jump before he could shoot her? She remembered a post she read once about how the worst thing a woman could do was get in the car. She'd already done that.

"I was locked up in Arena's basement for five days." He seemed to dissolve before her eyes, unwilling sobs breaking through tight lips. The car rumbled, inching onto the shoulder before he righted it.

Jessica clenched the armrests, afraid they'd crash. He must have been stalking her. He knew Brian had died and created a whole fantasy about it. Was he on K2 or one of those crazy-making drugs she'd read about? She closed her eyes momentarily, trying to calm down.

"They don't believe … I don't have the vaguest fucking idea where the money is." He took in a deep shuddering breath, visibly calming himself, too. His face was sweaty, eyes wide, shell-shocked almost as if he were the hostage. "I'm sorry. I haven't slept in days. Look, you know where the money is, and you have to give it back."

His words sounded like gibberish to her. Terrifying gibberish. She glanced surreptitiously out the window as the car turned onto a new road, her fear deeper with each mile he drove. She kept track of the turns. She knew the general terrain, that was a plus, but he was headed north toward more rural areas. He could kill her more easily the further they traveled this way. Her chest rose, breath short again. "Where are you taking me?"

He looked straight ahead as he drove. "Look, Brian worked for me and left unfinished business."

She restrained her expression of disbelief this time, trying to drag her mind out of a vortex of panic that was only making it harder to decipher what he was saying. "Was he your attorney?"

"In a manner of speaking. He was delivering money for me. It's gone, and the people it belongs to want it back."

Jessica looked sideways at him.

"They know who you are, and they'll hold you and Emily responsible. Just like I'm responsible. They won't let either of us walk away with their money."

Emily. He knew Emily's name, too. Had he read it in the obituary, too? She modulated her voice, "I'm sorry, but I don't know what you're talking about."

She looked at the landscape they passed. If she had any opportunity to escape, it would be fleeting and she'd need to act fast. He made another turn onto a quiet two-lane road bordered by woods. He pulled over and stopped on a wide dirt shoulder next to a copse of trees. He could kill her here. The blood drained from her face.

He put the car in park. "We structured it as a real estate deal."

"*What?*" Jessica's heart battered her rib cage. "Brian ... didn't do real estate."

He sighed and leaned his back against the driver's side door and looked in Jessica's eyes. "I'm going to tell you what's going on in case you really don't know, but let me explain a couple of things first. Brian was in deep, and if you bring the authorities into this, your bank account and everything else you own are gone. Federal asset forfeiture. They'll say it's all fruit of illegal gambling. The cops find out, they take it. From what I know about you, you wouldn't like that. And, believe me, the cops don't give a shit about the innocent widow and kid. Breathe a word and you'll end up broke and on a gangster hit list."

Jessica couldn't believe this was happening. A hit list? Illegal gambling? He knew Brian was doing real estate deals. It wasn't just a madman's fantasy. And now he was holding a gun on her, saying that Brian was a criminal and owed somebody money. Now *she* owed them money? Suddenly, the pieces fell into place with nearly an audible click in her brain. "Are you Jordan Connors?"

He cracked an ironic smile, and Jessica could see a glimpse of who this man might normally be. "So Brian did talk about me. My feelings were almost hurt. Look, there's only one thing to do to avoid the Feds and Jorge Arena. Brian had twelve million dollars when he died and, believe me, it did not go up in smoke. Brian was too careful for that. It's somewhere, and you need to find it before Jorge Arena comes for you and Emily."

"Twelve million dollars? Listen, no offense ... *Jordan*," she forced herself to sound friendly. "I still don't understand. That can't be true."

He exhaled in frustration and talked to her like she was an idiot: "Twelve million dollars needs to get to its rightful owner. ASAP."

Jessica's eyes met Jordan's, his gun only inches from her head. Jessica swallowed hard and eked words out. "You're saying that, when Brian died, he had twelve million dollars and it had something to do with a real estate deal?"

"You could say that, although the deals were just cover in case the Feds noticed the money moving."

She tried to process that. "And where am I supposed to find this money?"

"You knew him best. Think like Brian, figure it out."

"I knew him best?" She started to get angry—at this guy and at a Brian she obviously hadn't known. Rage shot out of her before she could stop it. "You've got to be kidding! I knew him best? I don't know what the fuck you're talking about. What do you think I'm supposed to do?"

Jordan's eyes shifted. His face—every muscle and tendon—went hard. "I have no intention of dying for you, Jessica … as much as I liked Brian. You and I are in this together. Find it or Arena will kill you, me, and everyone you ever loved."

She took in a harsh lungful of air, tears close to the surface again. Why did this whole shit-show make sense to her? Why did it feel like this man had given her the missing piece in a thousand-piece jigsaw puzzle that she hadn't even known was incomplete? Brian had been hiding things for a long time, she'd known it in her gut. It hadn't been irrational jealousy. She talked herself down: *Don't come unstrung, Jessica. You can put it all together once you get away from him, but you need to get away first.* Tears streamed down her face.

"Look, don't cry. I know this is out of your league, but I have it on good authority that you have a helper. Baby mama."

"What?"

"Lauren Davis. She's my next stop anyway. I'm sure she'll understand. It's the one interesting thing I learned while they had me cuffed in Arena's basement. He told me all about it when his guys got tired of kicking my ass. It was a surprising story, really, the way Brian always made her out to be the frigid, nagging first wife. You tell her Bobby Karate left a contract on the street for her, fifty thousand. Arena and his crew know where she is now. They'll buy the contract back for her if she helps. Otherwise, well, you can imagine. They'll cash in. She won't be able to hide in plain sight anymore."

"What? Lauren? She's a lawyer. What the fuck is a Bobby Karate?"

"Ask her. She'll know, and she knows the streets. It's like riding a bicycle. She'll help you. You've got forty-eight hours. After that, the Arenas and God knows who else will start making personal visits. Folks will do a lot for the amount of money that's missing."

Jessica took a deep breath, feeling as if she were clawing at the edge of a rabbit hole. Who were all these people she thought she knew? Brian?

Lauren? And she had one question that she needed answered. "Did Arena kill my husband?"

He laughed. "Why would he? You're not listening. They're out all that money and still need to pay it to the rightful owner. Brian wasn't stupid enough to cross them, and I can say one thing for your husband: he could be trusted."

Jessica nearly laughed. He could be trusted? By whom? By this insane yuppie gangster? She had no time to think about that now. She had more questions. "Did you know his partner, Steve? Did *he* kill Brian?"

"I don't know him. I don't know whether he killed Brian. But you gotta wonder—how could something that causes so much shit be an accident? They hadn't been getting along lately," Jordan said, thoughtfully. "Brian mentioned that. Damned if I know what happened though."

He shifted in his seat and reached to open his door, taking the keys from the ignition. "Don't go anywhere, Jessica. I need to take a leak. They punched me so many times in the kidneys, it's got me all fucked up. I have a few more things to tell you about how Brian did the deals. It might help. Then I'll drive you back to pick up my car. We're in this together now."

Jessica stared in disbelief as he walked away to a tree in the midst of a carjacking. She considered diving for her phone in the back seat or running, but her best bet would be to take no chances now that he seemed close to letting her go.

She watched his wiry back, mesmerized. Normally, she would have averted her eyes, but nothing was normal here on the shoulder of the narrow road, her kidnapper creating a steaming puddle amidst gnarled roots of an oak. After jumping up and down a bit, he walked toward the car. He pulled his pistol from the back of his waistband and opened the driver's door. Jessica felt a gust of cold wind. A sharp explosion rocked the air. Jordan let loose a sudden *humph* and flew sideways, falling.

She gasped back a cry. Her heart sprinting, she threw herself awkwardly over the table between the seats, pulling herself over the driver's seat toward the open door. Lying flat, the edges of the table digging into her belly, she peered out. Jordan was on the ground next to the car, face-down, blood blossoming around him in the dirt. She couldn't see the exit wound but it had to be worse than the small hole in the back of his coat. So much blood! Panting, with the side of her cheek against the seat leather, she took Jordan's wrist and felt for a pulse. None.

The sound of a car engine approached. They were coming for her. She saw the gleam of the car keys half under Jordan's waist. The puddle of blood was turning the dirt around him to a ruddy mud. She didn't see his gun, probably under him. The sound of the approaching car filled the air now. She flung her hand out toward the ground and grabbed for the keys. Getting a handful of wet dirt with the keys, she retreated backward like a retracting turtle.

The car's engine snarled, on top of her. It was too late to drive away. She hid her head under her hands, scrunched low, trembling, gritting her teeth against a scream. Then she heard the car speed up and keep going. She peered up, cautiously, and saw the glint of its bumper as it drove away.

She was alone with Jordan ... no, she didn't know that. The car could have been innocent, just passing. The gunman could still be waiting for her to lift her head up, could be in a tree or crouched low behind a rock. Dammit, she didn't know. But she had to get out of there. If the killer were still there, she'd be dead if she waited.

Without raising her head, she put the keys in the ignition and turned on the car. She listened, heard nothing but her own engine. Even the wind was still again. Heart jackhammering, staying low, she sat in the driver's seat, feeling every hair on her scalp, picturing the top of her skull vulnerable to a bullet. She could barely see over the dashboard. There was enough space ahead for her to go forward, clear the body, and veer onto the road without having to back up. She took a breath, her throat burning with the effort.

She pressed the accelerator, ready to dive across the seat if gunfire responded to the car's movement. She held her breath as the car began to roll forward. No shots. The door and back wheels were past Jordan's body now. Praying, she floored the accelerator in a billowing cloud of dust. The front wheels hit pavement with a swerve and screech. She righted herself in her seat, reached out to grab the door handle, and slammed the door shut.

She drove away as fast as she could, shouting to the car: "Go, go, go!"

When she reached a straightaway, she glanced in the rearview mirror. No one appeared behind her.

At an intersection with a wider roadway, she turned off the lane. After she'd blended into traffic and ridden without incident for miles, her sobs came out, sobs that made the road blur. But she couldn't allow herself that luxury—not yet. She wiped her tears away with the back of her hand and commanded herself to calm down.

She found Route 9D, which would eventually bring her back across the Westchester County line. She eased onto it, grateful for its familiarity, and began to process the information she'd received before Jordan's death.

A little voice spoke to her, saying: Go to the police, Jessica. Let someone protect you.

She considered the voice, but deep inside, Jessica knew she had already decided. At her deepest, instinctive, survival level, she knew that none of the old rules applied to her life anymore. Things like this didn't happen to people like her—their husbands didn't die, their husbands didn't have secret criminal lives, their husband's friends didn't kidnap people and get murdered right in front of them. But it had all happened, and there was no going back.

She could either fight for herself with every ounce of her strength, or she could die playing the damsel in distress the way she'd always done. If she chose the old wilting-girl card and called the cops, she would end up dead or as good as dead. She wiped away a tear. If she was going to take that path, she might as well have starved herself to death a long time ago.

So she drove, fighting off waves of panic that knocked her breath away each time she'd calmed herself down. The nauseating, thick smell of blood filled the car. She tried to keep her shoulder from touching the blood-soaked door as she drove and rolled down all but the driver's side window. She didn't want the blood that had gotten on the window getting into the door's inner workings.

She forced herself to breathe and think about what she had to do. The first thing was to bring the car home and hose down the door and the window. There was nothing to connect her to the murder and no reason anyone would check her car for DNA. So the car only needed to look clean. Getting rid of evidence had to be a crime, but she didn't care right now. She had to clean up the car and make her next move before Emily came home from school.

CHAPTER 22

At one o'clock, Jessica appeared in Lauren's office doorway. Lauren turned from the computer screen and jumped to her feet. "Emily. Where's Emily?"

"Oh, no," Jessica rushed toward Lauren, taking her arm. "Nothing's wrong with Emily."

Lauren gasped in lost air, "What are you doing here? What happened to you?"

Jessica moved closer to Lauren. Jessica's skin was corpse-white and her eyes puffy and faded without makeup. Her damp hair lay flat against her scalp. Lauren looked up into the frightened eyes of a woman she almost didn't recognize, so frightened yet so focused.

Jessica spoke softly, each word electric, "I'm in trouble, Lauren. Emily and you are, too. It's those real estate deals." Jessica turned back to the door, closed it, and told Lauren what Jordan had said.

Lauren's body vibrated with the shock of it. "You believe him?"

"What else should I believe? I obviously didn't know my husband."

Lauren leaned back in her seat, trying to calm herself. "I didn't know him either. He ran with a fast crowd in college, but him owing money to criminals, I can't even fathom it."

"Even if Jordan Connors getting killed doesn't prove he was telling the whole truth, there is one undeniable fact: Brian was into something with those real estate deals."

"And men were searching for something at the building," Lauren thought aloud. "If we believe the story that the money had to do with illegal gambling payments, Jordan Connors could have used straw companies as buyers and sellers to disguise somebody else's money. That would be a way to collect and make payouts. But so much money?" Lauren thought it through. Too many pieces were missing.

"He said a lot of people would kill for that kind of money."

"Well, it will be up to the cops to figure it all out now."

"What are you talking about?"

"What do you mean, what am I talking about? What happened with the cops?" The thought dawned on Lauren: "Why aren't you still at the police station?"

Jessica leaned forward. "I didn't call the cops."

"You're kidding ..."

"Think about it. It's true what Connors said about asset forfeiture, right?"

Lauren exhaled harshly, picturing the domino effect of the police finding out about Brian's activities. They could go after everything he owned. "Whoa, wait. I'm *not* sacrificing my daughter's safety for a bank account. That's out."

"Emily has a right to Brian's money. And there's your co-op, too, that Brian paid for, remember? We could all land in a homeless shelter." Jessica put her hand up to stop Lauren from talking this time. "But worse than that, we don't have enough to offer the cops. If I went to them and fingered Arena, they would make me set these Arena people up—wire me, get me in deeper, practically paint a target on my back—before they'd put me in the Witness Protection Program. If we're not killed helping the cops, Emily would have to be hidden away too. If we go to the police, the best-case scenario is that we all end up working in a clothing store in a Midwestern strip mall or something. We'll live a miserable, impoverished existence, always afraid of the Arenas finding us. And that's the best-case scenario.

"Why should we give up everything, our identities, our families, our homes? I'm innocent, we all are, and if those gangsters hadn't known that, they probably would have killed me when they had the chance. They were tired of Jordan. They only used him to find me and get a message across."

"It certainly worked."

Jessica closed her eyes angrily before returning to look at Lauren. "That means I have time. We can complete what Brian started. No one will hurt us if I stay calm and cooperate. Jordan said they have one cardinal rule—if you lose their money, you pay them back. Well, I didn't lose their money. I'm not the one who screwed up or violated their trust. So I have time at least. If I can't find their money, then we can consider calling the police. I'm doing it for you as much as anything, Lauren."

"I don't want you to do anything for me!" Lauren said. "You don't have any way to get them their money, and we have no choice but to trust the cops."

"There's another thing, Lauren. Jordan Connors talked about you."

"Me?"

"He mentioned a name that sounded like something out of a 1950s Hunger Games. Someone named Bobby Karate."

"What?!" Lauren popped up from her chair.

Jessica's eyes widened, taking in Lauren's reaction. "He said you'd know."

Lauren half-whispered, her throat closed with panic. "What?"

"He said Bobby Karate put a contract out on you. He said this guy, Arena, will buy it back if you cooperate, but otherwise they'll kill you and collect on the contract."

Hyperventilating, Lauren paced in the small space.

"I don't understand, Lauren. You need to tell me."

It took Lauren a minute before she could speak. "I had a boyfriend. He was a karate champion as a kid, that's how he got the nickname. He took me off the street, moved me in with him. I was a kid, Emily's age. He was a mobster, a made man. Do you know what that is?"

"Yes."

"I ran when I realized what he was into. I'd thought he was just dealing drugs." Lauren put up her hand when she saw Jessica's reaction to the idea that drug dealing was *just* anything. Lauren spoke quietly, adrenaline shushing her words. "He was a hit man. A few years ago, a true-crime book came out about him."

"You're kidding."

"He was way worse than I'd ever known. When I saw a news report about the book, I stopped in Barnes and Noble to look. I couldn't even read it all—it was so horrifying. It said he wasn't just a Mafia hit man. He was a psychopathic killer. He robbed women drug dealers and killed them. He did terrible things to them. I almost dropped the book when I read that. I shoved it back into the shelf. I mean, I'm a mom, a lawyer, I'm afraid of terrorism on the subway, just like the next person. That kind of life is not normal for me anymore and, even then, I never had any idea. Not that I wasn't scared of him when we lived together but I never knew the danger I was in. After I read the book, I had flashbacks about it for a year.

"I thought I was safe when they gave him a life sentence." Lauren paced a few steps and turned back to Jessica. "I was eighteen by then. I was relieved I'd never see him again. I can barely believe he was angry enough to put a contract out on me. And why would it still be out there after twenty years?"

Jessica sat in Constance's desk chair and stared at Lauren. "Brian told me you did drugs when you were a kid, that you were some kind of wild child from a wild family but …"

Lauren felt as if she were a teenager again, that the whole world was on the verge of falling down on her. "I didn't talk about a lot of it, even with Brian. I didn't want to bring all of that with me."

"Yeah, but—"

"Did you tell Brian everything about every guy you dated?"

Jessica gave Lauren a bemused look. "No … but I never went out with a killer."

Lauren waved it away, halfway conceding the point.

"Anyway, I'm in too deep—there's no going back," Jessica said. "If I call the cops and don't let them wire me up and put me in the line of fire, I'll go to jail for destroying evidence of murder, and Arena will still want to kill me. Who's going to protect me from mobsters in jail? And if the cops find out there's a Mob contract out on you, they'll make you work to get their protection too, if they even thought you were worth protecting. I need to find the money. I almost can't believe you'd want to trust the cops with your … background."

Lauren leaned her elbows against her desk and put her face in her palms. For Jessica's sake, she didn't say what she was thinking now—that Brian stashing the money would not have precluded a thief from torturing him for information about its location before Brian died. The money could be long gone. "What is it you propose?"

"I want to pick up Emily from school, I already have some of her clothes packed. You can keep her for a few days. She'll never object to missing school. You don't have an alarm system on your apartment, do you?"

"Never needed one."

"If they didn't know where I lived, my place would probably be safer. I have a sensor alarm for the lawn and the house is fully wired. I'm going to need it. After I bring Emily to your apartment, I'll go back home to wait in case they try to contact me. While I'm there, maybe I can find information, emails, receipts that would provide clues to where the money might be. And I can go back to his office if that doesn't work. Maybe he has the information about it in one of his files. Now that I know what I'm looking for, it could be hidden in plain sight. Bottom line, I'm going to find out where the money is and give it back to those people."

"Wait, let's take this one thing at a time. First, what would you tell Emily if she came back home to me?"

"I'll tell her the plumbing is screwed up and that we need to get out while they fix it. I'll tell her I'm going to stay at a friend's for a couple of days, and she'll go to your house. She'll be so busy celebrating the time off from school, she won't ask many questions."

"Emily will never buy that story." Lauren massaged her temples, a headache arriving. "But we'll get back to that. Let's move on to your next piece of insanity."

Jessica glared at her with an expression of furious exasperation that momentarily took Lauren aback.

"This thing about breaking into Brian's office," Lauren continued.

Jessica's chest rose, she took a deep breath, visibly calming herself down. "It's not breaking in. I have a passkey. I sign in and go inside like before. What's the big deal?"

"It is a big deal. Steve could have killed Brian. Who was in a better position to know what Brian was doing, and who's behaving really strangely? It's dangerous, it's illegal, and I doubt that Steve thinks of you as just the wife of a partner and friend, given the way he's been acting. What we need to do is go pick up my kid from school and get her out of there. That's the best idea you've had." Lauren grabbed Jessica's arm, feeling as if she needed to physically convey the point to Jessica: "You have no idea what you're dealing with here."

Jessica pulled her arm away. "Maybe I'm not as experienced with danger and dealing with killers, Lauren, but have you ever witnessed someone getting his head blown off? I've had my hazing, and I'm going to take care of this. I'm going to make this thing go away."

The phone rang. They both flinched at the sudden noise. Lauren lifted the receiver with trepidation. "Hello?"

She heard the voice of Gary, the bridge officer who managed Judge Quiñones' courtroom. "Lauren, we've got the Winston mom's attorney here with a 1028 motion for the return of her kids."

"What? Her kids aren't in foster care."

"Child Protective Services grabbed them again yesterday. A daycare teacher spotted a burn on the four-year-old. The kids have been talking up a storm. I guess they've had all they can take."

"No one called me."

"You've got to draft a petition for placement and get down here before court closes."

Jessica signaled, opening and closing her hand in the talk sign. Lauren held up her palm and looked away, trying to listen to Gary and figure out her next move at the same time.

"The judge is going crazy, wants you in here pronto," he said.

"Gary, I've got a family emergency. Either I'll be there, or someone will cover for me." Lauren hung up and swiveled toward Jessica, her brain spinning with the madness of having to worry about her job and the safety of children she didn't know when her own kid was in danger.

"Wait right here." She squeezed past Jessica. "I have to get someone to cover this case."

Jessica grabbed Lauren's arm. "Please, Lauren, you can count on me. I'll get Emily and bring her to your apartment."

"*No.*" Lauren's face felt feverish. She held up her palm. "She's my kid; you don't understand. Someone will cover for me."

Lauren walked into the hallway, looking in each attorney office. She passed a half-dozen offices, all empty. She kept walking, faster, tears imminent. The people who worked with her were always willing to look out for each other. If Lauren told any of them that Emily was in trouble, they would gladly help if they could. But she checked one office after the next—all empty, not even a supervisor. Everyone had gone back to court for the afternoon session.

Lauren turned left and checked the length of the next arm of hallway and doubled back on the far side of the partitioned-off central area where the support staff worked. She looked at her watch. She could go to court and find someone to take the case. She could quickly type out a form petition, shove it into the hands of the first attorney from her office she saw, and beg. But she didn't have time. If Jessica waited for her, Emily might get on the school bus before they got there. Lauren picked up her pace, heading back to her office.

When she neared it, she glimpsed Constance coming out and rushing away down the hall in the other direction.

"Connie," she called.

Constance turned, her face tense. "Can't stop. I'm late for a two-thirty trial in the Bronx. The judge is going to kill me."

Lauren waved at her as Constance fled and wiped the wetness from her eyes. She opened the office door and closed it behind her. Jessica turned from the window.

"Okay. Emily has keys to the apartment. Both of you wait for me there. I haven't decided anything."

"Don't worry, Lauren."

"Jessica, don't fuck this up, *please.*"

Jessica hissed, "What makes you think I'd fuck it up any more than you? You weren't saying that when you needed someone to take her."

Before Lauren registered the words, Jessica had pushed past and was gone. Alone, Lauren immediately regretted what she'd said. She should be grateful that Jessica gave a shit about Emily at all right now. For years, she'd dismissed Jessica as Brian's trophy-plaything, but there was a lot more to the woman than Lauren had realized.

Still, what the hell had Jessica gotten her into? No, Lauren mentally rephrased that in her mind: it was Brian who'd gotten Lauren into this. Fucking Brian. And besides anything else, she was stupid to think she could ever simply walk away from her teenage life. It didn't matter that she'd only been a kid. No one got to walk away from that kind of life as if it never existed.

CHAPTER 23

Emily cut Chemistry and Spanish, and walked home. It took her a half hour but it was worth it. She walked up the gravel path to the house, checking for signs of Jessica. Thankfully, the dogs weren't out and Jessica's car wasn't there, which saved Emily from having to play sick. She dug in her knapsack for her keys. For a change, her fingers found them quickly without a huge search, and she entered the house to the wet noses and snuffles of Hazel and Nuke.

"Hey girls," she said. A blinking light on the wall caught her eye when the door closed behind her. She crooned at the dogs, "Jessica's being paranoid again, isn't she?"

She turned to the burglar alarm and punched in the code number. She put her coat on the mahogany coatrack. "Let's go downstairs. We're gonna have such a good time."

The dogs came from behind and beat her down the stairs.

In her father's home office, she turned on the computer, dropped her knapsack on the floor, and cracked the sliding glass door. As the computer booted up, she pulled her pack of cigarettes from her knapsack and the ashtray from under the sofa. Tropical wallpaper appeared on the computer screen. Emily lit up and took the mysterious thumb drive from her backpack. Nothing made any sense anymore, but she was sure the thumb drive would explain things, explain the real estate stuff, explain how Steve—who'd always acted like her uncle—could have betrayed her. And Nicole. Emily had looked up to her. She was pretty, a Wall Street lawyer who did big deals. She could sail and fly a plane, too. Emily still couldn't adjust to the fact that Steve and Nicole never cared about her.

Emily took out Tabu's flip phone and called the only number in the phone's contacts.

Tabu answered, "Yo."

"It's Emily."

"Loli?"

"Don't call me that."

"Are you on his PC? I want you to search his programs. We can clone the app account on his PC and copy into the clone if it's installed there."

Emily searched. "It's not on his desktop ... not in his programs."

"Give me your IP address."

She knew how to do that, clicked the corner thingy that let her see all the apps. She typed "cmd" and read him the IP address that came up.

"I'm going to take over your computer. Just click 'okay.' Don't worry. I don't want your data and, besides, my little cousin likes you."

Emily blushed, surprisingly happy. "He does?"

"Loli, come on."

"Don't call me that." But she was smiling.

She clicked okay when a dialogue box asked whether she would allow remote access.

She sat back and watched while the PC's cursor started moving at light speed, searching for the encryption program. No more than two minutes passed.

"The app's not here. You were right," Tabu said, his voice echoing on his speaker. "The backup data isn't stored here."

Emily whispered, desolate, worse because of the false hope. "What can I do?"

"Does he have a laptop, another PC?"

"He has his job computer. His laptop is gone."

"His work desktop is your only chance then."

Hazel and Nuke began barking and ran for the gap in the sliding door. "Shit. I've gotta go. Can you help me if I call from my father's office?"

"Yeah, okay. But it will be a hundred more because we're gonna need to break his password there. You can give it to Hector when you see him. I trust you."

Emily heard tires on gravel outside and spoke fast, "I'll call you if I can get there."

She looked at the time on Tabu's burner phone before flipping it closed and throwing it in her backpack. Her last class would be letting out now, but neither the bus nor her feet would have gotten her home yet.

At the top of the stairs, she turned down the hall. She would be lying in bed with a stomachache by the time Jessica walked in. She picked up her pace. The ring of the doorbell startled her, turning her around midway to the bedroom. It wasn't Jessica. Jessica never forgot her keys.

***

Jessica sat at the curb in front of Emily's school. It was an old-fashioned building, red brick and covered with browning ivy. Kids streamed down the cement path that cut the school's manicured lawn in half. Jessica scanned the crowd, paying special attention to the kids who repeatedly halted traffic to light their cigarettes at the top of the stairs that led from the school's entrance. Emily would be one of them and should have been out already. She was usually the first one flying from school as if she took a head start before the dismissal bell. Jessica hadn't called, knowing Emily couldn't get calls during the school day, but she pulled out her phone now—the call went straight to voice mail.

She noticed a boy walking alone at the edge of the path. She had seen Emily with him before. She hadn't liked the look of him then and still didn't. He was clean-cut, but she could tell he couldn't be trusted. She was going to have a talk with Emily about him. Had he just passed something to one of the students, and received money back? Goddammit, Emily had been hanging out with drug dealers. Was it genetic or something? She tabled that thought for later, rolled down the window, and called out as the teenager passed, "Excuse me. Have you seen Emily?"

He pointed at himself. "Me?"

"You're friends with Emily, aren't you?"

He began to seem nervous. "I know her."

"Have you seen her?"

He shrugged, putting his hands in the pocket of his hoodie, under-dressed for the weather. "I don't have afternoon classes with her."

"Where could she be, do you know?"

"No, I don't know."

He had a hint of attitude in his voice now, which irritated her. She didn't have time for this bullshit. She got out of the car and stepped close to him, her eyes the same height as his. She spoke as softly as she could manage, "Look, you know something, and I don't have time for games. I need to find Emily, and she is obviously not out here. So, give."

"She wasn't in Spanish. I don't know."

"Damn." She started back to the car.

"Mrs. Silverman?" She turned back to the kid. "I think she went home to work on the computer. Please don't tell her it was me who said she cut Spanish."

"Don't worry about it." She opened the car door, trying to breathe.

He didn't need to worry about her telling Emily because she was going to kill Emily herself. She dialed Emily's number, which went to voice mail again. She texted: *Trying 2 call U. Call me back.*

Jessica forced herself to pull slowly from the curb and made her way through the teenagers who ambled across the street. She tapped out a hard, terrified rhythm with her palm against the top of the steering wheel. "I'm going to kill you, Emily."

When she reached the corner, she accelerated and turned with a screech. She sped toward home, chastising herself. She should have called the police. If anything happened to Emily, she would never forgive herself. Still, she wasn't calling the police now either, was she? No, she was in too deep. She would go to jail, and they would all lose everything.

Jessica leaned harder on the gas and barreled down tree-lined roads.

She formulated her plan: approach the house carefully. If things didn't look normal, she would make the hardest call of her life. For help. She imagined herself under arrest by the police. She braced herself for it as she turned and drove parallel to the golf course, almost home. A quarter mile and one more turn. Finally, up ahead, she saw the turnoff to the gravel drive. Her heart pounded. *Let Emily be okay.* A Mercedes pulled out of the driveway and onto the road, heading away from her.

"*Oh, God.*" Jessica sped up and turned into the driveway, gravel shooting out behind her.

The dogs ran to her when she opened the car door. Emily had to be home to let them out. Everything seemed normal, the dogs were calm, but they weren't watchdogs. She didn't even know if they would defend against attackers. Jessica ran for the front door.

The doorknob turned in her fist—unlocked. "Emily?"

The house was quiet.

"EMILY?"

Jessica looked in the empty kitchen on her right. Trembling, she turned left, held on momentarily to the smooth stairway banister that led up to her bedroom. She moved past the stairs toward Emily's bedroom at the end of the hall on the first floor. The hallway was dark even in midafternoon. Jessica flipped on the light switch. She tread softly, as if her footfalls would bring to life her worst nightmares. She wished she hadn't called out already, betraying her presence. She closed her eyes momentarily as she gripped the doorknob to Emily's room then screamed as it was suddenly ripped from her hand.

Jessica jumped back in time to see Emily standing at the open door, her adolescent you're-such-an-idiot look on her face. "Are you *okay*, Jessica?"

The blood rushed to Jessica's face. She grabbed Emily's arm. "What do you mean, am I okay? Why weren't you at school? Who just left? Did you have someone here?"

"Why don't you chill, Jessica? I can't believe you. I have a stomach-ache."

"Who was it?" Jessica tried to let her anger subside. Emily didn't say anything, and Jessica walked back to the front door to reset the house alarm.

Emily followed. "Are you all right, Jessica?"

Jessica turned around, trying to remember the reason she was supposed to give Emily for going to Manhattan. The kid was looking at her, waiting for an explanation, and there was no way she would believe a lie.

"I'm sorry, Emily."

"Yeah, right. I'm sick, and I have to get screamed at."

Jessica didn't believe Emily was sick, but that was the least of their problems. Jessica reached out gently this time and held Emily's arm. "We've got to go into the city. I came to school to get you."

Emily's eyes widened, scared. "My mother? Where's my mother?"

"Not your mother, your mother's fine. But we need to go to her house. There's been a problem." Jessica spit it out: "Your dad owed some money, and you're going there until it's straightened out."

"My dad owed money? Get out. He was rich."

"No, Emily, he was never rich. Not yet."

"Why do we have to leave because he owed someone money? Does this have something to do with his trip to Tortola?" Emily pumped her fists at her sides in frustration as if she'd let it slip.

"What?"

"Don't get mad, but I found out that Daddy went to St. Thomas and Tortola the day before … before the fire. He rented a boat with his PayPal credit card."

"PayPal? A boat?" Jessica shook her head, trying to think that through. She didn't know Brian had a PayPal credit card. He rented a boat? The whole thing was too much. "Look, we have to go now. I'll explain later. I already packed some clothes for you. They're in the car."

Emily went to her room and returned with her school knapsack. Jessica took a hard look out the kitchen window, scanning the lawn and the road beyond the trees for a flash of car chrome or any sign that someone was out there. She didn't see anyone. She and Emily walked to the car.

From the passenger seat, Emily handed her a sticky note. "That wasn't a friend of mine who was here."

Jessica looked down at the phone number written on the paper. "Who was it?"

"The guy said that a Mr. Arena or Areno, something like that, wants you to call him. Why didn't the guy just call instead of driving here?"

Jessica modulated her voice to sound nonchalant, or tried to. "Maybe he doesn't have the number." But the visit was a message that the killers were near and could reach Emily or her at any time. Jessica took the key from the ignition. "Don't move, Emily."

Jessica ran back to the house, opened the front door and called, sharply, "Hazel, Nuke."

The dogs galloped out and waited at the car's back door before Jessica reached it. Now that she had Arena's phone number, she'd be damned if she'd come back home again before this was over.

Emily frowned at her when Jessica returned to the driver's seat but said nothing. Jessica drove, watching the rearview mirror as much as the road ahead. No one followed. When they'd passed through the center of town, Jessica pulled to the curb in front of the vet's office and spoke to Emily. "Come on."

"I'll wait here."

"No." Jessica's voice came out stronger than she'd meant it to.

"Okay, whatever." Emily shrugged, humoring a madwoman, and got out of the car.

They both went inside the vet's office for the five minutes it took to board the dogs. Then they were on their way again. Jessica checked the rearview mirror compulsively, her heart lurching each time a car traveled behind them, until they blended into fast-moving highway traffic. As they traveled south, Jessica filled Emily in on the situation, editing out Jordan's murder and the contract on Lauren. Jessica hoped her drama-queen stepdaughter would be impressed enough by a threat of violence to allow Lauren and Jessica to protect her without a struggle.

Emily didn't say much after that. She stared out the window until they reached Washington Heights. A group of teenagers hung out in front of Lauren's building. They said a polite hello to Jessica, and Emily hugged a couple of them. But Emily didn't protest going upstairs. She unlocked the building's door and led Jessica inside.

CHAPTER 24

Lauren stood at the phone booth outside Part Nine of the family court.

"We're ordering Chinese," Emily said. "When are you coming home?"

"I'll be there as soon as I can. The judge went on a break."

Lauren put her phone away in her shoulder bag. The conversation was so mundane she had a hard time putting it together with what was going on. Really, she had a hard time putting any two thoughts together since she'd heard Bobby's name. She thought it couldn't get any worse when Jessica told her the story of being kidnapped and witnessing a murder. But it had. Lauren felt as if she'd been thrown into a sea of stinging men-o-war, memories flooding back, bringing old and new terror.

She'd met Bobby when she was still sleeping nights on a mattress in the disco at St. Mark's Place. He was picking up payment for a drug shipment at a pizza shop a block from there, not that she knew it for sure at the time. The place was packed, noisy with people coming and going—musicians, art students from Cooper Union, newly recovering addicts from St. Mark's, and hookers who worked Third Avenue.

"You living out here?" he asked when he saw her eyeing him over a slice of pizza, eating at a mini Formica counter that lined the small shop's wall.

She'd looked him up and down. "Why would you ask that?"

"You're comfortable here ... like you're in your den watching a game."

Lauren smirked. "What's a den?"

He edged closer to her, "Let me buy you a cup of coffee, and I'll try to explain it to you."

She'd ended up hanging around with him, riding in his Lincoln as he made stops at pizza shops. Bobby was older than the boys she'd been with until then, twenty-eight to her sixteen. With his black hair combed back and a cleft chin, he could have played John Travolta's part in *Saturday Night Fever*, only he was handsomer, with a daring power in his eyes and none of Travolta's dorkiness.

He asked questions about her, then talked in reams. "You know, Lauren, you could do a lot better than living out in the street with little boys who don't know how to take care of a woman. I got a nice crib. I could buy you beautiful clothes and jewelry. I know you think you're a girl, but you're a woman. You just need to learn how to be a lady."

Lauren began her lady-training in his apartment on the twentieth floor of a high-rise doorman building on the Upper East Side. He took her out to dinner and clubs and showed her off at family dinners. Until one of those family nights when she was sitting on a couch, smoking cigarettes and sniffing coke with a girlfriend of one of his buddies. The woman blabbed about Bobby's main source of income. "You don't know he's a hit man?" she'd asked, incredulously.

Lauren didn't believe it at first. But Bobby only sucked his teeth and stormed around the house calling the woman a fucking bitch when Lauren told him what she'd said. He never called the woman a liar.

After that, the apartment became a princess' fortified tower. Lauren reasoned and still thought Bobby must have loved her because for some strange reason he didn't kill her even after she started dipping into the pure dope he sold as a sideline. Heroin was the only escape for her. But once she started, she couldn't stop. It seemed every week Bobby slapped her around for being high when he came home.

"Killing people?" she'd screamed at him. "I do dope. You kill fucking people! What the fuck?"

He grabbed her and held his hand over her mouth. "Shh, shh, shh. I don't like when you curse at me."

His hand slipped over her nose. She couldn't breathe. She grappled with his hand, panicking, until he released her. She never knew whether his hand on her nose had been accidental, but after that, she knew she had to get away from him and hide, because there would be no peaceful breakup. Lauren fled to the only place she could think of. She checked herself into a residential drug-treatment program. They shipped her off to upstate New York for eighteen months, no forwarding address, at least somewhat protected by drug-treatment confidentiality. By the time she graduated the program and entered college, she'd learned that Bobby was in prison.

"Lauren," Gary, the bridge officer, called from the entrance to the courtroom.

Lauren looked at her watch. It was after six. She followed Gary into the courtroom. All she needed to do was concentrate on the Winston kids for a few more minutes. She had to make sure they didn't end up back home with their sadistic parents while the case waited for trial. That was turning out to be a lot easier than figuring out what to do about the tsunami that had struck her own life. A sense of desperation bore heavier on her by the moment. She'd been unwittingly living a lie for twenty years without the faintest hint that someone could have killed her at any moment. Her chronic sense of danger had returned as if it had never left. She didn't have a clue what to do. One thing Lauren could see coming, though, was a conflict between Jessica's needs, and Lauren and Emily's safety.

Jessica had injected herself deeper into the crisis by destroying evidence of murder. The cops could look at her as being involved with Brian's activities because of it. They might bust her for the evidence tampering if they couldn't get her on anything else. It wasn't something Lauren wanted, sacrificing Emily's financial security and maybe even their home to asset forfeiture. Lauren couldn't imagine giving up the life she'd worked so hard to create just to join the Witness Protection Program, but she would do it and call the cops herself if it were the only way to protect her kid.

Still, Jessica had been right about one thing: to get police protection, especially now that Jessica had committed crimes, they needed something to offer the cops. Lauren had nothing, even less than Jessica. She'd lived her whole adult life in a manner that ensured she'd have nothing, know nothing, see nothing to put her in danger again. The government didn't spend millions of dollars to put people in Witness Protection just because they *needed* protection. The government had to want you. You had to offer something. And the only thing Lauren had to offer was Jessica. Lauren didn't want to do that and, frankly, she doubted offering Jessica would be enough anyway.

"All rise," Gary called out. The judge entered the room.

A half hour later, the Winston kids safely in foster care, Lauren made her way downstairs to the courthouse lobby. The silence had a buzz to it, surreal after the drone of hundreds of conversations constantly going on in every corner of the building. Two court officers stood on post at the metal detectors, although no one entered the building at this hour. Next to them, a huge orange-and-white tomcat sat on the aluminum table where the officers normally inspected parcels. Lauren scratched the cat's neck before walking on, surprised by the secret life of the place after everyone went home.

Outside, Lauren turned right and crossed narrow, cobblestoned Leonard Street. No cars passed on the dark street. She walked alone on the high, stone-slab sidewalk. The mostly dark buildings towered close overhead. Her apprehension mounted. A picture flashed in her head: a man with a high-powered rifle aimed at her. Another with a handgun, darting out from a dark doorway. She'd been stupid not to spend the forty bucks on Uber instead of walking to the subway. She picked up her pace, even her loafers audible in the dead silence.

Up ahead, someone came around a corner, toward her. She took in sharp air. Then she saw a second figure next to him. A dog. They walked under a street lamp. She smiled. Carl smiled too, as he saw her.

"You have a way of just sort of being there, don't you?" she said, rubbing Mookie behind the ear.

"After the tourists and workers leave the neighborhood, Mook and I like to walk around what we Tribecans used to call the Outback." Carl looked up. "These office buildings are like canyons when they're empty. They remind me of that old Harry Belafonte movie. The one where he comes to New York after a nuclear holocaust and walks up and down the empty streets shouting hello and listening to the echo back. Tribeca isn't as much like that anymore, but the new condos don't seem to have many people actually living in them. I always thought there was something appealing about that movie, and the one with Will Smith alone in New York with the zombies."

"Very appealing." Despite herself, Lauren slipped her hand through the crook of his elbow. "Could you walk me to the subway? This place just doesn't have much charm for me tonight."

"No problem."

She felt a rush of comforting warmth with his hand covering hers, but she didn't want him to notice it trembling. She pulled her hand away, trying to make it seem natural. Her inner voice warned: keep things on the surface, Lauren. No matter how much she wanted to tell Carl everything and beg for help, and even if she'd jumped to unwarranted conclusions about him, she didn't know him well enough to trust him with life-and-death information.

They rounded the corner onto Broadway, which was also relatively empty of traffic and pedestrians.

"Why aren't you taking my calls?" Carl asked. "I thought we had a great time the other night. I hate to make a fool of myself by saying this, I mean it sucks to have to ask this, but I would have sworn we really liked each other. Did I get everything wrong?"

"I ghosted you," Lauren said.

"Why?"

Lauren stopped and looked at him. "Are you married, Carl?"

"No! Why would you even think that?"

"You used a burner phone with me. You had two phones."

His eyes narrowed for a moment, as if caught, but the impression passed just as quickly. "Lauren, no."

"Come on, Carl. There's no reason to have two phones unless you're hiding something."

"One was my work phone."

"For a sports bar?" she asked, incredulously.

"I never give up my personal phone number when I start a job. If they want me to use their device for security, I end up with a second phone."

"Security for a sports bar?"

"Look, take my number again, and I'll give you the number for the other phone, too. And I'm going to give you my address and apartment number, so you know I'm not married. You can visit anytime. Even now."

"Oh, no." Lauren smiled at him, feeling a far greater sense of relief than she had any business feeling after only one date with a guy. She took out her phone, "But okay."

Lauren put all Carl's information in her contacts and resumed walking. Her blood pressure calmed. Her fear of the street seemed distant, even unrealistic, with Carl and Mookie alongside her.

As they walked, Carl spoke. "How are things with your ex's estate?"

"Brian was screwing his partner's wife, and his partner closed his eyes to it. He needed the business Brian brought in—at least until Brian died and he got the business by default. It's amazing, even though we were divorced, Brian still managed to screw Emily and me by thinking with the wrong head."

"Wow."

Lauren blushed, wishing she hadn't mentioned her ex's genitalia. That must have broken all ten cardinal rules of dating. They turned onto Reade Street.

Carl looked in a restaurant window, crowded with people behind etched glass, then glanced back at her. "Did you ever think that maybe the fire wasn't an accident?"

"What?" The casual question didn't feel casual at all.

"A man who has one enemy for something as low as that, probably has others. Maybe people were waiting in line to kill him."

Lauren tried to respond as if she hadn't moved her daughter from home and school for fear of murder, as if there weren't a contract out on her. "It only happens like that in the movies, people lining up to kill the bad guy."

"I don't know," he said. "Sometimes people have secret lives that put them in with a bad element. It can be pretty hairy for the people close to them."

Her neck knotted, her back bristled. She didn't like the way the conversation was going and didn't know how it had gotten so close to the truth. Lauren spotted the lit green bulb above the iron rail of the subway entrance—saved by the bulb—and quickened her step. "I've gotta go, Carl." She turned to him, trying to smile but barely forming a slash across her face. "Thanks for walking me."

"Listen, Lauren, if it gets heavy and you want to talk … call." He put his hand on her arm and brought her toward him, the same electric intensity between them again.

"I have to go." She pulled away, looking quickly around to make sure no one had followed them, and ran down the stairs.

"Lauren—"

She waved, saw the confused look on his face, and kept going.

CHAPTER 25

In the living room overlooking West 181st Street, Emily paced like a caged lemur in the Bronx Zoo's Zanzibar exhibit. She turned on the TV, looked out the window, rummaged in her knapsack, and looked out the window again. Finally, she turned to Jessica, "I want to go to Daddy's office."

Jessica laughed. Emily had taken the words right out of her mouth. It had taken every bit of Jessica's willpower not to storm over to Brian's office hours ago. Where else could she look for information? She'd already turned the house upside down. Apparently, Emily had too.

Before Jessica could respond, Emily launched into a campaign speech: "You're not doing anything, and there are killers keeping me from going to school."

"School?" Jessica asked, dubiously.

Emily shrugged. "Okay, from my friends."

"We don't know they're killers."

"I googled about internet gambling and how criminals infiltrate websites. They're killers, Mafia or something."

Jessica's spine stiffened, but she didn't want Emily to sense how terrified she was. "You've been watching too many movies, Emily."

"What are we gonna do? You're just sitting around when we should be finding out where the money is."

"I'm going to call the people who came to the house, but I promised your mother that I wouldn't do anything else until we talked more
about it."

"That's the whole problem." Emily sat on the arm of the sofa, facing
Jessica. "If you wait for my mother, she'll never let us go to Daddy's office,
and she'll get us all thrown into the Witness Protection Program. I don't
know about you, Jessica, but I'm not leaving my friends. So, you guys
can forget about that. You can go sell movie-theater popcorn and live in a
trailer park in Idaho if you want, but I'll run away and come back here."
Emily slid onto the couch facing Jessica. "Please, we have to go to Daddy's
office. If we find out more about where he hid the money, we can give it
back, and my mother might go along because it's easier and safer than
calling the police. Anyway, I want to find out why Daddy died … if it
wasn't an accident. Please, Jessica."

A half hour later, Emily and Jessica checked in at the after-hours secu-
rity desk at Brian's office building. At the elevator, Jessica looked down at
Emily and said, quietly, "It was really painful coming here the first time.
I had good memories here."

Emily's eyes glistened. "I came here for Bring Your Daughter to
Work Day."

At the twenty-second floor, Jessica swiped Brian's ID at the glass
door, and she and Emily stepped inside. They walked empty corridors
and turned the last corner before Brian's office when a man rounded the
corner from the other direction and nearly slammed into them. Jessica
jumped backward, trying to catch her breath before he became suspicious
of her overreaction.

He was young, a recent law-school grad she'd never met. His tie and
collar button were open, and he looked quizzically at them. "Oh, sorry.
I didn't see you."

Jessica straightened up. "No problem."

He paused, probably wondering who they were there and how much
ass-kissing was necessary. "Do you need any help?"

"No, thanks." Jessica gave him her most condescending smile. "We've
been here late more times than I'd like to admit."

Jessica and Emily watched him go, then slipped into Brian's office. Emily headed straight to the desk. Half-lit office buildings towered outside the windows behind her. She picked up the picture of her and Brian. She studied it, her shoulders hunching, and put it down.

Emily's knapsack thumped to the carpet, and she sat in Brian's chair. She turned on his computer and slouched backward while the computer booted up.

"What are you doing?" Jessica looked over, surprised.

"I don't even need Tabu for this I hope," Emily whispered, although she could have spoken normally without anyone hearing.

A black screen appeared, then Emily was clicking within a menu.

"Tabu?" Jessica grabbed her hand. "What the heck?"

"I'm hacking into Daddy's computer."

"No! You can't do that!" "Wait, wait. Just a minute." Emily pulled her hand from Jessica's. She shoved up her sleeve and consulted notes she'd scribbled with ballpoint on the inside of her forearm. "I didn't want to pay Tabu for the easy stuff." She typed. "There were a bunch of videos on YouTube about bypassing passwords."

Windows bloomed on the screen.

"Oh my God." Jessica felt her face heating up with panic. "What—"

Emily had reached into her jeans pocket and pulled out a thumb drive, holding it up to show Jessica. "It's about this."

"What is that?"

"I don't know. It's Daddy's. I couldn't read it on his computer at home. I need to unencrypt it. I'll explain more, give me a minute. I promise, it will be okay." Emily took out a cheap flip phone from her backpack and sat it on the desk beside her. "Let me just check Daddy's list of files."

Jessica was anxious and shocked but more than a little impressed with Emily. Focused and all business, Emily had grown up before Jessica's eyes. Emily clicked into the PC's program list.

"Yes!" Emily half-shouted before shushing herself, staring at the computer screen. "That's it, a Crypt file. That's what Tabu said to look for." Emily made a call on the black phone. "Tabu, Tabu, it's here!" Emily listened to her friend on the phone. She googled a program name and downloaded it. "I've got it, Tabu."

Jessica started looking around, her nerves jangling. This thing with whoever-the-hell Tabu scared her, and it was taking too long. The program Emily was downloading said it was only 2 percent complete.

"Bro, it's saying there's two hours remaining on the download." Emily listened and turned to Jessica. "He said don't worry. It will only be five minutes. It was fast before."

Jessica started rummaging in Brian's desk drawers, needing to keep busy while they waited but not letting her eyes stray far from whatever might happen on the computer screen.

Emily spoke into the phone, "It's downloaded." A box appeared on the screen, asking whether to allow a person to control the computer remotely.

Jessica straightened up and grasped Emily's shoulder. "Are you sure?"

Emily held her finger over the phone's speaker again. "He's helping me. I don't know how to do it myself. Of course, I'm sure. He's already been on the house computer."

"You're kidding?"

"Listen, Jessica, if he wanted to steal, he could hack Target or Walmart. Stop worrying. I did my due diligence."

Due diligence? What did she know about that? And what if he did end up stealing from the firm? Jessica didn't care about the firm, but she didn't want to go to jail. Jessica sighed, letting go of Emily's hand. It was too late to turn back now, and she wanted to know what was on the thumb drive as much as Emily did.

Emily let Tabu control the computer. She sat back and covered the phone's mouthpiece again. "He's cloning the encryption app then he can download all Daddy's documents that are on the app onto the PC again. It will think we're Daddy and come up unencrypted."

The cursor began moving as Emily's hacker worked remotely on Brian's computer. Programs flashed on and off at high speed. Taking instructions over the phone, Emily inserted the thumb drive into the PC. A document appeared written in what looked like hieroglyphics.

More mysterious cursor clicks, and the document closed, then opened again.

In the light cast by the computer screen, Emily curled her hair on her finger the same way Lauren did when anxious.

Emily started to speak, "Jess—"

"Shhh," Jessica whispered, "Did you hear that?"

"I didn't hear anything."

"Someone walking in the hallway, maybe the cleaning lady. Just tell him to hurry."

"Tabu, hurry, we have to get out of here." Before he could have answered, Emily's face transformed with glee. She nearly bounced out of her chair. "*We're in.*"

***

In a ten-room house in Suffolk County, its living room overlooking a dock on Long Island Sound, Steve Cohen received a call. Anger infused the nerves in his face, his jaw clenching and his face growing darker. He clicked off the phone and turned to Nicole, dressed in a silk camisole she wore like a Brooks Brothers suit. Her opal-painted toes matched the carpet. His eyes lingered on them for a moment.

Nicole searched his face, her own expression hard and down to business. "What's going on?"

He loosened his tie and consciously relaxed his face. "Nada."

She ran her hand through her short hair. "Bullshit."

"Office business ... do you want to pick the color of the toilet paper now?"

"You can be such an ass sometimes." She turned to leave.

He watched her shapely legs, her walk powered with adrenaline even when she walked slowly. Steve pondered Nicole's legs, comparing her to his recollection of the gorgeous women at Home Game, so different from Nicole but no hotter. His mind returned to his last night out with Brian when Brian showed him around the seedy-chic casino upstairs, enticingly shady and exclusive like a Bernie Madoff investment fund. The tiny manager knew Brian and seated them in the VIP lounge where Steve and Brian could watch the poker players. High-class hookers rubbed the necks of the players. One whispered in a player's ear, her Stormy Daniels breasts brushing his shoulder.

Steve took a sip of his Stoli and put it aside. "I'm glad we have a chance to talk outside the office."

Brian tore his eyes away from the hookers. "Oh, yeah?"

"The congressman called."

"Needs money?"

Steve ignored the snark. For a lowlife, Brian could really get on a high horse. "They always need money. But it wasn't about that. He was concerned." Steve leaned toward Brian. "I'm concerned. He said you were talking down the Etta Houses settlement to our clients."

"Oh, that," Brian crossed his legs, relaxed, always self-assured when they talked about cases. "The offer sucks. It's not even close."

"He's worried you're raising their expectations. He wants the case settled. He has a lot of people to take care of there. Until they get a settlement, he has to figure out how to take care of them with taxpayer money. He wants the case out of his hair."

Brian leaned over, his eyes on fire. "Frankly, Steve, I don't give a fuck. *Your* congressman is not *our* client. Our clients need to be taken care of for the rest of their lives, eighty years or better for the kids, with trust funds that ensure they're protected if their brains are too lead-fried to make sound decisions for themselves. They need education, job training, therapy, medication, and a yearly income. Anything less than that, and I'm not letting it happen."

"They're going to live sad little lives no matter how much money we give them." Steve raised his index finger for emphasis, "I will not keep paying for discovery forever. The congressman wants this settled, and I'm in his corner on this. Get with the program, Brian."

"I'm not sure I can do that, Steve."

"I want you to think long and hard about that." Steve stood, furious, more because he still needed Brian than anything else. "I'm going to play some fucking poker."

He sat down at an empty chair at one of the poker tables, whispering to the busty hooker to get him some coke. As the dealer dealt him in,

Steve glanced over at Brian sitting in the VIP lounge, smirking, as if he were above a night of sex, drugs, and poker. Meeting Steve's eyes, Brian raised his drink in a gesture of a friendly toast, although it felt as friendly as a woman must feel when she toasts with a guy who's roofied her. It ended up being an expensive night filled with lousy coke and lousier poker hands, lasting long after Brian left to go home.

Steve's mind returned to the phone call he'd just received. Halfway up the floating stairs that curved to their bedroom, Nicole turned back, sneering down at him, "And Steve, if the color of the firm's toilet paper affects me in any way whatsoever, I will pick it."

The door closed behind her.

His face hard again, Steve thumbed into his cell phone and found the contact he wanted. He listened to it ring, "Not this time, Nicole."

***

Emily and Jessica watched Brian's computer screen fill with a chart of what looked like company names with numbers and other words in columns next to them. "What is it?" Emily asked.

Some of the names gave no clue about the nature of their businesses: Jansen-White, Inc., Samson Holding Co. But some were not so subtle.

"Look at that one." Jessica pointed toward the middle of the screen. "'Secured Boxes, Inc.' They're probably all private safety-deposit box companies. We should figure out which ones are in Miami. Brian must have stashed the money in a safe-deposit box."

"Would they let us in?"

"I don't know. The last column could be passwords. They're all gibberish words. Maybe all you need is the box number, password, maybe a key?"

Emily said goodbye to Tabu. "I'll throw it away. Someplace safe," she promised him and put the phone in her backpack. She clicked on the print icon and the printer hummed. She exited the file and put the thumb drive in her backpack, too. "I guess that's the catch, huh?"

"What?"

"The key."

"Yeah. But we've gotten this far." Jessica bent down and began to search furiously in the lower desk drawers she hadn't looked through yet, even though, logically, the key to the safe-deposit box would have been with Brian, probably burnt and lost after the fire. Jessica closed the drawer and straightened up. "We can call the Miami police and see if they have any of Brian's property. We never got his watch or wallet back either. It's only natural we'd call."

Jessica heard a strange noise again. Jessica couldn't tell whether it was from the hallway or the street outside. "What is that?"

Emily opened her mouth to say something but a crash sounded from the door. A flood of light bleached her features. Jessica and Emily yelped in unison. Jessica grabbed Emily and turned toward the door, putting her body in front of Emily's. A group of silhouetted figures stormed in, guns trained on them. The overheads flared on.

A man shouted. "Put your hands up, move away from the desk. You're under arrest."

CHAPTER 26

Blackout blinds kept prying eyes out of the casino above Home Game sports bar.

Carl paused at the podium inside the entrance and Daisy gave him a cheek-to-cheek kiss. "Carlito." Her voice was raspy.

"How's the baby?" he asked, looking past her, scanning the room. A sprinkling of men sat at the roulette tables; a couple more played blackjack; an off-duty call girl played the slot machines that were grouped in a corner. A table of marks and cons played poker.

Daisy smiled at the mention of her son. "Fine, thank you."

"I've got something for you," CB approached as Carl walked inside. He pulled Carl toward an empty blackjack table. CB wore a sharp navy suit shot through with iridescent highlights that glowed in the dim room. "Lucho Arena, I told you about him—Jorge's enforcer—he showed up before I opened. He went into my office bathroom with a paper bag and changed clothes."

Carl had done his research on Lucho Arena. Lucho was a mean bastard, liked being the muscle even though he was close enough to the center of power to let someone else do the dirty work. He'd been suspected of several murders back in the '90s when he was still in the drug game. Carl had seen the gruesome photos. They'd never been able to get enough evidence to charge him.

"Changed clothes?" Carl asked.

"Definitely. Same color pants but a different shirt and even a different jacket. He must have been coming from work, you could say. Word is that a guy was killed in Chinatown. I'd lay odds he was Lucho's vic."

"Did Lucho say anything?"

"He doesn't say much. But I heard him on the phone. Jorge's in some deep shit with the Chinese about the missing money. Their meeting didn't go well. In war, the best defense is a strong offense. But you gotta wonder what's up with that money that would make Arena and Lucho so hyped. Jorge's on his fucking period about it."

"The missing money?" Carl played it cool. "What more could be going on?"

"The possibilities are endless when it comes to Jorge sending money to a Chinese billionaire. Have you really looked into the Chinese dude?"

Carl took CB's question as rhetorical but wouldn't have answered it anyway. Xi Wen ran several businesses in China. Medical supplies, munitions factories, cell phone parts, and housing developments in the newly-born Chinese cities that had sprouted up around Chinese industries. Carl did wonder why Arena was so desperate to send him money, or at least why it was such a time-sensitive matter to settle up a gambling debt.

"So who got hit?" Carl didn't trust CB but he was starting to think the ASAC had done right to recruit him. CB had a knack for getting information. He was very motivated to cooperate. A pretty boy like him—weighing no more than 120 pounds—would have a tough time in jail.

"I heard the dead guy was from a Chinatown Tong that works for Xi Wen. I'm thinking they made the mistake of threatening Jorge." CB lowered his voice, "Did you know Jorge's father was in Trujillo's death squads in the DR? Jorge is literally a natural-born killer. It doesn't take much to get him started down a very dark path."

"Your family history makes his look like Mother Teresa's."

CB grimaced. "Leave my family out of this. We're three generations removed from any fake news you've heard."

Carl and CB walked back downstairs, passing the players who were focused on their cards, roulette balls, and shoulder rubs. At the bathroom adjacent to CB's office, Carl signaled him to stay back and used a hand-kerchief to turn the doorknob. He looked in at the pristine granite sink and marble floors without touching anything. He glanced inside an empty wastebasket. He returned to CB's office and called on his cell to see if the FBI computer showed any police activity in Chinatown. An agent con-firmed a street murder. Carl spoke into the phone, "We'll need a forensics crew here with a truck and the cable repair get-up." Carl turned back to CB. "You did well. You'll need to stay out of there until the morning when the crew can come in without calling attention to itself. Can you use another bathroom?"

"Yeah, sure."

Carl and CB headed back upstairs to the casino, which had started to fill up while they were downstairs. At a couch in the back, a group of men were giving drink orders to Daisy.

"That's Jorge and his cousin, Pedro," CB said, a slight jitteriness betraying CB's nerves at cooperating with the FBI now that he was physi-cally face-to-face with Jorge Arena. "Let's get this over with."

Jorge Arena was a large man in his fifties. Weather lines furrowed his face, softening pockmarks left from teenage acne. Carl thought his decades of illicit power had given him a commanding aura. Pedro was a big man, too, probably in his late forties. They both wore suits.

"Jorge, this is Carl," CB said in Spanish. "He's helping me out here."

Jorge nodded hello, not offering a seat.

"If you need anything," Carl said to Jorge, "just let me know." Carl signaled to Daisy to come over. "The next round's on me."

"Gracias," Jorge said. "And how do you know CB?"

"We went to City College together," Carl replied. "When we ran into each other again, we were both in the same type of business."

"Which is?"

"I work in clubs, but more than anything, I agent gamblers, book bets."

Jorge raised his eyebrows. "Quite a coincidence."

"Yeah, small world," CB cut in.

"If you'll excuse me," Carl said, having accomplished all he could on the first meet and greet.

***

An hour later, Carl met up with Rick and they drove downtown on West Street. Carl filled Rick in on what CB had said. "CB made a good point. This whole thing about the missing money doesn't sit right. Why wouldn't Arena try to tell Xi Wen to eat the loss? The money getting lost in transit must be a normal risk of doing business under the table. Like the cost of shoplifting for a department store."

"Millions of dollars?" Rick said. "Even a billionaire would want his money."

"True, but why would Arena be in such a rush to pay the money? You would think Arena could negotiate a discounted sum and that it would benefit him to take his time. It isn't like Xi Wen is going on food stamps if he has to wait."

Rick signaled, changing lanes to pass a slow car. "Lucho's Chinatown hit could be part of the negotiations. A shot across the bow."

"Jorge and Lucho have been busy today. This morning Jordan Connors was killed, tonight someone else. I think we're onto something bigger than we thought. There's a missing piece here. We know Arena infiltrated Jordan's website. What if Arena's guy had a look at the poker cards, intentionally lost a bet, and was really making a payment to Xi Wen, maybe buying something?"

"It's an interesting theory," Rick said.

Carl reached into his jacket for his phone and called into headquarters to see if the stingray had picked up any conversations at the bar when Lucho was there. An agent answered. After a few moments of narrowing down to the time Carl requested, she played back a call.

Carl recognized Lucho's voice, words edged with a slimy sexuality as he spoke to a woman. "*Hecho.*"

A woman's voice: "*Bueno.*"

"*La viuda?*" Lucho asked.

The Spanish word for "widow" froze Carl's lungs. It was the second time a question about the wife or widow had come up on audio. After the news they'd received from Westchester earlier in the day and the way

Lauren had acted, what were the odds of it being unrelated to Silverman's widow or even Lauren?

The woman responded, "Still no call since you went."

Carl hung up and spoke to Rick. "Jordan's good friend, Brian Silverman, vacationed in Tortola for one day with twelve million dollars and ended up dead; this morning in Westchester, someone called in a report of a possible carjacking at a strip mall. The perpetrator matches Jordan Connors' general description and the car was at least similar to Silverman's car, which is of course now driven by his wife. The caller was pretty sure of what she saw, but no one has reported her missing. What if Silverman was duped into thinking he was transporting a gambling debt but it was really something more dangerous and now—"

"You're jumping from one unproven assumption to another," Rick interrupted. "Jordan's body was found in a completely different county. We have a beige car, no usable description of the possible carjacker, and no victim. Just our luck there were no cameras outside the mall. What you've got, my man, is too little to get a tap on the widow or a warrant to look at her car. We are homing in on something big, and your mind is stuck on a tangent."

"I'd place a bet on it."

"You've been hanging out with too many gamblers. We'll find out more when we start getting forensics reports back on Jordan."

Carl's mind returned to the prospect of Lauren being caught up with Arena and the murderous crew who surrounded him, now adding in the Chinese Tong. "Listen, Rick, I know you want me to let it go, but Lauren Davis works out at our gym, for God's sake. Lucho was talking about *la viuda*, the widow. Jordan, too. Who were they talking about? Who was it Lucho visited? Lucho is a killer and he didn't seem too pleased. I get the impression that Jorge Arena isn't too pleased either."

"All you really have evidence of is that Brian Silverman knew Jordan and that Silverman went to great lengths—all the way to the Caribbean—to get laid. And now Jordan Connors is dead, so he won't be telling us anything different."

"We could bring Lauren Davis in, see if she knows anything. She'd cooperate. She's an attorney and a prosecutor."

"Tony Soprano's girl? Once a Mob chick, always … well, you know. Anyway, she's a Family Court prosecutor, not an ADA. She's not law enforcement. You have nothing on her—less than on the widow. I don't even know why you're hyped about her."

"Because I've got an instinct about this."

"No, you've got the hots for that girl."

Carl laughed. "That's total bullshit."

"Boy, I saw the way you looked at her at the gym. You need to watch your ass—and mine. If you screw up, they'll be looking at me like, *Why didn't you stop him?* Well, I've now officially suggested that you're a sick motherfucker in need of some serious therapy or some meaningless sex, one or the other."

"Thanks, bro. But it's Arena who needs some serious therapy. I think he's going off the rails. Even though I have to say he seemed cool as the Arctic when I met him."

They drove past the Meatpacking District, partyers crowding the cobbled streets. Despite himself, Carl thought about Lauren—laughing with her, holding her for just a moment. There was something special about her, but his encounter with her tonight confirmed that something wasn't right. Rick would have gone ballistic about Carl unofficially staking her out, so Carl couldn't mention how scared she'd seemed, how her hand had trembled when he held it.

Jessica Silverman was involved and, somehow, Lauren was too. If they didn't come in for help, and Brian Silverman had died with unfinished business, Arena would either kill them because they couldn't produce the money, or they could cooperate with Arena and end up caught in the Bureau's rapidly approaching conspiracy bust. And the problem for the women was that the US Attorney would charge them even if they cooperated with Arena under duress. Logic worked in reverse for the innocent ones: without a tap on their conversations, they would never prove they'd been threatened, and the forfeiture alone would make them irresistible. Carl knew he might be getting ahead of himself and the proof. But his gut told him that if Lauren was caught up the way he suspected, and if she helped Arena at this point, she wasn't coming out the other side of it with her life in one piece. She could easily end up in jail for a very long time.

CHAPTER 27

Wednesday, November 6

At 1:00 a.m., Lauren paced her living room, her heart on overdrive. Emily was in jail. Lauren felt the same aching powerlessness as the night Brian died, but worse now because one bad thing after the next had pancaked on her like a collapsing building, depleting her ability to cope. Her sanity was a thin veil at this point. Plus, although the least of her problems, this whole fiasco had made her see a truth about her own life: she was as alone in this crisis as she was as a kid when her father died.

Lauren felt so overwhelmed and frustrated, she wanted to pick up a chair and smash it against the wall just to release the pressure cooker of feelings. A drink would take the edge off, a glass of wine. *No*. Jesus, how did thoughts like that pop up after twenty years of not drinking or drugging? She pitched pumps, pantyhose, and a toothbrush into a gym bag. She rolled a suit and blouse tightly so they wouldn't wrinkle, and packed them inside, too. She ripped her phone charger from the wall and threw it in. She couldn't just sit in the house and wait all night or she'd go crazy. She practically ran out of the apartment door before she could think better of it.

She looked out her building's entryway for any sign of danger. At this hour, her neighborhood was entirely different than the gentrifying enclave it was during the day. Teenage drug dealers gathered in front of the all-night bodega next door to her building. Just her and them, which would normally be scary; but it was ironically reassuring to have any company on the otherwise empty street. She walked from her building, hoping the teenagers weren't so inebriated that they failed to see she was old enough to be their mother.

Lauren had bigger worries than harassment, although she was starting to have doubts about whether Jordan Connors had been telling the truth about the contract on her. He could have been lying. Why would Bobby put a contract on her? And, even if he did, why would a guy doing life in prison keep his money behind that contract just because she'd run out on him twenty years ago? The more she thought about it, the less sense it made.

Either way, contract or not, she had to get downtown to 100 Centre Street in the morning. Felony burglary and criminal trespass. The desk sergeant had told her what the charges were when she called the precinct after hearing Emily's hysterical one-phone-call on her voice mail. Lauren knew the routine. After arrest, Emily and Jessica would go from precinct cells to Central Booking. Then they'd be transported to the Department of Corrections' filthy, tomb-like bullpens under the Criminal Courthouse. They'd wait there for their case to be called for arraignment.

As an attorney, Lauren could have contact with Jessica and Emily after the Department of Corrections took custody at 100 Centre Street, but not before. By her calculations, that wouldn't happen until at least dawn. Meanwhile, she hadn't even thought of sleeping. She'd never sleep. So why try?

"*Mami*, I like your ass." A sixteen-year-old leered at her, holding his crotch, as she walked around the periphery of drug dealers.

Fuck you! nearly flew from her mouth, but she caught herself. She met the teenager's dangerous, marijuana-bleary stare and refocused her gaze straight ahead. A dozen teenage eyes followed her as if she were the ball in a tennis match. She walked to a cabstand further down the block, a line-up of idling cars between Fort Washington Avenue and Cabrini Boulevard. She opened the back door of the first apple-green car.

Twenty minutes later, she stood outside sprawling Independence Plaza, tall apartment buildings spanning several blocks in the far west side of Tribeca. She dialed Carl's number. "What are you doing? Are you sleeping?" she asked, knowing this whole unannounced-visit thing was inappropriate. He'd said he was just going home with his dog and that he wasn't dating anyone, but she knew it was risky anyway.

"Sleeping?" His voice was groggy but he perked up as if her voice had made him happy. "Yeah. What are you doing?"

She found herself crying. "I need to come up."

"You're kidding—you're here?"

"Downstairs."

A pause. "Come up."

Mookie barked at the other side of Carl's apartment door before she could ring the bell. Carl wore a T-shirt and sweats, holding Mookie back by the collar. "Sit, Mook."

Lauren put down one hand to touch Mookie's head and melted into Carl's arms, his muscled arms strong around her. She breathed in his scent, losing her mind. Their kiss was perfect, the kind of intense kiss-perfection that each person inexplicably knew the other felt too. They were both breathing hard when they separated. They looked at each other and laughed. She rubbed a tear away with her finger.

The living room was large by Manhattan standards. It was sparsely furnished, masculine in an inattentive way. A boy's bike and two skateboards rested against a white wall. Carl's bike was mounted on hooks. A few child's drawings were taped near the entryway to an alley kitchen. Lauren's eyes were drawn to a framed photo of Carl and his son.

The boy's dark eyes and thick black eyelashes were identical to Carl's. "He's gorgeous."

Carl smiled. "Alex."

"You look so happy with him."

"He makes me happy." Carl took Lauren's hand. "And I'm really happy you're here. Shocked, but happy."

Lauren lay her forehead against Carl's chest and let out a long sigh.

He wrapped his arms around her, leading her to a couch with a view of a dark shimmer of the Hudson in the distance. Mookie curled up next to Lauren's feet. Carl held Lauren, stroking her hair, as if he were trying to comfort her and keep his hands somewhere safe. "What's the matter? What happened?"

Lauren chose her words. "Emily was arrested."

"Emily?!"

"She was at Brian's office. She said they were collecting ... pictures, his personal stuff. I can't even describe this. Steve must have called the police. So much is going on, I can't think straight. I can't see her for hours. I just can't believe this is happening. I feel as if the walls are collapsing on us."

"Even if his partner was pissed off at your ex, who does something like that?" Carl seemed to be thinking out loud.

Lauren started crying again, and Carl kissed the wet of her face. Both of their hands ran over each other's bodies, swept up in each other as if by an outside force. Their breathing became heavy before they pulled themselves back.

Lauren caught her breath. "I'm going to the courthouse in a few hours. I could wait here."

Carl's olive complexion had flushed. "You're going to represent her?"

"For the arraignment." Lauren put her palms under Carl's shirt, feeling the smooth skin and hair over taut muscles. "Not until the morning. I can't do anything but wait."

She found Carl's mouth against hers, his hands against her bare back, his palm running over her butt. She groaned. Ready. Her cautious inner voice stayed blessedly silent. She felt his hardness through her own jeans.

He jumped up as if stung. "No, no. We can't do this."

Lauren took in the deep stress in his eyes. She straightened her clothes. "What?!"

"I really like you." Carl's face was red now. "But—look, I can't."

"You've got to be kidding."

Carl stood—as if he were going to put her out?

"Lauren."

She had reached her limit—hurt, pissed off, confused. "Oh, my God. You know what, I've had enough. There's something going on with you, and my plate is full." She jumped to her feet, needing to get away from him. "I'm sorry I came. I don't have the bandwidth for this. I'm sorry."

"Lauren, wait."

She grabbed her gym bag and coat.

"Please, Lauren, there are things I need to work out." He took her arm. "I can't talk about it now. Trust me."

"You've got to be kidding. Get your hands off me." The door slammed behind her before Carl had time to say more.

CHAPTER 28

Lauren sat the rest of the night in Bubby's, a rustic American all-night restaurant. She ate a few bites of eggs and cheese grits, avoiding the stares of the men who were drinking at the bar. She felt so angry at herself once again. What drew her to guys who were such a mess? Nothing she'd done had made Carl react like that. She was sure of that much. He acted as if he were a priest breaking his vows, tempted by a seductress. She had no plans of stepping foot near that kind of back-and-forth insanity. Finally, she was done. She was at a bottom with reaching for the nearest source of testosterone in a fucking storm. That was what she'd done when she was a kid, what she'd done with Brian too. Look where it had gotten her. They used to say in treatment that insanity was doing the same things over and over, expecting different results. She was officially insane.

Apparently Carl was too. He was as crazy as a bedbug. Unpredictable. Hiding something. Once again, she was glad she hadn't slept with him. Although she wasn't ready to ghost him this time. That had proved useless.

At 5:00 a.m., she changed into her suit for the day, balancing on one shoe at a time in the restaurant's cold bathroom while she put on her pantyhose. She drew a curious look from the waitress when she left in a business suit and pumps. The night's shadows still weighed on the city as she approached the Uber she'd called. The driver, wearing a kufi and trimmed beard, unlocked the doors and she got in.

The car sped east and north on empty predawn streets. She had one more thing to do before court. Having no clue what would greet her, she rode through Alphabet City, named for its Avenues A, B, C, and D. The car stopped across the street from Tompkins Square Park, four blocks from where she'd grown up. Alongside the park, gnarled oaks wove a moving web of light, street lamps shining through the gaps in their branches.

She'd passed Brownie's in cabs a few times over the years since she'd ceased frequenting the place two decades ago, but she'd barely glanced at it. It had been as distant to her as an alternate universe you forgot once you left. Glimpsed from the outside, it had always looked the same as it did now, grungy, with its windows blacked out and no sign to identify it.

The driver looked back at her. "Are you sure you want to go there?"

"Could you wait a minute for me to check if they're open?"

"Okay. But I don't think that's a place for nice people, ladies wearing suits."

Lauren paid him, wishing she could heed him. "I'm okay, thanks."

The morning was still dark outside, but when she pulled open Brownie's door, she entered true blackness like the entryway to a spook house. Her eyes adjusted and she reached for an inner door. A chestnut-complexioned bouncer—he must have been six four and over three hundred pounds—looked her over. House music boomed from speakers.

"Slumming?" he said, a snide half question, half comment.

"Is Brownie still here?"

"Where else would he be?"

Lauren walked by the bouncer, acting as if she'd passed his vetting. He didn't stop her. Unlike what the cabbie had said, suited-up lawyers and bankers did sometimes land at Brownie's. There was always a sprinkling of people who went from office to happy hour to night club to illegal after-hour spot to a spot like this that opened just before dawn when the after-hour clubs closed. Brownie's stayed open until midafternoon, closing just in time for happy hour. Manhattan offered an endless polar night to those on a death spiral.

The small club hadn't changed much since the mornings when Lauren had accompanied Bobby here. They were always treated as honored guests, continuing a night of drinking, drugging, dancing, and Bobby's networking with his nefarious associates. Lauren passed the long bar now, not seeing Brownie holding court on a stool as he used to do. Red velvet couches and cocktail tables lined a small dance floor. The hour was still early for Brownie's, only a few men and a couple of women with dramatic low-cut dresses sat at one table. The group sniffed coke openly, their eyes tracking Lauren as she walked along the edge of the dance floor. She looked away from their drugs, taking in their soulless eyes. She didn't look at their eyes long either, intuitively afraid of the attractive power of their darkness.

On the dance floor, two women danced close to each other, one masculine with huge breasts and belly, and the other feminine with a skirt barely covering her hips. The big woman moved her hips with slow grace against her dance partner.

Brownie sat in a dark corner with a bottle of champagne open in a bucket at his table. A gold-handled cane glinted next to him. He was no longer the stout man he'd been. He sat hunched over, looking around with rheumy eyes more fitting for a nursing home dayroom than an illegal after-hours spot.

He searched Lauren's face as she approached before he focused into an amused realization. "Is that you, Snow?"

Snow White. He'd been calling her that since he first came across her running the streets of Alphabet City, before she'd met Bobby.

She smiled but didn't reach down to kiss his cheek. Brownie's wasn't that kind of social atmosphere. It was a place for hustlers, truck hijackers, contract killers. It was a place where Lauren used to hang out, thinking herself strong enough to deal with all that, always afloat in a hidden sea of fear. A fear that had returned now as if it had never left. "Hi, Brownie."

"Well, well, well. I'd hoped you got away." He took in Lauren's business suit and face and gave her an approving look. "Maybe you did get away ... but I'm wondering whether you're making one big whopper of a mistake thinking you can test the waters again."

Lauren sat. "I'm not back."

"Good." He poured himself some champagne and put an index finger in the air, signaling to the bartender to bring her a glass.

"No thanks. I've got to be in court in a couple of hours."

His eyebrows arched. "So, what are you doing here … after all these years?"

"Listen, Brownie, trouble's found me."

He took a prim sip of champagne. "It has a way of doing that."

"Did you ever hear that Bobby put a contract out on me?"

"I heard that. Then you disappeared into thin air. I always hoped you got away and weren't just buried so deep no one came across you."

Lauren inhaled sharply, visualizing the image.

He went on: "I'm glad to see you're not. Bobby probably has a lot of bodies not found yet, women especially, and he was deeply pissed when you up and vanished on him. I'm not the only one who thought maybe the contract had already been fulfilled. Course, when you disappeared it was back before the internet made it hard to hide. It was a lot easier to vanish back then, which was lucky for you."

Lauren tried to tuck away her fear, digesting what he'd said. How would she ever hide now? Especially in plain sight, the way she'd done before. Her eighteen months in drug treatment, totally off the grid, had helped her more than she'd realized, putting time and space between her and any gangsters looking to make a fast buck. Later she'd used Brian's last name for much of her adult life. By the time Google alerts had become a thing, Bobby's contract must have been forgotten in some kind of Mafia cold-case file. "I didn't know about the contract, Brownie. I went away for a couple of years … to get myself together, started a new life. I'm out of the Life. But somebody wants to collect now. Damn, Brownie, why? Bobby's been in jail for nearly twenty years already."

"That he is. Life sentence. If he's lucky, he'll get out for compassionate release when he's ready to die. Rumor has it that you had something to do with that. Ergo the contract."

Lauren sat back, shocked. "No!"

"Word is the cops told him you were going to cooperate if he didn't plead."

"That's not true. I didn't know anything about what he was doing. I didn't even know he was arrested at first. I read the book when it came out, same as everyone else."

"He's in jail, but he's still got power. His name is good and so's his contract, apparently not forgotten anymore."

"I don't know what to do about it. Someone's blackmailing me to do a deal, or they'll cash in on the contract. My ex-husband got me into a bunch of shit. He was a piece of work."

Brownie smiled, benignly. "Even when you were just a kid, you always had a good head on your shoulders. But, Snow, you had a broken picker when it came to men. I guess some things don't change."

Lauren couldn't have agreed more.

Brownie put his drink down and sat back, thinking. "You can buy yourself some time by doing the deal the people want, but doing their bidding isn't a long-term solution. Even if they honor their bargain, now that you're on the radar, word will slip out and the next guy will go for it sooner or later."

"What do you suggest?"

"You have to buy back the contract."

"How do I do that?"

"Bobby's the one who can do that for you. And I'd venture to guess you'll have to pay the face value of it or something close to it."

"Jesus."

"He might help you," Brownie chuckled. "Or you could get the people threatening you to buy it back, if you got the juice to negotiate it."

They sat quietly for a moment.

Lauren leaned forward and kissed him on the cheek for the first time ever. "I've gotta go."

He grabbed her arm and pulled her toward him before she could straighten up. "You be careful with those folks. Handle them with care, the ones who're threatening you. You can do the deal to get them up off your ass ... 'cause folks like that don't just walk away once they set their minds on something ... but then you gotta do something about that contract and get out again, do you hear me? Once you're done with whatever mess drug you back down here, stay up above the sidewalk with the squares. Forget this life exists."

***

The casino closed shortly before dawn, although the Arenas were still upstairs hanging out and drinking. CB counted money at the glass desk in his dimly lit, windowless office. No knock. A man, tall and wide, filled the doorway. CB's breath caught in his throat. He steeled his face, forcing himself to relax. "Hey, Jorge, what's up?"

CB continued to count the night's receipts, although he'd lost count. He counted his breaths instead, trying to keep the air flowing. The problem with "turning state's" was that he was terrified, all the time. Jorge Arena paced on the far side of CB's desk, his imposing size and energy sucking away CB's courage like an evil spirit in a folk tale. Jorge didn't make social visits, not to CB at least. He had to fight back his paranoia before it got the better of him. He couldn't afford any unforced errors. CB had already hit information pay dirt tonight—he prayed he hadn't sparked Jorge's suspicion by asking Pedro and the others so many questions.

"I need to make a call." Jorge sat in an armchair and dialed his cell phone. It was probably a burner phone but even Jorge's burners were Apple, so you couldn't tell. Jorge didn't throw his wealth around, but he used it where it counted.

Jorge started right in talking, resuming a conversation midthought. "*Hijo*, you need to stay calm. The delivery is barely late. Be a man or they'll sense your weakness. It will be over soon." Jorge listened, his expression grave. "Let me speak to them."

Like CB, Jorge didn't have a Spanish accent unless he chose it. He wasn't born in New York, so his school-taught English tilted formal, hinting at a British teacher, but it was otherwise perfect. Jorge had attended the best schools in the DR and wasn't in the Life because he couldn't do anything else. He lived off the grid for the same reason some cowboys still did. He didn't want to answer to anybody. And he enjoyed the kill.

Jorge growled into the phone at someone. "I'm lending you my nephew. Keep him happy or your family in Queens won't have anywhere to hide. I know where they are. You fuck with mine, I will make Homeland Security look like Girl Scouts on a scavenger hunt …" He listened, scowling. "Girl Scouts. Fucking *Girl Scouts*."

When Jorge hung up, he turned to CB. "The *cabron* tells me he doesn't know what Girl Scouts are." Jorge sighed. "My nephew is staying in Africa, their guests."

CB weighed and measured each word before he uttered it. He couldn't seem curious. He continued to count the money, a cigarette perched in the corner of his mouth. "That's Tomás?" CB had played with several of Jorge's nephews during long summers in the DR.

"Yes. For now, it's just business with these Africans, them keeping Tomás. But it may turn ugly fast. My nephew is like the margin call in the stock market. Our stock has gone down due to our delivery delay and they need additional collateral. It's Tomás who brought me the buyers, a bunch of ISIS wannabes. He wanted a more active role in the family business. I was impressed with the magnitude of his deal, which we planned flawlessly." Arena shook his head with disgust as if to say that a flawless plan had still resulted in a shit storm. "You know Tomás' mother and my wife are sisters. They'll bring in the Santería priests if they hear of this. The praying will take over my whole house." Jorge chuckled, his mood lightening from black to gray. "I'll have to go stay at my girlfriend's." Jorge pointed, "Give me a cigarette."

"I thought the Chinese were the problem."

Jorge peered into CB's eyes. CB's heart plunged.

"Pedro talks too much." Jorge dragged on the cigarette, relaxing again. "Lucho made a bad situation worse, but I can't begrudge him. Andy Chow is the military leader of the Mott Street Tong. He's a cagey *maricon,* but he's a naturally rude person, talks too much shit. It's important to remain polite when everyone is well armed. He pushed Lucho too far. Now Chow is very pissed about what Lucho did. But if we get the money to their client, hopefully everything will be forgotten. It's all about the money as the saying goes."

CHAPTER 29

The streetlights still glowed outside Brownie's, but the sky had become sepia. A cold wind hit Lauren. A well-dressed group—men and women in black, wearing sunglasses although it was barely dawn—passed her as they entered Brownie's. Lauren paused, hearing birds singing in the park's trees. She remembered how much she'd hated that sound in the old days when she left Brownie's after an all-nighter of booze and coke. The morning birds rising before she'd gone to bed had been proof that her life was upside down.

She grabbed the cab the group of partyers had exited. The gray sky ripened into pink and orange as she rode downtown. Twenty minutes later, after a pit stop at McDonald's, she walked through the doors of 100 Centre Street. The normally bustling, fifteen-story criminal courthouse was eerily quiet. She passed an open concession stand, which offered coffee and magazines, the clerk nowhere in sight. Two court officers manned a long wooden table and metal detector. Lauren held up her attorney ID.

"Morning, Counselor," one officer said and signaled her through the metal detector, its alarms blaring and echoing in the cavernous lobby. The empty main lobby spanned the equivalent of a full city block, taking up the front half of the building's ground level.

"The Arraignment Part's that way?" Lauren asked the court officer as she pointed toward the second of three elevator banks, nearly a half block from where she stood. "It's been a while since I've been here."

"Yeah, walk past the elevators to the back lobby. Misdemeanor Part's on your left, Felony Part's on your right."

At the relatively small lobby area at the backside of the building, an officer sat behind a plexiglass window. A few worried families milled about. The two Arraignment Parts worked twenty-four hours a day. The arraignment provided defendants with their first shot in front of a judge after arrest, which often ended in a quick dismissal or a "time served" sentence but could also lead to an extended stay on Rikers Island.

Lugging her gym bag and two McDonald's bags filled with coffee, orange juice, breakfast sandwiches, and home fries, Lauren turned right toward the Felony Part. Emily would have eaten nothing but stale bologna-and-cheese sandwiches since her arrest. Lauren had brought extra food, knowing Emily and Jessica would need to share with any bullpen allies. That was the way it worked in the bullpens. Lauren's throat tightened. She just couldn't fathom how and when Emily crossed the line from Happy Meals to adult jails. Terrified at the trouble that had homed in on them, she pasted on a rigor-mortis half smile. If she was going to be effective today, she had to come off like an attorney, not a desperate mother.

She pushed open one of the heavy double doors to the Felony Part and scanned the large room, very different from the child-friendly Family Court. A dozen long, dark pews—scarred and worn like an old-fashioned elementary school desk—lined each side of a center aisle. Parents, girlfriends, and an occasional husband filled the pews. A wooden railing separated the gallery from the working part of the courtroom.

The Arraignment Part wasn't like courts people saw on TV, where everyone in the courtroom sat quietly while the judge handled the court's business. Here, people were doing all sorts of things within the front half of the room, walking around, negotiating, and maneuvering, even while cases droned on at the judge's bench. Harried Legal Aid attorneys and assistant district attorneys reviewed their case files and talked quietly into telephones at paper-cluttered tables that dominated the left side of the area. On the right side, two uniformed cops and a corrections officer sat at a table, reading the *New York Post* and chatting quietly. At the center, in front of the tall judge's bench, were traditional, scuffed defense and prosecution tables.

Presently, two prosecutors stood before the judge. One assistant DA in his late twenties was breaking in a newer female ADA. He whispered to her before each sentence she haltingly delivered.

The new ADA scanned paperwork in front of her. "The prosecution is hereby providing notice of the defendant, Craig Simmons' statement: 'I didn't cut the bitch. She had it coming for smoking the package.'"

The defendants, three of them, sucked their teeth then whispered intently into the ears of their court-appointed lawyers.

The judge ignored them and addressed the new ADA. "What's your bail offer, Counselor?"

The male prosecutor whispered into her ear again. She looked at the judge. "Forty thousand dollars each, Your Honor. The defendants have a long criminal record including prior assaults."

After a pointless argument by one of the defense lawyers, the three men were led, muttering, toward a door several feet to the right of the judge's bench.

The case over, Lauren approached a court officer who stood at the railing between the front and gallery. "I want to get down to the female bullpens." She showed her ID and signaled toward the door the three men had just gone through. "Is that the way?"

He unhooked the chain link between two halves of the wooden railing and stood aside. "You bet, through that door, the staircase to the left." He looked down at the McDonald's bags. "Special delivery?"

"If possible." Lauren knew to ask, not demand, while so far from her familiar Family Court. Every court had its own system of doing things that went beyond the law books. Her biggest job today would be learning how to make the wheels turn here, so she could get Emily and Jessica out as quickly and cleanly as possible.

He shrugged. "Ask the corrections officer downstairs. She'll probably let you. No glass bottles?"

Lauren looked down at her bags. "No."

"Good." He signaled toward the door with his head.

She crossed between the defense table and lounging police officers and pulled open the door. As it closed behind Lauren, an oppressive gray surrounded her. She descended the metal stairs to a set of bars that separated her from the female bullpens. The bars and the cinder-block walls were all gray. In the distance, women milled behind more gray bars, sat on gray metal benches and lay on dirty cement floors. More than fifty women were packed in the first bullpen, its bars forming a corridor between the bullpen and the outer gate where she waited.

The correction officer's keys jangled on her thick hips as she came to open the door for Lauren. "What's your client's name?"

"Emily and Jessica Silverman."

"Okay."

"Matron, matron," a bedraggled woman put sore-ridden arms through the bars of the first bullpen.

"Go to sleep, Sylvia, your prints aren't back yet." The CO swung the outer gate open for Lauren. "She calls me matron like in those old women's prison movies, thinks it annoys me. She's back here once a month, busted again, telling me 'matron, matron.' You'd think she'd be the one annoyed. Of course, she knows better than I do how long it takes for fingerprints to be processed and the DA to prepare the case." The CO pointed Lauren down the corridor. "That way, speak to the officer at the desk."

Lauren glanced through the bars of the first pen as she passed, checking to see if Jessica and Emily were in among the horde of prostitutes, addicts, and huge, masculine women. The scent of industrial-strength pine cleaner, unwashed bodies, and stopped-up toilets flared Lauren's nostrils.

A second heavyset CO hung up the telephone as she approached her desk. "Can I help you, Counselor?"

"Emily and ..."

"Mom!"

Lauren turned to a bullpen half the size of the other, within sight of the CO's desk. Emily stood at the bars, eyes darkly circled, hair matted. Looking haggard and skinny, Jessica leaned against the bars at Emily's left. On Emily's other side was a sink with a metal shelf above it. A deranged-looking woman with a multidirectional afro lay on the shelf. She scratched herself then stretched her legs until her filthy socks extended over the edge, close to Emily's head.

Emily turned and shouted at her, "Move your feet, *damn*."

The woman sat up. Lauren's muscles tightened, ready for anything, imagining the woman launching herself at Emily with Lauren unable to help. How long would it take the CO to get in there? Lauren held her breath, but Jessica snatched Emily and switched places with her. Jessica glared at the woman.

The woman sucked her teeth and muttered, "Stupid bitches." She rolled over and went back to sleep.

Lauren turned to the corrections officer who smiled, sympathetically. "Your daughter, eh?"

"Yeah. Can I give them food?"

"No bottles?"

"No."

"Go on." The CO pointed toward the pen. "We've been keeping an eye out, spotted them right away. But they've been handling themselves fine, all things considered."

"Thank you. How long do you think until their cases are called?"

"It's been a little busy, always is before elections—probably make court by nine or ten tonight."

Lauren took a harsh breath.

The CO shrugged and raised her palms. "Not my doing."

Lauren smiled, grimly. "I know." She walked to the crowded square pen. Nearly thirty women sat on its three benches, some sleeping with their heads on their knees, some staring into space. Another half-dozen women slept on the bare floor and still others stood and leaned against the bars. Lauren put her hand through the bars to the back of Emily's head and kissed her forehead.

Emily whispered, "Get us out of here."

"You've gotta hang on. It'll be a while."

"I can't, *please*."

"Just hang on, baby, you have to. It's going to be at least another twelve hours."

Emily sniffed back tears, keeping her face from dissolving in front of her cellmates, many of whom now watched the unusual bullpen visit between lawyer and daughter. "But you're a lawyer."

"You have to wait for the fingerprints to come back and for the DA to put the paperwork together."

Jessica sunk against the bars, as if losing her strength at the news of the hours still ahead.

Lauren turned to her, furious, even more so at the sight of her weakness. "Need I ask what my daughter is doing in jail, charged with a felony?"

"Need you ask why we're *both* in here for *hacking*. I had no idea what she'd planned," Jessica spit.

Lauren turned to look at Emily, "*What?*"

Tears pooled in Emily's eyes. "I'm sorry, Jessica."

Jessica whispered, "She hacked Brian's computer. I had no idea."

"I'm sorry, really, Jessica. I didn't mean—"

Lauren whispered, "I'm afraid to even ask what you two are talking about. They didn't charge you with hacking ... not yet. Burglary and criminal trespass, that's it."

Jessica sighed with relief. She reached for Emily, holding her. "I could have stopped you. I wanted to know too. I'm just scared." Jessica spoke softly to Lauren again, "Then building security must have called the police. I bet they checked with someone—namely that bastard, Steve—to see if we were authorized to be there. I still can't understand why he's doing this."

Lauren nearly shouted the truth: *because your low-life husband was fucking Nicole, that's why.* But she pulled herself back from that brink. She looked at Jessica, who was afraid for her life, disheveled, and exhausted. Lauren took in the sight of the exposed toilet in the corner of the bullpen. What a nightmare it must be for Jessica to use it in front of two dozen people, let alone these bunkmates. Yet, despite everything, Jessica was keeping her wits about her, trying to figure out what was going on and, most of all, trying to protect Emily no matter what Emily had done. Seeing Jessica put herself between Emily and the crazy woman, who outweighed Jessica by at least fifty pounds, had struck Lauren.

"Why did you go back there after we agreed?" Lauren asked.

"I didn't think we could get into any real trouble by just being there," Jessica said

"I convinced her," Emily whispered through the bars. "Daddy was sending messages to someone on the PlayStation about Tortola, and he was in Tortola the day before he died. I found a thumb drive of his, but I needed his office computer. Daddy had an encryption app on his work PC. I needed to get the IP address to clone the app and get his encrypted document."

Lauren stared at Emily, stunned, trying to keep up with her.

"I convinced Jessica to take me. It's not her fault. I didn't even tell her. We got this. Here." Emily pulled out a folded sheet of paper from her back pocket. "I stuffed it down my pants when the police came. They didn't care about it when they strip-searched me at the precinct. I took it out first, and they must have thought it came from my pocket. They weren't watching too carefully."

Lauren cringed at Emily's matter-of-fact description of the strip search but took the paper. "This was your dad's list?" she whispered. "So these are safe-deposit box companies. Brian went from New York to Tortola then to Miami—the money could be in one of these."

"When we were in Tortola," Jessica said, "Brian told me it was an offshore banking country. That could be why he went there."

Lauren searched her memory to recall a class she'd taken in law school that touched on money laundering. "The real estate transactions could have disguised the movement of money. They could have been Arena's or Jordan Connors' buildings that one of them was selling back and forth to himself. Brian must have come back with clean financial instruments, deposits slips or bonds maybe. If these are the safe-deposit boxes where he put them, we can cut a deal now."

"You can't cut a deal unless you have something to give them," Jessica whispered. "If we can find whatever Brian brought back from Tortola, we can get out of this mess a lot more safely by giving them back. We need to call the Florida police to see if they have any of Brian's property from the hotel. Would a key have burned?"

"What are you talking about, Jessica? *Please*." Lauren folded the paper, all the night's fatigue and fear weighing on her.

Jessica grabbed Lauren's arm through the bars and hissed, "You don't get it, do you, Lauren? No one is going to let us go on with business as usual—not the police and not Arena. We can't walk out of here and get our lives back. Our old lives are *over*. We've only got one shot."

"You don't even know what you're talking about, what you're getting us into," Lauren growled. "You don't know what it is to deal with these people."

Lauren didn't say more, not in front of Emily. From the snarl on Jessica's face, Lauren guessed Jessica wanted to remind her that she'd watched Jordan Connors get killed yesterday. Lauren put the paper in her coat pocket and passed the McDonald's bag through the bars.

Emily grabbed it enthusiastically, "You don't know how disgusting the food is here and there's nothing to drink. When we first came, they brought stale bologna sandwiches and milk containers like in school—only warm. There's not even any water in the sink."

Lauren noticed the remains of several milk containers and sandwiches scattered under the benches. Emily retreated to a bench and pulled out the Styrofoam containers. She passed a coffee to a scantily clad prostitute who had shoved over to make room for her. The woman's bare legs were covered with oozing abscesses from shooting up. Emily rose and handed Jessica an orange juice then sat back down to eat companionably with the woman.

Jessica balanced the juice with one hand on a horizontal crossbar and pulled a square sticky note from her pocket. "Listen, Lauren, you've got to call Arena. Here's his number. If they don't hear from me, they'll assume I don't want to talk to them. They could decide to kill us before I even get out of here."

"Goddammit, Jessica. We don't have any way to protect ourselves."

"Jordan was one of them—a gambler, a hustler. They kill their own all the time. Not people like us, not if we cooperate." Jessica looked around and stopped talking as a woman paced nearby. She looked back at Lauren and whispered, "Please, Lauren, tell Arena I'm in the hospital with depression or something. We don't want him to know where I am. He might have people here."

"Okay, okay," Lauren said, even though she doubted Arena looked at them as civilians who he wouldn't mess with. *People like us* didn't have contracts out on them. But that was yet another thing Lauren wouldn't say now. "I'll call and tell them we don't know anything, make them understand we're not a threat—but that's it. I haven't made a decision about what to do."

"Just get us time."

"Okay." Lauren put the phone number in her pocket with the sheet Emily had given her. "Look, it may be too early, but I've got to get back upstairs and see what I can find out about the DA's plans for your case."

"What are you going to do?"

"You have no criminal records, and we'll claim you were collecting items that belonged to Brian under the logical assumption that you were welcome at the office. I don't think they know about you being on Brian's computer. So the worst scenario is that the judge lets you go on bail while the DA brings the case to a grand jury or comes up with plea bargains. But release with charges still pending is not what I'm looking for. With all the problems we have, I want this case to disappear—completely and immediately. Steve will get the DA to drop these charges tonight or, come hell or high water, I'm gonna drag him over the coals like he'll never forget."

Lauren's anger closed her throat, feeling as if it could strangle her. She watched Emily sharing food with a prostitute who could easily have TB. "He's screwed with my kid for the last time, Jessica."

CHAPTER 30

In his bedroom, Carl reached sleepily for the phone that pinged next to his head on the nightstand. Gooseflesh rose on his bare chest as he swung his feet out of bed. Clearing his head, he looked out the window at sun-sparkled river water, a white ferry zipping across it. He clicked on the phone. "CB, what's up?"

"After you left, I found out what's going on. Pedro Arena was hanging around with a couple of the guys. He's one of Jorge's cousins, you met him. I opened a bottle of Dom for them, figured you could expense it. Daisy did some lap dances. A little cocaine and you know. Call me Father CB."

"That's amazing."

"Everyone likes a freebie," CB answered.

"What did he confess?"

"Weapons. It's all about a weapons deal."

"You're shitting me?"

"A war is close to breaking out between Arena's crew and a China-town Tong. The Tong is working for hire. The money that's missing? The Chinese poker player, Xi Wen, shipped out a whole boatload of weapons, literally. Missile launchers, grenades, long guns, that kind of thing. The Chinese guy is pissed because the weapons are out of his hands, millions of dollars in merchandise. He and the Tong think Arena is setting them up for a rip-off because he's late with his payment. The weapons are coming by boat from China to Europe and then they're supposed to go to Africa but they're sitting out in the ocean somewhere waiting for the signal about payment.

"And that's not all. Arena was the middleman and took half payment from the buyers. Jorge Arena told me the Africans who are buying the weapons don't know they're out their money yet, but they're worried because their delivery schedule's been pushed back. They're holding Jorge Arena's nephew for collateral. When they find out the money's missing, you can add a bunch of crazy pirates after Arena's ass … if Arena's sister-in-law doesn't kill him first for getting her son beheaded."

"So, they used Jordan's site—a rigged poker game—to do a weapons deal."

"It looks that way. For a smart dude, Jordan was unbelievably stupid. I don't think he had it in him to be part of this on purpose."

Carl agreed.

"Bottom line, Arena's under a lot of pressure. You better be careful. Anyone who gets in the middle of this crossfire is going to be in deep shit."

Carl started composing a to-do list in his head. "Good job, CB. I'll be coming up later when you open."

Carl hung up and called Rick to let him know what was going on, then emailed the ASAC, who would want a face-to-face. The City's medical examiner and forensics team were still working on the Chinatown murder and the Westchester medical examiner had Jordan's body. But any decisions on how they would deal with a weapons sale to probable terrorists or a terrorist state, two people dead already, was way above Carl's and the ASAC's pay grade.

Carl checked his Gossamer to make sure it was fully charged. It was a handheld device he could fit in a jacket pocket. Carl hadn't carried it with him yet because it was risky in case anyone wanted to check him for wires or weapons. But the Gossamer could identify all the cell phones in a room and allow him to key in on the telephones that belonged to Jorge Arena and whoever else in his crew came to the club. Then he'd be able to identify their phones and track their whereabouts. It could be valuable if a gang war were about to go down. They'd be able to see if a wave of Arena's guys were headed in the same direction. Carl would need to carry the Gossamer with him today. He could anticipate that directive from the ASAC.

Carl's phone rang again, the ASAC calling.

***

The courtroom was bustling when Lauren returned from the pens, following behind a line of male prisoners who climbed the stairs and filed inside. The cuffed prisoners took seats on a pew against the wall next to the door they had entered through. Lauren waited just inside the door until the current case finished. A baby-faced teenager stood at the defense table with hands clasped in front of him. His lawyer and the ADA talked with the judge at the bench.

"Okay," the judge said when the lawyers broke from their huddle. "Bail will be set at fifteen thousand dollars."

A middle-aged woman wailed in the gallery (the bail might as well have been a million), while the defense lawyer whispered something in the kid's ear. The kid nodded and put his hands behind his back. The court officer recuffed him. His face pained, the kid turned and chucked his chin goodbye to his mother before the court officer escorted him past Lauren and back to the bullpens.

Lauren took the opportunity between cases and looped around the defense and prosecution table. She approached a dark-mustached court officer who sat at a paper-covered desk next to the judge's bench. "Good morning. Do you have the charging papers on Jessica and Emily Silverman yet?"

He scanned a computer screen. "Not calendared yet. The rap sheet, bail investigation, and the DA's complaint have to come in before it gets to us. Are you gonna appear for both of them?"

"Yes."

He shoved two forms at her. "Notice of Appearance" was printed across the top of each form. Lauren filled them out and gave them back, now officially the attorney on the case.

"The clerk will post their names and docket numbers on the wall outside when all the papers are done. Then it'll be a couple more hours before the case is called." He chewed on a paper clip. "Won't be before tonight."

She thanked him and left. No matter how frustrating, there was nothing more she could do at court. Another shift of ADAs would be on duty by nighttime. Until then, she couldn't even chat with the ADA on the case to get more information, begin negotiations, and make sure he or she understood the ridiculousness of the charges. She had to get out of there or become one more pacing mother.

At the courthouse lobby's revolving doors, Lauren looked out before leaving the building. The cement landscape had brightened and filled with people heading to the area's courts and government offices. She walked two blocks to a Swedish lunch and coffee shop on Reade Street, across from the Federal Building. She ordered a latte and deliberated about the risks and benefits of where to sit. She decided on a quiet table near large windows with a view of the Federal Building that took up the entire block across the street. The window would allow her to assess whether anyone was watching her, with minimal risk. She didn't think she'd be gunned down through the windows in the heavily guarded area where cars were blocked from entering and explosive-sniffing dogs patrolled. It wasn't as if a person cashing in on a contract would be a suicide bomber who'd make a move here.

She dialed the offices of Cohen & Cohen. Especially during trials, litigators had to do their office work before and after the nine-to-five court day. With Brian no longer there to do all the actual work of the firm, she hoped Steve would be working and answering his own phone before his linebacker secretary arrived.

***

At the offices of Cohen & Cohen, Steve and Nicole pushed through double glass doors. Steve carried a brown paper bag containing coffee and bagels they would share before Nicole took a cab downtown to her own office.

Anger twisted his loyal secretary's face when she answered an apparently unwelcome call. "He's not here," the secretary said, looking up, watching Steve and Nicole approach down the hall. Bright sun shone through the floor-to-ceiling window where the hallway ended next to Steve's office. The sun silhouetted her face. Steve squinted against the glare as she mouthed, *Lauren*.

Steve dropped his attaché on a chair in front of his secretary's desk and handed Nicole the paper bag. Nicole frowned, her keen blue eyes following him.

Steve snapped his fingers and pointed toward a phone on a table that separated two waiting-area chairs outside his office. The secretary nodded.

"Please hold," the secretary pushed a button without waiting for a reply, and Steve walked to the phone.

Steve nodded, and they simultaneously returned to the line with Lauren, avoiding a double click.

"I take it you are aware of what happened last night," Lauren said to Steve's secretary.

"Yes, we are," the secretary responded, coolly.

"I need to speak to Steve."

"He has a trial starting in Wisconsin today. He's en route."

"Listen to me," Lauren snarled, "I don't care where he is or what he's doing. He needs to call the district attorney and make it fucking clear that this was all a mistake and that the charges need to be dropped."

"Excuse me?!" the secretary asked, as Steve's insides gnarled with rage, too.

"I said he better make it fucking clear." Lauren's voice raised, "Take this down. He makes this thing disappear, or I'll take out a full-page ad in the *New York Law Journal*. It will outline in detail the entire sordid story about how he treats the widow and orphan of his tragically killed law partner. Then I'll call every lawyer who refers him cases and make sure he never gets another fucking case in his life. Do you have that down?"

"Yes." The secretary's eyes met Steve's. He turned his back, not letting his secretary see just how truly fucking pissed he was by the nerve of that bitch.

"Good," Lauren said, curtly.

The phone cut off in Steve's ear without a goodbye. The secretary looked at the receiver before she, then Steve, hung up.

Nicole strode to Steve's side, her face red with her own anger for reasons he couldn't fathom. She spoke intently in his ear, "What the hell is going on?"

Steve grabbed her upper arm and pulled her into his office, away from his secretary's inquisitive eyes. "It's nothing."

"What did you do, Steve?" she asked as the door closed behind him. "What the fuck did you do?"

CHAPTER 31

Lauren caught her breath and looked out at the empty tables in the restaurant, a little shocked at herself. She had no idea whether her call would work—but it had felt great. Just a few days ago, she would have thought that cursing was unbecoming, unprofessional, but she had a feeling it was just right. She didn't have time to put on airs with that lowlife scum bucket and his minion secretary. While she still had the courage, Lauren pulled out the paper Jessica had given her. The phone number was in Emily's handwriting, and the catharsis Lauren had just felt vanished. These people had seen Emily. Emily had been completely at their mercy when they came to the house. The thought of Emily face-to-face with a killer sent a rush of terror through her. It would happen again if she didn't do something.

Lauren's mind kept replaying what Jessica had said—that their old lives were gone and they'd never get them back. Her chest hollowed out with anxiety as she called Arena's phone number, doing it now before she lost her nerve. She consciously moderated her breathing, hiding her fear.

"*Quién es?*" asked a man who answered the phone.

"My name is Lauren. I'm Brian Silverman's ex-wife. His wife is sick."

"What is wrong with her?" the man with a Spanish accent asked, suspicious, perhaps unsure whether Jessica had called the police, and Lauren was a cop. Jessica's excuse of depression was too weak. "She's sick. She can call you tomorrow."

"No," he said quickly. "Can you take care of her business?"

Lauren paused. The whole thing was insane. She wanted no part of this. But between Jessica and her, really, who was better equipped to handle it? "Yes," she said despite herself. "I can." She reasoned it out: convincing people—persuasive argument—was her strong suit. She suddenly felt more confident. If there was any chance of salvaging their lives, this might be it. "I can take care of her business, but she doesn't know anything, and you and I have our own business. I don't appreciate being threatened."

He paused. "No more talk on the telephone. You meet me. There is a bar. You go there at one o'clock and we will discuss it." He told Lauren the address.

"Are you Mr. Arena?"

"When you get there, you tell my cousin you are meeting Lucho. I am Lucho." The phone clicked.

***

At one o'clock, Lauren's Uber arrived at a long block perpendicular to the Intrepid Air and Space Museum. Lauren got out at the corner next to a car wash, allowing the Uber to continue up Twelfth Avenue. She noted her surroundings warily: an industrial street with a shuttered bagel factory, dirty warehouse buildings, and an empty outdoor parking lot. She came to a gray-and-purple awning without a name on it. It was as if the difficulty in finding the place morphed those who entered it into VIPs, in on a secret. She looked around. A half block away, groups of tourists waited at the light to cross the highway to the Intrepid. What could really happen to her in midtown Manhattan with so many pedestrians passing back and forth outside?

She opened the smoked-glass door. The place was John Wick sleek inside, peppered with tall glass tables and bar-height chairs, all vacant. A small, blond man, wearing a sky-blue muscle T-shirt, pulled on a black suit jacket as he came from behind the empty bar. Red backlights highlighted liquor bottles on the wall behind the bar and gave him a red tinge for a moment. He was the only one there.

Lauren had dressed down, wearing jeans, sneakers, and a work shirt under her wool peacoat. Still, he approached her as if she were a health department inspector. "May I help you?"

She nervously cleared her throat with a cough in a way she never had to do in court. "Um, I'm meeting Lucho here."

He paused, eyebrows arched, a flicker of fear passing across his crystal-blue eyes. But the expression was gone instantly, replaced by a smile that exceeded the occasion. He led her to a seat at the bar. "Sit down, sit down. I'm CB. I didn't know Lucho was coming. He's not here yet. Sorry, we're not even open yet, or I would give you some chips to play upstairs. We have blackjack, slots, roulette, poker."

Lauren nodded her head politely. Now that she'd said she was meeting Lucho, she was no longer the building inspector. Lauren figured CB took her for a girlfriend of Lucho's.

CB walked back around the counter, "What'll you have?" But before she could respond, his eyes cut toward the door. "Lucho. *Hola.*"

The well-groomed man who entered had dark eyes, an angular face, and thick, wavy hair to the nape of his neck. From Lauren's limited knowledge of Spanish, she thought CB was saying that he'd been keeping her company while she waited. She didn't need to know any Spanish to tell that the new arrival scared him. Like CB, Lucho also wore a suit, a very expensive suit. There was no sign of kindness in his eyes as he nodded at her, but she hoped the way he dressed meant they would talk business in a businesslike manner.

Lucho held his hand out, signaling toward a hallway. "Please," he said.

She walked ahead of Lucho down a hallway with tiny lights at the floor-boards. They reached a door with a small plaque beside it that said, OFFICE.

A room where no one will hear me scream. She forced the thought away, chiding herself. There would be no screaming.

When she came to the door, Lucho stepped close behind her, reached around and opened it. Her spine stiffened and she quickly walked inside to put space between their bodies. The small, square room was furnished with a glass desk, telephone, and a couple of cushioned chairs. Mirrors lined the walls. Through the mirror, she saw Lucho close the door behind him, scanning her, head to toe, a sexual assessment. "Your clothes, take them off."

"What?" The blood left Lauren's face. She turned back toward the door. She would never get past him.

"Your clothes." He smoothed his mustache, enjoying himself, although there was no hint of a smile.

He stepped closer and she stepped backward, hitting the wall.

"Strip."

Her heart hammered uncontrollably. "No."

Then he was across the little room and on her. She screamed and, without conscious thought, her fist shot out and connected hard with his jaw. She was stronger than she looked, and his head snapped back.

She pushed and tried to get around him to the door. She was almost there when he grabbed her, jerked her arm hard backward and threw her against the glass desk. Its edge painfully grooved the front of her thighs and she was bent over it, her back to him. His body pressed against hers and she cried out, trying to get away from him. Cold metal pressed against her neck. She heard the click of a safety and saw the glint of his gun reflected in the mirror.

"Shut up," he barked in her ear.

His entire body against hers, there was nothing more she could do. His hand reached around and roughly opened her shirt buttons. He grabbed one breast then the other and ran his palm down her belly. He opened her pants and his cold fingers reached her crotch. She began to cry, as he lingered there, feeling, groaning, before taking his hand out of her pants. He ran his palm down her pants legs and up her back.

"I need to check for wires, *mamita*. And you are *muy hermosa*." She felt his breath on her ear. "It is too bad so much money you owe. I would love *chocha* instead—you know, pussy. A little bargain. But Jorge would be very angry. He would say no *chocha* is worth twelve million dollars."

Then he was off her. Her chest heaving, Lauren righted herself and turned around, buttoning her blouse and zipping her pants, feeling as if every inch of her skin had been invaded. Lucho smiled as he watched her.

She silently talked to herself: *Do not panic, Lauren; if you're going to get out of here alive, you cannot panic.* "We don't have your money," she said as calmly as she could.

He tucked his gun into a shoulder holster inside his suit jacket. "But you will get it for Jorge. It is his."

"We don't know where it is, *if* Brian even had it."

"He brought bonds from Tortola. You can be sure of that. Now, you will complete delivery or you will die. Emily, too." His hips thrust out almost imperceptibly. "And that young one, she will get the *beecho* first, then I will bite off … how you say? Her neeples … before I kill her. My English not so bad, eh?" He smiled at Lauren as her face froze with horror. He watched her terror with the gusto of a customer at a strip joint.

She pushed words out. "I'll try."

"Jorge say to tell you he will buy the karate man's contract as commission for you if you bring our bonds. Jorge is much nicer person than me, but if you fail, Jorge's own family is at risk. Family always comes first, and he will not accept failure. You have two days, then you call. Do not think of calling the police." His hard eyes stared deeply into hers before he took her face in his hands and spoke in her ear, "The police cannot protect your little girl. She will never allow it, *si*? She will run away, back to her boyfriends, and I will be waiting for her and you. You call when you have the bonds. Here is a new number." He handed Lauren a card with a phone number and opened the door. "Go." Lauren wanted to remain calm but couldn't stop herself—she ran, feeling his eyes on her as she fled down the hallway. Her sobs began as she neared the door to the vestibule that led to the street. Almost to safety, the door opened. She slammed headlong into an entering man and let out a panicked half scream. *They weren't letting her go, they'd let her run toward safety for the fun of it.* The man held her arm tightly. She struggled, looking up.

Carl. Her head reared back. His eyes showed an instant's surprise. Then the expression was gone.

***

Over Lauren's shoulder, Carl saw Lucho's appraising gaze, familiar from surveillance photos. Lucho had one hand low behind his thigh. Carl started to reach for his gun but stopped himself. The place would explode right there with Lauren in the line of fire and Carl a step behind the man who already had his gun out. Carl loosened his grip on Lauren's arm.

"Get off me," she screamed hysterically, pushing past him and running out of the sports bar.

He looked after her for a second as casually as he could while he did a mental check on his own breathing. Then he turned back and walked inside, the door closing behind him. "You must have sold her one fucked-up piña colada."

CB approached, nervously. "Lucho, this is my assistant manager, Carlos."

"*Mucho gusto.*" Carl offered Lucho his hand to shake in the hope that he would put away his gun.

Lucho nodded and grunted acknowledgment. He didn't shake, but Carl breathed easier as he watched Lucho holster his gun inside his jacket.

"*Nos vemos,*" Lucho told CB.

Lucho gave Carl a long look as he brushed past close enough to invade Carl's body space. Carl felt the instinctive urge to attack or step away, both of which he resisted as Lucho walked out.

Carl's back bristled with warning. He moved quickly from the window toward the bar, picturing shots fired at him from the street even though the window was opaque. Carl tried to calm down and reason things out. He hadn't blown his cover. Lucho was just an asshole, pissing on bushes. Carl stepped behind the bar where CB had retreated. "What happened to that woman, CB?"

"*No sé.* How should I know?"

Carl grabbed a fistful of CB's Day-Glo T-shirt. "What do you mean, how should you know?"

CB struggled and landed on a stool, which rocked backward and nearly dumped him off before he regained his balance with a hand on the bar. He lowered his voice and angrily said, "How would I know? I heard her scream once. She came out crying. So, Lucho gave her some *beecho*, that's it. A quickie."

Carl barely kept his fist from crushing CB's face. He yanked the smaller man off his stool again and lifted him close. "Listen, you slimy motherfucker, you see her again, you text me, you hear? With a 911 code. You got me?"

"Yeah, I got you." CB pushed Carl's hand away. He took a step farther back from Carl. "So what's up with the girl, *compadre*?"

"I'm not your *compadre*."

Carl turned from CB, breathing hard, trying to come down from his last moments of panic. He leaned against the bar, his eyes on the ceiling. "Did you find out anything else about the deal?"

"They're trying to arrange a money drop-off with the Chinese dude's group. They want me to come. They need a crew they can trust not to rip them off. It's always hairy when money's exchanged. But some bitch is still supposed to have it." CB's eyes opened wide then narrowed. "Oh, I get it, I get it. That was the bitch, wasn't it? You have some out-of-control shit happening. You've got a whole international gang war about to break out over that money, plus now you're going to have ATF and Homeland Security wanting a piece of the weapons action, and there's some *gringa* running around ready to get herself killed. And you're thinking you've got to do something about it, but it could blow the bust." CB laughed. "You're all fucked up, aren't you?"

"Shut up, CB."

Carl walked away, down the hall. He wanted privacy to call Rick and let him know about Lucho being there. Carl pulled the Gossamer from inside his leather overcoat. At least he'd be able to identify Lucho's cell phone now, given that only three people other than Carl had been in the room and he already knew Lauren's and CB's phones. Still, would he let Rick or the ASAC know about Lauren? Carl needed time to think. He was shell-shocked from seeing her. She thought he was one of them and that he'd betrayed her. And it was true. He'd betrayed her all along and now he'd failed her. What if she really had been raped? He shook his head in rage and disgust at himself for being unable to protect her.

So now what were his options? They could get a warrant to listen in on her telephone. But at this point, Lauren was in too deep and so was he. It might not exonerate her, and the most likely thing she would say on audio was that Carl had been stalking her. That could easily get Carl fired or out-stationed to the North Pole. Carl's after-hours surveillance had violated the ASAC's orders. He'd gone totally off the reservation.

Carl entered the office and took in the sight of an overturned chair. He groaned. Carl's gut had been right about Lauren being involved. And CB was right. Everything had spun out of control. Lauren had come across information about Arena's money, or she had his money. Assisting weapons dealers would land her in prison for decades if it didn't get her killed.

Carl righted the chair and sat down at the desk, inspecting the read-outs on the Gossamer. He felt a glimmer of relief. Now that he could follow Lucho's and Lauren's movements, he'd know if the two were near each other and he'd have a chance at protecting her. He lay his forehead on his arms. That was a ridiculous plan. If the two did meet again, he couldn't ensure he'd be close enough to help. Rick had been on point all along. Carl really liked her, and it was interfering with his ability to think.

There was only one thing he could do: he had to get her out of town, out of the picture, and out of his head. For both their sakes, Carl had to warn Lauren to lay low and stay out of things. That was the only way they'd both get their lives back on track. And there was another reason why he had to talk to her—maybe a less important reason but it was driving Carl just as hard: he had to erase the expression of terror and betrayal from her eyes. The memory of it was already haunting him.

CHAPTER 32

The West Side Highway slipped by in a blur of speed and tears. Lauren hugged her arms and rocked in the back seat of a cab. She could still feel where Lucho's fingers had touched her. She could still see the images he'd painted of doing worse to Emily.

And then, Carl. She couldn't believe she'd been so stupid. Carl was the reason Lucho knew so much about her. She'd never seen Carl before Brian died. Then, suddenly, he was everywhere. And she, like an idiot, had told him practically everything about herself. But worse than that, she'd told him everything about Emily. *Fucking shit.* She let out a sob, hating herself.

Now, if she didn't do what these people wanted—that bastard Lucho was right—there was no way she could keep Emily safe. And Jessica had been right, too. There was no going back. Their lives had been snatched out from under them like a tablecloth in a magic trick. They had to find the bonds Lucho was talking about, and they had to figure out how to get them to Jorge Arena without putting themselves in even more danger. Lauren only hoped that Jessica was also right that the Arenas wouldn't kill civilians as readily as they killed their own, and that they'd think of her as a civilian.

Not sure of that at all, Lauren peered out the back window as her cab reached Washington Heights. There were a lot of cars behind hers. She couldn't tell if anyone had followed, but did it matter? They probably knew where she lived.

When she was alone in her empty apartment, she stripped off her clothes and turned on the shower, hoping to scrub away Lucho's hands. She stepped in, and the warm water covered her exhausted body—she hadn't slept in thirty-six hours, and she closed her eyes, nearly swooning with fatigue. The *Psycho* shower scene flashed across her mind. Only it was a gun and Lucho now. Yelping, Lauren grabbed a towel. She tried to calm herself as she dried off, then dressed.

She had to forget about Lucho and get down to business. Fighting through her near-fugue state of sleep deprivation and shock, she picked up her shoulder bag from the couch and took out the printed page that Emily had given her. She had guessed right about the bonds. Bearer bonds could be cashed by whoever had them, and they could be in huge denominations, so they were easy to transport. She scanned the list of company names, numbers, and what looked like code names next to them. Sitting at the table, she began plugging the company names one at a time into Google.

She hoped only one of the companies was in Miami. The first one was in Nevada, the next was in New Jersey. One didn't come up on Google at all. Lauren told herself she'd come back to it. She typed in the next entry: Jansen-White, Inc. A glossy website came up, depicting a reception area of red carpet and shiny chrome. It was a safe-deposit box company with a location in Miami. Pay dirt.

Lauren dialed the phone number. A woman answered in a sing-song receptionist's voice, her accent slightly southern. "Jansen-White, may I help you?"

"I'm considering renting a safe-deposit box."

"Yes, ma'am."

"How does it work? I've never rented from a private company before."

"Oh, well, it's very simple and designed with the client's absolute security and privacy in mind. The prices range from five hundred to two thousand dollars per year, depending on the size of the box. We have a vault that utilizes state-of-the-art security equipment and our premises are manned by an armed guard and subject to video surveillance at all times."

The woman's voice took on the intonations of a memorized recitation. "In addition, we guarantee your personal privacy by allowing you to gain access to your safe-deposit box through use of a PIN or code name that you choose, and only you know. Of course, we have a double key system. You have one key and our second key is required to gain access, which can happen only if you correctly input your PIN or code name and it corresponds to your box number."

Lauren looked down the list at the entries next to Jansen-White, obviously the box number and a nauseatingly cute code name: HazelNuke. Jessica's dogs. Now all she and Jessica would have to do was find the key to box number 276. Lauren thanked the woman, promising to call back after she'd had a chance to think over her safety-deposit box needs, and hung up.

Lauren looked up the rest of the companies and found one other in Miami, which didn't seem as likely. MapQuest put it a full hour away from the hotel where Brian had been staying, and Brian hadn't rented a car on his Visa or PayPal cards. Jansen-White was midway between Brian's hotel and the airport. She and Jessica would go there first.

Lauren searched flights to Miami. A morning flight wouldn't leave time for Jessica and Emily to make up for lost sleep after their ordeal, but they had to get to Miami before close of business tomorrow. After Lauren had selected flights and paid for them, she pulled up her Outlook calendar and began calling her coworkers to ensure her Family Court cases were covered for the rest of the week.

***

Braving the slow evening rush hour in a taxi, Lauren returned to the Criminal Court building. Her eyes felt weak and puffy from lack of sleep and crying earlier in the day. She paused outside the Arraignment Part and breathed deeply, trying to clear her head of the caffeine jitters. Caffeine was the only thing keeping her awake and oriented, but it also exacerbated her anxiety. A computer-printed court calendar hung on the wall, listing the names and docket numbers of the next fifty defendants to be called for arraignment. Emily and Jessica weren't on it.

Lauren turned back and waited in a line of a half-dozen people at the Correction Department information window. She gave a court officer Emily and Jessica's names through a grating in the plexiglass window. The man typed then stared at a computer screen. "Their prints are here but they don't have docket numbers yet."

"Is there anywhere I can check on the holdup?"

The man smiled, half-heartedly. "I wouldn't call this much of a holdup. If they don't get to court by morning, then maybe it's a holdup."

Lauren leaned toward the speak-hole. "There *is* a twenty-four-hour rule."

"That and a Metrocard will get you on the subway, Counselor."

Lauren sighed and began to walk away

"Counselor."

Lauren turned back to the window.

He pointed to his left. A few yards down, a door said AUTHORIZED PERSONNEL ONLY. He leaned forward. "That's the clerk's office, where they put all the forms in the right order and assign the case a docket number."

Lauren smiled, wondering what changed his heart. "Thanks."

She went to the door, knocked, and walked in. Four people worked at desks amidst a blizzard of paper. Despite the room's disorder, the clerks seemed efficient. Lauren spoke to a middle-aged woman at the first desk who had what seemed a permanent expression of exasperation on her face.

"We don't have your clients' files yet. The DA's prep unit has to finish with the files and send them to us." She looked at her watch. "They better hurry up, too, or the cases won't be called tonight."

Lauren lowered her voice and spoke as if confiding a painful secret. It wasn't difficult. "Emily Silverman's my daughter. What can I do? I'm not a criminal lawyer."

"Oh." The woman's eyes softened. "Look, the ECAB room is on the second floor—that stands for Early Case Assessment Bureau—the DA's prep unit. Technically, they don't like it when defense attorneys show up there, but sometimes if you're very polite, they'll tell you what's going on and even rush the paperwork for you. You can try. But get it done fast, honey."

Lauren thanked her and rushed out. She took the stairs and made her way down a hallway to the ECAB room. Inside, plastic chairs lined the wall where a sprinkling of complaining witnesses waited to meet with the staff that prepared and investigated the criminal complaints. A uniformed cop sat at an information window, his hazel eyes cynical but not unkind. She recognized the attitude of a thirty-year city employee. "What can I do for you?" he asked, gruffly.

"Could you check on the status of Emily and Jessica Silverman? I'm their attorney and there seems to be a holdup."

He swiveled in his chair and shouted into the air of a large desk-filled room behind him. "Anyone got Emily and Jessica Silverman?"

A voice shouted in response. "I had it, but Harold took it back."

He swiveled toward Lauren again. "Jeremy Harold is the ADA covering it." A hint of disdain in the cop's voice spoke volumes—the ADA's own side didn't like him. "Go figure why he pulled the file. Usually it's because there's something they screwed up or something that came up since they submitted it." He leaned forward, conspiratorially. "My advice is that you march over to Eighty Centre Street, seventh floor, straight to his office, and find out what's happening. I don't know you, so I figure you're new around here. My advice: put some fire under his ass."

Imagining missing their morning flight to Miami and fearful that the file had been pulled because they'd added a hacking charge, Lauren rushed down the stairs and through the lobby. Outside, the empty sidewalks and moonless sky took her aback. She hadn't realized it had gotten dark. She stood in the deep shadow of the Criminal Court Building. Not a soul walked the sidewalk. No cars passed. On the far side of the pocket park, its night-black pond the size of a backyard swimming pool, stood the Family Court where she spent her weekdays. She felt as if she were glimpsing her past life from a great distance. She yearned for normality.

She turned left under the pall cast by the Criminal Court Building. She wished the Criminal Court and brute-modern courts on the square had been built like the Federal Courthouse and New York Supreme Court, two blocks up. At least their wide stone staircases and columned facades hinted at a civilization that protected people. Lauren crossed Hogan Street, an empty lane running for the length of one block next to the criminal courthouse. Up ahead, 80 Centre Street, normally bustling with activity in its city government offices, would be virtually empty too. As Lauren walked, she tried to see around doorways for anyone hiding before she reached them. Trying to look natural, like any woman checking behind her on a dark street, she glanced backward every few steps, looking for anyone following.

She sighed with relief when she reached 80 Centre Street's ornate revolving door. She pushed, but it didn't budge. A sign stood on a pedestal in the lobby just inside the door: "Nighttime Access on Baxter Street."

Baxter Street? That was the narrow street that ran behind the line of courthouses. It fronted a park with a garden and playground that filled with Chinatown residents and Chinese music during the day. But the street was a no-man's-land, empty at night. Lauren groaned but quickly doubled back. Under normal circumstances, she would have been nervous walking alone on such a deserted block at night, but now her breathing shallowed and she found herself trembling. She'd had all the fear she could take for one day.

The thought occurred to her: if Arena's people saw her entering the district attorney's office, they might think she was cooperating with the DA against them. Lauren's throat and jaw tightened. They might shoot her at any time. She glanced behind her, quickly. No one.

But just as she turned her head to look forward again, a shadow moved at the periphery of her vision, in a doorway across the street. Her heart hitched.

She picked up her pace, straining to hear if there were footsteps behind her. Only the click of her own heels echoed off the dark buildings. She didn't know whether to run or try to act as if she hadn't seen. She looked back across the narrow street. The shadow moved again, separated from the building. A man crossed the street toward her.

She took off, hearing the squeak of sneaker rubber behind her now. She didn't look back. She sprinted, focusing on the building that housed the district attorney's office. The entrance would be just around the corner, a half block away. Lauren picked up speed, sure she could make it, even in heels.

She heard and felt the man right behind her. A hand grabbed her. She flailed her arm backward and twisted to the left to break his grip. Her right fist shot out, aimed for where his face would be.

Her fist slammed into his nose with a burst of power born of years of weightlifting, boxing classes, and adrenaline. She felt bone break under her knuckles. He let out a grunt and released her. She screamed, terrorized to see Carl again. But in her moment of opportunity, she pushed away from him using his body weight to launch herself backward into a pivot. Then she broke into a run.

She heard Carl run a few steps after her, calling her name. But twenty strides and she was around the corner and in the revolving door of the district attorney's office—with no idea how she would ever get out again.

CHAPTER 33

A security guard manned a beat-up desk. He looked up, seeming to assess her in her lawyer's suit, her face probably flushed and panicky.

"Everything all right, Counselor?"

Lauren's heart beat fiercely as she forced herself to walk toward him at normal speed across an ornate lobby with intricately carved vaulted ceilings. She calmed her breathing the best she could. "I got spooked out there, I guess. It's so dark, and a man surprised me. He stepped out of a doorway and asked for money."

"Do you want me to call the police? That's not the same as begging—scaring people."

Her breathing slowed down. "No."

He turned a ledger book toward her. "Going to the DA's?"

"Yes, thanks." She signed in and showed him ID.

He chucked his chin toward the back of the tall lobby. "That way."

She walked past the elevator banks to a corner of the lobby, out of earshot of the guard. Her heart still pounding, she dug her phone from her bag along with the piece of paper with Lucho's number. She had to make sure Arena didn't get the wrong idea from what just happened outside, or about her visit to the district attorney. She kept her eyes peeled on the elevators to make sure she didn't miss ADA Harold if he left for the courtroom.

Before hitting the phone's call button, she considered whether she should instead use this opportunity to ask for help. After all, she *was* in the DA's office. But she dismissed the idea. She couldn't do that, especially not while Jessica and Emily were in jail. If she raised one iota of suggestion that the supposed burglary had been connected to illegal gambling and murder, she wouldn't be able to pry Jessica and Emily out of jail. The DA would argue for high bail to give him time to investigate the true circumstances of the "break-in" and, add to that, the hacking. Then he might use the criminal charges and the bail as bargaining chips to make them cooperate, maybe without protection. No, there would be no help for them here.

She pressed the call button.

"Who is this?" A woman answered after a single ring.

"Lauren."

"Oh." She sounded interested, obviously knew her name. "Do you have something to tell Jorge?"

"Is he there?"

"No. You tell me."

"I'm working on things like I promised, but my daughter got herself into some trouble. Maybe you already know. I'm at the DA's office, I'm a lawyer. You guys know that. So don't get the wrong idea, please. I want the two days Lucho promised me."

"Okay …" The woman sounded bewildered.

"Are you authorized to say that? I don't know, maybe that's a stupid question. If you aren't, are you going to tell me?" Lauren muttered almost to herself, "This is crazy. I don't even know who I'm speaking to."

"I am authorized. You have nothing to worry about."

The call disconnected. Lauren hung up. That had to be good enough. She walked to the elevators and rode to the seventh floor in search of Jeremy Harold.

***

The elevator let out on a small waiting area with worn upholstered chairs and one gray metal desk, New York City government décor. Lauren rang a night bell next to a door and waited, prepared to try a longer, more annoying ring if the first one failed.

A man in a dark suit and bow tie looked out, his face gaunt, nearly anorexic. "Yes?"

"Are you Jeremy Harold?"

"Yes, who are you?"

"I'm Lauren Davis. I'm on the Silverman case. I understand you have it."

He opened the door for her and turned away, apparently meaning for her to follow. He looked back at intervals as he walked down the hall. "It will be ready in a few minutes. You didn't have to come here."

"You're required to get them to a judge within twenty-four hours of arrest. I believe we've passed that."

"File a writ of habeas corpus if it suits you—the judges never grant them." He looked back again. "Anyway, something came up. It was in the defendants' interest that I follow up."

Lauren followed Harold into a small, windowless office, annoyed at his tone, but more worried that they'd added charges. "What came up?"

"We're trying to speak to the complainant."

"Does that mean Steve Cohen called?"

"Yes. He spoke to one of our case investigators by phone. I've been trying to reach him back to ask him to come in to speak to me, but he's out of town."

"Then someone from your office confirmed there was no burglary."

Harold moved behind his neat desk, a picture of a plain woman and child on one corner of it. "Our policy is that we will not accept a complaining witness' withdrawal of the complaint unless we see them in person. Otherwise, it would be far too easy to frighten witnesses and stymie our prosecutions."

"Harold," she leaned over his desk and said his name with the familiarity of a first name. He looked annoyed. She picked up the photograph of his family. "Listen to me, *Harold*, this is not a domestic violence case or extortion. This is a woman and a *child* with no previous record, who entered with a key for one final visit to the dead father's office to take home the family photos from his desk."

He grabbed the picture and replaced it. "Ms. Davis, is it?"

"Yes."

"As far as I'm concerned, there are no *children* in Criminal Court. If they're old enough to do the crime, they're old enough to do the time. I will not seek dismissal. And in anticipation of your next question, we will oppose transfer of Emily Silverman's case to Family Court. Now if you will excuse me, I will complete the paperwork and get it to ECAB. You can expect the case to be called within the next couple of hours after the support staff finishes with it."

"You've got to be kidding."

"I kid you not. I have not seen the complainant, bail will be set, and I will seek an indictment within the allotted time."

"Okay." Lauren forced herself to keep her mouth shut, knowing it was futile to argue with him. But she would get the case thrown out if it killed her, and she'd rip Harold to shreds in court while she was at it. Of course, she couldn't discount the power of Harold's pettiness or his home-court advantage, but at least Steve had called, and the computer hacking had flown under police radar.

When Lauren reached the lobby, a court officer with gun in holster was about to push through a revolving door to leave.

"Officer," she called to him.

He turned. "Yes?"

"If you're going back to One Hundred Centre, could I tag along?"

He smiled. "Sure. Be my guest. It's way too lonely out there for you to walk alone."

Lauren looked around as they walked Hogan then turned up Centre Street. She saw no one. Perhaps that was due to her armed escort, but she hoped it meant Arena had pulled the troops back.

Once inside, she thanked the officer and stopped at the lobby concession stand. She waited behind a Jheri-curled pimp who looked like a throwback to the seventies, obviously there to post bail. She hadn't known guys like that still existed. He pocketed his change and turned from the counter. His hot dog already midbite, he winked at Lauren with his mouth full before walking away.

She stepped up and bought half a dozen microwaved beef patties, potato chips, candy bars, and sodas before heading down to the bullpens to see her kid.

***

At a small hospital on Gold Street, Carl sat with his head back against an orange vinyl seat. An ice pack soothed the throbbing pain of his nose and covered his eyes, turning the florescent room blessedly dark. He had a bitch of a headache, and the ice itself was uncomfortably cold, but he needed to keep the swelling down as much as possible.

Carl had caught a cab from Centre Street for the five-minute drive to the hospital. Without an open store or restaurant in sight to ask for napkins, he had bled all over himself, destroying his favorite denim shirt and coating the front of his leather jacket. He couldn't help but be peeved at Lauren, even though it wasn't her fault. When she'd hit him, she'd been terrified. That was what got to him more than anything. It made him feel such a burning desire to save her, it was as if a hand were squeezing his heart and wouldn't let go—especially now that he knew he couldn't help her. Carl breathed deep through his mouth, longing for nasal passages. Damn, that woman could throw a punch.

He hadn't even begun to come up with an explanation to tell Rick and everyone else for his raccoon black eyes and nose swelled beyond recognition. He couldn't fabricate an incident of physical violence like a bar fight or make the story job-related. Everyone knew fights weren't his style and, if he claimed it had happened on the job, that would only add to the lies he couldn't explain away if discovered. It was amazing how the first untruth—even a lie of omission—could lead you into a bottomless pit of lies. Carl wished it could all just stop already, but he had to think of another lie by morning.

Carl fought with his impulse to get up and walk out of the hospital without waiting to get his nose knocked back into shape. Carl had listened to a dozen names called and cracked his eyes open long enough to see people who'd arrived after him going inside. He'd seen the triage nurse a long time ago, and she'd obviously deemed him among the less important cases. On top of everything, he would be exhausted tomorrow. He hoped he'd be able to keep his wits about him. Tomorrow would be busy as hell.

Things were heating up on the case, and he had to concentrate. The Arena bust wasn't going to happen the way the ASAC had planned when he placed Carl undercover. He wasn't going to agent bettors for Arena and Jordan. The weapons deal had trumped everything. The Bureau and ATF would try to bust Arena when he gave the money to the Tong. It was Carl's job to find out where and when the money exchange was supposed to happen. One moment of sloppiness on his part could cost his team the bust. He'd already done all the screwing up he could afford on one case.

Ironically, the key challenge for Carl would be to stay away from Lauren. He wasn't crazy, and he knew he'd already gone too far. He'd jeopardized his career and the entire operation trying to help her, and he'd failed completely at that. Now, he told himself repeatedly, he had to stay as far away from her as possible. He didn't have another career lined up if he screwed this one up. He liked her, but he liked his life too.

Of course, it might be too late for him. In the end, he could only wait and see whether Lauren got busted and dropped his name. Hopefully, for her sake and his, Lauren would stay out of the crossfire. She was a strong woman with strong survival instincts. The throbbing of his entire face proved that. And her survival instincts might be their best shot. If they were lucky, Lauren had gotten the message loud and clear to get out of Dodge and lay low while she still had the chance.

***

At 10:00 p.m. Emily, Jessica, and Lauren sat on a courtroom pew set aside for waiting prisoners. Handcuffed, Emily and Jessica stared from deeply circled eyes, their mouths hard-set with fatigue and fear. After watching half a dozen cases, they were the only prisoners left in the courtroom aside from the addict currently before the judge.

Jeremy Harold stood at the prosecution table. The judge of the evening—a tanned woman in her fifties with shoulder-length hair and stiff skin—spoke with an exacting tone, discussing bail. The current defendant had been unlucky enough to have a bag of heroin in her pocket when the police arrested both her boyfriend and her on domestic violence charges.

Jessica leaned over and whispered, "This judge is tough."

"None of the drug and theft cases are like yours," Lauren answered.

"If there's bail, we have to go back inside while you get the money?" Emily spoke, tearfully, grasping Lauren's hand.

Before Lauren could answer, the bridge officer called out from where he stood in front of the judge's bench, "Jessica Silverman and Emily Silverman. Docket numbers ending in three-five-eight and three-five-nine."

"Don't worry," Lauren whispered in Emily's ear.

A court officer uncuffed Jessica and Emily. He led them to the defense table. Lauren stood to Emily's left, nearest the prosecutor.

Harold glanced disparagingly at Lauren before he spoke to the judge. "The charge is Burglary and Criminal Trespass, both in the third degree. The People are asking three thousand dollars bail for Jessica Silverman and five thousand dollars for Emily Silverman. The bail investigator could not establish Emily Silverman's community ties. No one answered at the telephone number she gave and she did not provide them with any others who could verify her residence and work or school enrollment. We did contact Jessica Silverman's parents, who verified she lives in Westchester County."

The judge looked to Lauren.

"Your Honor, I'm Emily Silverman's mother." Lauren glanced at Harold. His mouth opened then slammed shut. She looked back at the judge. "If the district attorney had checked his own paperwork he would have noticed that I was here at court and could not answer my home telephone. I'm not sure why no one called my cell phone."

The judge cracked a smile and turned to Harold. "Do you have an offer on this case?" She meant a plea bargain offer.

"No, Your Honor. We need more time to investigate the circumstances."

"Your Honor," Lauren broke in, "we would not accept any offer. The prosecutor cannot sustain his case and has skirted a violation of his professional duties here. Earlier today, his office received a call from the leaseholder of the commercial premises in which the defendants were found. The so-called complainant clarified that there had been no burglary or criminal trespass."

Harold cut in, "I have been unable to *see* the complainant to confirm this. My office has six days in which to indict on the felony charge after arraignment and we will continue our investigation."

"Your Honor, Jessica Silverman is the widow of an attorney who was killed in a fire two weeks ago. Emily is his daughter. They used the passkey to his law office and entered to gather his family photographs and personal effects. Jessica Silverman had previously received permission to do so. There was no unlawful entry, nor criminal intent. The arrest was a mistake, and the prosecutor knows that."

The judge looked at Emily as she spoke to Lauren. "Was that Brian Silverman?"

"Yes."

"A fine lawyer." The judge smiled sadly at Emily. "I read about it in the *Law Journal*." She turned to the ADA, whose face had flushed. She drew out her words, "Mr. Harold, let's not compound this family's tragedy nor a bad mistake. Were the defendants caught with any stolen property?"

"No, Your Honor." He rocked onto his toes as he spoke.

"Good." The judge leaned toward Harold, "If you get any real evidence, you can indict them, and we'll schedule an arraignment. I somehow doubt that will happen or that the defendants will be difficult to locate, if necessary."

"But, Your Honor—"

The judged raised her palm. "I am dismissing this case, Mr. Harold." She turned back to the defense table. "Good luck, ladies."

"Thank you, Your Honor." Lauren put her hand on Emily's back, "Let's go."

"We're done?"

"That's it."

A smile spread across Emily's face. Emily and Jessica grabbed each other and hugged, a closeness between them now that hadn't existed before.

Jessica reached out from the hug and squeezed Lauren's hand. "Thank you."

Lauren smiled and guided them toward the gallery.

***

Two bouncers stood nearby as CB, carrying the night's receipts, locked up the bar. They towered over him with the swagger of big men made bigger by shoulder holsters bulging under their jackets. But they also had an anxious edginess to them tonight, as if their swagger was cover for the fear that any sane person would feel if they worked for Arena under the present circumstances. CB activated the alarm system and made haste through the tinted-glass vestibule toward the front door before the alarm could engage.

"Shit!" The security guard on point stubbed his toe and had to right his balance as he pulled his gun out. "What the fuck?"

On the floor, he'd kicked a shoebox.

"Don't open it, don't open it." CB jumped back, thinking of explosives.

The box top was already ajar from the kick to its flank. They stopped and peered at its contents, shriveled and crusted in a nest of Godiva-chocolate tissue paper. A curdled-blood smell seeped out.

"Oh, fuck," CB bounced on the balls of his feet. "*Coño*. Holy shit."

Guns out, the three men backed into the bar.

His shirt plastered against his back, damp with sour sweat, CB called Jorge for instructions. The Tong had retaliated.

CHAPTER 34

"Good afternoon, ladies and gentlemen." The deep voice roused Jessica from sleep. "This is your captain again. We are currently approaching Miami International Airport, where the current local time is twelve twenty p.m."

Jessica stretched. She wore a sweatshirt and some high-water sweatpants, the bare skin between ankle and calf covered by leg warmers. Lauren's clothes. Jessica had thrown out the pants and blouse she'd slept in on the gritty bullpen floor. Even if she could have gotten them clean, which was doubtful, she could never have washed out the grimy memory of wearing them day and night hunkered down on the filthy cement. She'd washed her panties and bra, drying them with Lauren's blow-dryer, the bra still damp when she put it on. She still wore her own sneakers that she would throw away as soon as she got home to her closet, a closet smelling of cedar and normality. Jessica smiled. Brian would never have believed it if he'd seen her flying in Lauren's clothes, sitting in coach no less. But he wouldn't have believed her capable of handling anything she'd been through in the last few days. They both would have been wrong about that.

Jessica looked at Emily, who lay crunched in her seat between Lauren and her. Emily was fast asleep with her mouth open and her head in her mother's lap. The kid had been so courageous, and Jessica felt a pride in her that she'd never felt in anyone, Brian included.

Jessica and Lauren had decided to keep Emily with them for now, especially since they'd lost any possible tail, driving a roundabout route through endless city streets on the way from Lauren's apartment to Kennedy Airport. That was no guarantee of Emily's safety, but there was no guarantee anywhere. They both felt more comfortable keeping her close for as long as possible.

The plane dipped its wings toward blue ocean, the bright sun reflecting off the plane's wings. The ocean's beauty struck Jessica as surreal after her stay in hell, so recent that the smell still coated the inside of her nostrils. And things had only become more frightening last night when Emily left the room to shower and Lauren filled Jessica in about her own encounter with Lucho Arena. There was nothing Jessica feared more than being raped. She always imagined with dread trying to get help after a *second* rape. In her mind, at most, a rape victim got one chance to be believed. If even that. She hadn't. The thought of what happened to Lauren would have sent Jessica into a panic if she hadn't forced herself to focus. She reminded herself, repeatedly: if they stayed calm and did what needed to be done, it would all be over soon and they wouldn't be hurt.

Having no luggage to pick up, Jessica, Lauren, and Emily rushed through the airport terminal. Heavy tropical air hit them as they left the cool of the building. They grabbed a waiting cab.

Lauren leaned forward. "Four Hundred Northwest Second Avenue."

"That's thirty dollars."

"How much if we keep you for the afternoon, by the hour?" Lauren asked.

"A hundred bucks per."

"Okay." Lauren sat back in her seat.

"If we get done fast, are we going to the beach?" Emily asked.

"No," Lauren said.

Emily folded her arms in a fake sulk before breaking into a smile. All they planned to do was take care of business. Lauren had called, and the Miami police had said they had some of Brian's property. If they were lucky and found the key, they'd go to Brian's safe-deposit box and get on the first flight back to New York.

Emily whispered, "If we find the money, we should just keep it, run away to a tropical island or something."

Lauren laughed. "I think not."

"You'd miss your friends too much," Jessica said.

Emily leaned back low in her seat. "For twelve million dollars, even I could get over it."

Emily opened her window despite the cab's air-conditioning. Warm salt air rushed in, calming Jessica. She closed her eyes and leaned her head back for a moment, savoring the smell. But when the cab pulled in front of the police station, her nerves tingled with fear. If they couldn't find the bonds, what would they do? Lauren and she had agreed that there'd be no safe way to return to New York empty-handed. If they couldn't find the bonds, they would have to go to the police no matter what the cost to them. Lauren had already said she knew some criminal defense lawyers for Jessica, just in case. Lauren had said it lightly as if it were a joke, but both women knew it was all too real. Jessica had destroyed evidence of murder and obstructed justice. She'd watched enough *Law & Order* to know she would be in big trouble if they went to the cops.

Jessica wasn't the only one scared. Lauren had paced last night when she talked to Jessica alone. "What if we can't get them the money? What if we have to help the cops set up Arena to get you a no-jail deal? Would they even offer the Witness Protection Program for a gambling bust? You can't identify Jordan Connors' murderer. Even if they put us in Witness Protection, could I keep Emily in line? I don't think I'd ever close my eyes at night and be sure that Emily would be there in the morning. And would I practice law again? Would we have a choice of towns or jobs or homes? I don't think so."

Jessica cut her off, the one to calm Lauren down for a change. "We're going to find the bonds. It's not good to let our minds get ahead of us."

At the end of a short path, they entered a low-lying brick police station. A pregnant cop sat at a reception desk inside. She greeted them, checked their identification, and led them down a hallway to the property room. The property clerk shoved a form in front of Jessica through a gap in her bulletproof window. Jessica signed, and the clerk handed her a thick manila envelope. Then the pregnant cop brought them to an interview room with a steel table, barred windows, and a few wooden chairs.

Emily looked at the mirror that took up most of one wall and turned back to the cop. "Does anyone *not* know that's a two-way mirror?"

"You'd be surprised." The cop smiled. "They know, but lots of times people think no one is watching anyway. Do you?"

Jessica paused with the envelope in hand, her gut tightening. What would watching cops think of their plan to complete a failed gambling transaction? Why hadn't they left the precinct and rented a hotel room to look at the property? They weren't thinking enough like criminals. But then again, maybe this was the safest place, behind enemy lines … although it seemed as if everywhere was behind enemy lines now. Jessica's eyes met Lauren's and in that second, she knew they were both thinking the same thing, but they couldn't exactly tell the cop they'd changed their minds about using the interview room.

The cop took a long look at Jessica, then Lauren, and turned to the door. "I'll leave you alone." She winked at Emily. "Don't worry. No one's watching."

Once the door closed, they all sat. Jessica emptied the envelope onto the table and lost her breath at the sight of a half-melted key ring with several keys. Blackened coins fell out, too, bringing a charred odor. For the first time in days, horrifying images hit her of Brian waking up, screaming and burning.

"Oh, God," Emily murmured.

"We're looking for one numbered 276," Lauren said, gently, pulling the keys toward herself and beginning to look at them, one by one. There were four of them. "There's no number on any of these."

Commanding herself to stay on the business at hand, Jessica took the keys from Lauren and spoke softly, fingering through the keys, none of them looking like a safe-deposit-box key, "This one is the plane key, this one's our house, the car." She frowned. "I don't know what this is, it looks like a house key but—"

Lauren cut in, "You know how Brian kept things, Jessica. It could be the key to his college dormitory."

Jessica wondered why Lauren was so quick to cut her off about that. A thought flickered across Jessica's mind: Lauren was protecting her from something. Did Lauren think Brian had a pied-à-terre? Was there a key here to someone else's apartment the way Brian had Jessica's house key when he was married to Lauren? Jessica felt her eyes moistening.

Lauren took the keys and began putting the items back in the envelope. "Let's get out of here."

Once they were outside in the sunshine, Lauren spoke. "If we can't find the key, we'll need a court order to open the box if Brian even used his real name to rent it, and we could prove it was his. The IRS would have to be there, and it would take too much time even if we could avoid that."

As they resumed walking the path from the precinct to the waiting cab, Jessica's chest filled with anxiety.

Lauren glanced at her. "You look like 'dead man walking.'"

"What if I have to go back to jail?"

"It doesn't pay to let our minds get ahead of us," Lauren reminded her. Lauren opened the car door and stood aside for Emily then Jessica to enter. "We'll cover all the bases before we go home."

***

Lauren watched out the window as their taxi pulled into a hotel's palm-lined, crescent driveway. Emily wasn't the only one who could use a beach vacation, Lauren thought, or who'd like to run away completely. If only it were an option. Double glass doors automatically slid open as the two women and teenager approached. They entered the sudden cool of a lushly decorated lobby filled with potted palms and tropical colors.

Jessica leaned close to Lauren and said softly, "What was Brian thinking about when he walked right here? About me? Emily? About this other life? I'm so furious, Lauren, and so ... hurt."

"It's hard to picture him here," Lauren agreed, "making all kinds of major decisions, never giving us a say when he was risking *our* lives."

Lauren glanced at Emily, who seemed to be taking in their surroundings, probably listening more attentively than she was letting on.

A young woman smiled at them as they approached. "Welcome to the Key Biscayne Hotel."

"Thank you," Lauren said. "Is there a manager around?"

"I'm the assistant manager. Can I help you?"

"We're the family of Brian Silverman," Lauren said. "He was—"

The woman appeared pained. "Oh gosh, I know. We sent flowers, we felt so badly. Nothing like that has ever happened here before. I'm so sorry for your loss."

"Thank you," Lauren said. "We came to town to pick up his personal effects from the police and wondered if your staff had found any of his property."

"Yes." The assistant manager's eyes narrowed. "Didn't you get the letter? It went out a few days ago."

"I haven't been home," Jessica said.

"That explains it." The woman appeared relieved. "We wrote because we wanted to send the suitcase."

"A suitcase?" Lauren asked, surprised after the condition of the keys.

"Well, yes. There was a small hallway within the room that led to the bathroom and the door. The suitcase was in a closet there. It was pretty much untouched by the fire. The fire marshals and police took some things from the room and sealed it off until they ruled the fire accidental. But when we went in, we found it. I doubt any of the clothes are in usable condition after the firemen hosed down the place. But we didn't feel right … disposing of it, you know, without permission." She rang a bell and a young man came from a back room. "Freddy, would you watch the desk? I'm taking these ladies to Security."

A moment later, she led them across the lobby. The sound of pounding waves grew louder when they passed the lobby's open back. At the end of a long hallway, they reached a security room equipped with video screens and one sallow guard. The assistant manager used a key to open a windowless storage room with only a couple of bins and cartons inside.

"This is our lost and found." She walked to a closet, slid the door open and emerged, lugging a badly damaged suitcase.

Gray with smoke stains, it had dried into a moldy and misshaped version of its old self.

"That's Brian's," Jessica murmured.

The assistant manager nodded. "I'll leave you. I should get back to the desk. If you need anything or want to take it, tell the guard outside and we'll have the bellman bring it out front for you."

When the door closed behind the woman, Lauren knelt on the floor next to the suitcase, while Jessica and Emily stared, transfixed. "It's in bad shape." She unzipped with difficulty, the teeth catching. She had to work it open, pushing and pulling. "But if there's a key in here, it will be in better shape than the ones at the police station." She slid her palm through the suitcase pockets first. "Nothing."

She let the top flap fall open to the floor, exposing a moldy mass of clothing. Emily knelt next to her, sniffling, weeping a bit. Emily pulled out a pair of pants and began checking pockets. Lauren did the same. They piled the clothes between them on the carpet.

Jessica finally knelt, too, and carefully pulled a stained polo shirt from the mess. She put it aside, then lifted out a pair of khaki shorts. "Brian's favorites," she groaned. "How can I flip from hating him to missing him so fast?" She put her fingers inside the pockets.

Emily picked up a small jar of Vaseline, a hairbrush, and a safety razor, put them next to the pile. She checked the pockets of a sweat jacket. "Nothing."

"His watch and wallet haven't shown up either," Jessica said. "So many missing pieces to the puzzle …"

"Okay, let's try to think like Brian."

Jessica shook her head, angrily. "I didn't know him."

Emily chewed on her lip. "Maybe it's in his plane."

"His plane is still at the airport here," Lauren said. "But he wouldn't leave something in the plane if he needed it. I'm sure he didn't want to be seen extra times at the airport."

"Oh," Emily looked down at the pile of clothes then picked up the Vaseline. "Wait a minute. Hold up."

"What?" Lauren asked.

"Something I heard in jail. How they smuggle drugs into jail. They put them in a balloon inside …" Emily held the jar up to the light. "Yes," she cheered. "There's something here."

Lauren saw it, too. A black mass at the center of the petroleum jelly. She took the jar from Emily and opened it. She fished around inside with two fingers until she'd grasped what could only be a key. She pulled out the goo-covered key, in perfect shape.

"Unbelievable." Lauren hugged Emily. "You're something else."

Emily beamed.

Jessica looked at the key. "Number 276. Jansen-White's number. Do you think we can really get in there?"

"We've gotten this far." Lauren dumped the clothes back in the suitcase. She stood and brushed her sooty palms against each other. "Let's just do it before I get some sense."

"We can tell the manager to throw the suitcase out," Jessica said. "There's nothing to save here."

***

After a stop in the hotel bathroom to wash the smell of smoke from their hands, Jessica, Lauren, and Emily headed to Miami's downtown commercial district. Tall office buildings clustered on the horizon as they approached. The women left Emily happily eating tacos in a Chipotle at the base of one of the tall buildings. The sidewalks were empty, not many pedestrians out in the lung-sucking afternoon heat. Jessica and Lauren turned a corner and approached an office high-rise.

"These operations are probably designed to avoid questions," Lauren said. "I'm sure the company doesn't want to know whether we're the people who rented the box, as long as we have a PIN and key. I bet people even do drug deals, passing drugs and money by using burner phones, lieutenants, and safe-deposit boxes."

"You have a much better criminal mind than I do."

"You're not so bad yourself. You were practically the bullpen enforcer."

Jessica smiled, pleased that Lauren kept mentioning how she'd protected

Emily. It was possibly the best thing she'd ever done. "Yeah, well, I was scared then, and I'm scared now. And I am so damn pissed at Brian I could spit."

"Join the club. I'm scared, and I've been pissed at Brian for years."

Jessica glanced at her, then stared straight ahead, feeling a blast of self-loathing. "At me, too. You hated me. I can't feel sorry for myself about that, all things considered."

"It's a funny thing. I never really thought I was angry at you for what happened. I tried to tell myself I was above that, and it was Brian who violated his commitment to me. It's only since I've stopped being angry that I've noticed its absence."

"I didn't know you then, and ignorance was bliss for me. Ironically, I never intended for things to get serious with Brian or to break up your marriage."

"Really?"

"I was stunned how it turned out. I picked a married guy who lived thousands of miles away. You couldn't pick a more unavailable man. That's what I thought I wanted."

Lauren seemed to ponder that for a moment before speaking. "At some level, I must have wanted an unavailable man, too. Brian could have won a prize for unavailability, even if you were married to him. They say it's no accident when you pick someone like that."

"But it was ugly, what I did. Brian had a wife and kid … a really special wife and kid."

Lauren held Jessica's arm for a moment. "It's ancient history now."

Jessica felt Lauren's forgiveness physically, a warmth inside her and a lightness, as if gravity had let up a notch. "Thank you."

"And for the record, in my humble opinion, nothing you did was so bad that you deserved this. What Brian did was above and beyond."

They reached the building.

"We're crossing a line here, Jessica. We haven't really done anything illegal—at least not to further the conspiracy—until now. Once we touch the bonds, if we find them, it's a whole different thing."

Scared to death, Jessica pulled open the lobby door. "I'm already so far across the line, there's nowhere to go but forward."

They walked through a modern lobby to an office fronted by reinforced glass. Etched onto the glass were the elegantly scripted letters: JANSEN-WHITE, INC. Inside, a woman in a tailored black uniform sat at a lacquer desk, her black hair tied back into a sleek bun like the Russian spies in a James Bond movie. Jessica followed Lauren through the glass door and down a couple of carpeted steps to the reception area.

The woman watched them approach. "May I help you?"

"Box number 276," Lauren said, as if she'd been here a million times.

Jessica tried to breathe naturally, worried her mounting nervousness would screw up the great job Lauren was doing. The dark-haired woman brought out a small black box like the ones banks used to set up PIN numbers at customer service desks. "Enter your code name or PIN here."

Jessica took a quick look up at video cameras trained on them, probably belonging to an armed guard stationed on the premises.

Lauren keyed in the letters, H-a-z-e-l-N-u-k-e, the insultingly homey code name, of all things for Brian to think about while risking everything.

The dark-haired woman swiped the screen of a tablet, typed, and turned it toward them. She handed Lauren a stylus. "Just initial this."

Without pause, at a time when Jessica's hand would have been quivering, Lauren calmly scribbled and slid the tablet back across the desk.

The woman's eyes flicked to the screen, barely looking. She picked up the phone and pressed an intercom button. "Larry, we have a client for box 276."

A moment later, a door on the left side of the room opened and the woman signaled toward it. "Right in there."

Jessica and Lauren walked toward a man who waited inside the doorway. He had a shaved head and the demeanor of a police detective. It had been too easy, Jessica thought with panic, imagining an ambush of police waiting inside.

"This way." The man turned back down a hallway and the women followed him to a door.

They entered a room full of silver safe-deposit boxes, built into three walls. On the last wall, side by side, two more doors stood ajar. Two small rooms each contained a couple of chairs and a small table where people could sit to go through the contents of their safe-deposit boxes.

The man took them to box number 276 and turned back. "Insert your key here." He pointed to the top lock.

Lauren stepped forward, inserted the key, and turned.

The man turned his key and opened the door. He pulled out a bulky metal box and led them to one of the little rooms, where he placed the box on the table. He signaled to a button next to the door. "When you're finished, just ring this bell and I'll come get you."

He closed the door behind him, and the women were alone.

Lauren looked at Jessica. "Do you want to do it?"

"Open it? Not in the least."

"Okay. Here we go." Lauren opened the long metal lid. They leaned forward. A leather case was inside. It looked full.

Lauren lifted it out, opened its flap, and unzipped. She pulled out a thick manila file and put it on the table next to the box. She opened the file and they both stared at what looked like diplomas or award certificates. In blue letters, the top certificate said the issuer would pay fifty thousand dollars to the bearer. Cross Hair, Inc., was the issuing corporation.

"Crosshairs is right," Lauren said. "Thanks, Brian."

Jessica brushed her fingertips across the raised corporate seal on the first certificate. "Is this really worth fifty thousand dollars?"

"They're trying to get them badly enough." Lauren looked at the second certificate in the pile. It also said it was worth fifty thousand. Lauren thumbed through. "If there's twelve million, that means there are two hundred and forty of these here." Lauren handed Jessica half the pile. "We might as well count them now."

Five minutes later, they exited Jansen-White, Inc. Lauren carried her own soft leather attaché on her shoulder. They left Brian's empty satchel inside the safe-deposit box. They didn't want to leave with anything that looked different than what they'd brought in with them.

They walked to the front of the lobby and into the thick tropical air. Keeping a measured pace, they headed down the block to pick up Emily at the restaurant. Jessica glanced at Lauren. Despite her nonchalant expression and casual gait, Jessica couldn't help but notice how Lauren was white-knuckling her shoulder strap now that it was worth twelve million dollars.

CHAPTER 35

There was a buzz in the antiseptic air of the Federal Building's sixteenth floor by the time Carl arrived, midafternoon. Bright florescent lights speared through his dark sunglasses; but it wasn't Carl's headache or fatigue that made him feel a step behind everyone the moment he got off the elevator. It was the unmistakable energy that picked up the pace of the whole staff—from agents to the mailroom—before a big bust.

Rick rushed from their office into the hallway, nearly plowing Carl down. "Goddamn, what happened to you?"

A female agent brushed past. "Some girl finally got hip to the innocent act."

Carl felt a momentary surge of adrenaline: *They all know.*

"Come on, tell me on the way," Rick said, continuing to double-time it down the carpeted hallway with Carl at his side.

"It was nothing. I took an elbow in a pickup game at Chelsea Piers."

Rick shook his head. "Damn. What happened to the other guy?"

"Nothing. It was an accident."

"That's rough." Rick seemed satisfied.

Carl felt a flush of relief. "Where are we going?"

"The briefing room. A lot has happened. We're a go on Arena. There's a meet-up set for tomorrow between Arena and Xi Wen's people. We'll have a dozen squads to host them."

"All on what CB said?"

"No. We picked up audio from Lucho again. He said the documents are coming in. Straight-up code for money. Plus, Interpol believes the weapons are due into Calabria, Italy, traveling on a Chinese-flagged ship. Interpol is tracking that, and Homeland Security says there's been an uptick in communication from the African group that's supposed to be buying the weapons. It's confirmed that they're holding Arena's nephew hostage. Arena is the point person. An ATF agent in deep cover on the Tong side heard Arena's name, too. He thinks the Mott Street Tong killed one of Arena's men in retaliation for Lucho Arena hitting one of theirs. But that won't stop the deal from going forward. The Tong are Xi Wen's agents in New York. They won't sacrifice that payday for hard feelings. But if Arena doesn't get the money to the Tong, he's in for a shitload of trouble. He's apparently a week late already."

"Is Jorge Arena still using his phone?" Carl asked.

"No. It's gone. He probably drowned it. He's a careful guy, smarter than your average thug."

The two men walked into the briefing room, packed with squad leaders from their division, plus ATF and Homeland Security agents called in due to the weapons and international dimensions of the case.

The ASAC stood in front of the room and ran down the information Rick had told Carl. "The guns will never reach the States, but we'll have them all on conspiracy. For insurance, we're going to bust Arena's small-time bookies, a slew of new defendants dying to cooperate. We're not giving up on the bet-fixing, internet gambling, and extortion of the gambling websites, but what was previously the core of our case may end up just a wedge to get cooperation on the weapons conspiracy."

An agent raised his hand. "Are we depending on CB to lead us to the meet-up with the Tong?"

"Jorge asked CB to go," Carl said. "Arena trusts him."

"We've got CB and Lucho Arena," the ASAC added. "CB's at the Home Game. Lucho's home now. Lucho's phone is pinging away. He will hopefully keep it with him.

"Lucho's less disciplined than Jorge," Carl added.

Carl tried to act self-assured when agents addressed questions to him. Carl had gotten lucky, landing the informant and the bar that both panned out. Now he and Rick were in the thick of things, meeting with the big boys, all of them listening avidly to Carl and Rick's opinions on how the bust should go down. It could be the turning point of their careers. But Carl was too tense to enjoy a moment of it.

After an afternoon of briefings, Carl's face throbbed, he was sick of the constant ribbing about it, and he worried more every minute about what might go wrong. Worst of all, he worried that CB was right about them having a loose cannon—the widows—poised to screw up the works. He'd give himself less than even odds on coming out of this with his career intact. And that was the least of his worries.

***

At Kennedy International Airport, tourists flowed from the arrival gate. Gray and tense, Lauren, Jessica, and Emily stood out within the tanned crowd that exited the flight from Miami. With a force of will, Lauren kept her hand from clutching the shoulder strap of her attaché. They'd made it through the risky part, departure from Miami, the attaché passing through NSA screening without a blink from the agents. The bonds looked like innocuous documents, no reason to raise any red flags. But law enforcement didn't necessarily tell you when you were caught. Lauren envisioned hidden airport security, scores of cameras following their every step as the three turned down a corridor toward the exit sign instead of following the crowd to the luggage carousel. Lauren resisted the impulse to glance around for the cameras.

She spoke softly to Jessica, "She's going to my aunt's."

Emily leaned in. "You need me, Mom. I'll be safe."

"She can handle it, Lauren," Jessica said. "It will be easier for Arena to do things our way than deal with the attention if they hurt us."

"Face it, Jessica, if we were so sure of that, we'd just hand Arena the twelve million and count on a polite goodbye. She's going to my aunt on Long Island."

Outside, they walked the wide, curving sidewalk past a series of Third World airlines housed in a long terminal building. Jessica and Lauren walked quickly, Emily keeping up, not straggling and texting as she usually did. She was growing up before Lauren's eyes. Lauren would never have imagined that Emily having her life threatened, going to jail, and engaging in family criminal activities would be the thing to straighten her out. Maybe Lauren should patent it and do an infomercial: *Hey, parents! Are your kids cutting school, talking back, doing drugs? Well, have I got a cure for you!* Still, Lauren knew Emily was only a kid. It seemed like just yesterday when she taught Emily to cross the street. As far as Lauren was concerned, getting past airport security was the last risk Emily would take.

"Mom, I don't even know my aunt."

"You've met her, your grandfather's sister."

"I never even met my grandfather."

"We need Emily," Jessica said.

"Why? We put half the bonds in a safe-deposit box, bring the other half for goodwill, and set the terms for a safe drop-off of the key."

"You want to mail the key to ourselves? Come on, that would drag things out for two more days. They'd probably hold us hostage while they waited."

The thought drop-kicked Lauren.

"I wouldn't trust *my* life to the US Post Office," Emily said, the coup de grâce.

Lauren's breath hitched. Emily was right. So was Jessica. Lauren's idea for the drop-off made no sense.

"I would think that once they see the first six million," Jessica piled on, "we'd need to make it easy for them to get the other half of the bonds, fast. Otherwise we'll just piss them off."

They reached the parking garage and found Jessica's car. They drove the looping airport road toward a sign for Van Wyck Expressway.

"Okay, okay," Lauren said, anxiety thinning her voice as a plan began to map itself out in her mind. "I think I've got a way, one that should keep Emily safe." Lauren's eyes watered up. The idea of Emily taking any risk was beyond what Lauren could stand. She felt on the verge of sobs. The tables had turned, and Lauren was now the emotional mess.

"You all right?" Jessica asked.

"I feel like we're in hell. Can we wake up now?"

***

It was dark, and Carl was exhausted by the time he arrived at the sports bar to prepare CB. Arena had quadrupled security at the bar. Carl's nervous energy spiked as he passed so many of Arena's armed men. Carl followed CB down the back hallway to his office. Alone, CB leaned against a mirrored wall.

"Listen, CB, it's real simple. We've got your phone's identity code and can track it even when it's off. No one will be able to tell we're following you. So there's no chance we'll be spotted."

CB's face knotted. "I've done everything you asked. This is too much. You can't guarantee my safety. You wear bulletproof vests and jackets with FBI in block letters across your backs. But not me."

"All the agents have seen your picture."

"I'm relieved." CB started pacing. "But I'm not fucking doing it. Fuck it." CB stopped and thrust his two hands out in front of him. "Cuff me. I'm not doing it."

Carl sighed. He hated playing hardball and felt guilty about putting the poor guy in the crossfire, but Jorge Arena trusted CB and they couldn't have the entire bust depend on tracking Lucho's phone. These guys usually kept their personal phones with them even if they used a burner phone for a deal. Criminals were as addicted to their phones as everyone else. But with the amount of money and jail time at stake, Lucho could be smart enough to leave it home.

Carl leaned back on the edge of the desk. If Carl were in CB's position, he wouldn't want to go along with the plan either. But if Carl had been a criminal, he would have gone quietly to jail in the first place. Only a lowlife caused others to do the time for him when he was the one caught. That was what snitching came down to in Carl's mind. He'd never had much sympathy for informants. Still, Carl didn't want to see CB get hurt. He felt responsible for him and kind of liked the guy.

Carl's stomach burned as he spoke. "Listen, CB, if you refuse to do it, you're not only going to do the time for the kilo we caught you with, but when we bust the Arenas, you'll be charged with their conspiracy, too. Coconspirators do the time for all the crimes committed by their pals." Watching CB's face melt, Carl wished he sold cars for a living. "If you back out now, the US Attorney will charge you with conspiring to aid a terrorist organization. Word is that the African buyers have ties with ISIS. You'll end up in Super Max. A lifetime of solitary confinement. You'll never see the DR again, you'll never see your mother except through plexiglass, and the whore you had last week will be the last woman you'll ever touch. Plus, I can't vouch for my partner. One word on the street about you ratting, and you won't even be safe in prison."

"Shit," CB said, surrendering to becoming the rabbit in a dog race. "*Cabrones.*"

"Don't worry, there will be a hundred agents on this tomorrow."

CB exhaled loudly. "That's one of the top things I'm worried about."

CHAPTER 36

Friday, November 8

Lauren managed to catch a few hours of rest in her apartment. She was so exhausted from cumulative sleep deprivation that even her shot nerves couldn't keep her awake. Still, she'd been up for hours when Jessica appeared in the kitchen just after 8:00 a.m. Jessica wore new running tights, sneakers, and a sweater Lauren had ordered on Prime Now, which had arrived at 10:00 p.m. last night. Lauren had to dress more conservatively. She wore a pinstriped pantsuit and flats.

"Everything fit?" Lauren asked Jessica.

"Yes. It's amazing how grateful I am for things I never noticed before—like clean clothes and a shower. But I almost wish I were as listless and suicidal as I was last week. Maybe then I wouldn't feel so scared."

Lauren took a mug from an overhead cupboard, thinking how maybe Jessica's feeling suicidal was all about being scared. "Coffee?"

"Definitely. I'm addicted, although I probably don't need any nerve stimulation. Do you have any toast? I've been craving carbs as if I'm preparing for a marathon."

Lauren opened a loaf of bread, smelled it, and took out a few slices. "We're in luck."

Standing side by side at the counter, they were quietly spreading jam on toast when Jessica put down her knife. "I was raped in college … three fraternity guys." Jessica's eyes gleamed, and she pinched their inside corners with her thumb and index finger to stanch the moisture gathering there. "I *never* talk about it."

Lauren turned to Jessica and leaned against the counter, surprised by the turn in conversation.

"I was drunk, probably roofied. I was stupid. It was only my second week at college. I was just two years older than Emily. I didn't think about myself as only a kid. But when you look back, you realize. Do you know what I mean?"

"Yeah."

"Maybe I would have given myself a break if I had. I never forgave myself for being stupid enough to put myself in that position. I'd always done the right things before that. I was probably the only virgin on campus."

"I'm really sorry, Jess."

"When I reported it, I was hated—by the girls, too. It was before campus rape became a trending topic. Nobody thought it was rape. Who was to blame? They said I was drunk. I never even told my parents."

"God."

"I needed to say it out loud now. I haven't said it out loud for nearly fourteen years. I tried to put it behind me. I thought if I never talked about it, if I didn't even know any people who knew me then, it would be as if it never happened. That's why I don't have a Facebook page. The last thing I wanted was to know people who knew about it.

"But I never really left it behind. I stopped eating almost completely for months because I was afraid of losing control and getting fat. The connection between that and what happened to me is so obvious in retrospect. I can see now how I made sure I was always in control. It was so much easier not dating too. For a long time, that was my story. When I did start dating, I specialized in unavailable guys. They were 'my type,' and I didn't want a commitment. It took me by surprise when I spun out on Brian. I was all about being in control, but once it went the other way, I basically lost my mind. There was no halfway mark for me. It isn't Emily who needs therapy, it's me."

"Funny how I always imagined you walked with angels your whole life," Lauren said, "never going through any adversity like I did."

"I worked hard to make people think that ... and believe me, I know what happened to me is nothing compared to what you went through."

"I don't know. It's all hard," Lauren said. "And we both thought we could dust off our past and leave it behind."

Jessica's face hardened. "I swore after those guys raped me—and I still say it—I am *never* letting anyone do that to me again. Never."

Lauren sighed and leaned back against the counter, afraid. "The money has to protect us."

"People must do deals with Arena all the time and survive, right?" Jessica said. "Or he'd have no business."

Lauren felt a flash of dread about how things could really go. Words slipped out before she could stop them, "You haven't met Lucho."

"Fuck Lucho!"

Lauren looked at Jessica and, out of nowhere, found herself laughing. "If anyone had told us ... that we would be standing in my kitchen and you would be saying 'Fuck Lucho' ... about a murdering deviant gang member—would we have believed it?"

"Hell no." Jessica laughed, a deep laugh.

Tears of laughter, oddly coexisting with Lauren's dread, came to her eyes. "God, we're in the twilight zone." She took one of Jessica's hands. Her nail polish had chipped and peeled. "And look at your nails."

Jessica laughed even harder. "Shit, I can't go now, Lauren. I can't meet anyone. What kind of impression would I make?"

Emily stood in the doorway, her face scrunched, still adjusting to the morning light. "What's so funny?"

Jessica held up the back of her hand.

Emily looked from Jessica to Lauren, mystified. "You want to go to a nail salon?"

***

Jessica peered from the vestibule of Lauren's building, their laughter a distant memory.

Lauren looked at her. "We just have to go—no way to tell whether anyone's out there."

"We're still within deadline," Jessica said, trying to convince herself. Lauren had said that the longer they had the bonds, the more danger they were in. How many people knew they had them by now?

"There could be a lot of people beside Arena who would want twelve million unguarded dollars." Lauren spoke Jessica's thoughts, putting an arm protectively around Emily. "But Arena knows that and wouldn't have broadcast it. We just have to go."

Jessica saw Lauren checking behind them periodically as they walked toward their car. A harsh wind pushed at their backs, the morning sky scaled with deep gray clouds. Inside the car, Lauren flipped down her sun visor and looked through its vanity mirror. "Someone's getting in a parked car across the street. Emily, please stay low."

Emily slumped down in the back seat, tensely silent since they left the apartment.

Jessica turned on the ignition, resisting the impulse to slump low herself, thinking of how suddenly they'd killed Jordan Connors. She pulled out, glancing in the rearview mirror, unsure whether any of the cars that lined up behind them at the red light were following.

"That blue Honda has been with us for two blocks already," Lauren said. "Turn right."

They saw the cement wings of the George Washington Bus Terminal ahead. "Is he following?"

"I think so. Emily, don't look back," Lauren said, quickly. "Jessica, when you get close to the traffic light before the bus terminal, slow down and make the light when it's about to turn red. Turn right, onto the bridge."

"We're going to Jersey?"

"No."

At 179th Street, where cars entered the bridge, Jessica crawled toward a yellow light and took off as it turned red. She eased left onto the entrance to the bridge, no one behind her able to follow.

"Wait for it," Lauren said. "When I say, turn."

After the on-ramp, there was a left turn Jessica had never noticed. Always intent on merging into traffic to enter the bridge, Jessica thought she must have passed that unobtrusive left turn dozens of times without noticing it was there.

"Take the left, now," Lauren commanded.

Jessica took the turn with a screech.

Lauren pointed. "Make a U. Up the ramp."

They stopped on top of the George Washington Bridge bus station, hidden on the far side of a parked New Jersey Transit jitney. The red light they'd originally run was probably only now changing to green. They'd lost the car.

Lauren peered around. "Okay, let's give it two minutes, then we can pull back out and take the highway downtown."

"Now we've had the car chase," Emily said from the back. Despite her attempt to make a joke of it, she looked terrified.

***

They stopped at an ATM for cash, confident they weren't followed. On East Fifty-Seventh Street, Lauren left Jessica and Emily in the car. From there, it was smooth going. Just like Florida. In the lobby of an office building, down three or four marble steps, Lauren entered a glassed-in establishment. A receptionist greeted her. Lauren counted out five hundred dollars and followed a man to her new safe-deposit box. Then they stopped at a store on Lexington Avenue and Fifty-Fifth Street where she bought three burner phones. Lauren handed them to Emily in the back seat, who occupied herself with adding airtime to the phones and putting each other's phone numbers into each of their contacts. Lauren was glad she didn't have to deal with figuring out how to add the airtime now, even though it was apparently an easy enough task for even the least-educated drug dealer on the planet to complete.

"Here, Mom," Emily handed over the first phone.

"I can talk to them this time," Jessica offered.

Lauren spoke calmly but her stomach cramped with nerves. "I'm your lawyer, remember?"

Lauren took out her personal iPhone and went into the lined-yellow notes app where she'd put Lucho's number. She dialed on the burner phone and put her iPhone back in her coat pocket.

"*Bueno*," Lucho said when he picked up.

"It's Lauren."

"Ah." He was pleased. "Are you ready?"

"Yes."

"You know the sports bar. You meet me there."

"Can't we meet downtown? At a Starbucks near my job? It won't take a minute."

"Don't be stupid, *gringa*," he said with exasperation. "This is our business and this is a busy day. You do it like we say. No time for coffee. I will be at the bar in half hour and will take you to Jorge."

"An hour in case there's traffic."

"Okay."

Lauren hung up the phone, her chest aching with anxiety. She turned to Jessica. "Everything's set."

Moments later, Jessica pulled the car to the curb on Leonard Street, alongside the Family Court. Lauren heard the car doors lock behind them as she and Emily walked away from the car toward the courthouse entrance. Lauren had left her attaché in the car's passenger-side foot well. It struck her as insane, six million dollars just lying there with only unarmed Jessica to safeguard it. How many normal passersby would have become criminals if they'd known what was there?

***

Emily tried to relax. She followed Lauren past a line of families waiting to get through the Family Court metal detectors. The families were putting their pocketbooks and diaper bags on a conveyor belt to be X-rayed and walking through a metal detector, the line as slow as airport security. But there was a separate, shorter line for courthouse staff and attorneys.

The court officer stationed at the staff entrance recognized Lauren. "Good morning, Counselor."

"Hi." Lauren showed her ID and put her arm around Emily. "She's with me."

"No problem."

Emily wished her mother had kept her arm around her forever. She led Emily with a hand on her back through the staff entryway.

A packed elevator opened onto the fifth floor. When the doors opened, families, lawyers, and social workers got off with Emily and Lauren. Family Court was as crazy as Lauren had always told her, packed like Grand Central Station when the trains were delayed. Harried parents, loud children, angry couples, and lawyers; it seemed like everyone was in noisy motion while they waited for their cases to be called. Emily could see why her mother said she wouldn't stand out here. Nobody would stand out.

Lauren brought Emily to a long wooden bench where a woman and a bunch of her kids took up three quarters of it. The oldest kids were herding twin toddlers, who shrieked and tried to evade them. A middle child sat next to the overweight mother. He worked peacefully on a fried egg on a roll, which smelled of grease and ketchup. Emily felt a sad nostalgia for similar breakfasts she used to buy at the corner bodega near her old school in Manhattan, back when things had been normal.

Outside the nearest courtroom entrance, an armed court officer marked off names of people who waited in a line to report for their cases. Lauren had told Emily that once the families checked in, they sometimes waited all morning and afternoon for their cases to be called.

Emily spoke softly to her mother, "You're bringing them half the bonds?"

Lauren nodded, not looking at Emily. Lauren was scanning the room as if she were checking to see if anything was out of whack, like armed gunmen. *Sicarios* they called them on television. Under different circumstances, Emily might have made a remark about her mom's paranoia. Emily had always thought her mother overreacted to stuff, if Emily had the flu, if there was a string of burglaries in the neighborhood, if they heard sirens nearby. Her mother would get all protective and worried. Emily knew it had to do with things that had happened to her when she was young. Under normal circumstances, Emily might have asked sarcastically whether her mother was scanning the room for zombies. That would have hit Emily's brain as funny, but her mother didn't look in a laughing mood, and neither was Emily.

"I'll be waiting for you here," Emily said, gripping her burner phone within her jacket pocket.

"When I call and say everything's okay, someone will come, and you'll give him the key to the safe-deposit box."

"Okay."

"You can sit here all day. No one will notice you. Any sign of trouble, if anyone comes and I didn't call or if they try to get you to leave, you scream. Remember, they can't have a gun or knife even if they say they do. If you shout, the court officers will come running. They're always ready for trouble because of all the domestic violence cases here."

Emily knew her mother had to be upset, but she wasn't showing any sign of it. She had an expression on her face that Emily had never seen on her before, like a character out of *Mortal Kombat*: fierce—that was the word for it. Fierce and love. Emily forced herself not to think about the love part because her eyes were starting to well up. She couldn't let herself cry, not now. "What if no one comes and you don't call?"

"You go to Gary, the court officer from Judge Quiñones' Part." Lauren pointed discretely at a courtroom entrance at the far side of the waiting area. "You see him? Gary. He's over there."

A tall, skinny officer stood near the entrance to a courtroom, talking with the first person on a long line. He was smiling at the person. He looked nice.

"You tell him who you are, that I'm in trouble, and that you need to go to the Federal Building around the corner. Then you tell the FBI everything. But that won't happen, Emily. Just sit tight and I'll call you."

Lauren's eyes met Emily's. Emily could see in her mother's expression that staying fierce and loving Emily at the same time was hard for her too. Lauren kissed Emily on the forehead and squeezed her tight. "I love you, pumpkin."

And Lauren walked away.

CHAPTER 37

Jessica and Lauren rode northwest through Tribeca, Soho, and the Meat Packing District. In Chelsea, traffic stopped and started, slowing their progress.

"So it doesn't look like Steve was involved at all," Jessica said.

"You thought that too?"

"Couldn't help myself. When Steve turned on me, and Nicole pretty much disappeared, it felt as if Brian and I had divorced—you know how your husband's friends will divorce you too. But that's not supposed to happen when somebody dies.

"Being in jail gave me time to replay a lot of conversations in my head. We used to go out with Steve and Nicole all the time ... long weekends, sailing. Something wasn't right in the end. Steve was distant, even hostile. Brian and Steve had started to have disagreements about how to handle cases, and they argued over a lead-poisoning case. I know Brian was upset about it. Steve wanted to settle it and Brian didn't. It got so Brian liked Nicole better than Steve, although she always made me feel insecure. And then there was something else about her that made me"—Jessica seemed lost in thought—"uncomfortable. I tried to bring it up with Brian, but he totally dismissed me."

"Men get into a haze around women like her," Lauren said. "They can't see straight."

"Still, I never would have thought she'd betray—"

"Listen, next time you'll pick your husband *and* friends more carefully," Lauren said, thinking that she'd already said too much. She had to steer Jessica away from the subject. They couldn't afford the distraction, but she softened her voice, realizing she'd spoken too harshly. "We'll take care of Steve after."

Jessica sighed. "Really, nothing would surprise me at this point. And you can stop trying to protect me, although it's sweet. At this point, I wouldn't blink an eye if you told me Brian were hooking up with Steve. I'm so through with thinking I knew Brian."

"Okay," Lauren said. But she wasn't sure she believed Jessica and was still determined to err on the side of not surprising her. They rode in silence the rest of the way to the sports bar. Then Lauren pointed. "That's it."

Jessica nodded grimly and parked in an overpriced outdoor parking lot used mostly by tourists visiting the Intrepid or taking the Circle Line. The lot was nearly empty now. The attendant signaled them to a spot. When they stopped, Lauren clasped hands with Jessica for a moment low on the seat.

Lauren's legs felt weak as she stood upright on the pavement and closed the car door behind her. She crossed the street next to Jessica, trying not to think of what happened here last time.

The sports bar was half lit and empty except for a couple of large men sitting inside the door who looked like bouncers. CB's eyes opened wide when he saw them entering. *Why was he afraid? Did he know something they didn't?* Lauren nearly backed out of the door but felt Jessica's firm grip on her arm.

"You here for Lucho?" he asked.

"Yes," Jessica said.

"Sit." He pointed at an empty table near the bar.

CB went behind the bar and casually picked up a cell phone, although something about it didn't seem casual. He made a call and sat on a stool. He spoke softly into the phone, swiveling to give the women his back. Lauren assumed he was talking to Lucho, but she turned around at the sound of Lucho and another, stockier man entering behind them.

CB lurched to his feet with a Cheshire cat grin and called out, "Lucho, Pedro, *entren.*"

The sound of Spanish and the smell of cigarettes filled the air around her. Anxiety, almost a solid object, pounded Lauren's ribcage. She could sense Jessica stiffening next to her.

The heavyset one, Pedro, hung back, watching. Lucho stubbed out his cigarette in an ashtray on the bar. Lucho's eyes appraised Jessica, pausing at her breasts. He spoke to Jessica, "We will go to meet Jorge. You two go with Pedro. CB with me."

Lucho grabbed Lauren's attaché, ripping it away from her. She forced herself not to flinch, keeping her eyes steady on him. He opened the flap of her bag, looked quickly inside and smiled. "Good, Jorge will be happy." He turned to CB. "Let's go."

CB jumped to his feet and pulled a jacket from a hook. Jessica and Lauren rose from the couch. Lucho grabbed Lauren's arm with a harsh familiarity, like she was his bitch. "Come."

Terror shot through her at his touch, her blood rushing. She jerked her arm away but went with him toward the door. She looked back to see that Jessica was following. As they walked, Lauren coached herself: *It will all be over soon, it will all be over soon.*

Two cars were double-parked out front. Lucho opened the front passenger door to the first car and signaled to Jessica and Lauren. "Come."

Pedro didn't say anything, just entered the driver's side of the car and started it. Jessica got in the passenger side and slid to the middle next to him. Lauren followed her. As their car pulled away, she looked back. CB entered the second car with Lucho, two bouncer-types joining them in the back seat.

***

CB looked out the car window, having already given up on keeping conversation going with Lucho. CB had no idea where they were headed as they drove uptown on the West Side Highway along the Hudson River. He imagined his phone as if it were burning in his jacket pocket, attracting trouble like a rebounding rubber band. Fear jackhammered inside his body. He didn't like this. He didn't want anything to do with

Jorge's meet-up or the goddamn Feds. When they'd approached him to cooperate, he hadn't been able to bear the prospect of the decades in jail for his drug bust, but now he doubted the wisdom of his decision.

Lucho's phone rang, a reggaeton ringtone. The sudden music nearly launched CB from his seat. CB thought about the song. Where did Lucho get the time for messing with ringtones? Maybe one of his girlfriends had picked it out for him. Lucho balanced the phone with one hand on top of the steering wheel as he drove and looked at the number of the caller. He put the phone to his ear. A horn blew, and Lucho corrected his creep into the next lane.

CB swiped at Lucho's phone to keep him from talking and driving at the same time. "Watch the road, Lucho."

Lucho held it out of CB's reach. "Relax, CB. You too jumpy."

Lucho put the phone back to his ear. "Tito?" Lucho let out a laugh and turned to CB. "*Oye*, CB, it's Tito. Jorge's lawyer bailed him out this morning." Lucho turned back to the phone and listened. "*Si*, CB is here with me …" Lucho listened for a while. "*Si … no.*"

Lucho hung up. He looked over at CB, his eyes narrow as if Tito had pissed him off about something. For no reason at all, CB thought it had to do with him. But he hadn't seen Tito for months, and he had enough problems with the fucking Feds without worrying about some mother-fucker from the *pueblo* in DR who used to kick his ass every summer when they were kids.

Lucho hung up and made a sharp exit from the highway. As if CB hadn't been nervous enough, there was something new in the air. "Where are we going, Lucho?"

Lucho's voice had turned mean, every word laced with unexplained venom. "You know Jorge's nephew, my cousin, will die if we don't get this money?"

"Yeah, sure. I mean I hope not. We're going to get the money."

Lucho didn't answer. CB gripped the leather armrest as Lucho road-raged through streets in Washington Heights, past apartment houses with bodegas and bars on their first floor. Lucho accelerated and braked fast, making CB's stomach churn.

"I just wanted to hear that you know."

Lucho pulled under an overpass on Dyckman Street in Inwood, the shadowed sidewalk spattered with pigeon droppings from their roost within the steel girders above. Fencing ahead separated the wide dead-end street from a park.

"You wait here," Lucho said to the men in the back of the car. "You, come," Lucho said to CB and got out of the car.

CB's legs felt wobbly and he needed to pee. He didn't like this, didn't like the way Lucho was acting. CB had a bad feeling. This dead-end street without an easy exit wasn't a good place to do a high-dollar exchange. And why wouldn't the other men come with them?

CB could see the beginning of a path on the far side of the overpass, sloping upward toward the park. He ticked the seconds off in his head, his back stiff. Every second they were on foot—CB's phone emitting a slow-moving signal—brought them closer to the *federales* arriving and shooting it out with Lucho. CB didn't want to be in the crossfire when they tried to take Lucho down, especially in the middle of nowhere with no way to get out.

CB glanced beside him and saw an expression on Lucho's face that made him prefer to take his chances on a shootout. CB's breathing shallowed with each step. There wasn't a human being in sight. CB would have done anything to see a single person other than Lucho.

Lucho stopped.

CB peered around. "What are we doing here, Lucho?"

"You think we would not know, sooner or later?"

"What?" CB's heart plummeted, a lead weight.

"You were seen when you got busted. Tito saw you. You should have kept a better eye out if you was gonna be a pussy."

CB shook his head slowly, backing up toward the wall.

"You got busted." Lucho's phone rang again, muffled through the leather of his jacket pocket. Lucho yanked it out and slammed it with a loud crash against the wall next to CB's head. "The police are probably tracking this now, no?" Lucho lurched and hurled the crushed telephone over the fence into the park. Then he pivoted back around and pulled out a shiny .357 Magnum from his shoulder holster. He pointed it at CB's head. "You think we stupid *y los federales* think we stupid. But Jorge and me don't stay in business for twenty-five years being stupid."

CB began to cry.

"I know they got the *federales* coming fast right to where we standing now. Gotta be—'cause they know the money is coming. But I got big enough balls for this. One fucking *cabron*, I can handle." Lucho clicked off his gun's safety.

"*Por favor*, Lucho." CB's back pressed hard against the overpass' stone wall. He cried, "We're from the same town."

Lucho put the cold steel of the gun flush between CB's eyes. Hot urine coursed down CB's inner thighs, his wet legs giving way under him. The gun followed downward, pressing against CB's forehead as his back inched down the wall.

"You should have thought of that when you were planning for me and Jorge to go to prison and my cousin to die."

"No, Lucho, it wasn't like that."

Lucho leaned close to CB's face. "When I see your mother, I will tell her goodbye for you."

The gun muzzle pressed heavier against CB's skin as Lucho's arm straightened. Lucho backed up a pace to avoid blood spraying on his clothes. CB had time to know that, his last thought.

CHAPTER 38

Jessica and Lauren sat in the front seat of Pedro's late-model Mercedes Benz. Pedro hadn't said anything yet. His cologne—applied with a strong hand—filled the car. It was cologne that had been popular a few years ago, a scent ever-present at malls and cocktail parties. He wore a thick gold Rolex that peeked out from under the sleeve of his leather jacket as he steered, a watch not so different from Brian's—the one they never found.

Jessica observed the streets they passed in case they needed to find a way out in a hurry. She had long ago lost her sense of direction in this strange, hilly territory of the Bronx. At one point, they'd passed under the elevated train she and Lauren had seen last week. Jessica didn't know exactly where they were, but she didn't think they'd traveled a great distance from Manhattan. They'd seemed to circle more than anything.

An icy fear kept Jessica's muscles stiff and her mouth dry. She was trapped between Lauren and the silent man. She could feel the heat of his thigh against hers. At least he wasn't Lucho. He paled next to Lucho's frightening energy. She only hoped Lucho would stay away until Lauren and she were done and out of there.

The car traveled a wide street. Pedro turned right, uphill on a hairpin curve, and onto a narrower street of prewar apartment buildings and clapboard houses. The familiarity dawned on Jessica. At the center of an empty lot was the building with the scorched lobby they'd visited, the twelve-million-dollar building.

Pedro didn't say anything as he pulled into a spot two-thirds of the way up the hill and got out of the car.

"Brian's building," Jessica said when they were momentarily alone.

Lauren nodded, her mouth a downward parenthesis.

They left the car and followed Pedro across the street to the rubble-strewn lot. Jessica and Lauren followed Pedro between the building's two brick wings over the matted-down path through the courtyard. They entered the charred lobby with its stench of fire, human debris, and mold. There was no sign of the homeless woman from before, and Pedro headed to the opposite side of the lobby.

A sudden noise from behind spun Jessica around. The metal front door had opened then crashed shut. A little kid ran by, clattering up a staircase with a plastic grocery bag in hand. A door creaked open above and a quick rattle of adult Spanish drifted out before the door slammed shut.

The thought occurred to Jessica: if they had to run for help, would those people help them? A voice inside her head swiftly answered: *You don't know because you don't belong here. You should never have come here. Turn around, and get out now.*

Ignoring the voice, Jessica followed Pedro through a fire-widened doorframe into the freezing shell of the apartment she and Lauren had been in before. Wind whipped through the empty brick window frame at the far-right side of the room. The opening let in daylight, the rest of the windows still boarded up. Jessica's eyes burned with terror that she kept at bay with grim determination.

Pedro stopped at the center of the large room that had once been an entire apartment. He held up his palm, "Wait. *Viene* Jorge."

Breathe, Jessica commanded herself and turned back around in time to see Pedro walk toward the apartment's entrance. A man entered.

"Jorge." Pedro stepped forward, deferentially, and shook Jorge's hand.

A wiry man with a wooden gun butt sticking out of his jeans' waistband came into the room behind Jorge.

Jessica's inner voice—she recognized it as her father's voice now—

spoke up again: *You've made a mistake, Jessica, like usual. You're a screwup like your mother, a walking mistake, Jessica. And now you've really fucked up, just like you always fucked up.* But, Jessica realized with a start, that wasn't true. She'd hardly ever screwed up. She'd made some mistakes, but she was far from a fuckup, maybe too far from one. She looked at Jorge, at his arrogant bearing, as if he owned the whole goddamn world and an unexpected anger percolated from deep inside her, drowning out the berating inner voice. She, Lauren, and Emily had been royally fucked by everyone—by Brian, Steve, Jessica's father, and now this bastard standing in front of her. And they deserved better.

She met Jorge's dark appraising stare. His eyes flickered to her breasts and back to her eyes. She saw red. Right now, all she wanted was to know who in the hell had killed her husband and turned their lives into a goddamn mine field. This man had the answers.

***

CB had seen Lauren. He'd called Carl to tell him she was at the bar meeting Lucho. Lucho had already murdered someone just to send a message to the Tong. To Lucho, life was worth less than the cost of postage, at least other people's lives. And here Carl was, ready to make the biggest and most dangerous bust of his career, and Lauren was in the middle of it, with Lucho.

Carl gently rubbed the sides of his sore nose and looked out the car window. He and Rick were driving on Broadway past Fort Tryon Park, following CB's cell signal at a distance. Several times, Carl had almost told Rick about CB's call and everything else. But he couldn't chance screwing up his entire career or put Rick in the position of knowing—not unless it became a matter of life or death. The situation hadn't reached that point yet. If all went smoothly, the bust would go down without a shot fired. They had enough manpower to thoroughly overwhelm Arena's crew and the Tong, making gunplay unattractive even to those ruthless bastards.

Yet no one was expecting innocent women to be there. You held your fire a lot longer when you knew innocent people were likely to be in the crossfire. Of course, if Lauren and Jessica were there, the troops would assume guilt, not innocence, no matter what Carl said at this point. At least everyone knew to watch out for CB. Maybe they would look before they fired. But an informant wasn't really innocent in anyone's eyes either.

Carl looked down at his Gossamer, homing in on CB's signal. "Lucho's with him. They're about eight blocks northwest."

Carl didn't say the rest of what he was thinking: there were no other cell phones there. That meant Lauren wasn't with CB and Lucho anymore. Carl felt as if a vice had unclasped his lungs. Whatever she'd been doing at the bar could be over … unless something had happened to her phone.

Carl pressed the mic on his earpiece, "They're in Dyckman Park near the Henry Hudson Parkway."

"They're waiting for Arena there," Rick said.

"Yeah."

"We're getting feed from the drone, approaching the area now," a voice said in Carl's ear. Carl held his breath, waiting to hear what surprises the video might show.

Their car sped down a wide two-way street in a gentrified section of Inwood, its sidewalk cafés fallow in the November chill like a farmer's fields after harvest. They passed parking garages and industrial space on one side of the street and a playground and wooded hills on the other. Carl pulled his nine-millimeter from his shoulder holster. Their car stopped within sight of an overpass that supported the Henry Hudson Parkway above. A half-dozen Bureau cars converged from behind them, all proceeding slowly onto the dead-end street.

Carl's ear filled with the woman's voice again. "The drone's not showing anything. No one's here, not outside at least."

Carl looked at Rick. "It's too quiet."

Rick nodded.

The woman's voice: "We're going in."

Agents ran from their cars, all wearing windbreakers with FBI printed across the front and back. Several agents began looking in the cars parked on the block. As Carl ran, he couldn't help but notice the lack of luxury cars that Arena, Lucho, and the Tong members would have driven.

Silently, groups of agents ran forward, swinging around in an arch.

"Team Three," responded another female voice, "we have a body, west end of the underpass."

"Shit." Carl ran, hugging the wall of the tunnel, Rick following closely behind him.

Two agents stood over a corpse, face mangled, jacket open. Under the jacket, the dead man wore an electric blue T-shirt, soaked with blood.

Rick banged the side of his fist against the brick wall. "It was a setup."

Carl felt a moment of gut-wrenching guilt. Then fear settled deep in his spine. Where was Lauren? He grabbed Rick's arm. "Listen, we've gotta find Jorge."

"It was a setup. They found out about CB, told him a deal was going down, and killed him. Jorge's not around."

Carl shouted at Rick. "No, man, I was closest to this thing. Lucho said on the audio that they were expecting documents today. Documents is code for money. The weapons are on the move toward Italy. Something's going down today. We have to grab Jorge now."

Rick growled back, "Don't you get it? We don't know where he is, and they were probably just suckering CB to get him out here."

Carl could feel the stares of the other agents who were starting to gather and mill nearby, waiting for orders. Carl lowered his voice, "Hold on." He turned to the other agents. "I've got something before we toss it in." Carl went back to the car and entered a number into his Gossamer that he'd noted days ago. Agents gathered near his open door. Adrenaline poured though Carl. He envisioned disaster for himself, but Lauren's life was more important. The whole thing hadn't been a setup to sucker CB, or Lauren wouldn't have been with them today. He looked down. "I've got it. I've got a signal. Jessup Avenue in the Bronx. It's a signal associated with Arena."

He heard Rick behind him, talking into his radio. "Command, we're going to follow the signal Carl has and see if we can salvage things."

"Ten-four."

As Rick started the car, Carl knocked his knuckles in a frustrated rhythm against the passenger window. Rick cast a concerned glance at Carl before he pulled out. Carl ignored him, tense enough to spring through the windshield if he didn't keep a tight rein on himself. He thought back to the audio they'd heard yesterday. Lucho said the documents were arriving today. The women were delivering the missing money. What other explanation could there be for Lauren's cell phone signal placing her in the Bronx?

First Brian Silverman, then Jordan Connors, now CB. By the time the car reached the bridge that would bring them over the Harlem River to the Bronx, Carl was sure the only thing going down today was Lauren, and there might not be a damn thing he could do about it.

***

Jorge Arena was tall and stocky. He looked like kin to Pedro, except Jorge had salt-and-pepper hair and an air of authority and meanness that Pedro lacked. Jorge motioned Lauren toward him and pointed to her attaché. "Is this mine?"

"Yes." She stepped forward, willing her hand not to shake as she held it out to him.

"Good." He opened the flap and unzipped it. His wiry bodyguard stood close to his side, gun in hand now. Jorge looked inside then held the leather bag out to Pedro. "*Cuentalos.*"

"*Si.*" Pedro took the bag from Jorge. He knelt in a corner and began counting the bonds.

Now was the time to negotiate, Lauren coached herself. She had to tell Jorge that half the bonds weren't there before Pedro realized it and told him. She had to let Jorge know where the safe-deposit box was and where he could pick up the key. But before she could say anything, Jessica stepped toward Jorge. He looked curiously at Jessica and scanned her, head to toe, undressing her.

"Who killed my husband?" Jessica demanded.

What the hell? What was Jessica doing?

Jorge laughed, nothing friendly in the sound. "What?"

"You've got your money. Well, I want to know who killed Brian. You killed him or you know." Jessica's voice raised. "I've been through too much shit to leave here without answers."

Jorge shook his head and took a step closer to Jessica. "You are a stunningly stupid woman. Why would I kill your husband? Have you noticed how much trouble his death caused?"

Lauren glanced nervously back at Pedro. He still counted.

"Jordan, yes, he had to die." Jorge waved his hand in a dismissive gesture. "Mistakes—a few dollars lost, a few questionable hands of poker at my place—okay, but not this caliber mistake. And once we found you, we didn't need him anymore." Jorge moved closer to Jessica. "Anyway, my love, the fire was an accident. Your husband was smoking in bed."

Jessica stood tall, glaring at Jorge, her face red with fury.

"Jessica," Lauren tried to call her back. Lauren had a bad feeling about Jorge confessing Jordan's murder.

At the sound of her name, Jessica looked toward Lauren then back at Jorge. "The cigarette they found wasn't his brand, and his watch was never found."

Lauren gaped. Jessica had never told her about the cigarette brand.

A cruel glint in Jorge's eyes combined with a sexual leer. "He liked pussy, your husband."

Jessica blinked hard, her mouth snapped shut.

"He was with a *puta*, one of ours. We always kept an eye on things. He had a beautiful Cuban girl. They had a good fuck. Then she left."

Lauren looked back at Pedro. He was still counting—three quarters of the way through the pile. She stepped closer to Jessica, whose eyes glistened. It hadn't been true—what Jessica said in the car—that nothing Brian did could hurt her anymore.

"You ever had a cigarette habit?" Jorge asked Jessica without waiting for a reply. "It doesn't matter what brand you smoke if you run out. He bummed one from my girl and died smoking the wrong brand. There are worse things."

Jorge glanced around the women toward the back of the room, checking on Pedro's progress. Lauren began to speak again, to tell him the bonds were short, but Jorge interrupted. "The missing watch? Your husband trusted women too much, even hookers. He was the kind of moron who thought whores really liked him, that his package was so big and his technique so good that it wasn't just the money they were after."

Jorge chuckled. "But with hookers, it's always about the money, always. So, we learned that she took some liberties and stole his watch."

Jessica sucked back sobs.

"We spoke to the girl. After all, your husband was a valued employee. She didn't know that. But when we spoke to her, she admitted she put something in his drink, and he fell asleep. She took his watch. A Rolex. She said she didn't notice the cigarette burning. Like Jordan not knowing where to find the money, this mistake won't happen again."

Lauren paused, startled by the news: a prostitute had accidentally killed Brian.

"Jorge." From behind her, Pedro spoke fast in Spanish.

Jorge looked at Jessica then Lauren, his face flushing.

"We have the other half of the money in safekeeping," Lauren said more calmly than she felt.

"Really?"

"We need to be assured we'll be safe. This half is for goodwill. The other half is in a safe-deposit box. The key to the box can be picked up at Manhattan Family Court, fifth-floor waiting area. Our person will give you the key when I call and say we're safe." Lauren watched Jorge's face turn nearly a purplish shade, but continued, "Only one more thing. When you go there, leave the guns in your car. You'll have to pass through a metal detector to get in."

Stepping toward Lauren, Jorge snapped at Pedro. "Call Lucho *now*."

Pedro took out his cell phone and punched in numbers. He listened, shook his head. He said something to Jorge in Spanish then dialed again. Jorge nodded nearly imperceptibly to his bodyguard, who grabbed Jessica and put his gun to her temple. Jorge moved in and grasped a handful of Lauren's hair at the scalp, yanking her toward him. "Stupid whore. You want me to go to a courthouse? Right in front of the police?"

"Yes."

"Call them right now. Call your person. Get them here now!"

***

"Fuck," Carl spit the curse from his lips as their car had to slow at a red light on the Grand Concourse in the Bronx where crosstown traffic only sluggishly cleared for them despite their flashing lights.

Rick grabbed Carl's arm, speaking with a low but demanding intensity, "What's the problem?"

Carl wrenched his arm away.

"Don't lose your cool, Carl. It'll be our biggest bust, and we'll still end up transferred to Antarctica."

When the car was moving again, Carl fought with himself for one last moment, breathed in deep and braced himself. "Lauren Davis is out there. It's her signal on the Gossamer."

Rick slammed his palms against the steering wheel. "Goddammit, Carl, I don't believe—"

The radio came to life in their ears, a female voice. "This is Command. We've got something interesting here. The stingray picked up a call from Pedro Arena's phone, Jessup Avenue. The same place your Gossamer is sending us. And we've got some Tong members on the move too, headed that way."

Rick hit the gas, throwing Carl backward against the seat. The woman's voice spoke in their ears now, sending all the teams to the address. The blood drained from Carl's face, imagining the brutal Tong with Lauren too.

As Rick drove, Carl plugged in Pedro's cell phone identifier into his Gossamer, getting rid of the evidence that he was tracking Lauren. He trusted Rick not to tell. If Carl was lucky, no one would be the wiser that he hadn't been following Pedro's signal all along. That would be his last lie. He wasn't cut out for this shit. His heart beat a rap tempo. He was scared on so many levels.

Rick glanced at Carl and back at the road. His nostrils flaring, he spoke to Carl, "Spill it, everything."

CHAPTER 39

Jorge threw Lauren into Pedro's arms. His gun jabbed painfully into her ribs. She tried to reason things out but couldn't think with Pedro's hand running up and down her body, frisking her.

Released by the bodyguard, Jessica began screaming at Jorge, her face red. "You'll never get the key if you lay a hand on us. I don't give a fuck what you do, hell will freeze over."

Pedro let go of Lauren. Jessica's shouting filled the room. Arena's fist crashed against the side of Jessica's face. She fell. Arena stepped toward her. In that instant, Lauren knew what she had to do. She moved between Jessica and Arena, who looked hard at Lauren. By his shoulder, the sinewy bodyguard released his gun's safety and pointed it at Lauren's head.

Arena pulled out a switchblade and grasped Lauren's arm. "*Call.* For six million dollars, I'll leave you with railroad tracks for a face."

Lauren leaned even closer to Arena, the knife's point touching her cheek. She fixed her eyes on him. "I think not, Jorge."

Jorge's eyes flashed with rage. "What?"

Remembering herself as the girl who'd cleaned up her dead father's drug stash, the girl who'd survived in the streets, who'd lived with a killer, who stood up in court every day, she forced her voice out strong. "Have you thought about how we found the bonds?" She stared into his eyes.

"Brian was an excellent record keeper. He listed all the corporate shells you used to receive your payoffs from Jordan. And something tells me that's where you've hidden *all* your money."

Jorge's eyes narrowed.

Seeing his reaction, Lauren gained confidence, feeling as if she were in a powerful zone despite the knife against her skin. "The bottom line is that I'm not depending on just one person at the courthouse," Lauren lied. "My attorney will deliver the information to Federal Plaza at five p.m. if Jessica and I don't show up safe before then. Once the names of the shell companies are exposed, you won't be able to get the six million or any other money you were putting away for a rainy day. You'll be broke and on the run from a murder indictment … because the Feds will know exactly who wanted to hurt us and why."

Jorge's mouth closed into a tight slash. The knife point stuck deeper into Lauren's skin at her cheekbone. A trickle of blood ran down her face. The bodyguard's gun muzzle aimed at her head.

She lowered her voice for emphasis, "Tell me, how far will your cash-on-hand get you when you're hiding in the mountains of DR, paying off every cop, soldier, and politician who happens by? If you get that far."

***

Emily gripped her burner phone inside her jacket pocket. The Family Court waiting room was filled with people, standing and taking up every seat. She willed her phone to vibrate. She tried not to think of the possibility that she'd never hear her mother's voice again. She had the strongest urge to run out of the court and find some way to help, but she was keeping her promise and doing exactly what her mother said. Her mother said that she had to keep herself safe—for all their sakes. That meant doing nothing, no matter how hard it was.

A loud alarm slung Emily to her feet. The crowd reacted in a wave of noise. The court officers fanned out amongst them, flashes of uniforms in concerted movement. A public-announcement system called from above in between alarms, "This is a building-wide evacuation. Please proceed in an orderly manner to the emergency exits. Follow the instructions of court officers and building personnel."

The court officers opened stairwell exits. People moved, grabbing their kids and belongings in a fell swoop. A court officer with a megaphone announced over the repeated alarm and the noise of hundreds of families: "No running. Make your way quickly and quietly to the stairwells. No running please."

The throng surged toward the stairwells. Emily didn't see the skinny court officer, Gary, anymore. She hurried toward his courtroom.

"Miss, *Miss*," a short female court officer shouted Emily back. "That area is off-limits. You have to evacuate by the stairs."

"But—"

She sternly guided Emily away. "No buts. To the stairs *now*. Everyone has to evacuate the building by order of the NYPD."

Emily had a dark feeling. Would someone evacuate a whole building just for her? Just to get her outside the courthouse where they couldn't bring their weapons? For six million dollars? The thought made it hard for her to swallow. She considered hiding in a bathroom, but the officers were watching. And she felt safer in a crowd than left behind by herself. She entered the packed cement stairs, walking downward next to a mother and daughter of elementary school age.

***

The knife penetrated deeper into the skin over Lauren's cheekbone, the pain intensifying momentarily, then lightening up. Jorge released Lauren's arm in disgust.

A series of gunshots thundered. Lauren jumped back, her heart rappelling up her throat before she realized she wasn't shot. Jorge spun toward the apartment doorway and pulled out his gun. The bodyguard shouted in rapid Spanish over the noise.

Jorge yelled back, *"Vete, vete."* The bodyguard hit the wall near the doorway, looking out the apartment. He ran into the lobby.

More shots sounded out there. The percussion, then explosion, of each shot resonated against the walls. Jessica scrambled to her feet, still staggering and bleary-eyed from Jorge's blow to her head. Lauren grabbed her and spoke near her ear, "Gotta be a robbery, someone knew about the bonds."

They backed up, the full significance of a rip-off hitting Lauren. She'd seen the gory news stories of what happened when criminals robbed each other. They didn't leave witnesses.

Jorge and Pedro shouted to each other. The shots continued to rumble inside the building, each clap striking closer. Lauren looked around in panic. There was no cover and no place to hide. Jorge leaned against a wall, entirely focused on the entrance to the apartment and beyond.

Lauren signaled Jessica toward the window opening at the back of the room. If they got the chance, they could jump. It couldn't be more than a few feet to the ground outside, high enough to break an ankle if they were unlucky, but they had to take the risk.

Eyes still unfocused, Jessica steadied herself on Lauren but seemed to understand as they inched toward the back of the room. With Jorge's back to them, Lauren looked around to gauge Pedro's location. Pedro was a few yards from them, closer to the door. Pedro's eyes darted around, his gun out. Lauren and Jessica crouched near the back wall, waiting for the gun-fight to pull him and Jorge away, so she and Jessica could make their move out the window. They needed only the smallest moment of opportunity. Lauren prayed for just one moment of leeway.

Gunfire pounded right outside the apartment now. A man screamed. Jorge ran to the door, signaling Pedro to follow. The women scrambled toward the window just as blasts filled the room, one after the next. The women dove to the floor as shots burst from Jorge's gun. Return fire sprayed Lauren with splinters from a bullet that landed nearby.

Her hearing muffled, Lauren saw Jorge shouting, firing out of the doorway. Lauren yanked Jessica's arm, ready to run now. Return blasts ricocheted wildly around the room. Jorge lurched backward, his hands flying up and his gun firing wildly as he fell.

***

Within the cacophony of families flowing outward, Emily paused before she passed through the metal detectors that would lead her to the Family Court's lobby and outside. There was no sign of fire or smoke. No way this could be a fire drill or a real bomb threat. Her mother must have told Arena about getting the key from Emily, and now Emily was leaving the courthouse and its metal detectors. Armed men could be waiting for her outside. She had no idea what to do.

Court officers on megaphones urged the crowd on, "Please exit the building. Keep it moving."

Emily breathed in harsh air, realizing she wasn't safe from weapons inside the courthouse anyway. The officers had disarmed the metal detectors. Otherwise, they would have been ringing now that everyone was exiting through them. She allowed herself to be herded along by the crowd.

On the wide plaza in front of the court, people milled, a kaleidoscope of movement and conversations. Griping mothers formed ragged semicircles around the court officers demanding to know what had happened that was delaying their cases. Emily thought of going to one of the officers but knew they wouldn't take the time to listen to her now. People streamed across the street to wait in a pocket park until they received the all clear to return. Cars honked, trying to get through the jay-walking crowd.

Two large men moved into the families that filled the sidewalk instead of walking around on the curb. Emily spotted the men scanning faces. She groaned, her heart exploding in her chest. They didn't belong in Family Court. They had to be looking for her.

Someone grabbed her from behind. Her breath whooshed out of her.

Next to her ear, a man's voice: "Don't say a word." He pulled her backward, behind a column.

"Tabu?!"

***

Lauren and Jessica stopped short, still several steps from the window. The building went starkly silent, leaving a buzz in Lauren's ears. A man stood in the burnt doorway. In a blur of speed, he and a group of men, five in all, ran into the empty apartment. Asian men, wiry and fit. They strode in, shouting, guns trained on the women and Pedro. "Hands up, hands up."

Jorge was dead, and Pedro lay groaning on the floor, his pants turning maroon with blood. The new arrivals roughly frisked Pedro where he lay, checking his clothes and turning him from side to side to make sure he didn't have a gun under him. Two others grabbed Lauren and Jessica and ran their palms up and down their bodies, checking them for guns, too. Lauren fought back panic.

The leader, with a black-stubbled head and dressed in a stretchy cross between a sweat suit and evening wear, crouched near Pedro. The other men looked around, stone-faced, dangerously scared. The leader pointed to two of his men and, speaking to them in Chinese, waved them away toward the lobby, probably to keep watch.

Pedro moaned, his eyes slits. The leader crouched and put a hand on the scattered documents next to Pedro. He looked up with a grin at his friends and said in English, "Dudes, holy shit, yeah."

He picked one up and read it. He read a couple more and spoke excitedly in Chinese to his friends. His grin disappeared, and he waved his gun at the women and spoke to them for the first time. "We need to get out of here fast. Cooperate, and we will all be getting out, us first. Lie down. On your stomachs with your hands behind your heads."

The women didn't move fast enough.

He shouted, "*Now!*"

"Wait, please," Lauren put up her palm. She knew what happened when people lined up facedown on the floor. For the first time in this whole ordeal, she thought she was about to die. She pictured Emily. Alone. Things could not end this way. She could not leave Emily alone in the world. "Wait, please. I have a daughter. We both have young children."

Jessica looked at Lauren, her eyes opening wide as she caught on to what Lauren was saying.

"I'll do anything. We'll come with you," Lauren said, even though she knew these men would kill them no matter what if they didn't want witnesses. All she could do was buy time. "Please."

The leader gave Lauren a long look.

***

Tabu wore a black hoodie and sweats, his face unshaven. A gust of wind billowed his hood, and Emily could see how stressed he was. He'd been running. He was still breathing hard.

"This way," he told Emily, grabbing her hand.

They squeezed past the families who continued to exit the Family Court and slipped back inside the building. In the confusion, no one stopped them from threading their way through the muted metal detectors, past the elevators, toward the back of the courthouse. Tabu led Emily to a metal door and out into a cobblestoned alleyway between the back of the Family Court and another brick building.

"I smoked back here when I was your age." Tabu brought Emily behind an office-supply truck parked there, his breathing normal now. "I came to Family Court a lot."

Emily shivered with pent-up terror. "What are you doing here?"

"You didn't dump the burner phone like you promised," Tabu said. "I've been tracking you."

"I'm sorry. I forgot."

"But you know your father wasn't just a lawyer."

Emily nodded, wide-eyed.

"I didn't keep my promise either," Tabu said. "While I was in your father's computer, I looked around. What I saw made me worry about you. Your father took a sick plunge when he got involved with Jorge Arena. Arena is all over the dark web ... but fuck him, I have the home-court advantage there. His people called in the bomb threat that emptied this bitch out," he said, signaling to the courthouse. "When I realized you were here and they were on their way, I made it my business to beat them to you. Luckily, I was at work, not far from here."

"I need to get to the FBI," Emily said. "My mother ..."

***

The FBI car came to a halt at the curb at Jessup Avenue. Ahead, Lucho followed behind a couple of his men, walking toward the entrance to a scaffolded building.

"That's Lucho, let's go," Carl said.

"Yo, wait on the team."

"Right." Carl pulled out his nine-millimeter and ran from the car, not giving Rick time to stop him. He heard the faint rustle of Rick and other agents following.

It had been an hour since CB called. Carl didn't want that perverted bastard, Lucho, in there with Lauren, and the chances of a shootout would be far greater if Lucho were trapped inside with Jorge's men. Lucho would never let them surrender without a fight. They had to isolate him.

Lucho followed his men, who disappeared inside the building first. Lucho was halfway through the metal door when he checked behind him with a start. Carl sprinted over rubble toward him. Lucho began to draw his gun. But the movement of his arm stopped midway. Rapid gunfire from inside the building exploded in string-sentences. Bullets threw Lucho back against the door.

More gunfire, and Lucho hit the ground. A moment's pause and two members of the Mott Street Tong came out of the building's front door, jumping over Lucho, guns ready to meet whoever else had come with him.

Carl, joined by several FBI agents, shouted, "FBI! Drop your weapons!"

Carl saw the first flash of the Tong members' guns at the same instant that he and his fellow agents began firing.

***

Lauren heard automatic gunfire and what sounded like a grenade beyond the apartment. The leader shouted in Chinese to his men while clutching Lauren's attaché and stuffing fistfuls of bonds into it, some falling out. He didn't take the time to grab the rest. Instead of joining the fight outside the apartment door, the men ran with the attaché and leaped one after the next, a hand on the windowsill, out the window.

Lauren could see their backs receding as they sprinted toward the rear end of the building in the rubble-covered lot. She spoke to Jessica over the noise of the gunshots in the lobby. "We've got to get out of here." She was sure now that they had to get away no matter how risky. They would die here if the shooters reached them.

The women moved toward the window again when the shooting abruptly stopped. Lauren looked back, gasping, the silence buzzing in her ears. They were too late. The new attacker appeared in the doorway. He stood, his gun trained on them. He had a deformed face, bruised and swollen. Lauren looked closer and froze.

In that split second, her eyes met Carl's and she took in the letters F-B-I on his chest. She sucked in air and followed his gaze. He looked at the remaining bonds strewn across the floor. He looked to the open window.

In that instant, she could see pained indecision in his eyes.

***

Battle-charged adrenaline pumped through Carl. He looked at Lauren, the last few days flashing before him. His gut churned. He might as well have killed CB himself. He'd sacrificed everything—his marriage, his conscience—for the Job. Now this.

"Shit." He gave the slightest motion with his forehead toward the window.

Lauren turned toward the window.

"*Hold it!*" Rick appeared from behind Carl, an assault rifle in his hands.

The women stopped short.

He looked at Carl, "Sorry, bro—I didn't see that, not on my watch. Not on this crazy case." Rick aimed his gun at Jessica and Lauren while he walked toward Jorge and stuck a toe in his side, feeling for life. Rick looked across the room, taking in the semiconscious Pedro and the remaining bearer bonds, scattered nearby. "Hands up, ladies, please. You're under arrest."

More agents ran in. Pedro groaned as they turned him over and cuffed him behind his back. A male and female FBI agent rushed to Jessica and Lauren.

Carl averted his eyes from Lauren. He pushed a button on his radio transmitter. "Command, we need an ambulance."

Lauren and Jessica stood still, their hands in the air. Lauren heard clipped police sirens and distant shouting outside. The female agent spun Lauren around and shoved her to the wall. The man did the same to Jessica. The woman agent frisked them, her hands heavy and rough. Then the male agent wrenched their hands behind their backs and cuffed them.

"Let's go, ladies," the female agent said as she took Lauren and Jessica's upper arms and guided them toward the door. "Time for your new life—courtesy of the United States government."

CHAPTER 40

Thursday, November 28

The elderly federal judge looked down at Jessica and Lauren from his bench, which stood tall in a large, silent courtroom. Jessica still found it hard to believe that she, Jessica Silverman, had been arrested twice in one week. Unlike the New York criminal courthouse, polished mahogany and rich carpeting conveyed a sense of dignity to the federal courtroom that, unfortunately, didn't extend to her, the accused. Jessica saw Lauren turning back and smiling encouragingly at Emily, the only person seated in the gallery. Emily had insisted on coming and now anxiously curled her thick hair into dreadlocks over one shoulder. Jessica was nervous, too. Lauren squeezed her hand as if she'd read her thoughts.

After days locked up in the Metropolitan Correction Center, Lauren and Jessica had gotten out on bail, using their homes as collateral. They spent most of the week after that in the US Attorney's office for interrogation. The federal prosecutors had interrogated Emily for an entire day too. Thankfully, they didn't arrest her when she'd arrived at Federal Plaza babbling hysterically about Arena holding her mother and stepmother captive.

In the couple of weeks since, life had returned to a semblance of normality. Lauren had gone back to work, and Emily and Jessica had gone back to their lives in Westchester. Emily had ceased complaining about it and even attended school every day. She'd foresworn the wild life, she said, and they were all grateful to have until school let out in June before Emily and Jessica had to vacate the house, not that Jessica could afford the mortgage beyond that date anyway.

The elderly judge cleared his throat. He scanned the participants: Lauren and Jessica, their tailored lawyers on either side of them, and two Assistant US Attorneys at the prosecution table. "Counselors, I understand that an agreement has been reached."

The older of the US Attorneys spoke. "The United States has agreed to dismissal of all charges in the interest of justice based on the duress that led to the defendants' participation, the substantial evidence that they had no knowledge of the true nature of the conspiracy, and their subsequent cooperation."

Jessica and Lauren had nearly suffered nervous breakdowns when they learned they'd been charged with conspiracy to sell weapons. They were booked alongside Chinese gang members and Arena's men who'd survived. The FBI had been wrong that Arena had planned to meet the Tong. The Tong had come there to rob Arena. If they'd been successful, Xi Wen might never have known it was them who had stolen his money, and Lauren and Jessica would surely have been dead.

"As part of the agreement," the US Attorney continued, "Jessica Silverman will not oppose forfeiture of the marital residence, which was purchased with illegally secured gains."

Brian had prepaid a lot more on the house's mortgage than Jessica had known, over half a million dollars. The federal government was happy with how much money they were getting without a fight and, thankfully, didn't go after Lauren's apartment.

The judge wrote something, then looked up again. "Ms. Davis, I suppose it is superfluous to remind you … if you intend to remain a member of our profession, you should not appear before me again except as an attorney."

"Yes, Your Honor," Lauren replied.

"The cases against Jessica Silverman and Lauren Davis, docket numbers 18/10734 and 18/10735, are dismissed."

"*Yes*," Emily exclaimed from behind them.

Jessica let out a sigh of relief and hugged Lauren.

***

A cold, river wind blew across Centre Street. Jessica walked with Lauren and Emily through Greek-style courthouse columns and down wide stone steps. It was over. The FBI had won big. They'd intercepted the shipment of arms in Italy and twelve million dollars in bearer bonds. Jorge, Lucho, their bodyguards, and two Tong members had died, but Pedro had survived, and the FBI had caught the Tong members who'd taken the bonds. Pedro plea-bargained and turned state's evidence. That meant there was no one among the Arenas left to retaliate against Jessica and Lauren for their cooperation. But it also meant there was no one for the women to testify against in exchange for their freedom.

It was Emily who saved them from going to jail, her and her friend, Tabu. He brought Emily safely from Family Court to the Federal Building entrance on Worth Street. Before leaving her there, he asked for two things: one, not to tell the Feds he'd been involved and, two, not to tell them about the safe-deposit box and six million dollars until she and her mother had lawyers. He asked her to trust him on this, and she did. So Jessica and Lauren were able to voluntarily offer the bonds to the Feds later. That deal had saved them from prison sentences.

Warm air rushed up from the subway station as the women descended the stairs. Jessica's mind drifted. She had calls to make once she and Emily arrived home. She had to try to get out of the lease agreements for Brian's plane, hangar, and car, or she'd have to file for bankruptcy. Legal fees for their estate attorneys were eating away at what was left of Brian's money, and the FBI hadn't left much of that. And without proof of a profit-sharing agreement between Brian and Steve, the estate attorneys weren't offering any hope for a decent settlement.

Jessica looked over the side of the subway platform. "The train's coming already. I'm going to get used to this when I move here. I'll save a lot of money when I get rid of my car."

"Are you moving to our neighborhood?" Emily asked, still calling

Washington Heights home, especially now that she'd be moving back in June. "There's a dog run in Fort Tryon Park."

"Maybe. It could be within my budget if I'm that far uptown. I don't want a roommate, other than you when you sleep over. If I live nearby, you could walk over to babysit."

Lauren took a long look at Jessica. "I think you're starting to show." She smirked. "Mostly on top."

Jessica put her hand on her belly, already in love with the baby there.

"That's why I'm applying to NYU," Emily said. "I'm not going away to college. My sister will need me."

"It could be a boy," Lauren said.

"No way," Emily said. "I've got a feeling about this."

"Brian would have had a fit, can you imagine?" Jessica said. "I can hear the yelling in my head now. He would have said I did it on purpose."

"Didn't you?" Emily asked.

Jessica imitated Emily's New York accent, "Get out."

The train thundered into the station and they crammed into the car's front corner, standing room only. Jessica leaned her back against the door of the engineer's compartment. "So, this morning I was googling review courses for the medical school entrance exam."

"Really?" Lauren said.

"I have all the science classes I need and I had good grades in college. If I'm careful, I'll have enough money to stay home with the baby for its first year."

"*Her* first year," Emily said.

Jessica chuckled. "I'm sure I could carve out the time to study for the test. I could go to medical school the next year." Feeling a surge of excitement that their legal troubles were behind them, Jessica reveled in her freedom to think about any future for herself and her baby now. "It would mean student loans … a crapload of student loans. That's the main thing that worries me. But I always wanted to be a doctor, and if I could get through the last few weeks, I don't see why I couldn't get through medical school, pay back the loans, and raise a kid."

"I'll help," Emily said.

Jessica hugged Emily. "Thank you, Emmy."

"We'll both help," Lauren said. "You'll definitely need to live near us."

Jessica smiled broadly, really starting to believe she could do it. "Okay."

The train stopped at Union Square, crowds pushing out and pushing in.

"So, you haven't heard from Carl?" Jessica asked.

"Oh, God, he is so ugly," Emily said.

"Everyone's ugly when they have a broken nose," Lauren responded. "Emily and I saw him at the US Attorney's office, and he didn't speak. I think he has to stay away from me. It's still hard to believe it was all a lie between us, but I don't know why a guy lying still surprises me." Lauren turned to Emily, "Not that there aren't decent guys."

"I know, Mom. I get it."

The three left the subway at Grand Central Station and walked to their Metro North track through the vast Main Concourse. Lauren gave Jessica and Emily long hugs, only reluctantly letting them go before they missed their train to Westchester.

CHAPTER 41

Friday, November 29

Before dawn, Lauren's zip car headed north on the New York State Thruway, a slash of blacktop cutting through mountain ranges massed darkly on the horizon. By 7:00 a.m., signs appeared for the Clinton/ Dannemora Correctional Facility, a prison made famous by a headline-grabbing breakout a few years before. At 8:00 a.m., Lauren waited in line amongst wives, children, and parents. She placed her pocketbook on a metal table where a corrections officer searched it. A female CO patted Lauren down lightly after she walked through a metal detector.

Lauren filed into a large room along with the other visitors. She tried not to think about the horror stories she'd read about Bobby in the true-crime book. Round plastic table-and-chair groupings were set up at intervals in a room the size of a high school cafeteria. A moat of empty space around each seating group permitted private conversations and easy access for the corrections officers in case of funny business or violence. Dozens of visits had already begun, and the voices formed a low hum like the background music in a meditation video.

A CO directed Lauren to sit at an empty table to wait for her prisoner to arrive. She took in the room: the officers stood watching at the perimeter; behind them, vending machines full of microwaveable meals lined the walls; in one corner, prisoners and their loved ones could pose for photos in front of a sunset printed on a tarp pegged to a wall. Or they could choose a photo of a palm tree and pretend to sit under it. Lauren couldn't say what she was feeling at that moment. It was as if she'd been riding waves and been clobbered too many times. She was exhausted, and not just because she'd had only a couple of hours sleep the night before.

Prisoners filed in from a door at the far side of the room. When Bobby walked in, Lauren felt as if she were seeing time-lapse photography. From afar, he was a version of the thirty-year-old man she'd known, but as he walked closer, he morphed into a balding, fine-lined fifty-year-old with muscled arms and belly paunch. He wasn't shocked to see her.

"I was surprised I was on your visit list," Lauren said to him after he sat down and said a neutral hello. A prisoner had to submit the name and address of any proposed visitor, so the prison could do a security check, and the prisoner wouldn't have to see unwelcome visitors. Lauren was already on the list when she called the prison to inquire about visiting.

He smirked. "You've been on it for twenty years. You look good."

"Thanks." She didn't feel revulsion or fear the way she thought she'd feel when she saw him. She didn't feel as if she were talking to the sadistic serial killer described in the book, or to a guy who had put a contract on her. There was no evil energy that distinguished Bobby from anybody else.

"You come for dispensation?"

"Bobby, I had nothing to do with you getting busted. I didn't even know anything to tell the cops."

He glared at her. "Get the fuck out of here."

Lauren tensed up, thinking he might punch her, fast, before the guards could stop him. Worse than the idea of being hit, she was afraid that if he hit her, it would end their visit before she convinced him to cancel the contract.

"I left for drug treatment," she said. "And, really, I couldn't stomach the Life anymore."

"Word was that you were in the Witness Protection Program. Not just the Feds, but the word on the Street. A guy I knew saw you at the Federal Building."

"It was a ruse, Bobby. They bullshitted you. The guy you knew was probably the one working for them. If I were in the Witness Protection

Program, I wouldn't have ended up going to NYU in the Village with my real name. I was in drug treatment upstate when you got busted."

"That was a surprise, when I heard you were in New York all that time. I heard about it a few days ago." He sat and thought, his face turning ruddy as he processed how the Feds had gotten it over on him. "They had enough on me anyways. Fuck it. At least with the plea bargain, I'll be out for my golden years."

Lauren couldn't tell whether he was being facetious about his golden years. She doubted they'd give him parole before he was on his deathbed, probably not even then. But knowing Bobby, he had some cash stashed away to give him a future worth dreaming about.

"Mom and Pop both passed already," he said.

"I'm sorry, Bobby."

"We could start up again together. You could visit, and one day we could live our old age in Florida. I've got a place in Delray next to a golf course."

You've gotta be kidding, Lauren almost said it aloud. Putting to the side that he was a murderer, which was like putting aside an elephant beamed into your living room, she was light years away from even the idea of Bobby. He was locked up in a mental time warp, not just a physical prison. "I can't make this trip all the time, Bobby. It's a long way. I have a kid and a job."

He smirked. "Sure, you're right." But he let it go.

They talked for a while without rancor, mostly small talk about his family and friends who Lauren hadn't thought about for years. She walked away from the visit with the promise that the contract was canceled. She believed Bobby about that despite her rejecting his proposal, one that still boggled her mind.

***

Purple twilight reflected off a tall glass building when Lauren rounded a curve in forest-lined Palisades Interstate Parkway. The peaks of the George Washington Bridge appeared. She filled up the car's gas tank at a roadside station before heading over the bridge into New York City. She returned the zip car on 183rd Street and walked west, carrying a grocery bag filled with fruit she'd bought from a sidewalk vendor. Commuters flowed out of the subway entrance as she reached her block.

Lauren approached her building. She would have expected to feel happier, now that she was safe. She was pretty much broke, but she had gotten her life back, and Emily was doing great. Lauren felt sure she'd find a way to pay the bills. After traveling a bizarre memory lane with Bobby and after all she'd just been through, the miracle of her life had been catapulted into the forefront of her consciousness. She no longer took it for granted, and the first half of her life had ceased to be a distant dream she was running from. She could at last appreciate that her past was responsible for who she'd become. And that was a good result, whatever happened next.

Yet the illusion that she was satisfied with her life had shattered, too. She couldn't keep playing life neurotically safe the way she had for the last twenty years, shadowboxing with her fears. She'd been half living, or maybe three-quarters living, but there had to be more. A beautiful sunset like tonight was nice, even though she was alone, but sharing a sunset photo on Facebook was nothing like pointing it out to a warm-blooded human being. She'd felt lonely and discontented before Brian's death and hadn't even known it. Jessica had been right that there was no going back to her old life, or at least not to the oblivion of it.

She neared the glass door to her building. She put down her grocery bag and rummaged in her pocketbook for keys. A low shadow bounded at her, and she took a startled step back. Mookie tried to jump on her but quickly landed on all fours, his back half wagging in an off-balanced jig.

"Mookie!" She laughed aloud, petting him and looking around.

Carl walked toward her from where he'd been leaning on his car. She felt a long inner exhale, weeks of pain and yearning lifting. In that moment, even with his fading bruises, he looked like the finest specimen of a man she'd ever seen.

"Me and the Mook were in the car," Carl smiled at her, "and I kept getting these strange pictures flashing in my head: squirrels, then trees, then dog runs, and then I got it—Fort Tryon Park. Mook was trying to tell me: Lauren Davis lives near Fort Tryon Park. They have a great dog run there."

Lauren raised her eyebrows. "Mookie?"

"Absolutely. Mook said, 'Carl, you go over there right now—to 181st Street—you've got to beg her forgiveness, tell her everything just got out of hand, tell her you're sorry for lying to her and following her and—'"

"Saving her butt." Lauren stepped toward him.

Carl moved closer to her. "I tried, Lauren."

She put her hands on his chest, feeling the leather of his jacket and smelling the just-showered scent of him. "What about the FBI? I thought you'd get in trouble if you were seen with me."

Carl looked around and pulled her into the shadow of her building. "The case is over now." He brushed the hair from her face, smiling down at her. "So if you'll just refrain from future criminal activities, I know they'll get over it."

She laughed. "You'll have to keep a close eye on me."

"I promise."

Lauren thought he'd kiss her then, but he paused, strangely, as if conflicted again. Lauren tried not to overreact to it—she'd been a terrible mind reader when it came to him. "What?"

"There's one other thing I need to do ... before I go absolutely by-the-book straight."

Lauren frowned, even more confused.

"Come here." He brought her into the outer vestibule of her building, bringing Mookie along. "Can we step into the lobby?" he asked.

The way he was acting unnerved her. "Sure."

She keyed the lock and they entered the empty, prewar lobby with its ornate plaster moldings and high ceilings. They were alone there and out of sight of the street. Carl pulled a couple of pieces of paper from his vest pocket. The pages were folded in three like a letter. "When we search a computer," he said softly, "we dig deep. Nothing is ever truly deleted. You've probably heard that."

Lauren's heart beat hard as she looked quizzically at the folded papers in Carl's hand. "Yes, I've heard that."

"We came across this on Brian's computer," he said, handing the pages to her. "If anyone asks, you printed it up before we impounded the PC."

Lauren unfolded the papers. She quickly scanned the first page then took in the second page with Brian and Steve's signatures. "Oh, wow."

"Yup."

"Oh, wow! Brian's agreement with Steve." A smile spread across Lauren's face. She looked down again. "Brian is supposed to get fifty percent of the fees on the cases he brought in! Millions … tens of millions!" Catching her breath, laughing, Lauren grabbed her heart as the reality hit her. "Oh, my God! Oh, my God, thank you!" Tears filled Lauren's eyes.

Carl watched her. "This was my last foolish act."

Lauren reached for Carl, pulling him toward her. "Not if I have anything to do with it."

Carl's lips met Lauren's, and he wrapped her in his arms. Mookie sat heavily against their legs, nearly bowling them over.

EPILOGUE

Steve's Jaguar barreled through the Midtown Tunnel toward Long Island. Snow flurries melted on its windshield. Strips of tunnel light passed swiftly overhead and disappeared, tile walls seeming close enough to touch at each bend. Steve glanced sideways at Nicole.

"You're a fucking idiot, Steve. I can't believe you tried to cheat them, when you'd left that kind of ammunition around. A signed agreement with Brian? I don't mind that you're greedy, but being stupid is inexcusable."

"I don't understand why you insisted on settling so quickly," Steve said, fury thickening his voice. "I could have worn them down, stretched out their legal budget. Nine million dollars? I could have settled for half that in the end despite the agreement. We don't even have the Etta Houses money yet. The firm will be strapped for months." Steve turned on the windshield wipers to swat away horizontal snow as they exited the tunnel. "I can't believe you care so much about gossip—you hooking up with Brian. I barely care. Not to the tune of nine million dollars."

Nicole felt nauseous just remembering the call from Steve when he said Lauren and Jessica knew everything. She got off on danger. But, like a compulsive gambler, her downside risks became steeper as time wore on. She couldn't afford the price on this one. Thank God Lauren and Jessica only *thought* they knew everything.

When Nicole didn't answer, Steve raised his voice, "Get this, if you don't tell me what's going on, I'll back out of the settlement. I'll make them fight for it. That means every detail will come out in open court—with daily recaps in the media."

"You wouldn't do that."

He looked forward, the car speeding faster. "Don't try me."

"You can make back the money," she growled. "I didn't go to so much trouble just to have those bitches ruin us."

"What are you talking about? Spit it out, Nicole."

She took a deep breath. "When I went to him at the hotel that night, I didn't pass the reception desk. No one saw." Steve took a curve too fast, the tires slipping sideways. Nicole held on, fearful but excited by the nearly sexual thrill of telling. "Brian was so surprised to see me, although he was drunker than I'd ever seen him. I wondered whether he was doing heroin or Oxies—it was so unlike him. He could barely answer the door. We had a wild fuck anyway," she said, sadistically, "even wilder for him because I was his second woman of the night. Wild for me like a snuff film, frankly. Incredibly hot. Then we had a nightcap, and he fell asleep." She paused for the drama of it, making Steve wait. "If the medical examiner had noticed the drugs I put in his drink, the police would have blamed it on the prostitute. I took Brian's wallet, so they'd think it was a robbery. But I don't think the cops got that far. That's because when Brian passed out, I really did start the fire with a cigarette."

Steve cut his eyes to look at Nicole, his cheeks blotching with shock. "He was leaving you? You said you didn't give a shit about him."

She grimaced. "Come on, Steve." Nicole turned and rubbed her bare foot against Steve's crotch, noting his response. "Brian was leaving you. He said he'd have the cash soon to start his own firm. Or, get this, open a bar on some godforsaken desert island. But before he did, he planned to out you for that crazy deal you made on the Etta Houses."

"What?!"

"What did you think, Steve? That Brian would spend thousands of hours on discovery, combing through documents, interviewing witnesses, and *not* figure out that our congressman was on the take? He told me the congressman had taken a payoff, decades ago, to get Etta Houses built on that lead-infested dump. For God's sake, Steve, Brian wasn't going to put up with you and the congressman burying that case and underpaying *those poor people.*"

***

Two women, FBI agents from the Chicago field office, sat at a PC listening to audio in a sun-filled room. They leaned back in their chairs as if thrown there. The Etta Houses case had heated up fast. It was an investigation prompted by documents sent by an anonymous hacker who'd broken into Steve Cohen's computer network. The FBI had obtained warrants for taps on Cohen's home and car. But no one had expected this. One of the women wiped a sheen of sweat from the back of her neck as they listened.

"He didn't even tell Jessica about the Etta Houses problem," Nicole Cohen said, meanly. "Jessica was apparently too fragile to handle the stress."

"That's why you had a hissy fit about the burglary complaint against Jessica and Emily? You didn't want the attention? But why didn't you tell me Brian knew about the Etta Houses?"

"Why didn't I tell you?" Nicole Cohen asked, her voice edgy and sarcastic. "Because, Steve, you don't think outside the box when it comes to handling difficult matters. You'd have gone to prison and pulled my life down with you."

"I never thought he'd do that to me."

"If it's any consolation, Brian rivaled you in the nonthinking department. You should have seen him that night. He'd already told me he planned to report you, but he still believed I came to Miami to have sex with him." She chuckled. "He thought his sexual prowess bought far more female loyalty than I have to give to anyone."

A long pause, and Steve Cohen laughed. "I hated that bastard."

In the Chicago FBI office, the two agents laughed with him.

THE END

ACKNOWLEDGMENTS

To my extraordinary agent, Susan Ginsberg, for her wisdom, guidance, and warm support. To Richard Marek, who brought us together and believed my work merited it.

To the entire Writers House and Blackstone teams, especially my editor, Peggy Hageman (a true New Yorker and truly a pleasure).

To my sage readers, for their invaluable feedback: novelist Lorena Hughes, Eden Walker, Ellen Roberts, Elspeth Kramer, Bernadette Bridges, and Katy Garrabrant. A special thanks to my sister, Ellen Weinstat, always my first reader and cheerleader, and to my niece, Rachel "Clownfish" Bosamonte, for the inspiration.

Finally, I am also forever grateful to my guys, Shane, Kai, and Jerome Miller, for their love, patience, and companionship through the great adventure.

And to "Saint Mark's" and the "Harlem Circuit" for saving me.